THE MARGUERITE HENRY

Misty
Treasury

THREE COMPLETE NOVELS IN ONE VOLUME
BY MARGUERITE HENRY

Illustrated by Wesley Dennis

Simon & Schuster Books for Young Readers

Simon & Schuster Books for Young Readers
An imprint of Simon & Schuster Children's Publishing Division
1230 Avenue of the Americas, New York, New York 10020
THE MISTY TREASURY
Misty of Chincoteague text copyright © 1947,
copyright © renewed 1975 Marguerite Henry.
Misty of Chincoteague illustrations copyright © 1947,
copyright © renewed 1975 Morgan and Charles Reid Dennis.
Sea Star © 1949 Rand McNally & Company.
Stormy, Misty's Foal © 1963 Macmillan Publishing Company.
ISBN 0-689-82046-1
SIMON & SCHUSTER BOOKS FOR YOUNG READERS
is a trademark of Simon & Schuster.
Printed and bound in the United States of America.

Contents

MISTY
OF CHINCOTEAGUE

By MARGUERITE HENRY

Illustrated by Wesley Dennis

To
Paul and Maureen Beebe
Grandpa and Grandma Beebe
Eba Jones, Fire Chief
Wyle Maddox, Leader of Roundup Men
L. Quillen, Roundup Man
Wilbur Wimbrow, Roundup Man
Howard Rodgers, Roundup Man
Harvey Beebe, Roundup Man
Harold Beebe, father of Paul and Maureen
Ralph Beebe, uncle of Paul and Maureen
Delbert Daisey, Bronc Buster
Victoria and William Pruitt

all of whom really live on Chincoteague Island
and who appear as characters in this book

and a special dedication to
Three Chincoteague Ponies
Phantom
Pied Piper
Misty

All the incidents in this story are real. They did not happen in just the order they are recorded, but they all happened at one time or another on the little island of Chincoteague.

CONTENTS

PART ONE

BEFORE MISTY

Chapter 1

LIVE CARGO!

A WILD, ringing neigh shrilled up from the hold of the Spanish galleon. It was not the cry of an animal in hunger. It was a terrifying bugle. An alarm call.

The captain of the *Santo Cristo* strode the poop deck. "Cursed be that stallion!" he muttered under his breath as he stamped forward and back, forward and back.

Suddenly he stopped short. The wind! It was dying with the sun. It was spilling out of the sails, causing them to quiver and shake. He could feel his flesh creep with the sails. Without wind he could not get to Panama. And if he did not get there, and get there soon, he was headed for trouble. The Moor ponies to be delivered to the Viceroy of Peru could not be kept alive much longer. Their hay had grown musty. The water casks were almost empty. And now this sudden calm, this heavy warning of a storm.

He plucked nervously at his rusty black beard as if that would help him think. "We lie in the latitude of white squalls," he said, a look of vexation on his face. "When the wind does strike, it will strike with fury." His steps quickened. "We must shorten sail," he made up his mind.

Cupping his hands to his mouth, he bellowed orders: "Furl the topgallant sail! Furl the coursers and the main-topsail! Shorten the fore-topsail!"

The ship burst into action. From forward and aft all hands came running. They fell to work furiously, carrying out orders.

The captain's eyes were fixed on his men, but his thoughts raced ahead to the rich land where he was bound. In his mind's eye he could see the mule train coming to meet him when he reached land. He could see it snaking its way along the Gold Road from Panama to the seaport of Puerto Bello. He could almost feel the smooth, hard gold in the packs on the donkeys' backs.

His eyes narrowed greedily. "Gold!" he mumbled. "Think of trading twenty ponies for their weight in gold!" He clasped his hands behind him and resumed his pacing and muttering. "The Viceroy of Peru sets great store by the ponies, and well he may. Without the ponies to work the mines, there will be no more gold." Then he clenched his fists. "We must keep the ponies alive!"

His thoughts were brought up sharply. That shrill horse call! Again it filled the air about him with a wild ring. His beady eyes darted to the lookout man in the crow's-nest, then to the men on deck. He saw fear spread among the crew.

Meanwhile, in the dark hold of the ship, a small bay stallion was pawing the floor of his stall. His iron shoes with their sharp rims and turned-down heels threw a shower of sparks, and he felt strong charges of electricity. His nostrils flared. The moisture in the air! The charges of electricity! These were storm warnings—things he knew. Some inner urge told him he must get his mares to high land before the storm broke. He tried to escape, charging against the chest board of his stall again and again. He threw his head back and bugled.

From stalls beside him and from stalls opposite him, nineteen heads with small pointed ears peered out. Nineteen pairs of brown eyes whited. Nineteen young mares caught his anxiety. They, too, tried to escape, rearing and plunging, rearing and plunging.

But presently the animals were no longer hurling themselves. They were *being* hurled. The ship was pitching and tossing to the rising swell of the sea, flinging the ponies forward against their chest boards, backward against the ship's sides.

A cold wind spiraled down the hatch. It whistled and screamed above the rough voice of the captain. It gave way only to the deep *flump-flump* of the thunder.

The sea became a wildcat now, and the galleon her prey. She stalked the ship and drove her off her course. She slapped at her, rolling her victim from side to side. She knocked the spars out of her and used them to ram holes in her sides. She

clawed the rudder from its sternpost and threw it into the sea. She cracked the ship's ribs as if they were brittle bones. Then she hissed and spat through the seams.

The pressure of the sea swept everything before it. Huge baskets filled with gravel for ballast plummeted down the passageway between the ponies, breaking up stalls as they went by.

Suddenly the galleon shuddered. From bow to stern came an endless rasping sound! The ship had struck a shoal. And with a ripping and crashing of timber the hull cracked open. In that split second the captain, his men, and his live cargo were washed into the boiling foam.

The wildcat sea yawned. She swallowed the men. Only the captain and fifteen ponies managed to come up again. The captain bobbed alongside the stallion and made a wild grasp for his tail, but a great wave swept him out of reach.

The stallion neighed encouragement to his mares, who were struggling to keep afloat, fighting the wreckage and the sea. For long minutes they thrashed about helplessly, and just when their strength was nearly spent, the storm died as suddenly as it had risen. The wind calmed.

The sea was no longer a wildcat. She became a kitten, fawning and lapping about the ponies' legs. Now their hooves touched land. They were able to stand! They were scrambling up the beach, up on Assateague Beach, that long, sandy island which shelters the tidewater country of Virginia and Maryland. They were far from the mines of Peru.

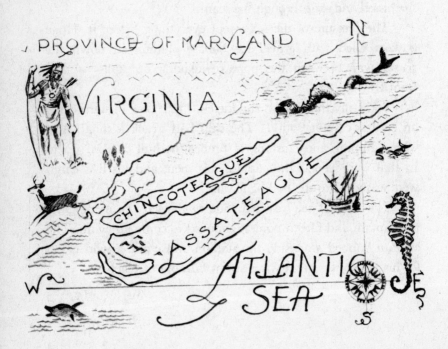

Chapter 2

THE ISLAND OF THE WILD THINGS

THE PONIES were exhausted and their coats were heavy with water, but they were free, free, *free!* They raised their heads and snuffed the wind. The smell was unlike that of the lowland moors of Spain, but it was good! They sucked in the sharp, sweet pungence of pine woods, and somewhere mixed in with the piney smell came the enticing scent of salt grass.

Their stomachs were pinched with hunger, but the ponies did not seek the grass at once. They shook the water from their coats. Then they rolled back and forth in the sand, enjoying the solid feel of the land.

17

At last the stallion's hunger stirred him to action. He rounded up his mares, and with only a watery moon to light the way, he drove them through the needle-carpeted woods. The mares stopped to eat the leaves of some myrtle bushes, but the stallion jostled them into line. Then he took the lead. So direct was his progress it seemed almost as if he had trodden here before. Through bramble and thicket, through brackish pools of water, he led the way.

The moon was high overhead when the little band came out on grassy marshland. They stopped a moment to listen to the wide blades of grass whisper and squeak in the wind; to sniff the tickling smell of salt grass.

This was it! This was the exciting smell that had urged them on. With wild snorts of happiness they buried their noses in the long grass. They bit and tore great mouthfuls—frantically, as if they were afraid it might not last. Oh, the salty goodness of it! Not bitter at all, but juicy-sweet with rain. It was different from any grass they knew. It billowed and shimmered like the sea. They could not get enough of it. That delicious salty taste! Never had they known anything like it. Never. And sometimes they came upon tender patches of lespedeza, a kind of clover that grew among the grasses.

The ponies forgot the forty days and forty nights in the dark hold of the Spanish galleon. They forgot the musty hay. They forgot the smell of bilge water, of oil and fishy odors from the cooking galley.

18

When they could eat no more, they pawed shallow wells with their hooves for drinking water. Then they rolled in the wiry grass, letting out great whinnies of happiness. They seemed unable to believe that the island was all their own. Not a human being anywhere. Only grass. And sea. And sky. And the wind.

At last they slept.

The seasons came and went, and the ponies adopted the New World as their own. They learned how to take care of themselves. When summer came and with it the greenhead flies by day and the mosquitoes by night, they plunged into the sea, up to their necks in the cool surf. The sea was their *friend*. Once it had set them free. Now it protected them from their fiercest enemies.

Winter came and the grass yellowed and dried, but the ponies discovered that close to the roots it was still green and good to eat.

Even when a solid film of ice sealed the land, they did not go hungry. They broke through the ice with their hooves or went off to the woods to eat the myrtle leaves that stayed green all winter.

Snow was a new experience, too. They blew at it, making little snow flurries of their own. They tasted it. It melted on their tongues. Snow was good to drink!

If the Spaniards could have seen their ponies now, they would have been startled at their changed appearance. No longer were their coats sleek. They were as thick and shaggy as the coat of any sheep dog. This was a good thing. On bitter days, when they stood close-huddled for comfort, each pony could enjoy the added warmth of his neighbor's coat as well as his own.

There were no wolves or wildcats on the island, but there was deep, miry mud to trap creatures and suck them down. After a few desperate struggles, the ponies learned how to fall to their knees, then sidle and wriggle along like crabs until they were well out of it.

With each season the ponies grew wiser. And with each season they became tougher and more hardy. Horse colts and fillies were born to them. As the horse colts grew big, they rounded up mares of their own and started new herds that ranged wild—wild as the wind and the sea that had brought them there long ago.

Years went by. And more years. Changes came to Assateague. The red men came. The white men came. The white men built a lighthouse to warn ships of dangerous reefs. They built a handful of houses and a white church. But soon the houses stood empty. The people moved their homes and their church to nearby Chincoteague Island, for Assateague belonged to the wild things—to the wild birds that nested on it, and the wild ponies whose ancestors had lived on it since the days of the Spanish galleon.

PART TWO

MISTY OF CHINCOTEAGUE

Chapter 3

THE PHANTOM

SPRING TIDES had come once more to Assateague Island. They were washing and salting the earth, coaxing new green spears to replace the old dried grasses.

On a windy Saturday morning, half-past March, a boy and his sister were toiling up the White Hills of Assateague Beach. The boy was taller than the girl and led the way. Their progress was slow. The heavy beach sand seemed to pull them back, as if it felt that human beings had no right to be there.

In the early morning light the two figures were scarcely visible. Their faded play clothes were the color of sand and their hair was bleached pale by the sun. The boy's hair had a way of falling down over his brow like the forelock of a stallion. The girl's streamed out behind her, a creamy golden mane with the wind blowing through it.

Suddenly the boy bent over and picked up a whitened, bow-shaped object. The girl was at his side in an instant.

"What is it, Paul?"

The boy did not answer. He kept feeling the object, running his fingers over it, testing the weight of it. Then he squinted

his eyes against the sun and looked out upon the thin line of blue where the sky and the sea met.

"Is it the bone of a horse?"

Paul looked down his nose in disgust. "Maureen," he shook his head, "aren't you ever going to grow up?"

"Is it an Indian bow washed white by the sea?" the girl persisted.

Paul hardly heard. His eyes were scanning the horizon.

"See a ship?" Maureen asked.

"Hmm," he nodded.

"I don't see anything. Where, Paul? What kind of ship?"

"A Spanish galleon," he said. "She's caught in a northeaster. Look at her pitch!"

"Oh, Paul," fretted the girl. "You are always play-acting." Then she added wistfully, "I hanker to see the things you see. Tell me what the ship's like. Make it a whopper."

"Can't see her now. She's lost in the swell."

He pushed the hair out of his eyes. "There she is!" he gasped, enjoying his own make-believe. "Her sails painted gold and there's a gold horse with wings at her prow. She's heading toward the shoals. She's going to crack up!"

"Oh, Paul!"

"What's more, she's carrying live cargo! Horses! And they're feared of the storm. I can hear 'em crying and screeching above the wind." He turned abruptly to his sister. "Now can you guess what I just found?"

"No. What?"

"Why, a rib bone, you goose. A rib bone of the Spanish galleon that was wrecked." Paul braced his legs in the sand and watched his sister's face. The result pleased him. Her eyes and mouth flew open.

"This is part of her hull. Fact is, it's her bones that caused the sands to drift higher and higher 'til they formed the White Hills we're standing on."

The girl looked around and about her. Everything was still and quiet on little Assateague Island. Their grandfather had brought the game warden to the island in his boat, and she and Paul had asked to come along. But now she wondered if they should have come. The men were seeing how the wild birds had weathered the winter. They were far to the north. No other creatures were in sight. Suddenly she felt a little chill of fear.

"Paul," she asked in a hushed voice, "do you feel like we're trespassing?"

Paul nodded. "If you look close," he whispered, "you can see that the wild critters have 'No Trespassing' signs tacked up on every pine tree."

"I wasn't thinking about the wild things," Maureen replied. She shielded her eyes against the sun and looked off in the direction of Tom's Cove. "Wish Grandpa'd come to take us back home to Chincoteague. It seems spooky-like to be exploring a ship's graveyard."

"I like exploring. I don't care if . . ."

Suddenly, from the pine thicket behind them came the sharp crackling of underbrush. Paul wheeled around, his eyes darting to an open glade.

"Watch the open place, Maureen! It's the Pied Piper and his band!"

With manes and tails flying, a band of wild ponies swept into the natural grazing ground. A pinto stallion was in command. He bunched his mares, then tossed his head high, searching the wind.

Paul and Maureen fell to the sand. They did not want the wind to carry their scent. They watched as the stallion herded his family like a nervous parent on a picnic. When he made certain that no one was missing, he began browsing. It was like a signal. His mares lowered their heads and settled down to the business of grazing.

Paul's eyes were fixed on the wild horses. They were cropping grass peacefully. But he knew that one strange sound would send them rocketing off into the woods. He and Maureen spoke softly, and scarcely moved.

"Do y'see the Phantom?" asked Maureen.

The very mention of the name "Phantom" set Paul's heart thumping against the walls of his chest. That mysterious wild mare about whom so many stories were told!

"No," he answered. "They're bunched too close."

"Do you reckon the Phantom's real? Or do you reckon it was some sea monster upset that boat last roundup?"

Paul gave no answer. Was the Phantom real? Sometimes he wondered. She had never been captured, and the roundup men did sometimes tell tall tales. Some had said she was a dark creature, dark and mysterious, like the pine trees. And some said she was the color of copper, with splashes of silver in her mane and tail. And some spoke of a strange white marking that began at her withers and spread out like a white map of the United States.

"Maybe," whispered Maureen, "maybe she got poor and died off during the winter."

"Her?" scoffed Paul, his eyes never leaving the herd. "Not her! Any pony that can outsmart Grandpa and all the roundup men for two years running can rustle her feed, all right. Recommember how Uncle Jed said his horse broke a leg trying to follow the Phantom at the roundup last Pony Penning Day?"

"Wish girls could go along on the roundup; maybe she wouldn't bolt away from another girl."

Paul snorted. "She'd leap into the waves and swim out to sea just like she did last year and the year before that." Then suddenly his face lighted as if an idea had just struck him. "But this year it's going to be different."

"Why is it?"

"Because," Paul replied, gripping the rib bone in his hand, "because I'm old enough to go with the roundup men this year. That's why. And if there *is* such a filly, I'm going to get her, and on Pony Penning Day she'll be in the corral with the others."

"For sale?"

"No, I'll tie a rope around her neck to show she's already sold. To me. To us," he added hastily, thinking of the cost of her. "She'll sell for around a hundred dollars, maybe."

"Oh, Paul! Let me help."

"All right, I will. How much money can you earn between now and Pony Penning Day?"

Maureen drew a quick breath. "I can earn as much as any boy. I can rake clams and gather oysters, and I can catch soft-shell crabs, and if Grandma doesn't need me, I suppose I could clean out people's chicken houses. I won't mind the work if ever we could *keep* a pony for our very own."

A little silence fell between them as they lay on their stomachs in the sand, their eyes fastened on the herd.

"I reckon we'd better keep our plans to ourselves," Paul spoke at last. "Then, if we don't get her—"

"Then nobody can poke fingers at us and laugh," finished Maureen. "Paul . . ."

"Hmm?"

"Why does everyone in school think we're lucky to live on Grandpa's pony ranch? Why is it?"

Paul was busy with thoughts of the Phantom.

"Do you reckon," Maureen went on, remembering to keep her voice low, "do you reckon it's because their families are watermen instead of horsemen?"

"Maybe."

"Or is it because Papa and Mama are in China and they think grandparents aren't as strict as parents?"

Paul was in a dream. He was capturing the mysterious wild mare. He was listening to Maureen with only half his mind.

"I reckon it's the ponies," he said at last. "But what fun is it to gentle a wild colt and just when he learns that you're his friend, Grandpa sells him and you never see him again?"

"I can't abide it either," said Maureen; "but there's something hurts worse."

"What?"

"It's when the colts are sold, right out from under their mothers. I get sick inside watching it."

"That's because you're a girl."

Suddenly Paul leaped to his feet. "Look!" he cried as a red streak broke from the herd and went crashing into the woods. "It's the Phantom! I saw the white map on her withers. I did. I did!"

For a full minute the pony was lost among the pines. Then out she came heading toward the White Hills. Behind her whipped the Pied Piper, and his ringing cry was a command.

"Run, Maureen! Run! He's a killer."

The boy and his sister flew down the hill, stumbling over dried brush and blackberry vines. As they reached the beach, they turned back and watched, breathless. Pied Piper was overtaking the Phantom. He was running alongside her. Now he was twisting into the air, lacing her with his forefeet. They could hear the dull pounding of his hooves against her body. Then they saw the Phantom turn. They saw the droop of her tail as she gave up her dash for freedom and meekly followed the stallion into the woods.

Long seconds after they were gone, the air seemed to quiver with the Pied Piper's bugle.

"I hate him!" cried Maureen, bursting into tears. "I hate him! I hate him!"

"Quit acting like a girl, Maureen! Pied Piper knows she's better off with the band. Even the Phantom knows it. Grandpa says horses got to stick together for protection. Same as people."

Chapter 4

SACRED BONES

"HALL-OO-OO!" came a voice down the beach. The boy and the girl turned to see Grandpa Beebe swinging toward them, his gnarled arms upraised like a wind-twisted tree.

"Paul!" he boomed. "Put down that bone. Put it down, I tell ye!"

Paul had forgotten all about the curved piece of wood. Now he noticed that he was clenching it so tightly it left a white streak in the palm of his hand. He dropped it quickly as Grandpa came up.

"How often do I got to tell you that bones is sacred? Even ship's bones."

"Is it true, Grandpa?" asked Paul.

"Be what true?" Grandpa repeated, pulling off his battered felt hat and letting the wind toss his hair.

"About the Spanish galleon being wrecked . . ."

"And the ponies swimming ashore?" added Maureen.

Grandpa Beebe squinted at the sun. "It's nigh onto noon-tide," he said, "and your Grandma is having sixteen head to dinner tomorrow. We got to get back home to Chincoteague right smart quick! I promised to kill some turkeys for her." He sighed heavily. "Seems as if the devil is allus sittin' cross-legged of me."

But he made no move to go. Instead, he squatted down on the beach, muttering, "Don't see why she's got to parboil 'em today." Then he took off his boots and socks and dug his toes in the sand, like fiddler crabs scuttling for home.

"Feels good, don't it?" he said, with a grin. He looked from Paul to Maureen and back again. "Yer know," he went on, and he began to rub the bristles of his ear, as he always did when he was happy. "Yer know, the best thing about havin' fourteen head of children is ye're bound to get one or two good grandchildren outen the lot."

"Grandpa!" reminded Paul. "Is it true about the Spanish galleon and the ponies? Or is it a legend like the folks over on the mainland say?"

38

"'Course it's true!" replied Grandpa, with a little show of irritation. "All the wild herds on Assateague be descendants of a bunch of Spanish hosses. They wasn't wild to begin with, mind ye. They just went wild with their freedom."

Maureen did a quick little leap, like a colt bucking.

"Then it's *not* a legend?" she rejoiced. "It's *not* a legend!"

"Who said 'twasn't a legend?" Grandpa exclaimed. "'Course it's a legend. But legends be the only stories as is true!"

He stopped to find the right words. "Facts are fine, fer as they go," he said, "but they're like water bugs skittering atop the water. Legends, now—they go deep down and bring up the heart of a story." Here Grandpa shoved his hand into the pocket of his overalls and produced a long stick of licorice and a plug of tobacco. With a pair of wire clippers he divided the licorice in half and gave a piece to Maureen and one to Paul. Then he cut himself a quid of tobacco.

There was a little silence while the old man and the boy and the girl thought about the shipwrecked ponies.

Then, almost in the same breath, Paul and Maureen blurted out together: "Who discovered 'em?"

Grandpa spat out to sea. "Why, I heard tell 'twas the Indians chanced on 'em first. They comes over to hunt on Assateague, and 'twasn't only deer and otter and beaver they finds. They finds these wild ponies pawin' the air and snortin' through their noses, and they ain't never seed no critters like that, blowin' steam and screamin' and their tails and manes a-flyin'. And the Indians was so affrighted they run for their canoes."

Grandpa Beebe began rubbing both ears in his excitement. "Then what, Grandpa?"

"Why, the ponies was left to run wilder and wilder. Nobody lived here to hinder 'em none, nobody at all. White men come to live on our Chincoteague Island, but Assateague was left to the critters."

40

Grandpa reached for one of his socks, then broke out in sudden laughter. "Ho! Ho! Ho!" he bellowed.

Paul and Maureen looked all around them. "What's so funny, Grandpa?" they asked.

Grandpa was slapping his thigh, rocking back and forth. "I jes' now thought of somethin' right smart cute," he chuckled, when he could get his breath. "Y'see, lots of folks like to call theirselves descendants of the First Families of Virginia. They kinda makes a high-falutin' club outen it and labels it F.F.V. But you know what?" Here Grandpa's eyes twinkled like the sea with the sun blazing on it.

"What?" chorused Paul and Maureen.

"The real first families of Virginia was the ponies! Ho-ho-ho! That's what *my* history book says!"

"Whee! Grandpa!" exclaimed Paul. "I like the way you talk about history."

Grandpa winked in agreement. "Nothin' so exciting as tag ends pulled right outen the core of the past."

"Did the first white men tame the ponies?" asked Maureen.

"No indeedy. Them first white men had no use fer the wild, thrashin' ponies. A slow-going pair o' oxen could do all the plowin' for bread corn and sech. Guess mebbe it was Bob Watson's boy of Chincoteague who fust tried to put a wild pony to plow. She was a dead ringer for the Phantom, too. But that was a long time agone."

Paul's heart turned a somersault.

"What happened to her, Grandpa? Did she gentle?"

"Did she gentle! Why, she jes' broke the singletree as if 'twas a matchstick, cleared the fence, and blew to her island home with the reins a-stringin' out behind her."

"Oh!"

"Some of 'em you jest can't gentle. Not after they've lived wild. Only the youngsters is worth botherin' about, so far as the gentlin' goes. Recommember that!"

Paul and Maureen looked at each other. They were thinking of their secret plan to own the Phantom.

Grandpa Beebe began putting on his socks and shoes. "Likely the game warden is done checkin' up on the wild birds. I promised to meet him at Tom's Cove afore the tide ebbs bare. But," he added, as he pulled on his boots, "I know my tides, and I'll give ye time for one more question."

Maureen looked to Paul. "You ask, Paul."

Paul jumped to his feet. How could he ask just one question when dozens popped into his mind? He began picking up fiddler crabs furiously, as if that would help him think. Finally he turned to Grandpa.

"It's about Pony Penning Day," he blurted out. "How did it start?"

It was plain to see that Grandpa Beebe liked the question. He began rubbing the bristles of one ear and then the other. "'Twas this-a-way," he said. "In the yesterdays, when their corn was laid by, folks on Chincoteague got to yearnin' fer a big hollerday. So they sails over to Assateague and rounds up all the wild ponies. 'Twas big sport."

"Like hunting buffalo or deer?" asked Paul.

"'Zactly like that! Only they didn't kill the ponies; just rounded 'em up for the fun of the chase. Then they cut out a few of the younglings to gentle, tried some ropin' and rough ridin' of the wild ones, et a big dinner of out-door pot pie, and comes on back home to Chincoteague. By-'n-by, they adds somethin' to the fun. They swum the ponies acrost the channel to Chincoteague and put on a big show. 'Twas so excitin', folks come from as far as New York to see it. And afore we knowed it, we was sellin' off some of the colts to the mainlanders."

"Why did they sell the wild things?" asked Maureen.

"Why!" echoed Grandpa. "Why, ponies was overrunnin' Assateague. They was gettin' thick as raisins in a pie!"

"That thick, Grandpa?" asked Maureen, her eyes rounded.

"Wal, maybe not that thick," grinned Grandpa.

"Don't keep interrupting Grandpa!" exclaimed Paul.

"Today it's jest the same," Grandpa said slowly. "Along toward the tail end of July, when the ponies is done with fightin' and foalin' and the watermen is tired of plantin' oysters, then we all get to hankerin' for a celebration. So the menfolk round up the ponies, the womenfolk bake meat pot pie, and there ye are! Only now, outside a few hossmen like me, the fire department owns most of the wild ponies. And a good thing it is for Chincoteague."

"Why is it?"

"'Cause all the money they make from sellin' 'em goes into our fire-fightin' apparatus."

44

Grandpa Beebe rose stiffly. "Come on, you two, I hain't got time to school ye. That's what me and Grandma pays taxes for. Besides, we been a-settin' here so long the sand is liable to drift up over us and make another white clift outen us. It's time we was gettin' back home to Chincoteague, and Grandma's turkeys."

Chapter 5

A PIECE OF WIND AND SKY

APRIL, May, June, July! Only four months until Pony Penning Day. Only four months to plan and work for the Phantom.

Suddenly Time was important.

"We got to lay a course and hold it," said Paul, as he whisked over the fence that same afternoon and began studying the ponies in Grandpa Beebe's corral.

Maureen slipped between the rails and caught up with him. "Quit talking like a waterman, Paul. Talk like a horseman so I can understand you."

46

"All right, I will. Grandpa's got eleven mares here. Six of 'em have a colt apiece, and the black and the chestnut each have a yearling and a suckling. Between now and July, how many colts do you reckon Grandpa will sell?"

"Probably all of 'em—except the sucklings, of course."

"That's what I figure! Now if we could halter-break the colts and teach 'em some manners, folks'd pay more for them, wouldn't they?"

"I reckon."

"All right!" exclaimed Paul as he sailed back over the fence. "Maybe Grandpa will pay us the difference."

That night at the supper table Paul looked up over his plate of roast oysters and caught Grandma's eye.

"Grandma," he questioned, "do you like a mannerly colt?"

Grandma Beebe's face was round as a holly berry and soft little whiskers grew about her mouth, like the feelers of a very young colt. She pursed her lips now, wondering if there were some catch to Paul's question.

"Paul means," explained Maureen, "if you came here to Pony Ranch to buy a colt, would you choose one that was gentled or would you choose a wild one?"

Grandpa clucked. "Can't you jes' see yer Grandma crow-hoppin' along on a wild colt!"

"Thar's yer answer," laughed Grandma, as she cut golden squares of cornbread. "I'd take the mannerly colt."

Paul swallowed a plump oyster, almost choking in his haste. "Would you," he gulped, "that is, would you be willing to pay out more money for it, Grandma?"

"Wa-al, that depends," mused Grandma, passing the breadboard around, "that depends on how *much* more."

"Would you pay ten dollars more?"

"If he was nice and mannerly, I would. Yes, I would."

"See there, Grandpa!" The words came out in a rush. "If Maureen and I was to halter-break the colts, could we—" He stopped, and then stammered, "Could we have the ten extra dollars for each colt sold?"

So dead a silence fell over the table that the *drip-drip* of the kitchen faucet sounded like hammer strokes.

Grandpa slowly buttered his bread and then glanced about the table.

48

"Pass your Grandpa the goody, Maureen."

All eyes watched Grandpa spread a layer of wild black-berry jam on top of the butter. Then he added another square of cornbread to make a sandwich. Not until he had tasted and approved did he turn to Paul.

"What fer?" he barked.

Paul and Maureen stared at their plates.

"Must be a secret, Clarence," Grandma pleaded.

Grandpa swept a few crumbs into his hand and began stacking his own dishes. "I ain't never pried a secret outa no one." he said. "And I don't aim to start pokin' and pryin' now. It's a deal, children, and ye don't need to tell me whut the money's fer until ye're ready to spend it."

Paul and Maureen flew to Grandpa and hugged him. For a moment they forgot that they were almost grown up.

The days and weeks that followed were not half long enough. Up at dawn, working with the colts, haltering them, teaching them to lead and to stand tied! Going to school regretfully and hurrying home as soon as it was out!

Now when a buyer came to look at the colts, Maureen did not run to her room as she used to do, pressing her face in the feather bed to stifle her sobs. Nor did Paul swing up on one of Grandpa's ponies and gallop down the hard point of land to keep from crying. Now they actually led the colts out to the buyers to show how gentle they were. They even helped load them onto waiting trucks. All the while they kept thinking that soon they would have a pony of their own, never to be sold. *Not for any price.*

April and May passed. School closed.

Paul and Maureen worked furiously for the Phantom. They caught and sold crabs. They gathered oysters when the tide went out and laid the oyster rocks bare. And most exciting of all, they "treaded for clams." In flannel moccasins to protect their feet, and wide-brimmed hats on their heads, they plunged into Chincoteague Bay. Sometimes they would whinny and snort, pretending they were wild ponies escaping the flies. Then suddenly they would feel the thin edge of a clam with their feet and remember that they were clam treaders, trying to earn money for the Phantom.

Paul learned how to burrow under the sand with his toes and lift the clam to the surface on the top of his moccasined

50

foot. But try as she would, Maureen never could do it. She raked the clams instead, with a long wooden rake. Then she dumped them into a home-made basket formed by spreading a piece of canvas inside an old inner tube. She kept it from floating out to sea by tying it to her waist with a rope.

Slowly, week by week, Grandpa's old tobacco pouch in which they stored their money began to round out, until it held exactly one hundred dollars. It never occurred to Paul and Maureen that the Phantom might escape the roundup men this year, too. They felt as certain of owning her as if someone had sent them a telegram that read,

SHIPPING YOUR PONY ON PONY PENNING DAY =

One early morning, when July was coming in, Paul cornered Grandpa hustling across the barnyard. He stepped right into Grandpa's path so that he had to stop short.

"Grandpa!" Paul burst out. "Will you rent me one of your empty stalls beginning with Pony Penning Day? I'll do a man's work to pay for it."

Grandpa roughed his hand up the back of Paul's head. 'Who you want it fer, lad? Plan to sleep in it yourself?"

Paul's face turned red. "I," he hesitated. "That is, Maureen and I are going to . . ."

"Wa-al?"

"We're going to buy—we're going to buy the Phantom on Pony Penning Day."

There! The news was out!

Grandpa threw back his head. He opened wide his mouth, ready to break out in laughter, but when he saw the grave look in Paul's eyes, he did not laugh at all. Instead, he let out a shrill "Wee-dee-dee-dee, wee-dee-dee-dee," as he pulled a handful of corn out of his pocket and spattered the golden kernels about his feet.

From all over the barnyard came wild geese and tame geese, big ducks and little ducks, marsh hens and chicks. The air was wild with the clatter they made.

"Can't no one catch the Phantom," Grandpa yelled above the noise. "For two years she's give the horse laugh to the best roundup men we got on Chincoteague. What makes ye think she's going to *ask* to be caught?"

"Because," Paul shouted through the din, "because the Fire Chief promised I could go along this year."

Grandpa Beebe stepped back a pace and studied his grandson. His clear eyes twinkled with merriment. Then a look of pity crossed his face.

"Lad," he said, "the Phantom don't wear that white map on her withers for nothing. It stands for Liberty, and ain't no human being going to take her liberty away from her."

"She wants to come to us," Paul said, trying to keep his voice steady. "Ever since that day on Assateague, Maureen and I knew."

A white striker bird flew up from the ground and perched on Grandpa's gnarled forefinger. Grandpa directed his remarks to the bird. "Can't fer the life of me see why those two want another pony Why, the corral's full of 'em. They're as much Paul's and Maureen's as anybody's."

Paul's lips tightened. "It's not the same," he said. "Owning a pony you never have to sell . . ."

The striker bird flew away. Paul and Grandpa watched in silence as it dipped and rose to the sky.

Grandpa stood in thought. "Paul boy," he said slowly, "hark to my words. The Phantom ain't a hoss. She ain't even a lady. She's just a piece of wind and sky."

Paul tried to speak, swallowed, and tried once more. "We got our hearts set on her," he faltered.

Grandpa pushed his battered hat to one side and scratched his head. "All right, boy," he sighed. "The stall is yours."

A moment later Paul was telling Maureen the good news. "Owning a stall is next best to owning a pony," she laughed, as they both went to work in a fever of excitement.

With long brooms and steaming pails of water, they washed the walls and the ceiling of Phantom's stall. They scraped inches of sand from the hard-packed floor, dumped it in the woods, and brought in fresh, clean sand. They built a manger, spending long moments deciding just how high it should be placed. They scrubbed a rain barrel to be used for a

watering trough. They even dug a "wickie"—the long, tough root of a brier that trails along under the ground.

"Phantom won't be frightened when she smells and feels a wickie halter," Maureen said. "It'll be much softer than rope."

Chapter 6

PONY PENNING DAY

PONY PENNING DAY always comes on the last Thursday in July. For weeks before, every member of the Volunteer Fire Department is busy getting the grounds in readiness, and the boys are allowed to help.

"I'll do your chores at home, Paul," offered Maureen, "so's you can see that the pony pens are good and stout."

Paul spent long days at the pony penning grounds. Yet he could not have told how or by whom the tents were rigged up. He hardly noticed when the chutes for the bronco busting were built. He did not know who pounded the race track into

57

condition. All he knew was that the pens for the wild ponies must be made fast. Once the Phantom was captured, she must not escape. Nothing else mattered.

The night before the roundup, he and Maureen made last-minute plans in Phantom's stall. "First thing in the morning," Paul told Maureen, "you lay a clean bed of dried sea grass. Then fill the manger with plenty of marsh grass to make Phantom feel at home."

"Oh, I will, Paul. And I've got some ear corn and some 'lasses to coax her appetite, and Grandma gave me a bunch of tiny new carrots and some rutabagas, and I've been saving up sugar until I have a little sackful."

In the midst of their talk, Grandpa, looking as if he had a surprise, joined them.

"I hain't rode on a roundup to Assateague for two year," he smiled, hiding one hand behind his back, "but I recommember we allus had a chaw and a goody after the ponies was rounded up and afore we swimmed 'em across the channel. Here, Paul," he said, with a strange huskiness, "here's a choclit bar fer ye to take along." And he pressed the slightly squashed candy into Paul's hand.

It was dark and still when Paul awoke the next morning. He lay quiet a moment, trying to gather his wits. Suddenly he shot out of bed.

Today was Pony Penning Day!

His clothes lay on the chair beside his bed. Hurriedly he pulled on his shirt and pants and thudded barefoot down to the kitchen where Grandma stood over the stove, frying ham and making coffee for him as if he were man-grown!

He flung out his chest, sniffing the rich smells, bursting with excitement.

Grandma glanced around proudly. "I picked the first ripe figs of the year fer ye," she exclaimed. "They're chuckful of goodness. Now sit down, Paul, and eat a breakfast fit for a roundup man!"

Paul sat on the edge of his chair. With one eye on the clock he tried to eat the delicious figs and ham, but the food seemed to lump in his throat. Luckily Grandpa and Maureen came downstairs just then and helped clean his plate when Grandma was busy testing her cornbread in the oven with a long wisp of straw.

"I got to go now," Paul swallowed, as he ran out the door. He mounted Watch Eyes, a dependable pony that Grandpa had never been able to sell because of his white eyes. Locking his bare feet around the pony's sides, he jogged out of the yard.

Maureen came running to see him off.

"Whatever happens," Paul called back over his shoulder, "you be at Old Dominion Point at ten o'clock on a fresh pony."

"I'll be there, Paul!"

"And you, Paul!" yelled Grandpa. "Obey yer leader. No matter what!"

Day was breaking. A light golden mist came up out of the sea. It touched the prim white houses and the white picket fences with an unearthly light. Paul loped along slowly to save his mount's strength. He studied each house with a new interest. Here lived the woman who paid Maureen three dollars for hoeing her potato patch. There lived Kim Horsepepper, the clamdigger they had worked for. Mr. Horsepepper was riding out of his lane now, catching up with Paul. All along the road, men were turning out of their gates.

"Where do you reckon you'll do most good, Bub?" taunted a lean sapling of a man who, on other days, was an oysterman. He guffawed loudly, then winked at the rest of the group.

Paul's hand tightened on the reins. "Reckon I'll do most good where the leader tells me to go," he said, blushing hotly.

The day promised to be sultry. The marsh grass that usually billowed and waved stood motionless. The water of Assateague Channel glared like quicksilver.

Now the cavalcade was thundering over a small bridge that linked Chincoteague Island to little Piney Island. At the far end of the bridge a scow with a rail fence around it stood at anchor.

In spite of light talk, the faces of the men were drawn tight with excitement as they led their mounts onto the scow. The horses felt the excitement, too. Their nostrils quivered, and their ears swiveled this way and that, listening to the throb of the motor. Now the scow began to nose its way across the narrow

channel. Paul watched the White Hills of Assateague loom near. He watched the old lighthouse grow sharp and sharper against the sky. In a few minutes the ride was over. The gangway was being lowered. The horses were clattering down, each man taking his own.

All eyes were on Wyle Maddox, the leader.

"Split in three bunches," Wyle clipped out the directions loud and sharp. "North, south, and east. Me and Kim and the Beebe boy will head east, Wimbrow and Quillen goes north, and Harvey and Rodgers south. We'il all meet at Tom's Point."

62

At the first sound of Wyle's steam-whistle voice, the sea birds rose with a wild clatter.

"They're like scouts," Paul said to himself. "They're going to warn the wild ponies that the enemy has landed."

"Gee-up!" shouted Wyle as he whirled his horse and motioned Kim and Paul to follow.

Paul touched his bare heels into Watch Eye's side. *They were off!* The boy's eyes were fastened on Wyle Maddox. He and Kim Horsepepper were following their leader like the wake of a ship.

As they rode on, Paul could feel the soft sand give way to hard meadowland, then to pine-laden trails. There were no paths to follow, only openings to skin through—openings that led to water holes or to grazing grounds. The three horses thrashed through underbrush, jumped fallen trees, waded brackish pools and narrow, winding streams.

Suddenly Paul saw Wyle Maddox' horse rear into the air. He heard him neigh loudly as a band of wild ponies darted into an open grazing stretch some twenty yards ahead, then vanished among the black tree trunks.

The woods came alive with thundering hooves and frantic horse calls. Through bush and brier and bog and hard marshland the wild ponies flew. Behind them galloped the three riders, whooping at the top of their lungs. For whole seconds at a time the wild band would be swallowed up by the forest gloom. Then it would reappear far ahead—nothing but a flash of flying tails and manes.

Suddenly Wyle Maddox was waving Paul to ride close. "A straggler!" he shouted, pointing off to the left. "He went that-a-way! Git him!" And with a burst of speed Wyle Maddox and Kim Horsepepper were after the band.

Paul was alone. His face reddened with anger. They wanted to be rid of him. That's what they wanted. Sent after a straggler! He was not interested in rounding up a straggler that couldn't even keep up with the herd! He wanted the Phantom. Then Grandpa's words flashed across his mind. "Obey yer leader. No matter what!"

He wheeled his pony and headed blindly in the direction Wyle had indicated. He rode deeper into the pine thicket, trying to avoid snapping twigs, yet watching ahead for the slightest motion of leaf or bush. He'd show the men, if it took him all day! His thin shirt clung to him damply and his body was wet with sweat. A cobweb veiled itself across his face. With one hand he tried to wipe it off, but suddenly he was almost unseated. Watch Eyes was dancing on his hind legs, his nose high in the air. Paul stared into the sun-dappled forest until his eyes burned in his head. At last, far away and deep in the shadow of the pines, he saw a blur of motion. With the distance that lay between them, it might have been anything. A deer. Or even a squirrel. Whatever it was, he was after it!

Watch Eyes plunged on. There was a kind of glory in pursuit that made Paul and the horse one. They were trailing nothing but swaying bushes. They were giving chase to a mirage. Always it moved on and on, showing itself only in quivering leaves or moving shadows.

What was that? In the clump of myrtle bushes just ahead? Paul reined in. He could scarcely breathe for the wild beating of his heart. There it was again! A silver flash. It looked like mist with the sun on it. And just beyond the mist, he caught sight of a long tail of mingled copper and silver.

He gazed awestruck. "It could be the Phantom's tail," he breathed. "It is! It is! It is! And the silver flash—it's not mist at all, but a brand-new colt, too little to keep up with the band."

The blood pounded in his ears. No wonder the Phantom was a straggler! No wonder she let herself be caught. "She's got a baby colt!" he murmured.

He glanced about him helplessly. If only he could think! How could he drive the Phantom and her colt to Tom's Point?

Warily he approached the myrtle thicket, then stopped as a hot wave of guilt swept over him. Phantom and her colt did not want to be rounded up by men. He could set them

free. No one had brought the Phantom in before. No one need ever know.

Just then the colt let out a high, frightened whinny. In that little second Paul knew that he wanted more than anything in the world to keep the mother and the colt together. Shivers of joy raced up and down his spine. His breath came faster. He made a firm resolution. "I'll buy you both!" he promised.

But how far had he come? Was it ten miles to Tom's Point or two? Would it be best to drive them down the beach? Or through the woods? As if in answer a loud bugle rang through the woods. It was the Pied Piper! And unmistakably his voice came from the direction of Tom's Point.

The Phantom pricked her ears. She wheeled around and almost collided with Watch Eyes in her haste to find the band. She wanted the Pied Piper for protection. Behind her trotted the foal, all shining and clean with its newness.

Paul laughed weakly. *He* was not driving the Phantom after all! She and her colt were leading him. They were leading him to Tom's Point!

Chapter 7

SHE CAN'T TURN BACK

TOM'S POINT was a protected piece of land where the marsh was hard and the grass especially sweet. About seventy wild ponies, exhausted by their morning's run, stood browsing quietly, as if they were in a corral. Only occasionally they looked up at their captors. The good meadow and their own weariness kept them peaceful prisoners.

At a watchful distance the roundup men rested their mounts and relaxed. It was like the lull in the midst of a storm. All was quiet on the surface. Yet there was an undercurrent of tension. You could tell it in the narrowed eyes of the men, their subdued voices and their too easy laughter.

Suddenly the laughter stilled. Mouths gaped in disbelief. Eyes rounded. For a few seconds no one spoke at all. Then a shout that was half wonder and half admiration went up from the men. Paul Beebe was bringing in *the Phantom and a colt!*

Even the wild herds grew excited. As one horse, they stopped grazing. Every head jerked high, to see and to smell the newcomers. The Pied Piper whirled out and gathered the mare and her colt into his band. He sniffed them all over as

70

if to make sure that nothing had harmed them. Then he snorted at Phantom, as much as to say, "You cause me more trouble than all the rest of my mares put together!"

The roundup men were swarming around Paul, buzzing with questions.

"How'd you *do* it, Paul?" Wyle Maddox called over the excited hubbub.

"Where'd you find 'em?" shouted Kim Horsepepper.

Paul made no answer. The questions floated around and above him like voices in a dream. He went hot and cold by turns. Did he do the right thing by bringing the Phantom and her foal in? Miserably he watched the Phantom's head droop. There was no wild sweep to her mane and her tail now. The free wild thing was caught like a butterfly in a net. She was webbed in by men, yelling and laughing.

"Beats all!" he heard someone say. "For two years we been trying to round up the Phantom and along comes a spindling youngster to show us up."

"'Twas the little colt that hindered her."

"'Course it was."

"It's the newest colt in the bunch; may not stand the swim."

"If we lose only one colt, it'll still be a good day's work."

"Jumpin' Jupiter, but it's hot!"

The men accepted Paul as one of them now—a real roundup man. They were clapping him on the shoulder and offering him candy bars. Suddenly he remembered the bar

Grandpa had pressed into his hand. He took off the wrapper and ate—not because he was hungry, but because he wanted to seem one of the men. They were trying to get him to talk. "Ain't they a shaggy-lookin' bunch?" Kim Horsepepper asked.

"Except for Misty," Paul said, pointing toward the Phantom's colt. "Her coat is silky." The mere thought of touching it sent shivers through him. "Misty," he thought to himself wonderingly. "Why, I've named her!"

The little foal was nursing greedily. Paul's eyes never strayed from the two of them. It was as if they might disappear into the mist of the morning, leaving only the sorrels and the bays and the blacks behind.

Only once he looked out across the water. Two lines of boats were forming a pony-way across the channel. He saw the cluster of people and the mounts waiting on the shores of Chincoteague and he knew that somewhere among them was Maureen. It was like a relay race. Soon she would carry on.

"Could I swim my mount across the channel alongside the Phantom?" Paul asked Wyle Maddox anxiously.

Wyle shook his head. "Watch Eyes is all tuckered out," he said. "Besides, there's a kind of tradition in the way things is handled on Pony Penning Day. There's mounted men for the roundup and there's boatmen to herd 'em across the channel," he explained.

"Tide's out!" he called in clipped tones. "Current is slack. Time for the ponies to be swimmed across. Let's go!"

Suddenly the beach was wild with commotion. From three sides the roundup men came rushing at the ponies, their hoarse cries whipping the animals into action. They plunged into the water, the stallions leading, the mares following, neighing encouragement to their colts.

"They're off!" shouted Wyle Maddox, and everyone felt the relief and triumph in his words.

Kim thumped Paul on the back as they boarded the scow for the ride back. "Don't fret about yer prize," he said brusquely. "You've got the Phantom sure this time. Once in the water she can't turn back."

But he was wrong!

Chapter 8

CAUGHT IN THE WHIRLPOOL

ON THE shores of Chincoteague the people pressed forward, their faces strained to stiffness, as they watched Assateague Beach.

"Here they come!" The cry broke out from every throat.

Maureen, wedged in between Grandpa Beebe on one side and a volunteer fireman on the other, stood on her mount's back. Her arms paddled the air as if she were swimming and struggling with the wild ponies.

Suddenly a fisherman, looking through binoculars, began shouting in a hoarse voice, "A new-borned colt is afeared to swim! It's knee-deep in the water, and won't go no further."

The crowds yelled their advice. "What's the matter with the roundup men?" "Why don't they heft it into deep water— it'll swim all right!" "Why don't they hist it on the scow?"

The fisherman was trying to get a better view. He was crawling out over the water on a wall of piling. It seemed a long time before he put his binoculars to his eyes again. The people waited breathlessly. A small boy began crying.

"Sh!" quieted his mother. "Listen to the man with the four eyes."

"The colt's too little to swim," the fisherman bawled out. "Wait! A wild pony is breaking out from the mob. Swimming around the mob! Escaping!"

An awed murmur stirred the crowds. Maureen dug her toes in her mount's back. She strained her eyes to see the fugitive, but all she could make out was a milling mass of dark blobs on the water.

The fisherman leaned far out over the water. He made a megaphone of one hand. "Them addle-brained boatmen can't stop the pony," his voice rasped. "It's outsmarting 'em all."

Maureen's mind raced back to other Pony Pennings. The Phantom upsetting a boat. The Phantom fleeing through the woods. Always escaping. Always free. She clutched the neck of her blouse. She felt gaspy, like a fish flapping about on dry land. Why was the man with the binoculars so slow? Why didn't he say, "It's the Phantom!" Who else could it be?

Now he was waving one arm wildly. He looked like a straw in the wind. He teetered. He lost his balance. He almost fell into the water in his excitement.

"It's the Phantom!" he screamed at last. "I can see the white map on her shoulders!"

The people took up the cry, echoing it over and over. "It's the Phantom! She's escaped again!"

Maureen felt tears on her cheek, and impatiently brushed them away.

Again the fisherman was waving for quiet.

"Hush!" bellowed Grandpa Beebe.

The people fell silent. They were like listeners around a microphone. "It's the *Phantom's* colt that won't swim!" he called out in a voice so hoarse it cracked. "The Phantom got separated from a bran'-fire new colt. She's gone back to get it!"

The people whooped and hollered at the news. "The Phantom's got a colt," they sang out. "The Phantom's got a new colt!"

Again the fisherman was waving for silence.

"She's reached her colt!" he crowed. "But the roundup men are closing in on her! They're making her shove the colt in the water. She's makin' it swim!"

Grandpa Beebe cupped his hands around his mouth. "Can the little feller make it?" he boomed.

The crowd stilled, waiting for the hoarse voice. For long seconds no answer came. The fisherman remained as fixed as the piling he stood on. Wave after wave of fear swept over Maureen. She felt as if she were drowning. And just when she could stand the silence no longer, the fisherman began reporting in short, nervous sentences.

"They're half-ways across. Jumpin' Jupiter! The colt! It's bein' sucked down in a whirlpool. I can't see it now. My soul and body! A boy's jumped off the scow. He's swimming out to help the colt."

The onlookers did not need the fisherman with the binoculars any more. They could see for themselves. A boy swimming against the current. A boy holding a colt's head above the swirling water.

Maureen gulped great lungfuls of air. "It's Paul!" she screamed. "It's Paul!"

On all sides the shouts went up. "Why, it's Paul!"

"Paul Beebe!"

Grandpa leaped up on his mount's back as nimbly as a boy. He stood with his arms upraised, his fists clenched.

"God help ye, Paul!" his words carried out over the water. "Yer almost home!"

Grandpa's voice was as strong as a tow rope. Paul was swimming steadily toward it, holding the small silver face of the colt above the water. He was almost there. He *was* there!

Maureen slid down from her mount, clutching a handful of mane. "You made it, Paul! You made it!" she cried.

The air was wild with whinnies and snorts as the ponies touched the hard sand, then scrambled up the shore, their wet bodies gleaming in the sun. Paul half-carried the little colt up the steep bank; then suddenly it found its own legs.

Shouts between triumph and relief escaped every throat as the little filly tottered up the bank. Almost to the top, her feet went scooting out from under her and she was down on the sand, her sides heaving.

Maureen felt a new stab of fear.

If only the big ponies would not crush her! That tender white body among all those thrashing hooves. What chance had she? What chance with the wild wind for a mother?

But all the wildness seemed to have ebbed out of the Phantom. She picked her forefeet high. Then she carefully straddled her colt, and fenced in the small white body with her own slender legs.

For a brief second Paul's and Maureen's eyes met above the crowds. It was as if they and the mare and her foal were the only creatures on the island. They were unaware of the great jostling and fighting as the stallions sorted out their own mares and colts. They were unaware of everything but a sharp ecstasy. Soon the Phantom and her colt would belong to them. Never to be sold.

The Pied Piper wheeled around Paul. He peered at the dripping boy from under his matted forelock. Then he trumpeted as if to say: "This sopping creature is no mare of mine!"

And he pushed Paul out of the way while the crowds laughed hysterically.

Dodging horses and people, Grandpa Beebe made his way over to Paul.

"Paul, boy," he said, his voice unsteady, "I swimmed the hull way with you. Yer the most wonderful and the craziest young'un in the world. Now git home right smart quick," he added, trying to sound very stern. "Yer about done up, and Grandma's expectin' ye. Maureen and I'll see to it that the Phantom and her colt reach the pony pens."

Chapter 9

ON TO THE PONY PENNING GROUNDS

IT WAS NOW mid-morning and the hot July sun was high in the heavens. The wild ponies stood with heads hanging low, tails tucked in. They looked beaten and confused. Only the Phantom's foal seemed contented. She slept, her sides rising and falling in the cool shade made by the mare's body.

"Rest 'em a bit longer," Wyle Maddox directed. "Then on to the pony pens."

Maureen sat watching, thinking. The little colt must never know the hungry feeling of being without a mother. But the hundred dollars? Would it pay for both?

She was jolted out of her thoughts with the cry, "Get-a-going!"

Onlookers fell back while Maureen, Grandpa Beebe, and the other horsemen surrounded the ponies and began driving them toward town. The Phantom broke at the start, her colt weaving along behind her like the tail of a kite.

"Please, God, don't let Phantom escape now!" breathed Maureen as she and Grandpa Beebe took out after them. But Phantom could not travel fast with her stilty-legged youngster. Maureen soon came upon them, hidden among the foliage of a kinksbush, the Phantom's proud, wild face and the colt's

comical baby face all framed round with green leaves.

With a shout she drove them back into the herd.

After that the mare no longer tried to escape, for there were no openings into the cool woods—only lines of cars and visitors forming a solid fence on either side of them.

Slowly and dejectedly the wild ponies paraded through the main streets of Chincoteague. Only the Phantom's colt seemed happy with her lot. She could smell her dam close by. Her stomach was stretched tight with milk. She was full of sleep. She kicked her heels sideways, dancing along, letting out little whinnies of joy. She seemed to *like* Chincoteague.

All up and down the streets the people came spilling out of their houses, shouting to one another as they recognized some mare or stallion from previous roundups.

"There's that pinto with the shark eyes."

"Look at the Pied Piper! His forelock's grown 'most as long as his tail!"

"See all the big colts!"

"Who's the chestnut mare with the white mark on her shoulders?"

"Not the Phantom! Not her!" they gasped in disbelief.

"It *is* the Phantom!" someone yelled in answer. "And she's got a colt! I saw 'em swim in!"

"And Paul Beebe caught her," someone else called. "I heard Kim Horsepepper tell all about it."

The excitement ran from house to house like a flame in the wind. "They got the Phantom! Paul Beebe got her! And she's leadin' a colt!"

Through the shouting, elbowing crowd, the slow parade went on—past stores and restaurants, past the white frame hotel, past the red brick firehouse which the colts of other years had paid for.

Maureen looked straight ahead. She stayed so close to the Phantom and her foal that when the foal looked sideways Maureen could see her long golden eyelashes.

At last the procession turned into the pony penning grounds. It moved quickly once around the ring. Then once

again, while children and parents and horse dealers hung over the fence. The children shouted at the top of their lungs.

"Oh, Dad! Buy me that colt with the star on her face!"

"I want the one with the white stockings!"

"I want the littlest one!"

Only the dealers were silent. They were thinking in terms of buying and selling.

Grandpa Beebe rode close to Maureen. "We got 'em here," he sighed sharply. "Now it's up to the men afoot."

Again that feeling of something pressing against her throat came to Maureen as she watched the men on foot drive the ponies out of the ring, separating the colts from their mothers. They herded the colts into small pens, giving the mares and stallions the run of a big corral.

Suddenly it was the Phantom's turn to be herded into the corral. She flew ahead of the men, never allowing them to touch her. Now two brawny men were making a grab for her foal. For long seconds the men held the foal high, their hands supporting her little round belly. Then they put her down, slapped her hip and sent her along with her dam into the big corral.

Maureen drew a deep breath of happiness. "The colt's too little to leave her mother. Too little!" she whispered into Grandpa's whiskery ear. "They'll let them stay together."

Then she hurried home to tell Paul.

"Paul's asleep," Grandma said, "and you leave him be. I got some butter beans warmin' fer ye and some nice fresh cornbread sittin' a-top the oven."

While Maureen ate, Grandma talked on. "I kin see you're boilin' over with things to tell, but they'll keep till you've ate. Between whiles I'll do the talkin'." She closed one eye in thought. "Let's see. Oh, Victoria Pruitt stopped by. Figgered you or Paul might like to earn some money helpin' her and Mr. Pruitt catch chickens. They're fixin' to ship 'em to Norfolk. But I told Mis' Victoria yer money pouch was fat as a tick."

Maureen's spoon fell to the floor.

"Oh, Grandma! The Phantom's got a colt and we got to earn a lot of money to buy her, too."

Grandma looked at Maureen's plate. She saw that the beans were gone and there was nothing left of the cornbread but a few crumbs. "Go 'long," she nodded. "Mis' Victoria wanted ye right much."

Maureen spent the afternoon chasing hundreds of chickens and cooping them up in little crates. By sundown her arms were pecked and scratched and her face streaked with perspiration.

As she walked home, clutching two dollars in her moist hand, she saw Paul riding toward her on Watch Eyes.

"Leg up behind me," he called out. "I got to go to the store for Grandma. You can help carry the things."

Maureen scrambled up behind her brother. "Paul!"

"Huh?"

"Do you reckon the firemen'll sell us both the Phantom and the little one?"

"'Course. The colt's too young to take away from the mare."

"But where'll we get the money?"

Paul slowed Watch Eyes to a walk. "I been working on it whilst I slept," he said. "What time does the sale begin?"

"It says half-past nine on the program."

"All right," exclaimed Paul, giving Watch Eyes his head "You and I'll get to the pony penning grounds at sunup. We'll wait there at the entrance for the fire chief. Soon as he comes, we'll say to him: 'We got exactly one hundred dollars, sir. We earned it in less'n four months. In four months more we can earn another hundred. Y'see, chief, we're fixin' to buy the Phantom—and Misty, too.'"

"Why, Paul! That's *exactly* what we'll do. It'll be just as easy as that." She threw her arms about Paul's waist. "Misty," she chuckled. "Who named the Phantom's colt?"

"She kind of named herself," Paul answered. "When I was in the woods there on Assateague, I couldn't tell if I was seeing white mist with the sun on it, or a live colt. The minute I knew 'twas a live colt, I kept calling her Misty in my mind."

"Misty!" said Maureen softly. "Misty," she repeated as they jogged along. "She came up out of the sea."

Grandpa was in the kitchen, standing before a mirror, trimming the bristles in his ears when Maureen and Paul came in with the groceries.

"Consarn it all!" he fussed. "Do you got to rustle them bags like cows trompin' through a cornfield? A fella can't hear hisself think, let alone hold his hand steady. This here's a mighty ticklish job."

"Why, Clarence!" exclaimed Grandma, "I've never seed you so twittery."

"Ef'n you had whiskbrooms in your ears, maybe you'd be twittery, too."

Grandma stopped basting the marsh hen she had just taken out of the oven and burst out in helpless laughter. "Whiskbrooms in my ears!" she chortled. And soon Maureen and Paul and even Grandpa were laughing with her.

"All right now," said Grandma, recovering her breath. "Maureen, you can set the potatoes to boil and lay the table. Lay an extra place like allus. Never know when some human straggler is goin' to stop. And bein' as it's Pony Penning Day you kin cut a few of them purty-by-nights and some bouncin' Bess fer a centerpiece."

No straggler came. Just the four of them sat around the table while a light wind played with the curtains. Grandpa became more like himself with each mouthful of the tender marsh hen.

"The reason I was jumpy," he confessed, "was account of thinkin' about that Phantom you children wanter buy. No one of sound mind ever buys a three-year-old wild pony. Why, Phantom's like the topsail on a ship—a moon-raker she is!"

The flapping of the curtain broke the little pause that followed.

"Besides," Grandpa continued, "My feet is killin' me. Reckon we're in fer a blow. A sou'wester come up this afternoon, and I never seed a nor'easter take no back talk from a sou'wester."

"If a thunder squall's a-brewin'," spoke Grandma, "the children got to stay home from the race tonight."

Paul's and Maureen's eyes sought Grandpa's, as much as to say, "How can you do this to us? Why, the race on the eve of the sale is almost as important as the roundup!"

"Oh," coughed Grandpa, "it'll be *after* the race afore the weather turns squally. And my advice is fer the children to go right smart quick so they kin mill around in the colt pens afore the race. They might find a critter with lots purtier markings than the Phantom."

Paul and Maureen leaped to their feet. They galloped around and around the table, stopping to nose Grandma and Grandpa like curious colts. Then they soberly promised to visit the colt pens, but in their hearts they knew there was room only for the Phantom and Misty.

Chapter 10

COLTS HAVE GOT TO GROW UP

As PAUL and Maureen stood inside the big corral, looking at Misty, they knew she was the finest-blooded foal in the world. Oh, the beauty of her! She was neither silver nor gold. She was both. And she had a funny white blaze that started down the left side of her face, then did a right-about and covered her whole muzzle. It gave her a look of wonderment and surprise. Like her mother she, too, wore a white map of the United States on her withers, but the outlines were softer and blended into the gold of her body.

They could have gazed at her forever, exclaiming over her gold eyelashes, her pink underlip, her funny knobby knees, her short flappy tail, the furry insides of her ears. But suddenly Paul was aware of an uneasy feeling, as though someone were eying him. Then he felt a hot breath on the back of his neck. Slowly he turned his head and came face to face with the Pied Piper.

For an instant neither the stallion nor the boy winked an eyelash. Pied Piper stared fixedly at Paul from under his long forelock. He was like a man peering out from ambush. Paul could see the white ring around the stallion's eyes, the red lining of his nostrils, the ears flattened. He could smell the wildness. He sensed that one false move, and a darting foreleg might knock him down as if he were a cornstalk. He opened his mouth to speak, but for a long time no sound came.

"Your baby," he spoke at last in the softest of voices, "your baby is—is beautiful."

The Pied Piper's ears twitched ever so slightly.

"You mean *our* filly!" corrected Maureen in her strong, high voice.

The Pied Piper laced his ears back again. He bared his teeth, breathing loudly.

"I'm not talking to you, Maureen," Paul whispered, his face pale. "Turn your head."

The Pied Piper's ears pricked once more. That curious soft voice!

"Oh," Maureen breathed, as she caught sight of the stallion. "Your baby is beautiful," she gasped. "And so is your mare."

"So are all your mares," added Paul for good measure. "Excuse us, sir, but we must see the race now." He and Maureen began backing slowly toward the fence.

Just then a stallion from another band came over to study the Pied Piper's family. The Pied Piper forgot Paul and

Maureen in the more important business of bunching his mares behind him.

"Whew!" said Paul breathlessly, as they scrambled over the fence, "that was a close one."

On the way to the race track they had to pass between the colt pens.

"We almost forgot our promise to look at the colts!" they both exclaimed in the same breath.

Hurriedly they squeezed in between the spectators and perched on the top rail of one of the pens. Their faces paled as they looked down.

Round and round the pen the colts were plodding, searching for their mothers, flinging their heads up, whimpering, trying to suckle anything their muzzles could reach.

"Why, they're as close packed as oysters in a barrel!" exclaimed Paul.

"They're children, lost and scared," said Maureen. "Let's go!" she cried through white lips. "Let's go! I can't abide the nickerin'. The young things are hungry."

Paul felt as if he were going to be sick. "I can't abide it, either," he said. Then his mouth thinned to a line and he doubled his fists. "I'm going to see the fire chief about this!"

The fire chief was a big, broad-shouldered man who walked with a cane. There were times when the cane seemed to dangle uselessly in his hands. But when he was tired, he leaned on it heavily.

They found him now in the center of a group of visitors, both hands gripping his cane. His face was sun-blistered and weary, but his eyes lighted when he saw Paul and Maureen.

"Here's Paul Beebe, the lad who swam the colt ashore," he explained to the little group. "And his sister, Maureen, who . . ."

The crowd shifted, began surrounding Paul, pelting questions at him. "Did the colt try to drag you down like a drowning person?" "How old is it?" "How wide is the channel where you swam across?"

Paul and Maureen scarcely heard the questions.

"What are you two looking so hollow-eyed about?" the chief asked as he drew the children aside.

"It's about the colts," Maureen stammered.

"Yes," said Paul. "We don't believe they should be taken from their mothers, and we aim to do something about it— if you'll let us, sir. We got lots of milk in the ice chest at home, and once we raised up a foal on a big nursing bottle and we still got the bottle. It's cruel to starve the young things."

The fire chief stood silent and thoughtful. He looked past the grounds and out to the bay, where the masts of the fishing boats formed spider-thin lines against the graying sky.

"I don't know if I can make you understand about this, but I'll try," he began slowly. "Colts have got to grow up sometime. Their mothers can't go on babying them all their lives. Haven't you two seen a mare tell her youngster to rustle his own living?"

Paul and Maureen nodded in silence.

"She can't tell the colt in so many words," the fire chief continued. "She just kicks him away. Gentle-like at first. Then good and hard if he won't understand. Sometimes she has to get pretty rough, especially when she's going to have a new foal in a few months."

"But those little colts . . ."

"Those little fellows," nodded the chief, "are old enough to fend for themselves. Separating them from their mothers is the kindest way we know to teach them how."

Paul and Maureen reddened. They felt very young and foolish as they thanked the fire chief for explaining things.

"Don't thank me, you two. When I was rising up atwixt a youngster and a grownup, the same question worried me every Pony Penning Day. Finally, I watched a mare tell her colt to grow up and then I quit worrying. Now I want you to quit worrying, too.

"Besides," he added as he pulled out his watch, "it's almost time for the race. Black Comet will be running any minute now. It's high time," he said, tapping his cane in the sawdust, "it's high time we islanders raised up a competitor for Black Comet. Things have been much too easy for him."

"Tell him now," nudged Maureen, her eyes shining.

"Chief!" said Paul, trying to make his voice behave. "Next year Black Comet will have a *real* competitor. Maureen and I want to buy the Phant—"

But the fire chief never heard what Paul had to say. His words were drowned by a voice blaring over the loud speaker.

"Tonight, ladies and gentlemen, Black Comet from Pocomoke is racing against Patches and Lucy Lee of Chincoteague."

Chapter 11

STORM-SHY

FEELING much happier, Paul and Maureen joined the throngs hurrying to see Black Comet. Black Comet was five years old. For three of those years he had been brought over from Pocomoke on the mainland to race for the Pony Penning crowds on the eve of the sale. And for three years he had won. Twice he led by several lengths, and once he led only by a nose. But always he won.

This night was no different. Black Comet pranced to the starting line, sure of himself. His jockey, too, was sure. They both seemed bored with the excited antics of the two other entries. One was a flashy black-and-white pony named Patches. He danced on his hind feet, bolted past the starting line, and had to be brought back again and again. The other entry was Lucy Lee, a nervous little mare.

Black Comet threw back his head and let out a high horse laugh at them as if to say, "You're wasting your time."

And they were! The race belonged to Black Comet from the start. He broke out in front and stayed there.

Maureen beat her fists on the fence rail. "Come on, Patches! Come on, Lucy Lee! Don't let Black Comet win every time!"

"Next year the Phantom will be in there!" Paul kept saying. "Next year the Phantom."

Just as Black Comet crossed the finish line, a bolt of lightning split the sky.

At that same instant Paul felt a strong hand grip his shoulder. It was Grandpa Beebe. His face was spattered with dirt and his clean blue shirt in ribbons.

"The squall ain't a promise no more," he shouted against the rising wind, "it's here! Paul, you stay and help the fire chief. Maureen, you come home with me.

"And Paul! If the storm gits too heavy," he called back over his shoulder, "you take shelter in our truck. It's backed up nigh to the colt pens."

The grounds burst into noise and confusion. The wind whined. It caught at the tent flaps, snapping them like whips.

White paper programs spiraled through the air, driven first one way, then the other. Children, over-tired and frightened, cried to be taken home. Thunder rumbled deep out of the heavens. Colts in their pens squealed. Stallions trumpeted.

Paul fought his way to the pony pens, dodging people, dodging pieces of paper which the wind swept into his face. He could scarcely see his way. The strings of colored electric bulbs waved back and forth, throwing weird shadows.

At last he came upon the fire chief, brandishing his cane and shouting directions: "Dan, you do this! Joe, you do that! Paul . . ."

Paul strained his ears to hear, but suddenly the skies seemed to open and rain fell in great torrents. The swaying lights went out, plunging the island into darkness.

"Everyone go home!" called the chief. "Nothing we can do now." A flash of lightning showed him limping toward his car.

Paul did not follow. The rain beat down on him fiercely. It felt cold and hard, like gunshot. How could Misty stand it? "She's so little," he thought. "She's bound to be storm-shy. I know what I'll do! I'll carry her to the truck and shelter her until the storm is past."

Warmed by his decision, he ran past the colt pens and on to the big corral. Lightning sizzled across the sky, flooding the earth with an eerie white. It showed the wild ponies, separated into four bands. Paul's eyes leaped from one band to another, trying to find the Pied Piper's family, but darkness

closed in. He held his breath, waiting for another flash. It came. It picked out the stallion's creamy-white mane.

Quickly Paul scrambled over the fence. He waited again, his eyes fastened on the spot where the Pied Piper's band stood huddled. He held onto the fence with one hand and made a watershed over his eyes with the other. He waited again for the lightning. It came tearing across the sky. He could see the Pied Piper's family as plainly as if it were daylight, but the Phantom and Misty were not among them. They were gone! Stolen! Some other stallion had stolen them! The thought flashed through his mind.

Shivering and drenched, he ran from one band to the other. He stumbled over tree stumps and fell flat in the water. His mouth was gritty with sand and mud. He went on blindly, feeling every hump in the grass, every fallen log; but nowhere in all that big corral could he find the tiny foal or her wild dam.

Running, slipping, falling, running, he made his way to the pony trucks. Most of the trucks were empty, waiting for tomorrow's sale. A few held a colt or two—big colts, big and shaggy.

Sick with fear for Phantom and Misty, he sought the shelter of Grandpa Beebe's truck to think out where they might be. Could Phantom have leaped the fence? Could Misty have rolled out under it? He stopped short. There, in the body of the truck, under a piece of tarpaulin, he felt rather than saw a slight stirring. He trembled, not from cold, but from fear that what he prayed was a mare and her colt would turn out instead to be bags of feed. He cried out for a flash of lightning. It came in a streak, filling the truck with yellow light. And in that split second Paul saw the Phantom and Misty, their heads lowered in a corner like children being punished at school.

He threw back his head for joy and let the rain beat on his face. So that was why Grandpa's shirt was torn and his face seamed with dirt! He had brought them to shelter before the storm broke.

Paul opened the door of the cab, half expecting Grandpa to be there. It was empty—except for Grandpa's old rain jacket that lay on the seat, and the strong smell of tobacco. He ripped off his wet shirt, his denim pants. His teeth chattered as he pulled on the warm, dry jacket. It was so long it almost covered his underwear. He ran around to the tailgate of the truck and steadied himself on the spare tire. Slowly, cautiously, hardly daring to breathe, he climbed up and over the tailgate and into the truck.

The storm blotted out any sound he might have made. But the Phantom sensed his presence. She neighed sharply to Misty, who caught her fear. Paul could hear the small rat-a-tat of her hooves.

He leaned hard against the stakes of the truck, every muscle tensed. Phantom would either charge him or stay as far away as possible. He waited, counting the seconds. He could hear the rain sloshing over the tarpaulin, spilling down the sides of

the truck. He could smell the steamy warmth of furry bodies. He could smell the sea. And in the occasional flashes of light,

he saw the copper-and-white tail of the Phantom sweeping nervously over Misty. Paul let out a deep sigh of relief. She was *not* going to charge him.

He never knew how long he stood there. He only knew that after awhile the Phantom no longer mistrusted him. She seemed to doze off for seconds at a time, as if she felt a oneness with him; as if she and her foal and this shivering, wet boy were fellow creatures caught in a storm, prisoners of the elements. Prisoners together.

Together! The word sounded a bugle in Paul. Time stood still. There was only the wind and the rain and the three creatures together! Together!

Aching to reach out and touch first the shaggy coat, then the silky one, he plunged his hands deep into Grandpa's pockets to stay the impulse. His fingers felt a firm, slightly sticky object. He squeezed it. He traced a few dried stems, then paper-thin leaves pressed solidly together. It was a twist of chewing tobacco! Quickly he pulled it out of his pocket. The spicy sweetness of molasses filled his nostrils. He took long, deep breaths of it. His mind was turning somersaults. Molasses! Molasses! How ponies love it! Often he had seen Grandpa cut a quid for Watch Eyes. With trembling fingers he broke off a sizable piece and held it on his outstretched hand.

For a long time he waited. When he could stand no longer, he sank down on the cold, wet floor of the truck, still holding his hand toward the Phantom.

He waited, motionless.

He listened to the storm bell tolling out in the bay, and to the rain swishing and swirling around him. He felt little

111

rivulets of perspiration run down his back. He grew hot and chilled by turns. His arm grew numb, then began to prickle as if hundreds of red-hot needles were jabbing him. His head reeled. It ached for lack of sleep.

And just when his hand was about to drop, he heard slow, questioning hooves placed one at a time on the floor of the truck. One step forward. Then a long pause filled in by the sobbing of the wind. Then another step. And another. Now a breath on his hand, now feelers sending chills of excitement up his arm, racing through his whole body. Now a soft muzzle lipping his palm. The tobacco gone! Lifted out of his hand by a pony so wild that she had upset a boat, so wild that for two years no one had caught her. A wild thing eating out of his hand! He wriggled his fingers in wonderment. All the numbness had gone out of them. He was not even trembling! Only this sharp ecstasy, this feeling that all of life was worth this moment. The roundup, the discovery of Misty, the swim across the channel—they all melted into this.

The moments rushed on. The storm quieted. Paul could hear the Phantom mouthing the tobacco. He tried to keep awake to enjoy the pleasant, soothing sound, but his eyes drooped. His breath steadied. He fell into a deep sleep, unmindful when the Phantom nosed him curiously from head to foot. Then she, too, began to doze.

At last Misty sank down in exhaustion. Her head fell across Paul's lap, not because she wanted human comfort, but because she was tired from the hard drive and the swim. The floor of a truck or a boy's lap were all the same to her, so long as her dam was near.

It was thus, at dawn, that Grandpa Beebe found them.

Chapter 12

THE SOLD ROPE

PAUL," whispered Grandpa in the low voice he used when children and wild animals were asleep. "Paul, boy . . ."

At sound of Grandpa's voice the Phantom neighed shrilly. Misty scrambled to her feet, swayed, then slid awkwardly along the floor of the truck. With a hungry little bleat, she found her mother's side and began nursing.

Paul opened his eyes, then quickly shut them. If this were a dream, he wanted to spin it out and make it last until the end of time. He wished Grandpa's voice would fade away, but it kept pricking him awake.

"Come, boy. Grandma is nigh crazy with worry over ye. The big pine tree fell atop the house last night and the Atlantic Ocean wetted our dooryard. I just couldn't come for ye till now."

Paul pulled himself up. His muscles ached. He could feel the wide stripes made by the boards of the truck across his back. He looked down at his long expanse of bare legs and suddenly remembered that he was wearing nothing but Grandpa's jacket over his underwear. He grinned at Grandpa.

Grandpa winked back. "I see you scamped my belongings," he chuckled. "It's any port in a storm, eh, lad?" Then he thought of his message. "Grandma's mixed some goose grease with onion syrup fer ye. Yer apt to catch a terrible fever," he quoted Grandma, but all the while his eyes were fondling the dam and her colt. "She says ye've got to come home and go to bed."

Paul felt the stickiness of his hand where the Phantom had nuzzled it. His voice tensed. "I can't leave, Grandpa. Today's the sale! We got to buy the Phantom and Misty."

"Maureen kin tend to that whilst ye get some sleep. I don't know what in thunderation made me protect that little feller fer ye last night. I must be getting addled in my old age. Now help me get the pair of 'em outen the truck and back in the corral so you can buy 'em legal-like at the sale."

But there was no need for help. With the truck backed up close to the corral gate, the Phantom flew down the ramp. She

115

smelled the rain-washed grass. She was crazy to get to it. Misty followed, a silver fluff of a shadow.

The pony penning grounds were waking up when Maureen rode in on Watch Eyes. Volunteer firemen were clearing the damage done by the storm. Trucks bearing licenses from Maryland, New York, North Carolina, Washington, D. C., were beginning to line up close to the colt pens. A few children, their faces still flushed with sleep, darted here and there, talking to themselves: "That little black pony. I could name him Black Beauty!" "I want the one with the white stockings!"

"How-do, Maureen," called Tom, who on ordinary days was an oysterer. "Yer up and about mighty early. Reckon yer sharpenin' your appetite for the big dinner this noon! Or mebbe ye come to buy my last two chances on the sorrel pony bein' given away Saturday." And with a great flourish he whipped the tickets out of his pocket.

Maureen could think of no answer. She was not interested in the sorrel pony, and she had forgotten all about the dinner to be served in the big dining hall on the grounds. She managed to smile at Tom and thank him politely. Then feeling of the money pouch around her neck, and the piece of rope over her shoulder, she stated her business quickly. "I came to see the fire chief," she said.

"Nowheres about. He's been and gone."

"Oh!"

"Anything I can do?"

"Reckon not."

"Wal, he'll be back afore ye can say Chincoteague Isle."

Tying Watch Eyes to a tree, Maureen wandered about the grounds, waiting for the chief. She stopped at the colt pens and noticed that several of the shaggy-coated youngsters already wore sold ropes around their necks. She noticed, too, that most of them were beginning to eat for themselves. Only a few were whimpering for their mothers.

The fire chief was right, she thought. They're learning to be grownups.

She felt good toward the whole wide world as she walked toward the big corral. She watched two stallions fighting— dancing on their hind legs, lashing out with their forelegs. A news photographer was getting a picture of them. Finally she climbed the fence and jumped inside the corral.

The wild ponies were refreshed by the rain. They thundered past and around her. They paid her no more attention than if she had been a small tree. She was nothing but an obstacle to avoid. She stood listening to the wild music of their hooves. She liked to feel the little gusts of wind made by their flying bodies. She liked the sight of their manes and tails frisking with the wind.

The Pied Piper's band was on the far side of the corral. He was policing his family, keeping his mares in a bunch. Maureen saw Misty stretched out at her mother's feet.

Her heart warmed at sight of them. She walked over to them, slowly, slowly. If she could slip the sold rope over Misty's head, it would save all the struggle later. The firemen had no

time to "ease up" to the ponies. With a hundred or more colts to sell, they had to work fast. Often two men had to pick up a pony by its tail and its head in order to fasten a sold rope about its neck. Meanwhile, the pony screamed and fought and struggled to get away.

Probably it *doesn't* hurt, thought Maureen, but I'd like to save Misty all that scared feeling.

Suddenly her eyes flew wide with horror. The Phantom was tugging at a rope tied around Misty's neck. A sold rope! "No! No! No!" Maureen shrieked. "Phantom!" she cried hysterically, "you're the only one who can un-sell her. Try harder! Harder! Harder!"

Phantom was doing her best. With her big yellow teeth she was trying to sever the rope, but Misty would pull away,

thinking her mother was playing. She opened her little colt's mouth, biting back, neighing fiercely.

Maureen looked around helplessly. Just then she spied the fire chief coming toward the corral with Tom at his heels. She ran to them. "Misty's wearing a sold rope!" she cried. "Misty's been sold!" Then her voice failed her.

"*Who's* been sold?" asked the chief, puzzled.

"Who?" echoed Tom.

"Misty!" she choked, trying to swallow her tears.

The fire chief knotted his brows. "Now suppose you tell me who Misty is," he said kindly.

"Why, she's the Phantom's colt, and Paul and I—we've been saving for months to buy the Phantom, and now we want both her and her colt. And we have a hundred and two dollars," she added breathlessly as she patted the money around her neck, "right here in Grandpa's tobacco pouch. And in four months more we can save up another hundred. I can go clamming, and I can catch soft-shell crabs, and Paul can shuck oysters, and Uncle Ralph will give us his night catch of fatbacks, and Paul and I can go up and down the streets calling 'Fat-backs for sale, nice fresh fat-backs for sale!'"

"Well, why in thunder didn't you kids tell me!" exploded the fire chief. Then his voice quieted. "I'm sorry, Maureen. I didn't know. Why, less than an hour ago a man by the name of Foster came through on his way to Norfolk. Had business there, he said, and couldn't get back until after the sale. I asked Tom here to show him around and he took a fancy to the filly's markings."

"He bought Misty?"

"Paid fifty dollars down," nodded the chief. "Insisted on buying the Phantom, too, just so the colt'll get a good start in life." He took a deep breath. "Tom and I," he added, "tied the sold rope around the colt's neck, but it's going to take a lot more than two of us to handle that Phantom."

Maureen watched the sun slide out from behind a low cloud and make diamonds of the raindrops on the grass. She turned her back on it. How could the sun shine when things went wrong?

The fire chief clasped and unclasped his cane. "I had no idea," he spoke quietly. "If you had only said something about it yesterday."

Maureen was about to leave, but Tom called her back.

"How's about taking my last chances on the sorrel?" he suggested. "There's a *gentle* critter. And ye'd still have a hundred dollars to spend on candy and things."

Maureen raised her eyes to Tom's. Then she smiled at him through her tears. She felt sorry for Tom. Guess he's never really wanted anything, she thought, as she slowly walked over to untie Watch Eyes.

Chapter 13

A PONY CHANGES HANDS

PAUL took the news without a word, but all the sunburn suddenly washed out of his face, leaving it pinched and white.

The day passed in a kind of dream. Both Paul and Maureen tried to stay away from the grounds, but something drew them there. Yet they no longer belonged to the happy crowds. They were onlookers now, like hungry people on the outside of a restaurant window.

Sick with longing, they watched colts being tugged and pushed and lifted into waiting cars. Some went off in station wagons, some in trailers, some in dealers' trucks. Many of them squealed and kicked and fought. A few were too frightened to struggle.

They stared fixedly as Grandpa bought a truckload of yearlings. "Soon we'll be gentling them—for someone else," Maureen whispered sadly to Paul.

The day that was to be so full of excitement dragged out. Even the merry-go-round with its brightly painted ponies and its brassy music did not help them forget. To Paul, the music kept wheezing, "You found and lost Misty! You found and lost Misty! You found and lost Misty!" To Maureen it was a noisy mockery.

"We'll have us another hoss family. Just as purty. Mebbe purtier," promised Grandpa Beebe as they sat at a table in the dining hall at noon. But Grandpa's words sounded bigger than his voice.

The ladies of the auxiliary hovered over them anxiously, heaping their plates with oysters and clam fritters, and great helpings of Chincoteague pot pie.

"Land sakes!" exclaimed a motherly person to Paul and Maureen. "What's the matter with you two young'uns? Such puny appetites! Take my Delbert now, he's on his fourth helping."

But try as they would, Maureen and Paul could not eat. The food that usually tasted so good lodged in their throats. Even Grandpa Beebe had no appetite. "Ef I didn't *know* 'twas plump oysters and rolled-out dumplings with chunks of chicken," he said, "I'd swear I was eatin' bran mash!"

In the afternoon there was the bronco busting. It was like any wild west show, except there were no mountains in the distance. Only fishing boats and the sea, and gulls flying, and a soft wind singing in the pines.

The wild ponies, crazed with fright, were let out of chutes. While the crowds gasped and shrieked, the ponies crowhopped. They bucked. They threw their riders at once, or

tolerated them for brief seconds. The people cheered madly when an oyster-tonger wearing a red baseball cap and holding a big unlighted cigar in his mouth stayed on his bronco for a matter of minutes. And just when he was doffing his cap and bowing to the crowds, the pony tossed him and his cigar and red cap high into the air.

An instant's pause; then such a whooping and laughter went up as he recovered his cigar and pulled his cap over his face, that it was heard by Grandma in the kitchen at Pony Ranch. Paul and Maureen watched, but they were not really a part of the laughing, cheering crowd.

Thursday night, Friday passed. The Pied Piper and all the brood mares except the Phantom were driven into the channel to swim back to Assateague for another year of freedom.

It was Saturday before Paul and Maureen were able to talk about their loss. They were in the dooryard, taking turns grinding clams for Grandma.

"If only I had never gone on the roundup," Paul said bitterly.

Maureen shook her head. "It was my fault. If only I'd gotten to the grounds at four, 'stead of five!"

"If only I'd told the fire chief the night before."

"What'll we do with the hundred and two dollars?" Maureen asked.

A long silence was broken by the squeaking of the crank.

"We could buy Grandma and Grandpa one of those electric

toasters," Paul said at last. "And we could save the rest to go to college on the mainland when we get grown."

"Let's do it," Maureen agreed, but without much enthusiasm.

Later that morning, as they were looking at electric toasters in a window on Main Street, they heard a man's voice call, "Hi, there!"

They turned around to see a station wagon at the curb, with a man and a small boy in the front seat. The man leaned past the boy and poked his head out of the window.

"Can you tell us where the fire chief lives?" he asked.

"Yes, sir," replied Paul. "He lives up the second street, third house from the corner. But I reckon he's still at the grounds. They're having the drawing on the sorrel this morning."

The boy's head shot out of the car. "The drawing's over," he exclaimed. "And guess what!"

"What?" asked Paul and Maureen.

"I won the pony!" he said breathlessly.

"That's right," nodded the man, who did not seem to share the boy's eagerness. "And now we've got to see the fire chief. He went off in his car before we could find him. By the way," the man questioned, "do you two know him?"

Paul and Maureen managed a smile. "Everybody knows him," they said.

The next moment they spied the chief's car turning in at a gas station on the opposite corner.

"I'll get him for you," Paul said, and he ran across the street.

"Hmm," mused the chief as he limped back with Paul. "Looks to me like Foster, the man from Norfolk. Only before, he didn't have a boy with him."

"Is he the one who bought Misty and Phantom?" Paul asked quickly.

The chief nodded.

By now the man and the boy had gotten out of the station wagon.

"How do," said the fire chief.

"Good morning," replied the man. He took off his hat and began twirling it nervously in his hands. He cleared his throat. Then he pulled a clean white handkerchief from his pocket and wiped his forehead.

"This is Freddy, my young son, and we . . ." He hesitated a moment, then hurried the words, "and we have a problem. You see, the other morning your man Tom sold us a chance on a pony, and I forgot all about it. That is," he laughed, "until this morning when I stopped off at the grounds to show Freddy the tiny foal I had bought for him."

"Tell him, Daddy! Tell him!" interrupted Freddy.

"Just as we stepped out of the car," Mr. Foster continued, "they were raffling off the sorrel colt, and—"

"We won!" shouted Freddy.

"No!" exclaimed the chief, and Paul and Maureen saw the tired look suddenly lift from his face.

"We won! We won!" cried Freddy. "Now tell him the rest, Daddy. Tell him!"

Mr. Foster spoke very quickly now as if the sooner told the better. "You see, sir, Freddy likes the sorrel pony because it is almost the color of my horse. He likes it better than the new-born foal."

Paul and Maureen could hardly breathe. They were staring at Mr. Foster as if they could not believe what they heard.

"Of course," Mr. Foster added, "I appreciate that Pony Penning Day is over and you may not have another chance to sell the little foal. In that case," he said, putting his hat back on his head, "in that case, why—we'll just have to hold to our bargain. Though what we'll do with *two* colts and how we'll get that wild Phantom home has me worried."

There was a long moment of stillness. An old man came along wheeling a cart of squash and watermelons. As the man went by, a dog lying in the doorway of the hardware store thumped his tail noisily. Across the street a juke box was spilling out the words, "Oh, give me a home where the buffalo roam."

Still the chief made no answer. Instead, he hooked his cane over Paul's shoulder. Then he took a notebook out of his

pocket and slowly, carefully, began thumbing through it, reading notations on each page. Finally he tore a leaf out of the book and took a fifty-dollar bill out of his wallet.

Handing the money and the page of writing to Mr. Foster, he said, "There was a boy and a girl had their eyes on the mare and her colt. I can't be sure," he said with a wink, "but I've a mind they still might be interested."

Maureen gave a little gasp. Then she picked up the astonished Freddy and gave him a sound kiss.

"Don't mind her," Paul said to Freddy. "Just girls' fribble." Then he grabbed the fire chief's hand and wrung it until his own ached. He shook hands with Mr. Foster, too, and even with Freddy.

At last he threw back his head like a spirited horse and let out such a loud whinny that it was heard the full length of Chincoteague Island.

Chapter 14

THE WICKIE

USUALLY a colt learns from its mother. It hears her whicker at sound of Man's voice. It sees her gallop to meet him when he comes down to the corral. It sees her lip Man's hand. Soon the colt discovers that Man represents the good things of life—delicious surprises in the way of sugar, carrots, apples. And presently it is trying to please Man, too; not only to be rewarded with something to eat, but to enjoy the tingly feeling of his hand or the pleasant sound of his voice.

With Phantom and Misty things happened the other way around. Misty accepted human beings right from the start.

Their hands felt good to her. She would brace herself, her forelegs splayed out, while Paul or Maureen gently stroked her neck or traced the white blaze on her face. She would lean toward them, asking in the only way she knew that the attentions never stop. Whenever they brushed her foretop or her mane, she lowered her gold eyelashes as if dreaming the most wonderful dreams.

"I declare," chuckled Grandpa. "That Misty 'minds me of a girl gettin' beautified for her first dance!"

Never was a colt more curious! A wickie was something to be investigated. First she nosed it. It tickled her colty whiskers and made her sneeze. Sneezing was fun. And one day, without knowing how it happened, she was wearing the wickie around her neck. It did not hurt! It did not hurt at all. Paul and Maureen were at the other end of it, and they were singing softly,

Come along, little Misty,
Come along.

Misty moved a step toward them, her ears pricked as if to catch the music in her name. And, wonder of wonders, she was rewarded with a lump of sugar as she walked along.

When Phantom saw that Misty was not being hurt, she would come forward, too. Nervously she would take what was offered and then back away, a safe distance behind her colt.

Grandma often came out to watch, with a dish of apples to pare or an armful of clothes to patch.

"This be the topsy-turviest pair I've ever seed!" she would laugh softly. "'Stead of the colt following its mommy, it's t'other way around."

It was days, however, before the Phantom would let anyone touch her. The mere placement of a hand upon her coat acted like an electric shock. She would bolt away, snorting in fright. But as August wore on, the horseflies became so vicious that she turned to Paul and Maureen for help.

135

"She's missing the surf," Paul said as they watched her trying to shudder her coat to drive the flies away. But the flies seemed to stick faster, drawing blood until Phantom was crazy with pain. They watched her sidle up to the other ponies on the ranch to get the benefit of their swishing tails, but the other ponies bunched up and ran away from her. She tried standing head-to-tail with Misty, but Misty's tail was so short and floppy that it was not much good.

Finally, when she was almost exhausted, she let Paul and Maureen flick the flies for her. She would offer first one leg and then another. And before the fly season was over, she had learned to "shake hands" like any circus pony.

Riding Phantom was quite another matter. Yet it, too, came about so gradually that she was quite unaware how it happened. First Maureen made a wide girth out of an old bedsheet and fitted it around Phantom's body immediately back of her forelegs. Once Phantom discovered that she could gallop just as fast with a band around her body, she no longer minded it. Next, Paul fastened a small sack of sand to the girth. Phantom tried in vain to back it off, but at last she seemed to realize that she could run as fast as ever with a sack on her back. After that she no longer fought it.

"If she'll carry the sand, she'll carry us!" Paul concluded.

And so it was. By the time frost came, they were riding her bareback, with nothing but a single "come-along" rope made of wickie.

"Phantom just won't take a metal bit in her mouth," Paul explained to Grandpa one evening as he and Maureen stood watching him trim one of his ponies' hooves.

"Great jumping mullets!" Grandpa exploded. "This pinto's forefeet has growed out so far I'm going to need my old-timey razor asides my snips. Maureen, you go git my razor. Now what was it you said about Phantom?" Grandpa asked as he waited.

"She just won't take a metal bit," Paul repeated. "We're still using the old wickie for bit and bridle both."

"Wa-al, ain't she travelin' where you want her to?" Grandpa barked, turning around to look at Paul.

"Oh, yes. We just lean the way we want to go and lay the wickie over against her neck."

"What more do ye want?"

"Nothing, Grandpa. Nothing at all. Maureen and I, we thought you'd be ashamed of us for not doing the job right— on our own pony."

"Ashamed!" bellowed Grandpa, straightening up and rubbing both his ears. "I'm so dang proud it's a wonder I ain't busted my suspender straps. Name me two other kids as has gentled a three-year-old wild mare."

Maureen came running with the razor.

"Walk!" commanded Grandpa. "How often do ye got to be told that if ye want to live to be a grownup ye should never run with anything as sharp as my old-timey razor?"

"Grandpa says it's all right!" Paul told Maureen. "Phantom doesn't ever need to know a metal bit."

"Not ever?" asked Maureen.

"Not ever!" repeated Grandpa as he wielded the razor in an expert manner. "I reckon she'll be happier without ever knowing."

Chapter 15

THE FIRE CHIEF PAYS A CALL

THERE WAS no question about Misty's happiness. She pranced around the ponies that came and went as if she knew that they were temporary guests, while she, Misty, was one of the family. This was her *home*.

When she playfully nipped the older ponies, they would lay back their ears until they saw who it was. Then they would whinny as much as to say, "It was only Misty."

She could be wild as a hare or gentle as a lamb. When the days grew brisk she would *gallumph* across the hard marsh, then suddenly she would stop stock-still, letting a gull light on her back while her nostrils quivered with excitement.

"Do you reckon Phantom is happy, too?" Maureen asked one day when the winter wind blew raw and cold.

"'Course she's happy," replied Paul. "Did you see me ride her down to the point before breakfast? She was neighing for joy. Her hooves hardly touched the earth."

"Oh, I know she's happy then, but . . ."

"But what?"

"Well, sometimes I see her leaning out over the fence— not yearning for the grass on the other side of it, but just looking away toward the White Hills and the sea."

"And is there something . . . ?" Paul asked after a little thought. "Is there something *far away* about her?"

"That's what I mean, Paul."

"I've noticed it, too," Paul admitted. "Sometimes when you can see the wild ponies frisking along Assateague Beach, she seems to be watching them. And it's kind of sad—like the time you wanted the doll with real hair at the carnival and you won the pencil box instead."

Maureen blushed. "Now that I'm grown up, I've almost forgotten about the doll. And Phantom'll forget her young days, too."

"Sure she will. We'll race her every day. She's happy then."

There was no doubt about it. The Phantom was wild with happiness when she raced. She showed it in the arching of her neck, in the upward pluming of her tail, in the flaring of her nostrils. Paul or Maureen had only to close their legs in on her sides to make her surge forward. Then she would skim the earth like the gulls she knew so well.

With the passing days the island folk began to notice her speed.

"Reckon Black Comet's going to have a little competition next Pony Penning," some said, wagging their heads wisely.

Others sneezed at the idea. "Phantom's got too much wildness in her," they said. "She's just as liable to jump the fence as run around the track. You can't depend on them wild ones."

Over in Pocomoke there was talk of the Phantom, too. In the schoolyards, across dinner tables, in the barber shops— everywhere the Phantom's name could be heard.

"She's built for speed," one mainlander admitted, "but I still favor Black Comet. He's used to the crowds. He knows how to snug along the fence. He knows how to save his power for the home stretch."

Spring came early to the little sea island. By the first week in April, myrtle bushes were covered over with a yellow fuzz and pine trees wore light-green finger tips to show another year's growth.

Phantom seemed to grow more restless as the season advanced. When Paul and Maureen came home from school they sometimes found her pacing around and around the corral, her head lowered. Other times she stood leaning far out over the fence, and there was a wild, sad look about her.

"Maybe she's looking for us," Maureen would say hopefully.

"Maybe!" nodded Paul.

One late afternoon toward the end of April the fire chief paid a surprise call.

"We 'spected you was coming!" exclaimed Grandma, her round face beaming. "See? Maureen's got a place all laid for ye."

The fire chief smiled. "One—two—three—four—five," he counted the blue-and-white plates around the kitchen table. Then he sniffed the ham baking, and he saw the heaping mound of oysters rolled in eggs and cracker meal and fried a golden brown. He moistened his lips.

"I'm staying!" he said.

There was not much talk while Grandma cut slivers of pink ham, dished up the oysters, and ladled hot gravy over the dumplings. And there was even less while everyone ate his fill.

At last the fire chief pushed his plate aside and lighted his pipe. "I've really come to see the owners of the Phantom," he said between puffs. "Wonder if they'd be interested in . . ."

At exactly that moment the fire chief's pipe went out and he had to stop in the middle of what he had to say. Slowly he found a match and relit it.

Paul's and Maureen's eyes were fixed on the chief's. They leaned forward on the very edge of their chairs.

"Wonder if they'd be interested in . . ." he stopped to puff and puff.

"Yes?" questioned Paul quickly.

"In racing the Phantom against Black Comet."

Paul's eyes caught Maureen's. Then their faces broke into a grin.

"Ho-ho-ho," chortled Grandpa. "I don't know who the joke's on. But these two been expectin' to race Phantom ever since last Pony Pennin'."

"Even before that," Maureen said gleefully. "Why, that morning over on Assateague when we first saw the Phantom, we talked about it even then."

Paul blushed. "Guess we just took it for granted you'd ask us."

The fire chief laughed heartily. "Well, now it's settled for sure," he said as he stood up to go. "Lucy Lee can't run this year. She'll be having a new colt along about then. And Patches has been sold to a dealer. So it'll be the Phantom against Black Comet and Delbert's chestnut filly, Firefly."

"And may the best hoss win!" prayed Grandpa as he nervously fingered the bristles of his ear.

Chapter 16

THE PULLY BONE

THE NEXT three months were filled with excitement for Phantom and her owners. Paul and Maureen were conditioning her for the big race. They fed her more liberally on grain. They rode her three miles each day, starting off at a slow jog, then trotting her, then asking for a burst of speed midway of the ride, then slowly jogging her back home again.

It was the early morning when the world was all red and gold with the rising sun that Paul and Maureen chose for Phantom's training period. They would take turns riding her —across the tundra-like beach, hard packed after a rain; up

147

and down Main Street, where her hooves sounded like sea
shells pinging against the pavement; over trails carpeted with
pine needles, where she made no sound at all.

They rode her out to the pony penning grounds, getting
her used to the feel of the track and the sight of the white fence.

Before long the Phantom came to be a familiar and glori-
ous sight. Her fame grew and spread. Now, on pleasant Sundays, visitors from the mainland began coming to see her.

Misty grew jealous of the attentions her mother was getting. She would nose in, trying to nip the buttons from the
men's coats or the flowers on the ladies' hats. One time she

lifted a hat all covered over with roses and dropped it in the water barrel.

This brought Grandpa Beebe running with a handful of gunnysacks. He pretended to be angry as he rescued the dripping hat and tried to dry it off with the sacks. "Paul and Maureen!" he would shout in his thunderous voice. "Hain't you never going to drive any sense into that Misty's head? She'll grow up thinkin' she's a baby all her days. Never seed a critter so mettlesome!"

As July came in and Pony Penning Day drew near, something came between Paul and Maureen. If Paul worked around the barnyard, Maureen made some excuse to go off down to the oyster boats to see if the men had brought up any sea stars in their oyster tongs. And if Maureen worked at home for Grandpa or Grandma, Paul went off treading clams for Kim Horsepepper or catching sea horses.

"What's the matter 'twixt Paul and Maureen?" Grandma asked Grandpa one night after the house was still.

"I don't know fer sure, mind ye, but I suspicion it's about the race," Grandpa replied.

"Why, I thought 'twas all settled. Hain't the Phantom goin' to run?"

"A-course. But the catch is—who's to ride her?"

"They both hankering to ride?" questioned Grandma.

"That's my guess," Grandpa nodded.

Finally, on the Monday morning before Pony Penning, Grandma asked the question right out. She and Maureen were hanging up clothes at the time, while Paul, perched on top of a chicken coop, was silently whittling a pole into a clothes prop.

"Which of ye," Grandma said, as she removed a clothespin from her mouth, "which of ye will ride Phantom in the big race?"

A long silence was the only answer.

"Well! Well!" said Grandma brightly. "If ye won't state yer rathers, I got a fine idea."

Still no answer. Maureen shook the creases out of a table-

cloth as if her life depended on it. Paul kept on whittling furiously.

Just then Grandpa Beebe came by. He glanced around sharply. "Why's everyone so hushed?" he asked. "Except fer the flappin' of the clothes I'd think 'twas Sunday meetin'-time."

"Why, I just asked who's to ride Phantom come Pony Penning Day," replied Grandma, hanging her clothespin bag on the line and looking from one to the other.

"Oh," and Grandpa strung the little word out until it seemed to have springs in it. He dropped the posthole digger he was carrying and toed it with his boots.

Seconds went by.

"If I wasn't in my seventy-three," he shook his finger, "if I wasn't in my seventy-three going on my seventy-four, I'd settle the hull matter and ride her myself."

Grandma straightened up from the clothesbasket.

"Clarence!" she said, speaking loud enough so her voice would reach Paul. "Seems like somethin' told me to save the pully bone from that marsh hen. It's hangin' above the almanac in the kitchen."

Grandpa slapped his thigh. "Nothin' could be fairer than a pully bone!" he exclaimed. "The one that breaks off the biggest part gits to ride."

"I'll fetch it," Maureen called over her shoulder as she disappeared into the kitchen. She came out holding one end of the wishbone very gingerly, as though it might break off in her hand.

"Now then!" Grandpa cleared his throat nervously.

Grandma picked up the empty clothesbasket, then set it down again in the very same spot.

"Now then," Grandpa repeated, "stop that gol-durn whittlin' and step up, Paul."

Paul's legs seemed as wobbly as a colt's. He came forward very slowly, and his hand shook as he grasped the other end of the wishbone with his thumb and forefinger.

"Squinch yer eyes tight," Grandma directed. "Make yer wish. And when I count three, *pull!*"

Paul and Maureen each took a long, deep breath as they clutched the tiny wishbone that was to decide their fate.

"One," Grandma counted slowly. "Two it is—and three!"

With a slight cracking noise, the wishbone broke. The larger half was in Paul's hand.

He gave a whistle of joy. Then his face sobered as he caught sight of Maureen, who was burying her half of the wishbone in the sandy soil. She looked up, trying to cover her feelings with a little smile.

"You won, Paul," she said, blinking. "You'll ride her better anyhow."

Chapter 17

WINGS ON HER FEET

THE LAST Wednesday in July dawned hot and still. Another Pony Penning Day had come!

By sunup the causeway between the mainland and Chincoteague was choked with traffic—trucks, station wagons, jeeps, cars of every description, bringing visitors to the island. They watched excitedly as the wild ponies swam ashore after the roundup. They lined the streets to see the procession to the pens; they cheered the bronco busters. But even after these events were over, the crowds kept on coming. For this year the big event was the race. Phantom was running! A wild sea horse against the sleek, well-trained Black Comet, winner for three years.

Toward evening a light wind came up, whisking sheep clouds before it. The sun was a huge red balloon hovering over the bay as Paul and Maureen, riding double on Phantom, turned into the pony penning grounds.

Maureen slid to her feet, and before she could whisper a word of encouragement into the Phantom's ear she was caught like a fly in a web. Her schoolmates, her uncles and aunts— everyone wanted to be with her during the race. They felt sorry for her because she was not riding. They seemed to wrap themselves about her until she could hardly breathe. Oh, how she longed to be by herself! Then she could race *with* Paul and the Phantom! Only by being alone could she *be* Paul and Phantom both.

It was the voice over the loud speaker that came to her rescue. "Tonight, ladies and gentlemen!" the voice blared. "Tonight Black Comet from Pocomoke races against Firefly and the Phantom."

Everyone began running toward the track. Maureen slipped away from her friends and lost herself in the crowds. She wedged her way into a small opening between strangers and soon she was standing at the rails, her stomach against a fence post. She heard strange voices all about her. But now there was no need to listen to them. They were as unimportant as the little insect voices of the night.

She drew a deep breath as the names of the three entries were announced again.

"There comes Black Comet!" the cry went up on all sides. "There he is!"

She saw Black Comet amble out on the track, aloof and black as night. He seemed bored with the entire business. Maureen would not have been surprised to see him yawn.

Now Firefly, a tall, rangy mare, pranced nervously to the starting post. Maureen's eyes passed over her lightly, then lingered on the Phantom who was parading to the post with dignity in her manner. She seemed unaware of the crowds, as

if for her they did not exist. Her head was uplifted, her nose testing the winds, her body trembling. She could not understand the delay. She snuffed the wind hungrily. The wind was calling her, yet Paul was holding her back.

At last the signal was given. A roar went up from the crowd. "They're off!"

"Black Comet at the rail," came the clipped voice over the loud speaker, "Phantom on the outside. But it's Firefly who's taking the lead!"

From then on no one could hear the announcer for all the yelling. The changeable crowds were calling, "Firefly! Firefly!"

Firefly held the lead the first quarter, then Black Comet shot forward and pulled out in front.

Maureen dug her fingernails into the fence rail. "Phantom!" she prayed. ' Oh, Phantom! Get a-going! It's a race."

But the Phantom was not running a race. She was enjoying herself. She was a piece of thistledown borne by the wind, moving through space in wild abandon. She was coming up, not to pass Firefly and Black Comet, but for the joy of flying. Her legs went like music. She was sweeping past Firefly now. She was less than a length behind Black Comet.

The people climbed up on the fence rails in a frenzy of excitement.

"Come on, Black Comet!" screamed the crowds from Pocomoke. "Come on!"

"Gee-up, Phantom!" cried the island folk.

Maureen was no longer an onlooker. She was the Phantom winging around the curve, her nostrils fire-red in the dying sun. She was Paul, leaning forward in a kind of wild glory.

She was drawing close to Black Comet. Now she was even. She was sailing ahead. She was over the finish line. She was winner by a length!

The crowds grew hysterical. "It's Phantom! Phantom! She won!" But there was no stopping the Phantom! She was flying on around the track.

The voice over the loud speaker was laughing. "Only once around," it was saying. "Only once around." Paul pulled back on the wickie and spoke softly in Phantom's ear. Gradually he brought her to a stop.

Maureen was laughing and crying too. The crowds pushed past her, dived between the rails, flocked around the Phantom. They yelled and thumped one another on the back as the judge handed Paul a purse.

Paul felt of its bulging contents. Then his eyes swept the crowds.

"Here—here I am!" cried Maureen.

Every eye turned to see whom Paul wanted. When they discovered Maureen, standing on the top rail of the fence like a bird on a twig, friends and strangers, too, clapped and cheered. In an instant Paul was riding through the little opening they had made. With the fence as a mounting block, Maureen swung up behind Paul.

The island folk went mad with happiness.

"Hoo-ray for Paul and Maureen!"

"Hoo-ray for the Phantom!" they rejoiced.

But Paul and Maureen found only one face in all that sea of faces and heard only one voice in all that blur of noise. It was Grandpa Beebe's. "Git home," he bellowed. "Tell Grandma."

All the way home Paul talked to the Phantom. "Do you know," he murmured, "do you know you won twelve whole dollars? And we're going to spend it all on you?"

"We could buy her red plumes, and ribbons to braid in her mane," suggested Maureen.

Paul leaned far forward to get as close as he could to Phantom's ear. "We could buy you shiny brass and leather trappings," he said. "You could be handsomer than any horse in the king's guard."

The Phantom let out a long whinny into the deepening twilight.

Paul laughed and laughed. "Want to know what she said?"

"What'd she say, Paul?"

"She said, 'Buy that toaster for Grandma and Grandpa. As for me,' she said, 'all I want is wings on my feet!'"

Chapter 18

A WILD BUGLE

IT RAINED fitfully during the night following the race. By morning the rain stopped and the sun broke through softly in slanting rays, drawing the moisture upward in thick curtains of mist.

After the excitement of the day before, matters on Pony Ranch were settling down to their usual routine. Paul and Maureen were busy with chores, Paul repairing the chicken house and Maureen scrubbing the water pans. Misty tagged first one, then the other—like a puppy with two masters.

163

Close to the fence stood the Phantom. She kept lifting her head upward, as if to worship the miracle of the sun drawing water. From time to time Paul took sidelong glances at her.

"Let's take turns racing her as soon as our chores are done," he called to Maureen. "You can be first."

Maureen smiled to herself. She knew that Paul was trying to make it up to her for not riding in the race. She hurried with her chores. Then, with Misty at her heels, she hung her apron on the clothesline and went to get the wickie.

When the Phantom caught sight of the wickie she whinnied, then stood trembling while Maureen slipped the rope-like root between her teeth, brought it under her chin and tied a square knot. It was strange how gentle Phantom could be. But even in her gentleness there was a wilding look in her eye, as if only her body were inside the corral while her real self lived somewhere far away.

Grabbing Phantom's mane, Maureen jumped onto her back.

"Ready!" she called to Paul.

Paul dropped his hammer and came running to let down the bars of the gate which fitted into horseshoes nailed to the fence posts. Phantom pawed the ground nervously as if irked by Paul's slowness.

With one bar down, Maureen put her heels into Phantom's side and Phantom sailed over the hurdle and out upon the marshy plain.

Misty tried to follow but Paul pushed her back. "Soon
we'll be racing you, too," he promised, combing her foretop
with his fingers. "But today we got to make Phantom happy."

Then he carefully replaced the top bars, climbed over the
fence and wandered out to a lone pine tree. There he stood,
leaning up against the tree, waiting his turn. His blood quickened as he watched Phantom whip across the little point of

land that went down to meet the sea. Around and across and up and down the flat tongue of land she swept, like the sea mews that soared overhead.

At last Paul waved them in. "My turn now!"

At exactly the moment when Maureen turned Phantom over to Paul there was the sound of a ringing neigh in the distance. It speared the morning stillness. It seemed to come, not from the sea, but from the Spanish galleon, back across the ages.

Phantom's ears pricked. She jerked her head in the direction of Assateague Island. Tremblingly she listened. The bugle came again, strong and clear. It brought Grandpa Beebe bounding over the gate, running toward Phantom.

"It's the Pied Piper!" he yelled. "He's coming to git the Phantom."

Paul and Maureen strained their eyes toward the island of Assateague, but all they could see were the white spumes from the billows, and skeins of mist rising from the sea. Then suddenly one of the whitecaps seemed to be flying free. It was the foaming mane of the Pied Piper, racing in with the billows.

"Git on Phantom's back!" Grandpa called. "Whup her, Paul! Whup her hard! Maureen! Git that gate open!"

Her heart pounding, Maureen flew to the gate. As fast as she could, she let the bars down, at the same time shoving Misty back. "Paul!" she cried. "Get a handful of her mane. Ride her toward Misty."

With a gasp of anguish she looked back. Paul was not trying to hold Phantom. He was slipping the wickie out of her mouth. He was giving Phantom her freedom.

"Oh, Paul!" screamed Maureen. "Hold her! Hold her! Don't let her go!" But her words were lost. The Phantom's whinnies were high with excitement. The Pied Piper was heading straight for her, his neck thrust forward, his head down, his eyes hidden by that long creamy foretop.

Grandpa waved his hat, trying to head him off, his arms whirling like a windmill. The Pied Piper veered around him. Then he snorted and trumpeted to the heavens.

"Paul!" bellowed Grandpa. "You'll be tromped down. Git outen the way!"

But Paul stood there as if caught in the Pied Piper's spell.

For a moment the Phantom hesitated. She looked obediently to Paul, her master. Then that wild bugle sounded again. It seemed to awaken some force within her, creating a curious urging in her mind. A shudder of excitement went through her. She twisted her body high in the air as if she were shaking herself free—free of fences that imprisoned, free of lead

168

ropes, free of stalls that shut out the smell of pines and the sound of the sea.

An impatient whinny escaped her. She whirled past Paul, then ran flying to meet the Pied Piper.

The air went wild with greeting. Deep rumbling neighs. High joyous whickers. The stallion and the mare were brushing each other with their noses, talking together in soft little grunts

and snorts as animals will. At last the Pied Piper nipped her thigh, urging her forward. This time the Phantom did not hesitate. She flew toward her island home. Only once she turned her head as if she were looking backward.

"Take good care of my baby," she seemed to say. "She belongs to the world of men, but I—I belong to the isle of the wild things!"

For long seconds, Paul and Grandpa and Maureen stood stock-still. They watched the Pied Piper plunge into the surf until he seemed part of the flying foam. They watched the Phantom until all they could see was the white map on her withers. Then the map smalled until it, too, was lost among the whitecaps of the sea.

The air about them quivered like a violin string. Then suddenly the string snapped, and the everyday world was all about once more. Grandpa was no longer the wiry man who had bounded over the fence. He was himself, gnarled and a little stiff-legged as he walked to the gate. Paul followed along behind him, and some of the Phantom's happiness seemed to shine in his face. He had given her the freedom she longed for.

Maureen lowered the bars of the gate for them, then put them back in place.

With one accord the old man and the boy and girl went to the Phantom's stall. It was not empty. Misty's quizzical little face with its funny blaze was peering around at them. She came trotting out of the door and gave Paul's face a great

swipe with her wet tongue. It was as if she had said, "Why is everyone so quiet? I'm here. Me! Misty!"

She reached out for Maureen, too, and as Maureen turned her cheek to be nuzzled, she noticed a few copper-colored hairs from Phantom's tail caught in the half-door of the stall. Winding them into a circlet, she fastened them above the manger.

"Guess she was just a Phantom after all," Maureen spoke quietly.

"'Course she was," Paul said.

Grandpa began working hard at the bristles in his ears. "Ye done the right thing, children," he said huskily. "Phantom wuz never what you'd call happy. She belongs to Assateague. But Misty here, she belongs to us."

At mention of her name, Misty sidled over to Grandpa and scratched her head up and down against his broad shoulder

How good it was to be the center of attention! She went from one to the other, butting her face gently against Paul's pocket, asking for a kernel of corn, lipping Maureen, nipping the brim of Grandpa's battered old hat.

"Phantom was a good mammy," Maureen said. "She stayed with her baby as long as she needed to. Colts got to grow up sometime," she declared, her thoughts slipping back to what the fire chief had said.

Misty seemed to sense the importance of this moment. She backed away from the group, her head uplifted, not toward the sea and the island of Assateague, but inland, toward the well-pounded trails of Chincoteague. Her whole body quivered as if she saw a promise of great things to come—of races won, of foals tagging at her side. Overcome by all the excitement in store, she kicked her heels in ecstasy and let out a high, full whinny of joy. It sounded for all the world like explosive laughter.

Paul gave a little gasp.

"What did she say?" Maureen asked quickly.

"I never!" Paul's eyes widened in disbelief.

Grandpa clapped his hat far down on his head. "Land sakes, Paul! You never what?"

"Reckon I never heard a pony talk up so plain. Why, she just laughed deep down inside her. 'I'm Misty of Chincoteague,' she said, plainer'n any words."

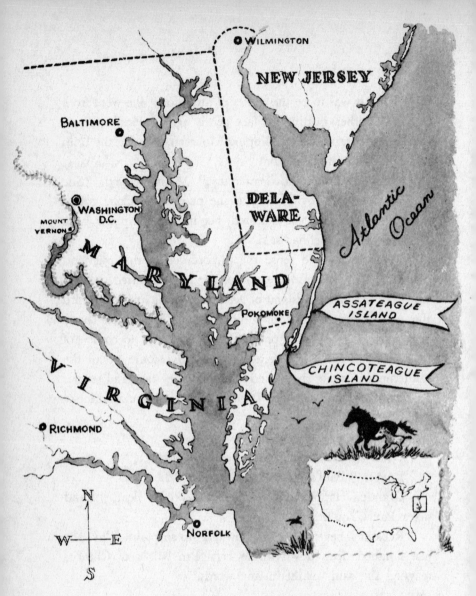

Four miles off the eastern shore of Virginia lies the tiny, wind-rippled isle of Chincoteague. It is only seven miles long and averages but twenty-one inches above the sea.

Assateague Island, however, is thirty-three miles long. Just as Paul Beebe says, Assateague is an outrider, protecting little Chincoteague from the rough seas of the Atlantic. The outer island is a wildlife refuge for wild geese and ducks and the wild ponies.

For their help the author is grateful to

VICTORIA PRUITT, Island Historian, Chincoteague Island

MRS. W. E. DAVIS, known to everyone as Miss Mollie, Chincoteague Island

CAPTAIN JACK RICHARDSON, for many years with the United States Coast Guard on Assateague Island

BOB WILLIAMS, who helped me find people and places, Chincoteague Island

ALFRED TAPSELL, seventeen years before the mast in the British Merchant Service

WAYNE DINSMORE, Secretary, Horse Association of America

J. NORMAN JOHNSON, Meteorologist, U. S. Weather Bureau

MILTON C. RUSSELL, Head, Reference and Circulation Section, Virginia State Library

H. H. HEWITT and ROBERTA SUTTON, Chicago Public Library

DR. CHESTER J. ATTIG, late Head of the History Department, North Central College

C. E. GODSHALK, Director, the Morton Arboretum

MARY ALICE JONES, Children's Book Editor, Rand McNally & Company

MR. AND MRS. ROBERT H. QUAYLE, Wayne, Illinois

LOUISE COFFIN, Wayne, Illinois

GRACE LUENZMANN, Wayne, Illinois

ROBERT V. NEVINS, Brookville, Massachusetts

JUNE BECKMAN, Naperville, Illinois

GERTRUDE JUPP, Milwaukee, Wisconsin

MR. AND MRS. L. C. FERGUSON, Hammond, New York

SEA STAR
Orphan of Chincoteague

SEA STAR

Orphan of Chincoteague

BY MARGUERITE HENRY

Illustrated by Wesley Dennis

To

IRVING JACOBY

CONTENTS

LAST PONY PENNING, I went to Chincoteague a second time. My purpose was to work with the movie men who were planning to film the book of *Misty*. I had no thought of writing another Chincoteague story. *Misty*, I thought, was complete in itself. Let the boys and girls dream their own wonderful sequels.

And then all my resolves burst in midair. Early on the morning after Pony Penning, a lone colt with a crooked star on his forehead was found at Tom's Cove. His mamma "lay on her broadside, dead."

Except for the sea mews and the striker birds, the colt was quite alone, one little wild thing, helpless against the wild sea.

And there, in that wild moment at Tom's Cove, the story of Sea Star was born of itself.

M. H.

SEA STAR

Orphan of Chincoteague

Chapter 1

BRAIDS AND RIBBONS

PAUL WAS separating each silver hair in Misty's tail. At
his feet lay a little pile of blackberry brambles which he had
removed, one by one.

With an air of secrecy he looked around quickly to make
sure no outsider could overhear what he was about to say. But
he and his sister, Maureen, were quite alone in the barnyard
of Pony Ranch — except for the wild fowl and the ponies.
There was no need at all to whisper, but Paul did whisper, and
he seemed to be laughing at a private little joke of his own.

"How'd you like to see Misty's tail braided?"

"Braided!" Maureen dropped the gunny sack with which she was brushing Misty's coat and stared. "How silly! Whoever heard of a wild Chincoteague pony with a braided tail!"

"Nobody except you and me." Paul looked around again, chuckling to himself. "Nobody'll ever know except the guinea hens and ducks and geese, and who listens to them?"

Surprise crept into Maureen's voice. "How'd you guess, Paul?"

"Guess what?"

"That I've been hankering to do Misty up like those pictures we saw in the paper, the ones of the horses at the big show?"

Paul laid the comb he had been using on Misty's rump.

"Mental telegraphy, of course. Miss Vic says when two people think the same thing it's mental telegraphy."

"She does?"

"Yes. And I believe it!" Paul's voice no longer whispered. It chortled in amusement. "For two nights now I've been dreaming Misty was a famous steeplechaser, and we had to braid her tail and mane and trim off her fetlocks and whiskers and clean her coat until if you patted her hip you couldn't raise a single puff of dust. Not a puff."

Maureen dipped a corner of the gunny sack in a pail of water and began scrubbing Misty's knees.

Her words came jerking out to the motion of the scrubbing. "We'll tie her braids with fancy ribbons. We'll put a wreath of flowers round her neck—like Grandpa says they do at the big races over on the main."

14

Paul giggled. "Grandpa'd say we're chuckleheads, but let's do it, anyway! Then we'll take pictures in our mind, and afore anyone else sees her we'll shake out her tail and her mane and let the wind rumple 'em all up so she looks exactly like a Chincoteague pony again."

Though scores of ponies came and went on Grandpa Beebe's Pony Ranch, Misty stayed. For she belonged to Paul and Maureen. They talked to her as if she were human, and often it seemed that she talked back! Now, as if she understood their plans, she spun around, kicked the comb from her back, burst through the unfastened rope fence, and headed for the marshland, her mane tossing in the sea breeze.

Disturbed by her motion, the barnyard went wild with noise. Guinea hens, geese, ducks — wild ones and tame ones flew into the air with a great clatter. A bunch of ponies in the corral who, a moment before, had been dozing in the sun, alerted and were off, following the silver direction-flag of Misty's tail.

"My stars!" laughed Maureen. "That Misty's got the sharpest ears and the knowingest mind of any pony I ever did see. Look at her. She's gone wild as her mother—bucking and leaping and kicking her heels at our plan."

Watching Misty, Paul and Maureen thought a moment of her mother, the famous wild Phantom on near-by Assateague Island. Then Paul said, "But Misty is not really wild; in two minutes she'll be back, asking for those braids and ribbons."

Maureen did quick little capers of her own, mimicking Misty. She stumbled over the pail, spilling out half of the water before she rescued it. "Look at her!" she said, a little out of breath. "She's the same color as the flowers of the kinks bush. And she floats on the wind, like they do." A note of anxiety showed in her voice as she went on. "You think the other ponies get jealous of Misty?"

"'Course not. They don't ever get jealous of a leader. Grandpa says it's the first time he's seen a mare colt to be the leader."

They watched the older ponies trying to follow Misty's antics. The more Misty galloped and bucked and twisted her body into the air, the more Paul's and Maureen's laughter rippled out over the marshland of Chincoteague Island.

"The big ones are clumsy as woods cows beside our Misty!"
Maureen said.

Now Paul threw his head back and let out a shrill whistle. It was as if he had roped Misty with his voice. She jammed to a halt. Her head and tail went up. Then she wheeled and came flying in, the rest of the band stringing out behind her.

Maureen and Paul ran for the gate. When the entire bunch was safely inside, they fastened it securely.

Misty flew on past them to the entrance of her stall. There she settled down to earth like a bird after flight. She watched the other ponies go to a big open shed which they shared. Then she stood waiting at her manger, waiting for the little reward of corn and the pleasant scratchy feeling of the gunny sack.

Maureen went back to work, this time on Misty's muddy hocks. "We got to hurry, Paul," she said, "before Grandpa gets back from Watson Town. I promised him I'd do Grandma's work today."

Paul did not answer Maureen. His words were for Misty's furry ears. "You're fierce and wild and wonderful when you come in all blown, your nose snortin' white flames like a dragon. I wonder if even Man o' War could have been as exciting looking."

Maureen stopped scrubbing and stood up in thought. "No, Paul," she said slowly. "I reckon even Man o' War didn't have as much fire."

Misty, impatient with all the talk, moved over to a wash tub that was turned upside down and placed her forefeet on it. "Here, you!" she seemed to say. "Do I have to do *all* my tricks for a few kernels of corn?"

She lifted a forefoot high, pawing the air.

Paul caught it and shook it vigorously. "How do, Misty," he said, bowing very gravely. "I failed to see you in church last Sunday. Hope you weren't ailing."

Misty lipped Paul's straw-like hair to see if there was any taste to it. Finding none, she nudged his head out of the way and reached for the niblets of corn that he now produced from his pocket.

From all over the farmyard chickens and hens came running, pecking up the little kernels Misty dropped.

"Now she's clean and had a good run; so we can ready her for the show," Paul said. "That is, if you can find any ribbons."

Maureen was in and out of the weathered house beyond the corral before Paul had three strands of forelock ready to braid.

"Here's lots of ribbons," she called. "They came tied around Grandma's presents when she was in the hospital. She brought them home for me to do my hair, but I've been saving them up for Misty." She spread them out on the up-turned wash tub. "Let's use all different colors."

Misty liked the attention she was getting. She preferred the company of humans to that of the other ponies. They tried to sneak her ear corn, and nose into her water barrel. But the boy and the girl—they neither snatched her food nor drank her water. They brought it instead!

She nipped their clothes playfully as the friendly, awkward hands braided and looped her mane and forelock.

"My fingers get all twisted," Paul complained, "but if stable boys over on the main can do it, so can I."

"Why, your braids look better than mine, Paul. You've looped yours underneath instead of over on top. But my bows are tied better, I think. Now let's do her tail."

Misty snatched little colt naps as they worked on her tail. A fresh wind from the sea fanned her face. It fluttered the ribbons on her forelock and mane. Every little while she would shake her head and make the braids dance. Then she would give a high horselaugh into the pleasant July morning.

When the tail was tied in red and pink and blue ribbons, Maureen went off to gather an armful of flowers from the patch of Bouncing Bess at the side of the house. The stems were thick and strong, and she braided them so that the flower heads came close together, making a huge pink wreath.

"It's funny," she thought to herself, "I've done this often in my mind. The Bouncing Bess. Grandma's ribbons. The skinny little braids. It's as if we'd planned it all out together."

On the way back, she tried the wreath around her own neck.

"Prettier than a wreath of roses, don't you think, Paul?"

"Bigger, anyway," he said.

Together they placed the flowers around Misty's neck. Then they stood back, running their eyes over the picture before them—the wreath hanging down almost to Misty's knees, the tiny silver braids with dozens of gaily colored bows.

Paul grinned broadly, both a little ashamed and a little proud of his handiwork. "Jumpin' grasshoppers! No one would know her from a blue ribbon winner. Why, her pedigree is busting out all over!" He half-closed his eyes, reciting, "Misty —out of the Phantom by the Pied Piper."

"Who before that?"

"Pied Piper out of the Wild Wind by the Wild Waves . . . Out of . . ."

Maureen's laughter bubbled. "We haven't got time to go all the way back to the ponies that swam ashore from the wrecked galleon. Come on! Let's make believe I'm the man who leads the winner before the grandstand, and you're the jockey."

A handful of ribbon lay at Paul's feet. Quickly he picked out a wide band of purple satin and fastened it across his shirt like a jockey. Then he climbed up close to Misty's withers so he would not be too heavy for her. He bowed to the imaginary crowds, bowed again and again, as Maureen led Misty around

the corral. Now he was accepting the imaginary silver cup while the people went mad with applause. He closed his eyes, listening to the sound of it. It was deafening. It roared and roared in his ears until they hurt.

"Paul! Paul!" Maureen shouted above the noise. "Open your eyes. It's a plane. Heading toward us. It's going to land. Paul! Right here at Pony Ranch!"

Chapter 2

THE SILVER PLANE

PAUL STARTED from his daydreams. Misty was trembling under him, prancing in fear. He slid off and blindfolded her with his hands. The spear of light in the sky was a silver plane. It came darting in, landing down meadow, taxiing toward them.

As it settled to a stop, three men scrambled out. One stayed with the plane. The other two came walking toward Pony Ranch, looking around and about them like men who had suddenly landed from Mars.

Maureen gazed awestruck. "Reckon something's the matter of their engine?" she asked.

Paul looked and gave a nod. "Or maybe they meant to land at the Government base on the other side of the island." He turned Misty loose and started for the plane at a dead run. Maureen was close at his heels.

Now that the whirring monster was still, Misty was full of curiosity, too. Ears pricked forward, she jog-trotted alongside Paul and Maureen, the wreath bobbing against her chest. The other ponies followed at a cautious distance, but when they reached the gate, Misty drove them back. Then she rejoined the boy and girl.

"It's like history," Paul said as he ran. "Columbus and his party lands and the natives go out to meet them."

Maureen laughed nervously, "They don't look to me like faraway people."

Now the two men and the boy and girl were close enough to study each other. Uncertainly they all stopped in their tracks and stood very still on the narrow spit of land. In the sudden quiet the sound of rustling grasses and channel waves skipping into shore grew loud and distinct.

Paul and Maureen waited, listening.

"Good morning," said one of the men, with a smile as warming as sunlight.

"How do," nodded Paul and Maureen solemnly.

The man who had spoken was low-voiced, and his blue eyes were very young and very old. The look he gave them was not the look a grownup gives to boys and girls, but one that friends save for each other. "My name is Van Meter," he said, "and this is my associate, Mr. Jacobs."

Mr. Jacobs was a tall man, and his eyes were dark and deep like the sheltering coolness of a pine grove. "How do," he said, repeating Paul's and Maureen's way of greeting.

Misty broke the awkward pause that followed. A bug flew into her nose and she snorted it out so fiercely that her braided forelock flew straight up.

They all laughed and the strangeness was gone.

"This must be Pony Ranch," said Mr. Jacobs, looking at the fences and sheds as if he carried a blueprint of them in his mind.

"It is!" exclaimed Maureen.

"And you must be Paul and Maureen Beebe."

The boy and girl nodded in wide-eyed amazement.

"But this pony," said Mr. Van Meter, his eyes taking in the wreath of Bouncing Bess and the braids and ribbons, "it can't be! No, it can't possibly be—Misty!"

Paul picked up a piece of marsh grass and twiddled it between his fingers. "It *is* Misty," he said, embarrassed by the silly ribbons and wreath.

Mr. Van Meter was plainly disappointed. As he turned his head he caught a glimpse of a little herd of wild ponies frisking along the beach of neighboring Assateague Island. He gestured toward the wind-blown creatures. "I expected to find Misty with her mane and tail blowing in the wind," he said, talking more to himself than to the others. "And I hoped she'd have some of the mystery of the sea in her look."

"Oh, but she does!" exclaimed Paul and Maureen together. Quickly they lifted the wreath of flowers from her neck and began loosening her braids.

Maureen glanced up shyly as she worked, "We just wanted to see how she'd look if she won a big race over on the main."

"And how *do* you think she looks?" asked Mr. Jacobs.

The boy and girl were shaking out the strands of hair.

"You say, Maureen."

"No, you, Paul. Do you like Misty all prissied up with ribbons and things?"

Paul answered easily. "Even before we started, we knew we'd like her better with her mane and tail free."

"Good! So do I." Mr. Van Meter smiled with his eyes. "Now, will you take us to meet your Grandpa Beebe?"

"He's gone up the island to Watson Town. Grandma's been having trouble with her biddies, and he wanted to talk to Miss Vic about them."

"Oh."

"He sometimes gets hung up talking," explained Maureen, "but nearly always he comes back pretty quick."

"Perhaps," suggested Mr. Jacobs, "we could talk to Mrs. Beebe until he gets back."

Paul shook his head. "She's gone to Richmond with Clarence Lee."

"Yes," added Maureen proudly. "Our uncle, Clarence Lee, Jr., is going to go to college. He may learn so much he could be a preacher!"

The strangers seemed to be turning matters over in their minds. There was a little pause before they spoke. "Perhaps you would like to hear our mission," Mr. Van Meter finally said.

"Oh!" Maureen looked surprised. "Are you missionaries?"

Paul snorted. " 'Course not, Maureen. Whenever are you going to grow up? Mr. Van Meter means that maybe we'd like to know why they came to our island. And how they know all about us and Misty," he added.

Maureen blushed. "Please to come and sit down on the benches underneath the pine trees," she invited politely.

Together they walked over to the pine grove at the side of the house while Misty, free of her wreath and halter, kicked up her heels and trotted off to sniff and snort at the strange silver bird resting on her private exercise ground.

The two men watched her with a pleased expression. Then Mr. Van Meter took a snapshot out of his billfold and passed it to Paul and Maureen. "These are my two children," he said. "Last Christmas they were given a book that told the legend of a Spanish galleon wrecked long ago in a storm, and how her cargo of Moor ponies swam ashore to Assateague Island, and how descendants of those ponies are living wild and free on the island today."

Paul and Maureen looked up from the picture. "That's just how it happened," said Maureen.

"Don't talk, Maureen. Listen. Listen to what's coming. Maybe it's going to be something good."

"It *is* good," Mr. Van Meter went on. "My boy and girl kept telling me about the roundup of the wild ponies you people of Chincoteague have every year."

"It's this week!" Paul blurted out.

Mr. Van Meter nodded as if he knew all about it. "Finally I got as excited as my children, so excited that I talked it all over with Mr. Jacobs. We want to make a movie of it."

Paul and Maureen just stared. They could scarcely believe their ears. A movie made about the wild ponies of Assateague! Then Maureen became thoughtful. "Would Misty be in it?" she asked. "She was born on Assateague, but she's not wild any more."

"That's why we are here. We'd like to use the real Misty in the picture, the little colt that was in the book."

Now Maureen clapped her hands for joy and Paul leaped to his feet, letting out his shrill whistle. Misty came flying in, asking questions with her ears. He whispered the good news to her, laughing to see her ears swivel this way and that, as if to catch every word he was saying. Then she was off again, circling the plane and browsing all around it as if she were afraid it might eat her grass.

"We knew you'd like it," said Mr. Van Meter. "That's what we came to see your Grandpa about. We want to buy Misty."

"Buy her!" Two heads jerked up as if they were on puppet strings.

"Yes, we'd like to take her back to New York in that plane— on Friday after Pony Penning. You see," he explained, "the roundup scenes over on Assateague and the swim of the ponies across the channel we want to make down here. But all the close-up scenes could be done better in our studio in New York. It will take months, because colts can't work long at a stretch."

"But why," Paul cried, "why would you have to *buy* her?"

"Because," Mr. Van Meter said soberly, "we'd want to keep her a while after the screen play is made. We'd want to take her to schools and libraries where boys and girls could meet her. We'd want to fix a stall for her in the theaters where her picture was showing so that they could see the real Misty. It might be a long time before she could come back."

"Yes," added Mr. Jacobs, "and you are grownup enough to know that we would have to buy her to carry out our plans. We would have to be responsible for her."

The two men were like jugglers. But instead of balls, they were using words, tossing them back and forth over Maureen's and Paul's heads. Always the words seemed out of reach.

Mr. Van Meter said, "We had a feeling you might want to share Misty with boys and girls everywhere."

"Boys and girls who have never seen a real pony," Mr. Jacobs continued.

It was Mr. Van Meter's turn now. "Sometimes when I

hear children in New York talk about Misty, it seems she no longer belongs to a boy and a girl on an island, but to boys and girls everywhere."

The words kept flying, back and forth, higher and higher. "Misty has grown bigger than you know," Mr. Jacobs said. "She isn't just a pony. She's a heroine in a book!"

Paul pounded his fists against the rough hard bark of a pine tree. Maureen turned her back on the men, digging her bare toes in a bed of moss.

"There, now," comforted Mr. Van Meter, "if you do not want to sell her, we will think no less of you."

A silence came over them all. It grew deeper and deeper. Even the hens and chickens stopped scratching, and far down the marshland Misty lay down to sleep.

The sound of a chugging truck was welcome relief.

"That'll be Grandpa," Paul said.

Grandpa Beebe brought the truck to a stop. He got out and squinted down meadow at the silver plane. He took off his battered hat and scratched his head in puzzlement.

"Grandpa! Oh, Grandpa! Come!" Paul and Maureen shouted, panic in their voices.

Grandpa came swinging toward them. "What you two bellerin' about?" he yelled right back at them. "Ye sound like a couple bull calves caught in a bob-wire fence."

"Oh, Grandpa," cried Maureen, throwing herself on him, "they want to make a movie of Misty, and they want to buy her and take her away. Oh, Grandpa!" The words lost themselves in great heaving sobs.

Grandpa put Maureen away from him. He strode over to the two men and faced them eye to eye. "If I was a younger fella," he exploded, shaking a gnarled forefinger at them, "I'd give ye more'n a battle of words. Ye should be downright ashamed o' yerselves. Grown men come to hoss trade with childern! Oncet when I was a mere little boy in my nine I went out to Hog Island and I come upon some nestes, fish hawks' nestes they was, and I stole some eggs outen 'em. That night I woke up in the dark and I felt mean and shriveled inside. And that's how you two should feel now."

The men started to speak, but Grandpa waved for silence.

"Why, Paul and Maureen here has raised Misty from a teensy baby. I reckon Misty figgers they're her pappy and mammy." He clapped his hat on his head and looked from one to the other. "Why, Paul here saved Misty from drownding and oncet he stayed a hull night in a truck with her, and him and his sister bought her with their own earned money. You city fellas maybe wouldn't understand, but livin' out here on this lonely marshland, why, Misty's the nighest to a friend these childern got."

"But, Mr. Beebe, we do understand—" Mr. Jacobs started to say more, but Grandpa turned his back and talked to the boy and girl.

"Mind the time Misty got in the chicken swill and et all them green apple peels and got the colic? Mind how we three had to stay up walkin' her and walkin' her all the night long?"

Maureen blew her nose.

"I do, Grandpa," Paul said. "And I recomember last Christmas when we fixed cardboard antlers to Misty's ears and slung two gunny sacks with toys pokin' out of 'em over her back. Recomember?"

"I do!" Maureen spoke up. "And she had holly berries

36

tucked in her mane and jingle bells tinklin' from her halter."

Grandpa Beebe's voice gentled like a thunderstorm turned into a spring rain. He included the two strangers in the circle now. "Yep," he chuckled. "We took her right smack into the church for the childern's Christmas party. You should of heard the childern laugh to see a pony in church. But one o' 'em spoke

up mighty cute. No bigger than a turnip that kid weren't, and his voice was jest a mouse-squeak, but he come up to Misty an' he said, 'The little Lord Jesus was borned in a stable, and He'd like as not let a pony come to His house.' Then Misty passed the presents around from her packs."

"Stop!" cried Mr. Van Meter. "Can't you see the more you tell us about Misty the more we want her?"

But Paul and Maureen and Grandpa went on as if they had not heard. "Mind the time we brought her into the kitchen," Paul asked Maureen, "and Grandpa was washing his face over by the mirror, and when he looked up there was Misty laughing over his shoulder?"

Grandpa slapped his thigh. "I tell ye, fellas, 'twas the funniest sight I ever see. I looks up at that shaggy face in the mirror and thinks I to myself, 'Great guns, I'm gettin' whiskery!'"

Grandpa cut his laughter short. "What in tunket am I laughin' at? This ain't funny! Now you two strangers tell yer story and be right smart quick about it. Me and Paul got to go down the peninsula today."

Mr. Van Meter looked to Mr. Jacobs and Mr. Jacobs sent the look back. "You tell it, Van. You have children of your own."

Patiently, Mr. Van Meter told the whole story from start to finish. He explained, too, that his company was young and struggling and could afford to pay only two hundred and fifty dollars for Misty. "But," he added quickly, "if the children do not wish to sell her, we shall think no less of them."

"Thar's yer answer, then. We'll help ye all we kin with yer picture-making, but Misty's next to the Bible with us. Why, she's got the map of the United States on her withers, just like her wild mommy, the Phantom."

"And," added Mr. Jacobs very quietly, "the marking on her side is in the shape of a plow, like the state of Virginia."

Grandpa looked surprised. "Call her in, Paul."

Paul let out his shrill summons. It roused Misty from her sleep. She listened for the whistle again. This time it came louder. She thrust her forefeet in front of her, got up sleepily and came lazing in.

Grandpa took hold of her forelock. He turned her around

"By smoke!" he exclaimed. "She *has* got the marking of Virginia on her. The shape of a plow it is." He grew tongue-tied for a moment. Then he smiled. "I'm sorry I was snappish and made such a big to-do. But," he added sternly, "the answer is still no."

"Grandpa," suggested Paul, "don't you figure they could find a good colt to buy at the Pony Penning sale after the roundup?"

"'Course you could," Grandpa told the men. "And Paul and Maureen'll help ye all ye want during Pony Penning time. They'll be glad to run yer errands and tell ye where the ponies will be druv, and where they'll be swum acrost the channel. Now we got lots of work to do. Maureen's got to do the cookin' for her Grandma, and me and Paul have got big business down to Cape Charles." He started to walk off. "You two goin' up in that air buggy or could we drop ye off uptown?"

"We'd like a ride to the inn uptown," Mr. Van Meter told Grandpa. "Our pilot friend is anxious to be off for Norfolk as soon as he finds out if we are welcome here."

"Well, ye're welcome to go about yer picture taking, all right. Come along. We'll go down and tell yer friend. Then I'll drop ye off at the inn."

Chapter 3

A MILL DAY

MAUREEN WENT into the house. It was hard to settle down to her chores until the plane was gone. She heard its engines warming, heard it roar down the point of land. She ran to the window to see it take off, blowing the grass into ripples behind it.

Two cameras and a little cluster of luggage were left behind. Paul and Grandpa, Mr. Van Meter and Mr. Jacobs, each picked up a load and carried it to the truck. Now the truck was moving away too, and soon Pony Ranch was bathed in silence.

Maureen put on Grandma Beebe's apron, wrapping it

twice around her and tying it in front. The breakfast dishes were still on the table, beds unmade, rugs rumpled on the floor. She looked around, wrinkling her sunburnt nose. "I'd rather clean out the pony stable and all the chicken coops than clean house!" she thought to herself.

But it was seldom Grandma Beebe left Pony Ranch, and Maureen had promised to take her place. She lighted the flame under a big pot of beans. Then she stood in the middle of the floor thinking.

"I wonder—" she said out loud in the quiet of the house. "No!" she stamped her foot. "No, we couldn't sell Misty. We just couldn't." And she turned briskly to the unmade beds.

Meanwhile, Paul and Grandpa had left the two men at the little frame inn and were driving across the causeway, leaving Chincoteague Island far behind.

All the way down the long peninsula to Cape Charles no mention was made of Mr. Van Meter and Mr. Jacobs. It was almost as if they had never dropped out of the sky at all.

"Mighty nice cabbages in that patch," Grandpa would say. "And the 'taters'll soon be ready to dig, I reckon."

"Uh-hmm," Paul would answer. "How many ponies you figure to sell down to Cape Charles, Grandpa?"

"Oh, a whole flock, likely. Tim Button wants to use 'em to hawk his garden truck through the streets."

"Grandpa?"

"What is it, boy?"

"Why do the people over on the main say *herds* of ponies, and we say *flocks?*"

"Why!" thundered Grandpa, taking one hand off the wheel to rub the spiky white whiskers in his ears, "it's 'cause Chincoteague ponies is different, that's why. They fly on the wind like birds. But," snorted Grandpa, "the horses over on the main — they be earthbound critters."

Pleased with the answer, the boy fell silent.

A truck cut in ahead of them. It was packed solidly with dark red tomatoes. Paul counted the crates, guessing at the number of tomatoes in each, then at the total tomatoes in the truck.

The day was slowly raveling itself out. Big Tim Button had changed his mind about wanting to buy the ponies. "Sorry, Beebe," he twanged through his nose, "but I just signed some papers to buy a couple secondhand trucks." And he threw out his chest, slapping the papers in his pocket as if he were not sorry at all.

Tired and discouraged, Grandpa and Paul headed for home. On the way they stopped at the ferry station to pick up Grandma and her friend, Mrs. Tilley, just back from Richmond. Paul had to climb into the body of the truck to make room for them.

He made believe he was a pony being shipped away. He could poke his nose right into the cab because a colt had already done that and broken the glass in the window. Paul looked between the beards of wheat that decorated Grandma's hat and giggled to himself. If he were a pony now, he would rip off the wheat and eat it. Then, like as not, he would trample the hat.

He looked at Grandma to see if she would mind. But her eyes were absently following the fields along the road. He doubted if she would care at all. Mrs. Tilley, however, was lively as a wren, chattering and wagging her head, opening her purse, shutting it again, fussing with her packages. She would fly into a fit if a pony ate her hat. Paul grinned at the thought.

Then he turned his back and sat down quickly to squelch the idea. He dangled his feet over the tailgate and watched the road unroll like a bolt of white ribbon behind them.

It was almost sundown when they turned in at Pony Ranch.

Grandma sniffed audibly as soon as the truck door opened. "Paul! Run into the house, quick. The pot of beans is burning!"

Heavily, she got out and walked up the steps into the house. Maureen met her. "You got the best smellers in the whole world, Grandma! The beans were just fixing to burn, but you saved 'em."

With a kiss and a pat, Grandma whisked off Maureen's apron and tied it around herself. "There!" she sighed, "I'd sooner have bread and molasses and burned beans to home than fine vittles on the main."

At supper that night when Grandpa had finished his plate of beans and spooned up every drop of molasses, he turned to Grandma. "How about yer trip, Ida? How does it feel to have a boy in college?"

"I—don't—know," answered Grandma, with a long pause after each word, "I just don't know."

"Well, where's Clarence Lee, Jr.? Ain't he got hisself all enrolled in that fine school?"

Grandma exchanged a glance with Grandpa, then nodded her head toward Paul and Maureen as if she did not want to discuss the matter in front of them.

"Oh," chuckled Grandpa, "if it's the childern ye're worried about, ye can forget them. They done a heap of growin' up today."

Grandma put down her fork. "I would feel better maybe if I did talk things out," she said, looking from one to the other. "They were mighty nice to me there at the school." She paused, then rushed on. "But the tuition money — it's got to be paid ahead of time. Seems like the school is so overcrowded. There's more young men want to enroll than there's places for 'em to sit down."

"Why can't they bring in stools and folding chairs," interrupted Grandpa, "like we do when the church is full?"

"I spoke of that, but they just smiled at me." Grandma let out a big sigh. "I've had a mill day, Clarence. Seems like my heart's been tromped on. I did so want Clarence Lee to go to college and be a preacher."

"Where's the boy at now?"

"He stayed to Richmond, trying to raise the money. But, Clarence, I'm all worried up. He's got to take some kind of tests and he's trying to earn a pile of money at the same time. Some boys can work hard and study too. But they ain't had the bad pneumonia. Besides, most of them just get the gist of what they're studying. Clarence Lee, now — well, he's got to go deep down."

"Ye say a pile of money, Ida. How much do ye mean, exactly?"

"Three hundred dollars."

"Three hundred dollars!" echoed Grandpa.

"I know, Clarence. The grass was late coming this spring, and ten of your best mares died off. I know. . . . But it was a pitiable sight to see him walk out that door, looking lost and lonely, like a colt cut out from a big bunch of his friends."

"Dang it all!" raged Grandpa. "Ef only Tim Button had taken them ponies. All I got to my name is fifty dollars."

46

Paul and Maureen had long since stopped eating. They looked up from their plates at the same time and suddenly their glances locked. Then, white-faced, they nodded to each other.

"Grandma," Paul spoke very quickly, as if he were afraid he might change his mind, "two movie men were here today. They came to buy Misty."

"For two hundred and fifty dollars," added Maureen.

Grandma's coffee cup was half way to her lips. She set it back down again without touching it.

"You didn't sell her!" she exclaimed, aghast.

"Well, practically," Paul said. "As soon as they give us the money."

"You see, Grandma," Maureen explained very carefully as if she were talking to a little girl, "Misty really doesn't belong just to us any more. She's grown bigger than our island. She's in a book, Grandma. Now she belongs to boys and girls everywhere."

"Yes," Paul's voice warmed. "They want to take her to schools and libraries for children to meet — children who've never seen a real pony."

"I should think you'd have wanted to horsewhip the men," Grandma said to Grandpa.

"Oh, he did, Grandma, but when they told how much Misty meant to poor little city children, well, what could he do?" asked Maureen.

Paul sat up very straight, thinking out his words carefully. "We want to give the money to Uncle Clarence Lee," he said, "and when he gets to be a great big preacher, maybe he'll want to send Maureen and me away to school."

"And if he does," came Maureen's high voice, "I'll study to be a horse doctor."

Grandpa seemed to have a choking spell. He pulled out his red bandanna handkerchief; it almost matched his face.

"Consarn it all," he spluttered and gulped, "I must of got one of them kinks-bush catkins in my gullet."

"Clarence, did you *let* the children sell Misty?"

Grandpa Beebe took a long time folding his handkerchief and getting it back into his pocket. Then he looked sideways, from Paul to Maureen and back again. He cleared his throat. At last he said, "What else could I do, Ida? Misty is theirn. Besides, them men was dead right!"

The silence around the little table seemed never-ending. It was Grandma Beebe who broke it, speaking very softly. "Now I know what you meant, Clarence, when you said the children done a heap of growing up. They had a mill day, too."

Again the silence held them together while each one braved his own thoughts. Suddenly, a sharp siren pierced the quiet. It went through the house like a streak of lightning.

Grandma clutched the table in alarm.

"Don't be so twitchy, Ida. You know that was just the fire whistle calling volunteers to ready up the Pony Penning Grounds."

"Oh, I plumb forgot about all the big doin's."

"Grandma," asked Maureen, "could I go with Paul to help the firemen?"

Grandma laughed, but there was a catch in her voice. "To-night I guess I'd let you move the sands of the White Hill if you had a mind to. Go along. All of you. I got a mighty big letter to write to Richmond."

Chapter 4

THE PICTURE-TAKERS' PLANS

OUT THE kitchen door, down the steps, through the barnyard, Paul and Maureen ran.

Geese and turkeys, guinea hens and chicks, flew out of their way. Pigs ran snorting and squealing into the pens. But the ponies came running toward them, jostling each other to be first. Some pinned their ears back, driving the others away. To them Paul and Maureen meant good things. Corn. Water. A good hard gallop.

Misty bustled in among the other ponies, scaring them away with her threatening teeth. She wanted to get closest to Paul and Maureen.

"You're the littlest one," Paul whispered, "but you act the biggest." He laced his fingers into her mane and led her into her own stall. For a second his face tightened. "Maybe," he told her, "when you come back from New York, you'll be old enough for me to ride."

He dropped a handful of corn into her feed box and while she was busy nibbling it, he quickly closed the door behind her.

Maureen had already bridled Watch Eyes, the pony with the white eyes. She held another bridle out for Paul.

"We got to find Mr. Van Meter and Mr. Jacobs before they meet Grandma," she said.

Paul took the bridle. He sorted the ponies with his eyes and selected Trinket, a lively mare, taller than the others. He slipped the reins over her head and the bit into her mouth. He fastened the cheek strap. Then he vaulted up, ready to go.

Grandpa, pitchfork in hand, came to see them off.

"Ye done a big thing," he said, his eyes warm with admiration. "We can't keep nobody to the end-time, anyhow. They got to grow up. And usually they got to go away." He shoved his pitchfork in the soil and cleaned off the tines slowly to help his thinking. "Now the way for us all to take the sting off our thoughts is to keep busy as hummer-birds. We got to get so plumb tired we can't lay awake by night. We'll jes' turn in, turn over, turn out. That's what I'm going to do!"

Fastening the gate, he brandished his pitchfork over his head and was off, singing in a husky voice,

> *"Oh, they're wild and woolly and full of fleas,*
> *And never been curried below the knees. . . ."*

Down the lane, along the hard-packed trail to the Pony Penning Grounds, Paul and Maureen rode. The sun was slipping into the pocket of the horizon. Dusk was gathering, but Watch Eyes and Trinket knew their way. Often they had been entered in the races during Pony Penning Week. When they reached the grounds, they turned in of their own accord.

"You're early for the races," a man in a fisherman's cap laughed up at Paul and Maureen. "By the way, did two men find you? I understand they're picture-takers, come all the way from New York."

"They here now?" asked Paul.

The fisherman pointed his finger toward the pony pens. "They're down yonder in the big pen, conferencing with the fire chief."

52

Paul and Maureen could see them now. Mr. Jacobs sitting on the fence, writing in a notebook, Mr. Van Meter nodding to the fire chief while his eyes wandered over the empty pens and out across the water to the masts of the oyster boats.

Paul and Maureen rode up to them. The faces of the men turned quickly.

"Hello, you two," Mr. Van Meter called.

The fire chief mopped the sweat beaded on his forehead. "I'm mighty relieved you've come," he said. "Wilbur Wimbrow just asked me for a wiry somebody to do a special job for him. That's you, Paul. And the ladies of the Auxiliary need you to help wash dishes in the dining hall, Maureen."

"We did come to help, Chief," Paul answered, fixing his eyes on the ground, "but mostly we came to tell the movie men we changed our minds—about Misty."

Mr. Jacobs hastily stuffed his papers into his pocket and looked up with a startled expression.

Mr. Van Meter ran a fingernail across the rail of the fence to scratch out his thoughts.

"You—you haven't changed your minds?" asked Maureen in sudden alarm.

"I don't know," said Mr. Van Meter. "Your grandpa, how does he feel about it?"

"Why," gulped Paul, "he told Grandma at supper tonight that you were dead right."

Both children nodded, not daring to trust their voices.

Mr. Van Meter put out his hand. He reached up and took Maureen's first, then Paul's. "It's a deal, then," he said in a very quiet voice, "and I think you know we'll take the best possible care of Misty. We'll fly her to New York the day after Pony Penning."

Paul and Maureen counted the days in their minds. They had less than a week.

After a little while Paul said to the fire chief, "We'll tie Watch Eyes and Trinket. Then we want to go to work."

The fire chief saw the look in their eyes. "Wilbur Wimbrow is over near the track, Paul," he said with understanding. "He's having trouble installing the loud-speaker. And the ladies are cleaning the cupboards, Maureen. Seem's like you two must have sensed how shorthanded we were tonight."

All that week, day after day, Paul and Maureen spent at the Pony Penning Grounds, helping Chincoteague get ready for its big celebration. Paul liked working alongside the volunteer firemen. They were broad-shouldered and strong; yet they treated him as if he were one of them. When they needed someone to squeeze into a small spot, they never said, "We could use a youngster here." Always it was, "Paul, he can do it for you. He's wiry as any billy goat."

Once or twice Paul caught himself whistling as he worked. Then suddenly in the midst of a tune he would remember, and fall silent.

Maureen worked in the hall where the huge Pony Penning dinner was to be served. All the dishes had to be washed, and fresh white paper tacked on the long tables. Cutting and tack-ing the paper was fun, but washing the stacks upon stacks of dishes unused since last Pony Penning seemed a waste of time to her. "Why don't we just dust them off?" she suggested in a small voice.

When everyone laughed, she slipped away to Pony Ranch to help Grandpa. She found Mr. Jacobs there, sitting in the doorway of the corn house, taking notes on the backs of old envelopes.

"Could I ask something?" she said shyly.

Mr. Jacobs looked up and gave a friendly nod. "I'd like that. Ask all the questions you want."

It was always hardest to begin. Maureen twisted one leg about the other uncomfortably. "Is New York," she blurted out at last, "is New York a place where the sea winds blow?"

Mr. Jacobs answered quietly and earnestly. "Yes," he said, "but not as softly as here."

"And could a pony—I mean, could a body smell the sea?"

Mr. Jacobs' eyes grew deep and thoughtful. "Yes, sometimes. But you've got to sift it through city smells. It's far away, like something in a dream."

Misty butted right into their conversation. Grandma's white curtains were on the line, and Misty had swooped under them. Now she came waltzing along, trailing the curtains far out behind her like a wedding veil.

This sent Maureen and Mr. Jacobs off into peals of laughter, and brought Grandma out on a run. She caught up her curtains to wash them all over again without so much as a cross word for Misty.

The days flew by, but the nighttimes did not go quickly at all.

"Did you hear a lot of owls whooing last night?" Maureen asked Paul on the morning before the roundup.

"'Course I did. Anyone would hear screechy critters like that. But what was even louder was the apples making a thud when they fell."

"Do you . . . do you hear them, too, Paul?"

Paul nodded. "I counted eight. And twigs a-snapping like rifle shots, and the ponies tearing the grass as noisy as Grandma ripping old bed sheets to make dust rags out of them."

In the midst of their talk, Mr. Van Meter came driving up in an old rented car. He got out and sat down on the kitchen stoop so that he was looking up at them.

"We plan to take the roundup scene tomorrow," he said. "We're anxious to get good shots of the roundup men driving the wild ponies to Tom's Cove over on Assateague Island. You've been on the roundup, Paul. You'll know where we should set our cameras. Will you help?"

Paul lifted his chin and stood up very straight. "I'll help," he said.

"Mr. Jacobs will go with you," Mr. Van Meter went on. "But I'll be waiting here on Chincoteague to get pictures of the ponies swimming across the channel. Maureen, will you help me? You could tell me just where the ponies will land."

"I have to be here," Maureen answered. "After the wild ponies are swimmed across, I always help drive them into the pony pens."

"Good! Then everything's settled. Paul will meet Mr. Jacobs at Old Dominion Point at seven-thirty sharp, and I will meet you there a little later, Maureen."

The boy and the girl nodded politely.

"It'll be just as exciting as going on the roundup," Paul said, but his words were braver than his voice.

"It's funny," Maureen confided to Paul after Mr. Van Meter had driven away, "instead of hating Mr. Van Meter and Mr. Jacobs, I like them. I like them both."

"I do, too," admitted Paul. "And sometimes when I hear Grandma brag on 'Clarence Lee at college' I feel good inside."

"Like the time you turned the wild Phantom loose and let her go back to Assateague?"

"Yes, like that," Paul said.

Chapter 5

CAUGHT IN THE PONY-WAY

ON THE dawn of the roundup day, Paul tiptoed to his window. He crouched on the floor, his arms resting on the sill. A full yellow moon, flat as a tiddlywink, hung low in the western sky. A grayness was rising in the east and the sea, too, was a ball of gray cotton. It was the hour the roundup men would be leaving Chincoteague, loading their mounts onto the scow that would ferry them over to the island of the wild things.

In his mind Paul could hear the sound of the motor and the waves slapping against the heavy timbers of the scow. He could hear the blowing and snorting of the horses, the clipped, nervous speech of the men. Once he had been one of them. Singlehanded, he had captured the wild Phantom and her baby, Misty. How long ago that seemed! He wondered if the Phantom would be caught this year. His body broke out in sweat just thinking about her. How beautiful she was! How hard he and Maureen had worked to tame the wildness out of her! But in the end they had given her back her freedom.

"Some critters is made to be wild," a voice said behind him.

Paul scrambled to his feet, startled.

It was Grandpa Beebe in his nightshirt. "I couldn't sleep for thinkin' about Misty's mamma," he said. "So I tipped to yer room. Figured ye might be awake."

"Grandpa!"

"Yes, boy."

Paul's words came in a rush. "Grandpa! If you hopped Watch Eyes and galloped to the mooring place, you could stop the scow. You could join the roundup. You could," Paul whispered tensely, "you could make sure the Phantom escaped."

The little bedroom was very still. Paul could not see Grandpa's face, but he could hear his troubled sigh.

"'Tain't like ye, Paul," Grandpa said at last. "'Twould be downright dishonest. Besides, when the roundup men comes upon the Phantom, they'll be puny as dustin' straws in a blow. Ye can almost count on her escapin' this year. She's been caught oncet. She ain't goin' to let it happen again. Now slip on your pants," he said. "Ye can help me do the chores afore ye have to meet the movie men."

Sharp at seven-thirty Paul was waiting at Old Dominion
Point. A few early visitors from the mainland were tramping
about expectantly, asking questions of each other.

"How did the wild ponies get to Assateague in the first
place?"

"When was the first Pony Penning held?"

"I heard it's the oldest roundup in the United States and the
biggest wild west show of the east!" said a man with a kodak
in his hands and three children at his heels. "It's different, too.
They swim the wild ponies across to Chincoteague."

Paul walked away. He could not bring himself to talk
about the roundup and Pony Penning. "It's sacred, kind of,"
he said to himself. "And it takes somebody like Grandpa or
Miss Vic to make folks understand about it." He was glad
when he heard the chugging of a motor and caught sight of Joe
Selby's oyster boat with Mr. Jacobs and a stranger aboard. He
rolled his pants above his knees and waded out into the water.

"Halloo-oo-oo," he shouted, waving his arms. "I'm here!"

The boat nosed over and he clambered aboard. Mr. Jacobs
was barefoot, too, and he was ripping open cartons of films.

"Paul," he said, "this is Mr. Winter, one of our cameramen,
who came down to Chincoteague last night."

Paul looked up at the lean, serious young man. His shy

"how do" was lost in the sputter of the engine as the boat turned and headed out into the channel.

"And you know Joe here," Mr. Jacobs nodded toward the man at the tiller.

Paul smiled at the weather-creased face of Joe Selby. Many a time he had gone oystering in this very boat.

"I hear Grandpa Beebe is a pretty good weather prophet. What did he say, Paul? Clear skies?" asked Mr. Jacobs, squinting anxiously at the clouds.

Paul blushed. "I didn't ask him." How could he explain that he and Grandpa had been more concerned with Misty's mother?

"Well, Joe here thinks it won't rain. Never has rained on Pony Penning Day. Never will, he says."

The talk stopped.

The wind dried Paul's wet legs. He shivered a little from cold and excitement. He watched the people on Chincoteague blur into a cloud, then watched the cloud slowly wisp out until it stretched far up the beach.

Ahead of him lay the waving grasses of Assateague, and on and beyond the pine woods and the sea. If he half-closed his eyes, the tops of the pines became the mane of a horse and the White Hill the cap of a rider, and the whole island was riding in advance of their boat, looking after her like any outrider, protecting her from the mighty waves of the Atlantic.

Suddenly the motor went quiet, cutting off his thoughts.

"We're in the shallows now," Joe called out. "Close as we can get to Tom's Cove."

Camera on shoulders, film held high above the water, the two movie men jumped overboard.

Paul followed. The soft bottom squinched up between his toes. How different this was from going on the roundup! Instead of pounding over the marshland, shouting and driving the wild ponies, here he was, splashing ashore, as peaceful as on a Sunday school picnic.

But Mr. Jacobs was not calm and quiet, and his eyes were no longer dark and cool. They threw sparks like horseshoes on a pavement.

"Paul," he said sharply, "from which direction will the ponies come? We want to set our cameras close enough to catch the wild look in their eyes."

Paul thought carefully before replying. "The roundup men drive 'em down to that little grazing ground yonder. But they come from"—he wheeled around and pointed a finger to the deep woods that formed the backbone of the island—"they come from . . ."

Paul's sentence hung in mid air. A rolling boom of noise! Dust clouds swirling! And hulking out of the woods some dark misshapen thing! It might have been a prehistoric monster or a giant kicking up clods of earth for all the form it had. But whatever it was, it hugged along the ground like puffs of smoke on a windless day. Now the shape fell apart! It was the men on horseback driving the wild herds to Tom's Cove. They were coming earlier than anyone had expected. Much earlier.

Paul and the two men were blocking the pony-way! The

ponies would be coming right at them. How could he get the men and the camera to safety?

A daring thought crossed his mind. Let them stay in the pony-way! Let them stay! Let the wild things come dead-heat at the camera. "They got horse sense," he thought. "They'll split around us."

He skinned off his white shirt and buried it in the sand. The ponies must not shy away from a billowing white object.

"Follow me!" he shouted, running directly toward the noisy, swirling mass.

The cameraman was young. He could run almost as fast as Paul, even with a clumsy camera to carry. Along the hard-packed sand, across the meadow marsh, up a little rise the three of them ran.

"Here!" shouted Paul, pointing to the camera.

It was too late to explain his plan. The dark racing monster was no longer a nebulous thing. Wild ponies and men on mounts were taking shape, coming around the horseshoe curve of Tom's Cove, splitting the air with yells and whinnies and pounding hooves, like thunder rolling nearer and nearer.

Mr. Jacobs was standing close to the cameraman, his eyes darting nervously from the oncoming ponies to the overcast sky. He nodded to Paul that he understood. If the plan worked, the ponies would break up in two bunches around the camera. He would get a closeup of the wildest scene of the roundup.

And suddenly the sun struck through the clouds like a powerful searchlight. Manes, tails, sweating bodies were highlighted with red and gold.

"Now! Now!" Paul heard himself yelling. "This is it!"
Why was that cameraman so slow? What was he waiting for?
Was there ever a sight so wild? It was wilder than thunder and
lightning. Wilder than wind.

He clenched his hands behind him to keep from knocking
the camera over. This man Winter was as cold as his name.
Paul hated him. He had given up going on the roundup for

him, for a man who stood frozen. A man who waited, waited,
waited, when all around him the wild things were blowing and
screaming.

And just when he could stand the delay no longer came the clicking, clicking sound of the camera close in his ear. Mr. Winter was grinding now. And just in time. The ponies were plunging at him, their eyes white ringed, their nostrils dilated until the red lining showed like blood. Now they were splitting in two bunches, swerving around the camera, coming so close that their tails whisked it.

Paul drew a long breath of relief as he turned to look at Mr. Jacobs.

"He knows just when," laughed Mr. Jacobs weakly.

Chapter 6

HORSE-DOCTOR PAUL

THE PONIES began to slacken their pace. They were coming to the sweetest grass on Assateague. The roundup men, almost as blown as the horses, drew rein.

Suddenly Paul forgot the cameramen; he was a horseman now. "Look!" A choked cry escaped him. "A mare's hurt, terrible hurt. Look at her limp. Her colt can outrun her."

He raced across the wiry grass to the men resting their mounts. "What's the matter of her, Mr. Wimbrow?" he called anxiously.

Mr. Wimbrow took off his fisherman's cap and wiped the perspiration from his forehead. "Heel string's cut," he said tiredly. "Likely she cut it on an oyster shell."

The mare tucked her forelegs beneath her and lay down to rest, as if she knew the roundup was only half over. She was a pinto with splashy black and white markings. She might have been beautiful, but now she was just a crippled captive. A captive who seemed content to rest while her puzzled colt and stallion watched over her.

"You going to swim her across the channel?" Paul asked.

"Reckon we will," Mr. Wimbrow said. "The salt water will clean the cut better'n any man-made medicine."

Paul nodded. If Wilbur Wimbrow thought swimming wouldn't hurt the mare, it wouldn't. He turned to study the milling mob of ponies, watching the stallions gather in their own families. Every now and then a mare would break away, and the stallion would herd her back into his band with galloping hooves and bared teeth. At last they were all neatly grouped like classes in school.

"I hanker to see the Phantom," Paul thought aloud, "but I hope I don't!" He wondered at himself. One time he had so wanted to capture her. Now he so wanted her to remain free. He could not bring himself to ask the men if she had been caught. From one bunch of ponies to another he went. There were blacks and chestnuts and bays and pintos, but nowhere among them was Misty's beautiful wild mother with the white map on her withers.

"She didn't get caught!" he whispered with a fierce gladness. He wanted to throw back his head and whinny his relief to the whole wide world.

Instead, he belly-flopped in the grass, laughing softly to himself. The sun poured down on his back, warmed him through. All around, the wild creatures were grazing, their legs scissor blades, opening and closing, opening and closing, as they moved from one delicious clump of grass to another. Paul felt strangely comforted. Out here on Assateague, with the wild things so near, he could push aside unhappy thoughts. Maybe Friday would never come. He pulled a blade of grass and slid it between his teeth, savoring the salty taste. For a long time he lay quite still, lulled by the wind and the waves and the pleasant sound of the ponies cropping the grasses. It was not until

he heard boats starting up their motors that he went back to
the cameramen.

"The tide's ebbing bare," he told them. "The men'll be driving the ponies into the water soon. They're going to need all the

boats to make a kind of causeway for the ponies to swim from Assateague to Chincoteague."

He dug up his shirt, shook it free of sand, and pulled it over his head. Then he waded out to Joe Selby's boat.

Everything was working according to plan. The boats, spitting and sputtering, were lining up to form a sea lane across the channel. On the beach the roundup men were closing in, drawing a tight circle around the ponies. A sudden explosion of lusty yells, and now the animals were plunging into the sea! Men's cries mingled with the screaming of ponies and the wild clatter of birds overhead. The channel was boiling with noise.

Paul's eyes and ears sharpened. He felt he belonged neither to the roundup men nor to the cameramen. He was an excited onlooker, like the visitors from Norfolk, from Washington, from Philadelphia. He watched the hurt mare and her colt stumble into the foam. The water seemed to revive the mare.

"Look at her colt!" he laughed aloud. "He's getting a free ride!"

Sure enough, the colt's muzzle was anchored firmly on his mother's back. It seemed to comfort the mare, to give her new strength.

Four or five tow-headed boys were swimming alongside the ponies. They wanted to be ready in case a foal needed life-saving. They remembered how Paul had rescued the drowning baby Misty. But this year the colts were expert as swimmers in a water carnival, and not one needed help.

The first ponies were scrambling up the beach at Chincoteague now, their coats curried by the water and the noonday sun. The blacks were no longer shaggy and dusty but took on the shininess of satin, and the chestnuts glistened like burnished copper.

"Slick as moles!" Paul laughed to himself.

He wanted to get to them quickly, eager as any sightseer. "Let's put in to shore," he yelled to Joe Selby.

The scow with the roundup men was landing alongside them. Wilbur Wimbrow's arm went up, signaling for Paul to come.

The boy welcomed an excuse to be with the horsemen. "They need me," he said to Mr. Jacobs as he leaped over the side of the boat.

"That hurt mare's got to have some first aid," Mr. Wimbrow told Paul. "Your fingers are fine as a mother-woman's. Us men'll hold her quiet while you lay these cigarettes in her cut. The tobacco'll burn it clean."

He handed two cigarettes to Paul and took the bandanna handkerchief from around his neck. "You can use this for a bandage," he said. "It'll stay the blood."

Grandpa Beebe, gathering his rope, stepped up behind Mr. Wimbrow. "Leave me rope the hurt mare fer ye," he said.

Mr. Wimbrow was glad of fresh hands to help. "After we doctor her," he told Grandpa, "I'd like it if Paul and Maureen'd lead her over to my place. If she's driven to the pony pens along with the mob, she's liable to get tromped on."

"Better off by herself," Grandpa agreed. "What you want done with her colt?"

"We'll drive him to the Pony Penning Grounds with the others. He's big enough to be sold with the other colts."

Grandpa Beebe easily roped the mare. Then he talked to her in the voice he saved for wild things. "Easy there. Easy, girl. Ye're not hurted bad."

The crowds closed in to watch.

"Why don't they shoot her?" asked a well-meaning visitor wearing Oxford glasses.

"Why!" barked Grandpa. "For the same reason yer family didn't aim a gun at ye when ye lost yer nacheral sight."

The people cheered for Grandpa and pressed in closer.

"Go ahead," Mr. Wimbrow nodded to Paul. "We got her."

Paul tore the paper from the cigarettes. He picked up the hurt leg, bending it at the knee. Gently but firmly he laid the tobacco in the cut. It was good to be helping, not just watching. Now he knew how good Grandma must feel when she took care of a sick neighbor. Maybe he and Maureen would both be horse doctors when they grew up. Maybe they would live in the old lighthouse on Assateague. Then they could see whenever a wild creature was hurt. All these thoughts spun around in his mind as he tied the bandanna securely.

"Paul, you leg up on Trinket now," Mr. Wimbrow said. He beckoned to Maureen, who was mounted on Watch Eyes and holding Trinket for Paul. "Then you two lead the mare down behind Old Dominion Lodge so's she can't see her colt go off without her."

Grandpa and Mr. Wimbrow tied a connecting rein between the hurt mare and Trinket and Watch Eyes. Then they faced her out to sea while the roundup men roped her colt and headed for the Pony Penning Grounds. A little moment and it was over. The trembling of the mare quieted. Her neighing became no more than a whimper. She limped numbly along between Watch Eyes and Trinket.

"Paul," said Maureen as they headed for Mr. Wimbrow's house, "seems this mare's got enough trouble without having her colt taken away from her too."

Paul was busy trying to hold Trinket to the slow pace of the mare.

"'Course she's got enough trouble," he said at last, "but up to Mr. Wimbrow's house she won't be able to hear the colt whinkerin' for her all night long." He rode on in silence for a moment. Then he added, "Maybe it's like a twitch."

"What's like a twitch?"

"Humpf," snorted Paul. "You wanting to be a horse doctor and don't even know what a twitch is."

"I do too know what a twitch is. It's nothing but a piece of rope twisted around a horse's nose to make him forget where his pain's at."

"Well," said Paul, "this mare's foot probably hurts so bad she can't fret about losing her colt."

Maureen nodded her head.

Chapter 7

THE BEST KIND OF WINKERS

GRANDPA WAS already at home when Paul and Maureen arrived. He was trying to seem very happy.

"Childern," he shouted, "look-a-here. Ever see such a whopping big watermelon? And it's frosty cold, asides." He held it high to show that it was beaded with icy sweat. "Grandma says if we're going to eat it in our hands we got to stay outside." He winked happily.

Grandma Beebe came out of the house with a pan of steaming water, a bar of brown soap, and washcloths. She set the pan on a bench in the shade. "Now," she said brightly, "wash up good, and let the wind dry you off. I been making a plummy cake for the Ladies' Auxiliary and my kitchen's hot as a griddle. Out here it's nice and cool." She looked up at Paul and Maureen. "What's the matter of you two? You glued to Watch Eyes and Trinket?" But she smiled as she said it.

Paul and Maureen slid to their feet and led their mounts to the big shed.

"Don't let your ponies stomp on my biddies," Grandma called after them.

There was a chorus of neighing as the horses that had been left behind greeted the ones that had been away. Misty's neigh was a high squeal of happiness. Paul and Maureen stopped to rough up her mane and stroke her nose. Then they hung up their bridles and joined Grandpa at the wash bench, while Misty tagged along.

"There's a letter come from Clarence Lee this morning," Grandma was saying as she laid a red-checked cloth on the picnic table. "He's in the college all right, studying to be a minister."

"A minister, eh?" Grandpa Beebe straightened up and planted his feet wide apart. "I'm a-danged," he laughed softly. "To think I sired a minister! Why, I'm that proud I'm liable to go around with my chest stickin' out like a pewter pigeon."

"You mean pouter pigeon, Clarence."

"Well, let's not gibble-gabble. We got us a lot of watermelon to eat. And I've brung some new little carrots for Misty."

Grandma had made crab cakes and baked them in clam shells, and she had black-eyed peas and corn pone with wild honey. And Grandpa was all excited about the deep pink of his watermelon and the blackness of the seeds. "'Taint only something noble to look at," he exclaimed, "but whoever tasted a melon so downright juicy and sweet?"

Pony Ranch seemed to draw close about Paul and Maureen. They could not help feeling comforted by Grandpa's and Grandma's happiness.

Maybe, if no one thought about Friday, it would never come. Maybe they could go on picnicking forever, with Misty coming to them and offering to shake hands until all the carrots were gone, and the chickens fighting over the watermelon rinds and rushing for each seed that was dropped.

"I declare!" Grandma said, her eyes fixed on the whirling chickens. "It took me to be a grownup afore I figgered out why they call that shoal up north of here 'Hens and Chickens.' It's plain as the nose on your face that they do it 'cause the water swirls and closes in like hens and chicks after a morsel to eat!"

Grandpa clucked his tongue in admiration. "Ida! I never knowed the reason either!"

When the picnic was over, Paul got up and stretched himself. He squinted at the sky between the pines and found the position of the sun. "They're just about fixing to call the bronc-busting contest over at the Pony Penning Grounds," he said to Grandpa. "Reckon I'll ride."

Grandma caught her breath. "Don't let him do it, Clarence," she cried in alarm. "He'll be killed outright."

"There, there, Ida." Grandpa's voice was the same one he had used on the hurt mare. "He'll not get killed. Leastaways, not outright," he grinned. "Y'see, Ida, Paul and Maureen is like nervous hosses. They got to wear winkers to keep from seein' things comin' up from behind. My grandpap used to say" —and here Grandpa Beebe began rubbing the stubble in his ears as if he were enormously pleased with his memory— "he used to say, 'Clarence, keepin' busy is the best kind of winkers. If ye keep busy today, ye can't see tomorrow comin' up.' That's what he said."

Underneath his eyebrows Grandpa's eyes had a merry gleam. "Go 'long, Paul. Pick out a tough pony and ride 'im till he's dauncy. I'd sure give my last two teeth to trade places with ye."

Chapter 8

A WILD ONE FOR WILD-PONY PAUL

WHEN PAUL and Maureen rode into the Pony Pen-
ning Grounds, the loud-speaker was blasting at full strength.
"Ladies and gentlemen, Jack Winter of New York City is
making his way over to the chute."

"That's the cameraman!" Paul told Maureen excitedly.
"He's going to ride in the contest!"

They tied their mounts quickly, running to the corral just
in time to see the young New Yorker come bolting out of the
chute on a white spook of a horse. His hands were clutched in
the horse's mane, and he was gripping hard with his knees. But

his feet were not locked around the pony's barrel. He looked like a rider in the bareback class at a horse show.

Paul was screaming at him, "Lock your feet around his belly. Lock your feet around . . ."

But his words thinned into nothing. The white spook had planted his forefeet in the earth and was lashing the sky with his heels. One second . . . two seconds . . . three seconds . . . four, five, six, barely seven seconds, and Mr. Winter was plummeting through space, then falling to earth with a thud.

A bugle of triumph tore the stillness that followed. Then the freed animal went snaking around the corral until a round-up man roped him.

Shakily Mr. Winter got to his feet, stumbled out the gate held open for him, and lost himself in the crowd.

"Give a big hand to Mr. Winter, folks. That's all he'll get," called the voice over the loud-speaker.

The crowd responded with spirited applause.

"Who'll be next, folks? The ten dollars still stands. Who's next?"

Paul's arm shot into the air, but no one saw it.

The voice kept prodding. "How about Delbert Daisy?"

People all around Paul and Maureen were making remarks. "Delbert tried it last year," someone said. "He's too smart to try again."

"I'm a cowboy from Texas," a man with a ten gallon hat drawled, "but I be dogged if I'm ready to pick me a homestead. I'm a reg'lar bronc rider, used to a halter and a belly rope for anchor."

Another stranger agreed. "No siree! No thousand pounds of wild horseflesh under me without something to hold on to. Not me!"

"Who's next, folks? Who's next?" the voice hammered.

The crowds around the corral were banked solid. Paul could not wedge between them to climb the fence. He and Maureen finally wriggled underneath it.

Inside the corral Paul's hand went up again.

This time everyone saw.

"Look, everybody! Paul Beebe's next," the voice bawled out. "Ten dollars to Paul if he can stay aboard for thirty seconds. Stand back, Maureen. That's his sister, folks. Stand flat against the fence, Maureen."

Maureen clutched at her throat. They were going to let her stay in the corral! She stood back as far as she could, leaning hard against the rails, with the people pressing against her on the other side.

"Let out a wild one for Wild-Pony Paul!" came the voice.

Paul was gone. He was climbing the fence of the chute, swinging his leg over an unbroken pony, gripping the strands of tangled mane as if they were reins.

"Who's he riding?" someone cried.

There was a pause.

Then the announcer's voice cracked with excitement. "A wild one it is! Red Demon—a she-devil on hooves. Those aren't her ears, folks, they're horns!"

A hush of expectation fell over the onlookers.

"Be you ready, Paul?"

A thin voice answered, "Turn 'er loose."

Every eye was riveted on the closed gate of the chute. Now it burst open and Red Demon, a chestnut with a blaze, shot out bucking and twisting. In a quick flash of seeing, her white-ringed eyes swept the corral. Suddenly she spied a tree at the far end. She hurtled toward it, not straight like a bullet, but in a tortuous, weaving line, calculating, deadly.

Paul tried to capture the rhythm of her muscles. He leaned back, gripping with his thighs, pushing inward and backward with his knees, turning and twisting with her, writhing like a corkscrew.

The crowds watched, horrified. This was the thrill they had come to see.

Maureen hid her face in her hands, listening. She heard the earthquake of hooves as the Red Demon headed for the tree, heard a man's voice rasp out, "He's going to get hung up in that pine!" She waited for the crash, but there was none. Stealthily she peered between her fingers. They were not going to crack up! The wild pony was swerving around the tree and Paul was making the spine-wrenching turn with her. He was still on!

Now the weight of Paul enraged Red Demon. Birds and flies could be removed with a swish of the tail. But no mere swishing would remove this clinging creature. There had to be violence. She brought her head and shoulder to the ground, then jerked up with a sudden sharpness. The boy's head jounced down and shot up in unison.

A woman shrieked.

Maureen grabbed the back of her own neck. She felt as if it had been snapped in two.

"Hang on!" she screamed. "Hang on!"

Red and glaring, the hot sun struck down on the two wild things. It seemed to weld them together like bronze figures heated in the same furnace. They were all of one piece. The boy's arms were rigid bands of bronze, and his hair did not fly and toss with the rocketing of the pony—it hung down, sweat-matted between his eyes, like the forelock of a stallion. It was hard to tell which was wilder, boy or pony.

"Fourteen seconds . . . fifteen seconds," the voice over the loud-speaker blared.

And still the two figures were one, the boy's arms unbending, his legs soldered in place.

That lone tree at the end of the corral! It seemed to bewitch Red Demon. Again she rushed at it, head lowered as if to gore it with her devil ears. A thousand throats gasped as she whiplashed around it again, and then once again, each time missing by a wink.

And still Paul held on.

"Twenty seconds . . . twenty-one seconds . . ."

The power of the sun seemed to strengthen as the seconds wore on. Now it fused the two wild creatures, making molten metal of them. In fluid motion, horse and boy were riding out the fire together. Together, they dipped and rose and spurted through space, now part of the earth, now part of the sky.

Maureen felt her knees giving way. "Please! Please! Someone stop them! Oh, stop them!" She tried to brace herself

against the fence to keep from falling. The beat of Red Demon's hooves continued to pound hard and steady in her ears. She closed her eyes for a second, then opened them.

Something was happening! The molten mass was bursting in two. Everything went black before her eyes. When next she opened them, Paul was lying beside her. Then they were both picking themselves up, laughing feebly. Paul was no longer the bronzed rider on a bronzed horse. He was a dirt-streaked, pale-faced boy in faded jeans.

All about them half-frenzied visitors were swarming over the fence rails, men and women laughing and crying both, asking questions and answering themselves. And over and above the noise, the voice on the loud-speaker never stopped. "Thirty-three seconds! Thirty-three seconds! Paul rode her dizzy. The ten dollars goes to Paul Beebe."

Chapter 9

OFF IN A SWIRL OF MIST

PAUL SPOKE in breathless jerks as they edged away from the crowd. "I'm going to give the ten dollars—to Mr. Van Meter—to see that Misty has some carrots each day," he told Maureen.

But Mr. Van Meter refused the money. "We'll see that Misty gets her carrots, Paul. You save your money for something very special," he said with a wise look.

"What would that be?"

"I don't know, but something special always turns up when my youngsters have ten dollars saved. Now you two better go home. You've had a hard day."

The sun was throwing long shadows by the time Paul and Maureen arrived back at Pony Ranch. There was not much talk during supper that night, and afterward the boy and girl were too tired to enter Watch Eyes or Trinket in the night races to be held at the Pony Penning Grounds.

Paul helped Grandpa water the ponies while Maureen sat on a chicken coop drawing pictures of Misty. She worked with

quick strokes because Misty seldom remained still. While the pony was drinking at the water barrel, Maureen drew a side view of her, the side with the map of the United States on it. And while she tagged after Paul, Maureen sketched a funny little back view—the softly rounded white rump and the long tail that swished from side to side when she walked. Maureen laughed aloud as she tried to put the swishes on paper.

Paul and Grandpa came to look over her shoulder.

"By smoke! I'm a jumpin' mullet if there ain't a strong favorance to Misty!" Grandpa said.

"It's not bad," Paul agreed.

"Don't she look like a little girl wearing her grandma's long dress?" Maureen giggled. Then her face sobered.

Paul was staring at the pictures, at all of them. "You can make me some — if you like," he said in a low voice.

Misty went back to the water barrel for another long, cooling drink, then stood quite still watching Maureen sketch and erase and erase and sketch. The evening breeze was stirring. Soon Misty would settle down to the business of grazing by moonlight. But right now, when it was neither night nor day, she was content to snuff the winds and to look about her.

She came over to Maureen and breathed very softly down her neck. She nudged the bread board on which the drawing paper was tacked. Then, as if she were posing, she turned her head slightly, looking out over the marshland, waiting for night to close in.

Maureen sketched on. The pricked ears, the blaze on her face, the soft pink underlip with its few lady whiskers, the mane lifted by the small wind.

At last she had four pictures for Paul and four for herself. She started to say good-night to Misty, but Grandma was watching from the doorway.

"Let's see what you've done, Maureen," she called out. "As a girl I was always one for drawing, too."

Maureen showed Grandma the pictures and smiled at her

praise. Then she put the ones for Paul on a shelf in his room and went to her own room. There she laid her page of sketches on her pillow, and fell into a deep, exhausted slumber.

Toward morning, sounds pecked at her sleep. She dreamed she was riding Red Demon on an oyster-shell road, and the tattoo of hooves pinged sharper and sharper in her ears.

She awoke to the sound of hammer strokes. With sudden anxiety she was out of bed, dressing, hurrying to join Paul and Grandpa. The hammer strokes could mean but one thing. They were building a crate for Misty. She must get to them quickly —to see they built it big enough, strong enough.

"If I don't have to eat any breakfast," she pleaded with Grandma, "I'll make up for it tomorrow. Honest I will."

To Maureen's astonishment Grandma agreed. "No griddle cakes this morning," she said. "They'd stick in your throat and lump in your stummick. Only this tiny glass of milk."

Instead of an everyday glass tumbler, Grandma was pouring the milk in the ruby-colored glass, the one her own grandmother had left her. Maureen somehow managed to drink all of it.

When she burst out of the house, the floor of the crate was already built.

"Maureen!" Grandpa called to her. "You hurry down marsh and gather driftwood. Paul, you look in that bunch of scantlings. See if there's anything we can use. I'm a-danged if lumber around Pony Ranch ain't scarce as two-headed cats."

The finished crate was an odd-looking object. Uprights had been splintered from an old gate, laths taken from a deserted chicken roost, and driftwood from who knows where; but so much care and measuring had gone into the making of it that to Paul and Maureen and Grandpa it did not look rough-made at all.

"Snug, ain't it?" said Grandpa, forcing a smile. "And Paul's gathered a big enough bundle of salt grass to last her the hull day."

"'Member when we readied the stall for Phantom?" asked Maureen very softly. "Readying a crate is not . . . is not . . ."

Grandpa snapped his fingers. "Consarn it all!" he sputtered. "I plumb forgot the pine shatters. Paul and Maureen, you gather some nice smelly pine shatters from off'n the floor of the woods. Nothin' makes a better cushion for pony feet as pine shatters. Besides, it smells to their liking. *Every*thing'll smell to her liking—salt grass, driftwood, pine shatters."

Taking the wheelbarrow and an old broom, Paul and Maureen headed for the woods.

"Grandpa can think of more things for us to do!" Maureen scolded as she swept the pine needles in a heap.

"It's just his way of putting our winkers on, Maureen."

Scarcely were the pine needles dumped onto the floor of the crate than Grandpa pointed to the sky.

"Be that winged critter a gull or a plane?"

The beat of engines was the answer. A silver plane came sweeping down on Pony Ranch, now circling it, now banking, now turning into the wind, landing, taxiing right up to the gate!

Barnyard creatures flew screeching into the air. The older ponies ran snorting for their shed. Only Misty stood her ground. She had seen this strange silver bird before. She had snuffed it carefully from its big nose to its twin tails. There was nothing at all to be afraid of.

Mr. Van Meter and Mr. Jacobs jumped out of the cockpit. They nodded a good-morning to Grandpa, then came right over to Paul and Maureen.

"It makes it easier," Mr. Jacobs hesitated, then tried again. "It makes it easier," he said, "knowing you two *want* to share Misty with boys and girls everywhere. Van and I were saying this morning—if we didn't know we were going to make thousands of children happy, we certainly wouldn't make two sad."

"Maureen!" commanded Paul, and there was something of Grandpa's tone in his voice. "Here's some corn kernels. You

stand by the crate and slip your hand between the boards."

Maureen did as she was told.

"Now hold out the nibbles and call to her."

Maureen's voice faltered, "Come along—little Misty," she sang brokenly, "come—along."

Misty hesitated only an instant. Then she stepped onto the friendly pine needles and walked into the crate.

It took Grandpa and Paul, Mr. Van Meter and Mr. Jacobs, and the pilot, too, to load the crate onto the plane.

Maureen stood watching, looking and thinking and trying not to do either.

Suddenly she felt a pair of warm arms folded close about her. She turned and buried her face in Grandma's broad bosom. "Oh, Grandma," she sobbed, "I feel just like a mother who has borned many children. But Misty is my favorite. And it hurts to have her grow up and leave us . . . without even looking back and whinkerin'. She's—" Maureen burst into tears, "she's even eating her grass!"

"She don't understand, honey," comforted Grandma. "She's just a young 'un, all excited in her mind. Children and ponies both get all excited with traveling and their boxed lunches. They seldom cry when they go off. It's the ones left behind does the bellering. Now blow your nose good and don't let Paul see you cry."

After the crate was safely stowed inside the plane, the men came back out and looked from one silent face to another.

"Now we will say good-bye to you all," Mr. Van Meter said quietly. "We will do everything we can to keep Misty well and make her happy. She has a big job in life now. She's got to be a sea horse more than ever, leaving a little trail of happiness in her wake wherever she goes. She's got work to do!"

"Please," asked Maureen, "always each night whisper in Misty's ear that we'll be here a-waiting for her when she's ready to come home."

"Think of it!" said Paul with a crooked smile. "Misty's the first one of the family to see our islands from the air." He turned to Mr. Van Meter. "Do you suppose you could point out the White Hill to her from the air so's she could see where the Spanish galleon was wrecked?"

"I think we could, Paul."

"Then you could tell her how brave her great-great-great-great granddaddy and mammy were; how they swum ashore from the wrecked galleon in a raging storm."

"We'll tell her that, Paul."

"Gee willikers," Grandpa's voice cracked, "git agoin' afore we changes our minds and hauls Misty back out."

Mr. Van Meter nodded. He signaled to the pilot to start up the engines. Then he and Mr. Jacobs stepped inside the plane.

"And be careful," bellowed Grandpa above the noise of the engines, "'bout letting big chunky kids ride Misty too soon. Recomember she's a young 'un yet."

The plane nosed the wind and roared along the narrow spit of land, the sound of its engines deepening as it climbed. It passed over a lone, wind-crippled pine tree, then up and up and out across the channel, away into the blue distance.

"She's over the White Hill!" shouted Paul into the wave of silence that broke over them.

They watched until the plane was swallowed in a white cloud of mist.

"Now ain't that just like a storybook?" Grandpa crowed, while he rubbed the bristles in his ear. "When Paul fust seed her she was all tangled up in a skein of mist, and now she leaves in a sudden swirl of it. Don't it ease the pain of her goin'?"

There was no answer. None at all.

"Don't it?" he insisted, pulling his hat down low over his eye. "That is, somewhat?"

Chapter 10

ALL ALONE AT TOM'S COVE

For THE space of a few brief moments, the little huddle of those left behind stood rooted. Whether they still heard or only imagined they heard the purring of the plane, no one knew.

Grandpa let out a sigh that seemed to come from his boots. "Hmpf! You folks can stand here a-moonin'," he said at last, "but as fer me, I got to hyper along to the Pony Pennin' Grounds. This be one of my big days. Some of the strangers from over on the main may want to buy a partic'lar pony with a partic'lar markin', and might be I'll have jes' the one fer 'em. Come along, Paul and Maureen."

Paul shook his head. "If you don't care, Grandpa, I don't believe I want to see any ponies today."

Grandma cleared her throat. "Clarence," she said, "I promised the Ladies' Auxiliary to bring some oysters to the Pony Penning Dinner this noon and to fry 'em myself. If you can spare the children, I'd like to have them take the little boat and gather some Tom's Cove oysters for me. I want to be sure they're good and plump and right fresh out of the sea."

Listlessly Paul and Maureen followed Grandma to the house. They put on their high rubber boots. They took the flannel gloves and the baskets she offered.

As they walked to Old Dominion Point, they stared blindly at the familiar sights. The beach was deserted now except for the little white striker birds tippeting along the shore on their red feet. The milling crowds of yesterday were gone. They were at the Pony Penning Grounds.

In silence the boy and the girl climbed in a small boat with an outboard motor. Paul cast off the mooring line. He started the motor. It sputtered and stopped. He tried again. This time it chugged evenly.

They were sculling the waves now, heading across the inlet. Paul looked dead ahead. He saw a fishhawk strike the surface of the water in front of the boat, then rise again with a fish so large he could hardly fly with it. He saw the lighthouse of Assateague, like some giant's dagger stuck in the island to keep it from floating out to sea. A circle of buzzards wheeled low over Tom's Cove, making a racket that could be heard above the beat of the motor. Idly Paul pointed to them.

104

Maureen nodded. She cupped her hands around her mouth. "Likely something dead. A shark, maybe," she called to him.

"Something's alive, too," he called back. "It's keeping the birds from swoopin' down."

Now they were so close to Tom's Cove they could distinguish the shrill chirring of the hawks and the high whistle of the osprey. Paul's indifference was gone.

"The live thing's a baby colt!" he cried.

He shut off the motor and beached the boat. He made a sun visor out of his hand. And there, not a hundred yards away, standing quiet, was a spindle-legged foal. It had a crooked star on its forehead. And as it stood there with its legs all splayed out, it looked like a tiny wooden carving against a cardboard sea.

Maureen spoke Paul's thoughts. "He's like the little wooden colts Mr. Lester makes for Christmas." Then she looked down at the quiet thing lying in the sand. Her voice fell to a whisper. "It's not a shark that's dead."

"No," said Paul, "it's his mamma."

They started out of the boat, but when the foal heard the *plash-plash* made by their rubber boots, he gallumphed away, fast as his toothpick legs would carry him.

"Don't go after him, Maureen. He's afeared. Stand quiet. Might be he'll come to us."

Paul's plan worked. When no one gave chase, the foal minced to a stop, then turned his wild brown eyes on them. The crooked star on his forehead seemed to widen the space between his eyes. It gave him an expression of startled wonder.

A quiet stillness lay over Tom's Cove. Even the circle of birds had stopped their screaming. Paul and Maureen made no move at all. They stood as still as the wooden stakes that marked the oyster beds.

Cautiously, as a child who has lighted a firecracker comes back to see if it will explode, so the foal came a step toward them. Then another out of wild curiousness, and another. When Paul and Maureen still did not move, he grew bold,

dancing closer and closer, asking questions with his pricked ears and repeating them with his small question-mark of a tail.

Paul's laugh of wonderment broke the spell. "Say! He's somethin'! A fiery little horse colt!"

At sound of Paul's voice, the foal took fright and shied so sharply that all four of his feet were off the earth at once. Then he high-tailed it up the beach.

"He's sassy for one so little," Maureen laughed. "How long do you reckon he's been alone?"

"Not long. His mamma 'pears too old to stand the running yesterday. She's got an F branded on her hip—belongs to the fire company."

"What'll we do, Paul?"

"Don't know. I'm a-thinkin'."

"Let's take him back and bottle-feed him."

"'Course we'll take him back! But how do we rope him without a rope? How do we round him up without a horse? And even should we catch him, how do we hold him in the boat? He'll be lively as a jumpin' bean."

Maureen was fumbling in her mind for an idea.

"We got to gentle him quick," Paul said.

"Grandpa says nothing takes the wildness out of a creature like sea water."

"That's it, Maureen! That's it! We'll drive him into the channel. Then we'll swim out and tow him in."

Their eyes fastened on the colt, Paul and Maureen worked off their boots. "You stay on this side of him," Paul whispered excitedly. "I'll circle wide around on the other side. Then we'll close in and drive him into the sea."

The foal's gaze followed Paul as the boy went around him in a wide arc. Now the three creatures were forming the three points of a triangle, the colt at the tip and Paul and Maureen back at equal distances on either side.

Paul stopped, took a deep breath. Then like any roundup man, he gave the signal. His wild screeching whoop tore jagged holes in the morning. Quicker than an echo came Maureen's cry. They both charged the foal, arms waving and voices shouting at the top of their lungs.

The wild creature stood frozen an instant. Then he became a whirling dervish, spinning around and around in an ever-smalling circle. The roaring humans were coming at him from

both sides, closer and closer. With a gallopy little gait he
headed out into the water.

Splashing after him, yelling at him, Paul and Maureen
drove him out beyond his depth.

"He can swim!" gasped Maureen. "Look at him go!"

For a few brief seconds the baby colt headed out into the deep. Paul and Maureen watched his tiny pricked ears and the ripple he stirred, making a little V in the water. Suddenly the ears drooped.

"Oh, Paul! He's done in!"

With long strokes the boy and the girl were swimming toward the foal. He was no longer a wild thing, skittering away from them, no longer a brave little horse colt pointing his nose to the sky. He was a frightened baby, struggling to keep from being sucked under. He wanted to be rescued. Exhausted with thrashing and kicking, he let the human creatures swim near. The girl's hand touched him, held his nose out of water. The boy took a firm hold of his forelock. It was thus that the three of them came swimming back to shore.

"Maureen!" Paul spoke jerkily to get his breath. "I'll hold Lonesome. You get our boots."

Still holding the tiny forelock, he shook the water out of his own ears. The foal shook his head too, fiercely, as if he could match anything Paul did. Paul laughed at him, and strangely enough the colt let out a funny little laugh too, until Tom's Cove was a jubilant echo of human and horse laughs.

Now Paul placed his arms under the foal's belly and lifted him into the boat.

Maureen stood dripping wet, watching. "Don't call him Lonesome," she said. "That's too sad of a name. Let's call him Sea Star."

Paul seemed to be talking to himself as he took Maureen's

rubber boots and pillowed the colt's head on them. "Why, that name's exactly right," he said. He burst out laughing again. "An hour ago we didn't want to look at a pony. Now this orphan has wound himself around us just the way sea stars wind themselves around oysters."

"Oysters!" clucked Maureen. "We plumb forgot them."

"Grandma won't mind," Paul said. "Or will she?"

"'Course not. She'll say a new-borned colt without any mamma is a heap more important. But the ladies of the Auxiliary will mind; they're counting on Grandma's oysters."

Paul found an old gunny sack in the boat and began drying off the foal. "Tell you what, Maureen. We'll take turns watching Sea Star. You can watch him first, while I fill my basket. Then it'll be my turn to watch. Besides, the tide's slacking. Soon the oyster rocks'll ebb bare. Oysters'll be thick as pebbles. In no time we can fill our baskets."

The little colt's sides were heaving as he lay in the bottom of the boat. Maureen knelt beside him, two wet creatures side by side. "You're all done in," she whispered as she combed his mane with her fingers. "Why, your mane's nothing but ringlets. It's curly as your tail—even though it's drenched." She laid her head alongside his. "I can hear your breathing," she said. "It sounds like the organ at church before the music comes out. I kind of feel like I'm in church. The blue sky for a dome. White lamb clouds." She leaned over and traced the star on his forehead. "My, how you'll miss your mamma!"

As if he understood, the little fellow bleated. He scrambled to his feet. When the boat swayed, he tried to plant his legs far apart like a sailor's. Then his knees buckled and he was lying on Maureen's boots once more.

In the distance Maureen could see Paul scrambling over the rocks, picking up oysters, quickly throwing them into his basket. Now he was running back, his basket full.

"It's my turn to watch Sea Star," he called out.

Maureen put on Paul's wet boots. They were too big, but she did not mind. She sloshed along in them, singing at the top of her voice.

> *"Periwinkle, periwinkle,*
> *Come blow your horn;*
> *I'll give you a gold ring*
> *For a barrel of corn."*

Paul sat on the edge of the boat, fondling the colt with his eyes. Occasionally he looked out toward Maureen gathering oysters. But he did not really see her. He was busy in his mind, thinking of the firemen's brand on the mare, thinking of the ten dollars he had won in the bronco-busting contest. He was buying the biggest nursing bottle they had in the store uptown. He was buying milk. He was giving Misty's stall to Sea Star. He was . . .

"*Whee - ee - ee - ee - n - n - n!*" Sea Star was drying out. He was hungry. He was crying his hunger to the whole wide world.

Maureen came running back. "My basket's almost full," she panted. "Let's get a-going. Sea Star's got to eat."

Chapter 11

THE LITTLE TYKE

WHEN GRANDMA BEEBE looked out the kitchen
window, she dropped the egg whisk in her hand and did not
bother to pick it up, even though it was making little rivers of
egg yolk on her clean swept floor.

She rushed out the door and stood on the stoop. Her mouth
made an "O" in her face as she watched the strange three-
some turning in at the gate. Paul and Maureen looked to her
as if they had been swimming with their clothes on. And wob-
bling along behind them on a lead rope made of vine was a
tiny brown colt.

117

"We picked your oysters, Grandma," called Paul.

"And we covered 'em all over with seaweed so they'd stay cool," Maureen said, waving a piece of the seaweed.

Grandma did not seem interested in the oysters. She was looking right over their heads, clear over to Assateague, up to the place where the pine trees met the sky. "The burden is all rolled away," she said quite plainly.

Paul and Maureen caught each other's eye in surprise. They had half expected Grandma to look upon Sea Star as another burden. Instead, she seemed glad to see him! She was coming down the steps now, lightly as a girl.

"You been so long gone, children," she said, "I been beset by worriments. Now I know." Her face broadened into a smile. "You found a lone colt. Ain't he beautiful with that white star shining plumb in the center of his forehead?"

"We had to drive him into the sea afore we could catch him," Maureen told her.

"Land sakes!" laughed Grandma. "You not only catched him, you gentled him! Here, hand me those baskets. I'll shuck my oysters while you make the little tyke comfortable."

She took the baskets and disappeared into the house.

Paul carefully lifted Sea Star and carried him into Misty's stall.

"He's so tired," Maureen said, "he's not even whiffing around to get acquainted."

It was so. Sea Star did not poke his nose into the manger nor smell the old dried cob of corn at his feet. He just stood, rocking unsteadily.

Paul was bursting with things to be done. "I'll get fresh water, Maureen, and some of Grandpa's Arab feed mixture, and a bundle of marsh grass. You get milk from the ice chest, and see if Grandma's got a nursing bottle."

Long legs ran excitedly in opposite directions.

"No," Grandma pursed her lips thoughtfully in answer to Maureen's question. "Yours was the last nursing bottle we had need for. I sent it away in the mission barrel."

Maureen waved her arms in despair.

"But that's no never mind," Grandma said quickly. "I got a bottle of bluing here. We'll just rinse that out good, and we'll cut a finger off my white kid gloves for a nipple."

"Oh, Grandma! Not your beautiful gloves Uncle Ralph sent you on Mother's Day?"

"The very ones. I don't wear gloves, anyway, only on a funeral or a wedding. It's lots more important that orphan colt gets some good warm milk inside him. He's all tuckered out."

"He's spunky," Maureen said. "He ran away from us quick as scat."

"You put some milk to heat and stir in a little molasses," Grandma said. "Between whiles I'll make as fine a nursing bottle as ever money would buy."

A truck rattled into the lane and ground to a stop. Grandpa Beebe's booted feet came clumping up the steps and his voice carried ahead of him:

> "Oh, they're wild and woolly and full of fleas
> And never been curried below the knees . . ."

119

"Ida!" he bellowed through the screen door, "the ladies is askin' when ye're comin'. Ain't ye ready?"

Suddenly he caught sight of the bottle. "What in tunket ye two doin'? Don't tell me another grandchild's been left to our doorstep!"

"Why, that's exactly what happened," laughed Maureen. She took Grandpa's hand and pulled him down the steps. "Come quick, Grandpa! My sakes, you're harder to lead than a new-borned colt. Quick, Grandpa! Paul and me—we got the wonderfulest surprise for you."

Grandpa let himself be pulled across the barnyard and into the corral and up to Misty's stall. Then he stopped dead. For a long time he just stood there staring from under his eyebrows as if he had never seen a newborn colt before.

A rapt smile slowly spread over his face. "I'm a billy noodle!" he said softly. "As purty a horse colt as I ever see."

"Ain't he young?" asked Maureen.

Grandpa clapped his hands on his hips and grinned. "That he is! Carries hisself in nice shape, too, fer one so young."

Paul explained. "He belongs to the fire company. His mare was layin' on her broadside, right on the beach at Tom's Cove, Grandpa. Looked to be an old mare, white hairs growing around her eyes. We got ten dollars, Grandpa, and I—we, that is—you reckon the fire company will let the colt go?"

"Dunno, childern," Grandpa answered. "That's not what's important now. What's fust to my mind is, can anybody keep him? 'Tain't easy to raise up a baby colt without any mamma. Will he eat fer ye? Here, let me try that grass, Paul."

Gently Grandpa placed a few wisps in the colt's mouth.
He tried working Sea Star's muzzle. "Go on, li'l shaver," he

coaxed. "Start a-grindin' with yer baby teeth. First thisaway,
then thataway. 'Tain't half so dry when ye get to chawin' on it.
And it's got a delicate salt flavor. Yer ancestors thought it was
right smart good. Whyn't you jes' keep a-tryin'?"

The kitchen door squeaked open and Grandma's voice called out, "Maur—een! Your milk's warm."

"Coming, Grandma."

Grandpa stopped Maureen with his hand. His clasp was so firm that the fingers left white bands when he took them away. "Maureen, no!" he ordered. "I oncet raised up a colt on a bottle. 'Twas a horse colt, too, just like this one. And by-'n-by I couldn't poke my nose outen the door but what he'd come gallopin' at me, puttin' his hard little hooves on my shoulders, askin' fer his bottle."

"I think that would be cute," Maureen said.

"It *was* cute," Grandpa admitted, "that is, at first it was. I'd laugh at him and play with him, and like as not go back in and warm up some milk fer him and put 'lasses in to make it taste mighty nice.

"But," Grandpa's voice grew stern, "when that colt was comin' on six month, 'twasn't cute any more. He got too sniptious for anything, and he growed so strong that when he put his hooves up to my chest 'twas like bein' flayed by a windmill. Why, if I didn't have something to give him he got ornery. Dreadful ornery. He'd nip and bite and have a reg'lar tantrum." Grandpa sighed. "Never could do a thing with that colt. Had to sell him up to Mount Airy to a dealer who wished he'd never clapped eyes on him."

Maureen said wistfully, "It would have been such fun to feed him, and poor Grandma's cut a finger off her new gloves and fixed up a nice bottle for him."

"Well, you tell yer Grandma ter just sew that finger right

back on! We ain't goin' to have no spoiled brat-of-a-colt around here. Our colts got to be nice and good."

Paul bit his knuckle, trying to keep back the hot words. "We're starving him, Grandpa. He'll die!"

"Shucks, Paul, we ain't even give him a chance. He'll be eatin' gusty-like afore sundown. Now here's what we'll do. I'll make a mash outa our Arab mix and leave it in the stall fer him, and he's got this nice salty grass, and a good bed to lie on, and the sea wind fluffin' up his mane."

Grandpa picked up the bucket with the Arab feed mixture in it. "Come," he urged, "you jest snuck away and let him be all by hisself fer a little while. Like as not he'll lay down and have a real refreshin' sleep, and when he wakes up he'll begin mouthin' things and find 'em good! He'll forget he's a baby and get all growed up in a hurry. I've seed it happen time and time again."

"Does it *always* happen that way?" Maureen asked.

Grandpa grew tongue-tied. He stood, absently riffling the Arab mixture between his fingers. "Most always, child," he said at last. "Now it's gettin' on fer dinnertime and I got to take yer Grandma to the Dining Hall. The ladies is a-waitin'." He turned to go. Then came back. "Hurry and change yer wet duds or folks'll think I grandsired a couple mush-rats. Then ye can ride over to the dinner on Watch Eyes and Trinket. We'll leave the little shaver be. By the way, what's his name?"

"Sea Star," said both children at once.

As they closed the stall door, Sea Star sent a high little whinny out after them.

"Ain't that cute?" chuckled Grandpa. "He's a-whinnerin' fer ye already. My, but he'll be glad to see ye when ye come back. Ye're goin' to have a high-mettled horse colt there," he added.

"That is, pervided the fire chief is agreeable to yer deal."

Chapter 12

RISKY DOIN'S

THE SMELL of good things floated out of the Dining Hall—oysters and clams frying, dumplings simmering in vegetable juices, chickens and sweet potatoes roasting. The steaming vapors ran like wisps of smoke past the noses of the people waiting in line. The line moved slowly, like a snake trying to wriggle into a hole too small for it. Paul and Maureen and Grandpa were part of the line. As it crept forward, Grandpa tried to make talk.

"Paul! Maureen! Stop yer worritin' and snuff up!" his voice rolled out strong. "Get a whiff of what I calls perfume. Don't it make ye feel like a coon-hound hot on a scent?"

The boy and the girl did not need to answer. People all
around them were following Grandpa's advice—inhaling the
teasing odors in quick little sniffs, laughing and agreeing with
him.

126

Grandma's friend, Mrs. Tilley, stood at the door taking tickets. She greeted the Beebes warmly when they finally reached the entrance. "You three set up to this table right by the door. It'll be cooler and you can see the visitors come in hungry and go out full as punkins."

The Dining Hall was a big, low-ceilinged building with an endless number of long tables, covered with the white paper Maureen had tacked on them. But now the white was almost hidden by great serving dishes of golden oyster fritters and clam fritters and crisp chicken and dumpling puffs and bowls of brown bubbling gravy.

Talk seesawed back and forth from one table to another. Home folks from the island and strangers from the mainland were visiting like old friends. They all seemed to be laughing, throwing their heads back, showing strong teeth like colts, or teeth crowned with gold, or toothless gums, but all laughing.

Always. each Pony Penning time, it was the same. People on all sides of them laughing and making fun. But each year for Paul and Maureen there was a colt nagging at their thoughts, stealing their appetites.

A little white-haired man whose cheek pouch was bulging like a chipmunk's leaned across the table to Paul. "I'll trouble you to pass me the chicken and dumplings, Bub." He waggled his head toward the kitchen. "If they're figuring eight pieces and four people to a hen like they useter do," he piped in a thin voice, "I'm goin' to discombobolate their figuring."

Paul passed the chicken and dumplings.

Grandpa tried to lower his voice. "Childern," he smiled in understanding, "jest 'cause somebody ter home is off his feed 'tain't no reason why ye should be off yers. Now let's us dig right in, and when we've slicked our plates clean so's Grandma and the other ladies kin tell we liked their cooking, then we'll hunt up the fire chief and ask him right out plain whether he don't think Sea Star was sent straightaway from heaven to take Misty's place."

Maureen and Paul smiled back at Grandpa. He never seemed to fail them. They bent their heads over their plates and ate. To their surprise the food tasted good. The oysters were so slippery they did not stick in their throats at all. And they drank glass after glass of tea.

"I guess we had Grandma's fritters," Paul said. "Hers are the prettiest brown."

After dinner the fire chief was nowhere to be found in the milling crowd, so Grandpa stepped up to the announcer's stand in the center of the grounds. "I'll thank ye to call out the fire chief's name in that squawker contraption," he said to the announcer.

"Calling the fire chief!" the voice rang out above the noise of the people and the music of the merry-go-round. "Calling the fire chief! He's wanted at the announcer's stand."

This brought the fire chief weaving his way through the crowd. He was nodding to visitors at right and left, and the cane which he carried when he was tired was nowhere in sight.

The people made way for him until he reached the stand. Then Grandpa Beebe stood in his path.

"Was it you wanted me?" the chief asked.

Grandpa nodded.

The chief's eyes crinkled. "Clarence," he said, "ain't this the best crowd we ever had to Pony Penning? Weather's good, too, and everything's running along smooth as honey on a griddle cake."

Paul and Maureen hung a little behind Grandpa. Paul was tying knots in a piece of string, and Maureen stood twiddling her curls in the wrong direction. When the fire chief caught sight of them, he came a step closer and lowered his eyes to theirs.

"I know you two are feeling sad about Misty, but you done a fine thing. Besides, she'll come home swishing her tail behind her—maybe not for a few years—but one day for certain. Chincoteague ponies is like Chincoteague people. Once they gets sand in their shoes they always comes back."

"That ain't what's eatin' 'em, Chief. I'll let 'em tell ye theirselves while I go make arrangements fer shipping one o' my ponies that's goin' all the way to Sandusky, Ohio."

There was a little silence while the fire chief and Paul and Maureen followed Grandpa with their eyes. They watched him tack back and forth in the sea of people like a sailboat, his old battered hat the topgallant sail. When he was lost to view, Paul and Maureen suddenly felt adrift.

The fire chief drew them to a bench away from the crowd and motioned them to sit down, one on each side of him. Then he helped them with a question.

"You folks at the pony sale this morning?"

"No," Paul answered. "We were oystering over to Tom's Cove."

"So?"

"Yes, sir." Paul spoke quickly now. "And lying on the beach was a mare with the brand of the Fire Department on her."

"Was she solid brown, with no white on her at all?"

"Yes, sir."

"Except she was getting white around the eyes," Maureen spoke up.

"Was she a very good mare, Chief?" Paul asked.

"That she was! Raised up frisky colts. A new one each year. Always hers brought the highest prices at the auction." The fire chief's voice had a faraway tone. "Guess she helped buy a lot of equipment for the fire company," he said. "This year she and the Phantom were the only mares who didn't get rounded up. We figured the Phantom was too smart, but we feared for the brown mare."

A slow tear showed at the corner of Maureen's eye. It grew fuller and rounder and finally spilled over.

"Come, come, child. That mare was full of years. She'd had the free and wild life for nigh onto fifteen years. Don't cry about her, honey."

"I'm not. It's her new-borned baby I'm thinking about."

The fire chief was silent for what seemed a long time. "Hmmm," he said at last. "Had a colt, did she?"

"A baby horse colt," Paul answered. "A beauty! All brown except for a white star in the middle of his forehead. His name's Sea Star."

A smile played about the fire chief's lips and his head nodded as if he saw the spindly legged foal standing all alone at Tom's Cove with the sea at his back.

"Sea Star!" he chuckled. "I declare! You young ones pull just the right name out of the hat. How d'you do it?"

"It was Maureen," Paul said. "I was thinking of calling him Lonesome, but that was too sad of a name. Maureen just said his name right out. 'Sea Star' she said, without even thinking."

Paul shoved his toe in the sandy soil until he almost bent it back. "Chief," he said, "will the Fire Department, you think, sell off the little colt? To us?"

The fire chief pinched his lip in thought. He closed his eyes for a minute. "Sometimes," he said, talking more to him-

132

self than to Paul and Maureen, "sometimes the whole Department has to be called together so's a matter like this can be laid on the table for discussion."

A little groan escaped Maureen.

"That's the way of it in most cases." He was about to say more, but one of the roundup men came up, his eyes reddened.

"Got my specs knocked off during the ropin' this morning," he said. "Wonder, Chief, if you could do something about the nosepiece. It's broke."

"Lucky you ain't bug-eyed," the fire chief laughed, "or you'd lost more'n your specs. I'll see they re fixed for you."

He turned back to Paul and Maureen, going right on where he had left off. "Then there are times," he said, "when a thing's so clear we'd only be wasting the men's time if we called up a meeting."

"Yes?"

"This, now, is one of those times," the chief said. "A decision's got to be made quick when a pony's too young to fend for itself. By the way, where's Sea Star now?"

"He's in Misty's stall," Maureen said.

"And," Paul looked at the chief gravely, "we've got ten dollars from the bronc-busting contest, because Mr. Van Meter wouldn't take the money to buy carrots for Misty." Paul leaped to his feet as if an idea had just burst in his mind. "Mr. Van Meter said we might need it for something very special, and Sea Star's it!"

There was a waiting silence while the fire chief opened up a roll of peppermints and offered them to Maureen.

Paul clenched his fists in impatience. He made himself look straight into the fire chief's face. "I reckon we'd need lots more than ten dollars," he said bitterly. "That is, if you'd sell him at all."

Again a little whirlpool of silence while the chief absently folded the tinfoil around the peppermints. "Now I view the matter like this," he spoke at last. "It's risky doin's, laying out money for a colt under three months. Mighty risky." He pocketed the peppermints. "No," he said thoughtfully, "the Fire Department wouldn't think of taking a cent over ten dollars for an orphan. I'm sure on it. Besides," he added, "that baby needs you two! Needs you bad."

Paul and Maureen looked at each other. They wanted to thank the fire chief, but the words would not come, not even in a whisper.

Maureen found her voice first. "Oh, Chief . . . !" she gulped, then could say no more. She threw her arms around his sun-creased neck and whispered an unintelligible thank-you in his ear.

Paul reached for one of the chief's hands and shook it hard. Then he slid his hand into the pocket of his jeans and took out the neatly folded ten-dollar bill.

Chapter 13

NO ORNERY COLT FOR US

WHEN PAUL and Maureen returned home they found everything in the stall just as they had left it. The Arab mash untouched. The grass in the manger undisturbed. The water bucket full. And huddled in a corner of his stall, his head hanging low between his knees, Sea Star was sobbing out his lonesomeness in little colt whimpers.

Maureen's face went red and her lips tightened. "We tried Grandpa's way," she exploded. "Now I'm going to fetch that bottle."

"No, you ain't!" a voice behind them spoke sharply. Maureen hardly knew it for Grandpa's voice, and the sharpness hurt because it was so seldom used.

"I've been doctor-man to my hosses since afore you two was borned." A fierce light of pride came into his eyes. "In all my days I raised up only one colt to be mean and ornery, and I promised myself I'd nary do it again. Ye've got to trust me a mite longer. Ye've just got to. Chincoteague ponies is wiry. Tougher than you think."

He stooped down on one knee and looked eye to eye with Sea Star, putting his gnarled fingers underneath the ringlets of the colt's mane.

The colt turned his head and sniffed. Memory told him there was no need to be afraid. He accepted Grandpa and Paul and Maureen as if they were no more nor less than the little wind that sifted in between the chinks in the siding.

Grandpa's eyes were unyielding as he straightened up. "How many Pony Pennings," he asked, "can you two recomember?"

Paul and Maureen thought a moment, counting up on their fingers.

"Seven," Paul said.

Maureen said, "Seven for me, too." Then at a surprised look from Grandpa, she changed her mind, "Well, five for sure, Grandpa."

"All right. Five times ye've *both* seed the wild ponies swimmed across from the island of Assateague to Chincoteague, ain't ye?"

The boy and girl nodded, while Sea Star tucked his forelegs beneath him and lay down on his side. He soon fell asleep to the drumming of Grandpa's voice.

"And five times," the voice went on, "ye've both seed the mares druv into the big pens and the colts cut out and druv into the little pens."

Paul and Maureen nodded again, their eyes watching the foal's sides rise and fall.

"And each time after the cuttin' out was over with, ye've heard the colts bellerin' fer their mammas."

Maureen clapped her hands to her ears as if she could hear the sound now.

Grandpa did not stop. "The youngsters go millin' around in the pens hungerin' and thirstin' and refusin' to tech the water and grasses the firemen pervides. But," and here Grandpa began rubbing the bristles of his ear, "but before the week is out, what *always* happens?"

"The colts are eating nice as you please," smiled Paul.

"That's the right answer, Paul! Now I know you're a hossman!"

Maureen slipped her hand inside Grandpa's. "We'll wait, Grandpa, afore we think about that nursing bottle again. Sea Star'll be eating like a stallion by the time the week is over, won't he?"

Friday passed. The crowds trickled out of the Pony Penning Grounds and over the causeway to the mainland.

Saturday came, and the mares and stallions were let out of the big pens and driven back home to the island of the wild things. The few unsold colts were driven back, too. They were older, wiser, able to fend for themselves.

At Pony Ranch, Sea Star dozed the hours away. Unlike the other colts, he seemed to have grown littler, younger.

Saturday night came. Darkness drifted down softly over Chincoteague. The moon rose slowly, unrolling a broad carpet of silver out across the Atlantic.

It found Paul's bed and tickled his face with its beams. He turned to the wall, but the moon would not be put aside. It rode through his sleep. In his dreams he was flying on a moonbeam, lighting a path through the woods for the Phantom, lighting a schoolyard in New York where crowds of children were pressing in on Misty, stroking her neck with grubby fingers. He was lighting a desk in Richmond where Uncle Clarence Lee sat bent over papers and books.

Then suddenly the moonbeam became a silver lance and Sea Star was dancing in the prick of light it made. Now the

silver lance was cutting the grass in wide swaths, showing the colt how tender it was, and soon Sea Star understood. He began ripping it, grinding it with his baby teeth.

Paul awoke. He listened sharply. It was only the wind shaking the pine needles.

He jumped from his bed. He looked out over the flat tongue of land where the silver plane had landed. The moon was still shining brightly. He dressed and quietly opened the door of his room. The guinea hens were beginning to wake. They were clacking loudly. Paul was glad. Now his footsteps would not waken Grandma and Grandpa. He passed their closed door. He came to Maureen's door and almost collided with her. There she was, tiptoeing out into the hall.

"What you fixing to do?" whispered Maureen.

Paul's sheepish grin was lost in the dark. "Sh!" he said, putting his finger to his lips. "I'm going to make a warm gruel."

Maureen's mouth flew open. "Why, that's exactly what I was fixing to do!"

In single file they stepped wide of the boards that creaked and came down into the kitchen. A light glowed brightly over the stove and there was Grandma stirring oatmeal porridge and reading her Sunday school lesson as she stirred.

"Well, I never!" she gasped at the two surprised faces before her. "I thought I was seeing owls. I just got up early to prepare my lesson," she explained. "Come sit down and eat a morsel of porridge. Though I *was* fixing it for someone else—a four-footed critter."

Maureen caught Grandma's hand and clasped it tight between both of hers. "Oh, Grandma," she said, "you're the understandingest grandma in the whole wide world."

Paul fumbled under the sink where the pots and pans were kept. He found an old one that had lost a handle and held it up for Grandma.

She looked at it and nodded. Then she spooned out a big helping of the steaming meal and sprinkled a handful of brown sugar over the top of it.

"Go along, you two. Our breakfast can wait until after you coax Sea Star. Always and always it'll be the same here, I reckon. The ponies comes first, then the people. Go along while I memorize my text." Her words trailed out after them, "'And the angel of the Lord stood among the myrtle trees . . .'"

Chapter 14

THE GENTLEMAN FROM KENTUCKY

SEA STAR refused the porridge.

Maureen said, "He spits it out as if 'twas vinegar."

"He was somethin'!" Paul said. "Just look at him now. Ribs showing like a squeeze box." He turned away, stumbling across the barnyard, and headed for the piney woods.

Maureen followed at a distance. The sun was rising. Long shafts of sunlight slid through the trees, gilding one side, leaving the other black. The piney litter underfoot deadened the sound of their feet. Maureen watched Paul's fists go to his eyes and brush something away with the back of his hand.

142

"Ain't the cobwebs bothersome this time of morning?" she said, coming up to him.

"Sure are," Paul replied, keeping his face ahead. "For a girl, you're right observing."

"Oh, thank you, Paul. I didn't aim to be a tag-along, but I couldn't bear not to come. I figured you'd be brooding something in your mind."

Paul slowed his steps. "I been brooding all right."

"Sure enough?"

The boy nodded.

"What you decided, Paul?"

Paul's voice began to sound more like his own. There was a wild note of hope in it. "One Pony Penning a gentleman was here all the way from Lexington, Kentucky. And he got to talking manlike to me and Grandpa. He had a big nurse-mare farm."

"A nurse-mare farm?"

"A nurse-mare farm."

"What's that?"

"Quit interrupting, Maureen; I'm trying to figure something out. You just listen."

"All right, I will. But oh, Paul, make it good!"

Paul cuffed the pine branches with his hands as he walked, sending dewdrops flying in every direction. It seemed to ease his feelings and loosen his tongue. "This gentleman," he said, "owned lots of draft mares and jennies, and they most always had young 'uns tagging at their heels. Then when a fine Thoroughbred colt from one of the big racing stables near by lost its mamma, why, then the gentleman would rent out one of his mares and the little Thoroughbred would eat off her. He'd grow big and strong."

"Oh, Paul! It's beautiful!" Maureen heaved a loud sigh.

144

"Now all we got to do is rope a mare over on Assateague and rent her from the Fire Department."

Paul snorted in disgust. "'Taint as easy as that. A wild mare'd kick the living daylights out of an orphan colt. She'd want her own colt back, or none at all. She might even kill another colt."

"What if . . . " Maureen gasped with the wonder of the idea that had come to her. "What if the mare couldn't kick? What if her heel string was cut and she couldn't light out with the other heel?"

Paul let out a low whistle. "Why, she wouldn't have a leg to stand on!"

Maureen was beside herself with excitement. "Let's go right back and . . ."

"Wait!" said Paul. "The man told me and Grandpa lots of other things. He said that if the nurse mare didn't want to adopt a strange colt, she could hold herself all tense-like and the milk just wouldn't come out. And besides, the mare with the cut heel has still got a mighty good set of teeth and she could bite. Bite hard." Paul opened his jaws and snapped them sharply together. The sound sent a shiver through Maureen.

"What we got to do," Paul said, "is to make that mare *want* to take on Sea Star for her very own. *That's* what we go to do."

For several minutes they followed along the winding path in silence.

Maureen slipped past Paul, her bare feet making no noise at all. "Hmpf!" she taunted. "If your man from Kentucky was so awful smart, how did he do it?"

Paul did not answer right away. He kicked a pine cone along the path with his toes until it scuttered behind a tree trunk. He peered into a deserted redbird's nest. "I recomember now!" he said as if he had found the answer among the twigs and rootlets of the nest. "He told us he used to rub the colt all over with sheep dip. Then he'd rub the mare's nose with it, too. He'd trick her into thinking the colt was hers 'cause they smelled the same."

Now the words were tumbling over each other. "He told about a lady stable owner, too, who was in the perfume business, and she rubbed a mare and an orphan colt with the same perfume, and the mare took on the colt."

Maureen halted, nodding to herself as if she had discovered something very wise and secret.

"Paul! Whiff! Like this." She drew the pungent odor of the myrtle trees deep into her lungs, and laughed as she blew it out again. "What smells so good and perfumey as our own myrtle leaves?"

The wind had picked up the fragrance from the thicket of myrtle trees ahead and was blowing it in their faces. Now they both threw back their heads like colts and snuffed it in greedily.

A muffled, rustling sound! A crackling of brush! A sudden stirring in the clump of myrtles!

Startled, Maureen touched Paul's arm and pointed to the swaying branches. They both hung back, motionless, listening. The feathered *whish* of bird wings? The pawing of a wild deer? An otter? Questions went unasked as the sound faded out, then began again.

146

"Might be Grandma's lesson come true," whispered Maureen in awe, "might be the angel of the Lord standing among the myrtle trees."

"It *is!*" shouted Paul. "It's Grandpa Beebe!"

Chapter 15

A HAUNTIN' SMELL O' MYRTLE LEAVES

THERE CAME an answering shout, and a familiar face with white, spiky whiskers peered out of the frame of myrtle leaves. The face rimpled into a sudden smile, and a voice rolled out strong:

> *"Oh, they're wild and woolly and full of fleas*
> *And never been curried below the knees. . ."*

"Childern!" laughed Grandpa. "Ye come just in time to help. I got some empty gunny sacks here and I want 'em filled plum full o' . . ."

"Myrtle leaves!" cried Paul and Maureen in the same breath.

Grandpa nodded in surprise as he gave one sack to Paul and another to Maureen. Then he reached toward a branch, talking as he stripped the leaves. "Once there was a gentleman here from . . ."

"Lexington, Kentucky!" Paul filled in the words, grinning.

Grandpa's head turned around and his eyes went wide. "And this gentleman had a . . ."

"Nurse-mare farm!" Paul and Maureen shouted in unison, like actors in a play.

Both hands suddenly went up to Grandpa's ears and he began rubbing the bristles hard. "I ain't a-pridin' on myself," he chuckled, "but now I know fer sure there's somethin' of the best of me in the both of ye!" His laughter bubbled low, then rang out in the stillness of the woods.

It was good to have work to do. Old gnarled fingers and young smooth ones worked swiftly, stripping off the long narrow leaves, filling the bags.

Grandpa brought out his knife and cut off vines that got in their way. "I couldn't sleep last night for worritin' about that little fella," he said. "Whenever I dropt off, I drempt. I'd be combin' his curly mane with my fingers and feelin' of the little ribs stickin' out like the ribs of Grandma's bumberella. Then right smack out o' nowhere came the man from Kentucky nosin' into my dreams. He tolded all over again how that lady rubbed perfume on a nurse mare and an orphan colt. And next thing I knew, I was sittin' up in bed a-whisperin' to myself,

'What in tunket has a more hauntin' smell as our own . . .'"

"Myrtle leaves!" exploded Paul and Maureen.

Grandpa's eyes twinkled. "Yes, sir! There's somethin' in this mental telegraphy all right."

Hands worked faster and faster, filling the bags. Now they were half full.

"Jumpin' mullets! I clean forgot to tell ye who the nurse mare's goin' to be." Grandpa's voice rose and quickened with his fingers. "Last night while the moon was ridin' high, I snuck out the house in my bare feet, horsebacks over to Wilbur Wimbrow's and fetches him out o' bed.

"'Wilbur,' I says to him, 'little Sea Star is bad off. He's gettin' mighty poor. Won't eat. How about puttin' him to the mare that got her heel cut?'"

"What'd he say?" Maureen glanced up, watching Grandpa's face intently.

"Wilbur was never one to mince words. He says to me, 'Clarence, you an' me is 'bout the oldest roundup men we got in Chincoteague, and we both knows mares is notionate critters. They take a notion they don't like a colt and they'll have no truck with it.' Then he minded me of the time we tried to get a mare to be a foster mamma and she jest skinned back her ears and lit out with her heels and like to a-kilt the little stranger."

Maureen gasped.

"But we took a lantern out to the barn and I made sure that the mare was still favorin' her near hind leg. Then I looked at her milk bag and saw 'twas swelled with milk. Wilbur, he followed my glance."

"What'd he say?" Paul asked, scarcely above a whisper.

"He just sort of grunted. Had to admit she wasn't lackin' for milk. 'But will she give it?' he asked.

"Then I told him how we'd smash up some myrtle leaves and

152

souse the colt all over with the oily smell of 'em, and we'd rub the mare's nose with it too, and maybe she'd think 'twas her own colt come back to her."

Paul and Maureen let out a deep sigh.

"Stop, childern!" commanded Grandpa. "We got enough leaves here to souse a whole flock of ponies. Let's git a-goin'."

As they hurried back along the path, Grandpa forgot all about breakfast. He was busy with plans. "Maureen, you bareback over to Wilbur Wimbrow's. He's waitin' to help ye with the mare. Me and Paul will fix up the colt till he smells like a whole clump of myrtle. Then we'll hist him into the truck and bring him to his new mamma."

When Maureen was up on Watch Eyes and had gathered the reins in one hand and taken the bag of myrtle under her arm, Grandpa waited a moment before opening the gate for her. He beckoned Paul over to his side. "If you two was jes' little childern," he spoke to them slowly, thoughtfully, "I wouldn't have you to worry. But bein' as ye're nigh growed up, I got to tell you this idee *might* not work." Then his voice rolled out like a steam calliope. "Git a-goin', child. What's keepin' ye? Are ye glued to the earth?" And he slapped Watch Eyes on the rump.

Maureen spurred him with her heels. "Giddap, Watch Eyes. Faster! Faster! You can help."

Watch Eyes liked the idea. He stretched out as if he were racing his own shadow. It was all Maureen could do to turn him in at Wimbrow's lane. He wanted to go on and on into the morning.

The clatter of hooves brought Mr. Wimbrow out of his house, carrying a steaming pail in one hand and a wooden bowl with a potato masher in the other.

"Morning, Maureen," he said. "Put Watch Eyes in that stall next to the mare."

Maureen looked up into the lean, weathered face of the roundup man. She gave him a small nervous smile as she led Watch Eyes to the empty stall.

"I'll need you to grind up the leaves," Mr. Wimbrow said. "Here's our potato masher and a bowl. I was just fixing to bathe the mare's heel. You can sit in the doorway and work. It'll do the mare good to begin getting a whiff of the myrtle."

Maureen pounded and beat the leaves. The fragrance filled her nostrils until it wiped out the smell of the disinfectant Mr. Wimbrow was using.

Her eyes slid over the mare as she worked. She saw how Mr. Wimbrow had tied her to a corner of the stall to keep her from moving about and using the hurt leg. She saw the mare turn her head to watch what was going on. But there was no sharp interest in the way she watched. It was the same look that Sea Star had—a sad, dulled look as if nothing at all mattered.

"This cut ain't healing like it should," Mr. Wimbrow worried aloud, sloshing the water over it with his hand. "Some say we should put ice packs onto it. Some say we'd ought to plunge it in hot salt water. I'm doing the best I know how." He sighed, feeling along the tendon. "But what I think is, she's a-grievin' so she ain't even trying to get well."

He threw the bucket of water out of the door and came back to tie up the heel with a clean bandanna. "Likely it'd be better if you rubbed her nose with the myrtle," he said. "She's still got the wildness in her. She thinks of me as someone who keeps bothering that hurt foot. But you, now," he smiled down at Maureen, "you can be a messenger from the woods, bringing gifts of myrtle."

Maureen's hand trembled a little as she scooped up a mound of crushed leaves and slowly went around to the mare's head. She held out her hand just far enough away so the mare had to reach for it. Suddenly the nostrils began to quiver. That familiar fragrance! It seemed to stir memories of the warm places, deep in the woods; memories of the life-giving myrtle, green when all the grasses were dried. She lipped a taste of it, and as she rolled it on her tongue Maureen rubbed oily fingers around one of the mare's nostrils. At the touch of fingers she drew back snorting, her muscles twitching in fright.

Maureen's heart was thumping wildly now. She waited for the mare's fear to pass, waited seconds before the quivering nose reached out again and she could rub the other nostril.

Back at Pony Ranch every hand was busy. Paul grinding the leaves in Grandma's clam grinder, Grandma sewing bags of cheesecloth, and Grandpa stuffing them with myrtle.

"If anybody'd ever said I'd be sewing on the Sabbath day," Grandma said to herself as her needle flew, "I'd have low'd my head in shame. But here I am, sewing for all I'm worth, and out in a stable against my ruthers. Queer how a young 'un can nudge in and upset all your notions."

"That's the way of it," Grandpa chuckled softly. He nodded his head in Paul's direction. "And don't it beat all how fast Paul's a-grindin'? The sweat's rollin' off him. If 'twas clams, now, instead of myrtle leaves, he'd be cool as a cowcumber and there'd be mighty few clams grinded."

"That's what I admire about Paul," Grandma said with certainty. "When something important's at stake, he pitches in."

A look of understanding shuttled between Paul and Grandma.

All this while Sea Star drowsed in a corner of the stall. The smell of myrtle excited no memories in him. Sometimes he cried in his sleep and woke himself up. Then listlessly he would watch the strange doings of the humans.

"Now, Paul," Grandpa said, "ye can grab a bag of myrtle and rub Star from stem to stern whilst I hold him. Mind ye, don't miss a hair." Putting one hand under the foal's muzzle and grasping his tail with the other, Grandpa lifted him to his feet. "Go to it, Paul. I got him steadied."

Paul began rubbing, timidly at first, then vigorously.

"Why, I believe he likes it," Paul laughed, a little awed, and

he began asking questions like sparks bursting from a fire.
"Does he look more fawn than colt to you? His star, it shines
bright on his forehead, see? What makes colts' knees so funny
and knobby? Reckon he'll have a left mane like Misty's?"

There was no time for Grandma or Grandpa to answer
one question before the next fell.

The boy stopped a moment, standing quietly. Then he squatted on his heels and went to work on the foal's face. "Look at me, Sea Star," he said. "When Misty comes back home, you and she can be a team. Misty and Star. Sound pretty to you? And you can run like birds together and you can raise up foals of your own, and Maureen and I can race you both and we won't care which wins. And . . . I guess I need a fresh bag, Grandma. This one's all squinched out."

Occasionally Sea Star fought for his freedom, but it was a weak little fight, as if he knew he had no place to go if he were free.

He let Paul rub his colty whiskers with myrtle. He let him put some of it in his mouth, but he neither chewed nor swallowed it.

"Guess you won't be needing me any more," Grandma said, picking up the clam grinder and her spool of thread. "I'll go in and read over my lesson just once more. Be sure to come back in time to get me to my class," she called over her shoulder.

Grandpa nodded absent-mindedly. Then he buried his nose in Sea Star's coat. "Yep," he sniffed, "if I closed my eyes, I'd think I was right spang in a clump of myrtle. Now, Paul, carry him to the truck. I'll hyper on ahead and let down the ramp."

All during the ride to Wimbrow's, Paul quieted Sea Star with his voice. "You just lean up against me," he said. "Never knew the roads were so bumpity. But I'll stay close to you for comfort. Once I spent a whole night in a truck with Misty. I'd do it for you, too," he breathed into the silky ear.

Chapter 16

LET'S DO SOMETHING

INSIDE WILBUR WIMBROW'S gate Paul set the colt down on the grass. To Paul's surprise, he followed along to the barn as if an invisible lead rope held them together.

Looking at the weak little colt, Mr. Wimbrow shook his head. "Sure is slab-sided," he said. "Let's *do* something!" He turned to Grandpa. "Ought we to blindfold the mare?"

"'Tain't no use. Sea Star's about the color o' her own colt. We'll coax in with him and put him right onto her. Maureen and Paul, you kin look on — if you back up against the wall and stay put."

Matters were out of Paul's and Maureen's hands now. All they could do was to watch the two men wise in the ways of animals.

The stall came alive with expectancy. Mr. Wimbrow tuned his voice down low. He was trying to make it sound natural, but Paul and Maureen felt a tightness in it. "I'll hold the mare's head so she can't turn round and bite," he said. "Clarence, you put the little fellow where he belongs."

He followed his own directions. He took hold of the halter rope close to the mare's chin. He stood there, waiting, without speaking any more.

Grandpa drew in his breath sharply, overcome by the importance of the next few moments. He placed his roughened hand on Sea Star's neck, urging the little fellow forward, inside the doorway of the stall. He turned him gently around, so that Sea Star's nose was at the mare's flanks.

Then he took his hand away.

There was no sound, except for a greenhead fly drumming against a water pail. No one moved. Not the two men nor the boy or girl. The world outside did not exist. There was just a dull, spiritless mare, a weak and hungry foal that did not belong to her, and over all, the pungent fragrance of myrtle oil.

Now the mare filled in the silence. With a sound no bigger than a whisper she began snuffing and blowing and snuffing in again. She tried to turn her head.

Wilbur Wimbrow looked at Grandpa, his eyebrows asking a question.

Grandpa Beebe's head nodded yes.

Mr. Wimbrow let go the rope. The mare could turn her head now. She brought it around slowly toward Sea Star, looking. Now her breathing was quick, as if she had just come in winded from a gallop. And then in the middle of a breath came a quiver of sound. It was like a plucked violin string. It was pain and joy and hunger and thirst all mixed into one trembling note. She and the colt were one! A high neigh of ecstasy escaped her. Fiercely she began licking Sea Star's coat, scolding him tenderly with her tongue all the while.

"My sakes! Look at your coat, will you! Scraggy as anything. No shine to it at all. You been neglected. But I'll make you shining again!" Her tongue strokes said all that and more. She almost upset Sea Star with her mothering. She was shoving him around to suit herself. He was swaying like a blade of grass in the wind.

Paul and Maureen could hardly breathe. Every sound, every motion, seemed sharp and clear. The fly buzzing against the pail, and from some distance away a mocking bird weaving a morning song.

Now Sea Star was questing with his nose, with his lips, moving slowly in toward the mare, drawn in toward her, crying a thin, plaintive mew. Suddenly the crying became a joyous snort—a snort of discovery. He had found the warm bag of milk! He was suckling!

Excitement ran through the stall like flame. Suck! Suck! Grunt and suck! A little brush of a tail flicking back and forth to the rhythm. It said, more plainly than any words, "This is good, good, *good*, I tell you."

162

For a long time no one spoke. It was enough happiness just to listen to the smothered grunting and to watch the flappety tail. At last Grandpa heaved a great sigh and smiled from one to the other as if they had all come through a great crisis together.

"Jest listen to that little fellow goozle," he said. "That mare gives a lot o' milk, too. Never knew one to take on a colt like that."

"He'll never be no stunted colt now," Mr. Wimbrow said.

"Less'n he drinks so much he'll get stunted carrying it!" laughed Grandpa, relief written on his face.

The mare paid no heed to the voices at all. She had so much to do. Licking and brushing Sea Star's coat to make up for the lost days, and talking all the while in little nickers.

Paul swallowed two or three times before he could make his voice sound like his own. "Sea Star's having his Pony Penning dinner today," he said shakily.

Maureen nodded happily, "And didn't that mare have sharp smellers? She put me in mind of Grandma."

Grandpa caught his breath at mention of Grandma. He squared his hat on his head. "We got to get on, Wilbur. Ida's a great one for gettin' to her Sunday school class on time." He took a final look at the mare. "Most always ye got to watch a nurse mare and an orphan for two-three days afore ye can leave 'em together, but the way she's chattin' over little personal matters with him . . . well, he ain't no lost star now "

Mr. Wimbrow nodded. "Soon as I think the mare can hobble along on her own power, I'll lead 'em both over to Pony

Ranch. The children can keep her until Sea Star grows up."

Paul walked out of the stall alongside Mr. Wimbrow. "We'll be glad to pay rent for her like the big racing stables do," he said. "'Course, we can't pay so much."

Mr. Wimbrow roughed his hand over Paul's head. "Really should be the other way around," he said. "The colt saved the mare's life. He come just in the nick of time. She's got something to get well for now."

Chapter 17

OPEN THE GATE

GRANDMA WAS under the pine trees, stirring something in an iron kettle over a fire. She seemed neither ready to go to church nor ready to stay at home. She was wearing her Sunday hat, and over her Sunday dress she had tied a big apron. The smell of chicken steaming with wild onions curled out of the pot. As Grandpa's truck drove in she stopped stirring and waited for the family to come to her.

"You don't need to tell me," she cried. "It's *good* news! Paul's hair is rumpled as a kingfisher's topknot, Grandpa's wearing his hat backside to, and Maureen's been twisting her curls the wrong way. You don't need to let out a peep," she said with shining eyes. "Sea Star's eating! Now we're going to

167

eat, too. We're going to have us a real old-timey Pony Penning feast. You know, you forgot all about breakfast."

Paul and Maureen laughed. They *had* forgotten about breakfast.

Grandpa rubbed his stomach and smacked his lips in pleased anticipation. "To me it smells like outdoor pot pie, simmerin' full of goodness."

"Might be," Grandma said.

Maureen looked into the pot and began stirring. "But, Grandma, what about your Sunday school class?"

"The Lord understood, and so did Mrs. Tilley. She's going to substitute teach for me."

"Ida!" Grandpa scolded in mock sternness, "I never thought I'd live to see the day when you'd get high-toney on yer own family."

"High-toney?"

"Yep, high-toney. Seems to me that when ye wears yer best hat to a outdoor picnic . . ."

Grandma threw her apron over her face and laughed until the tears came. And soon the whole pine grove echoed with laughter.

"Here, Maureen, lay my hat in on my bed. Then you can take the biscuits out of the oven and dish up the Seven Top turnip greens. Clarence, you and Paul slick up. Oh, I haven't been so happy in a week! I've got a hungry family again."

When the picnic table was set and the plates heaped with the chicken pot pie and greens and hot biscuits, they all sat down, Grandpa and Grandma on one bench, Paul and Maureen on the other. Hungry as they were, they did not eat at once. They turned to Grandma, waiting for a word from her.

Grandpa's voice boomed his loudest to hide his real feelings. "Ida, I reckon ye can say grace at a picnic jest as well as to any other time."

Grandma stood up at the end of the table. Her eyes began

to twinkle. "I feel like a colt," she admitted almost shyly. "You know how choicy they are when first they begin to eat? You give 'em some grasses, and they go picking out certain ones that seem saltier than the others, and maybe they hunt for a little bunch of lespedeza."

Paul laughed. "That's just the way they do, Grandma."

"Well, so long as you're not my regular Sunday school class, I'm going to pull out wisps of goodness from the Good Book here and there. 'Tain't the formal way to do, I know. But it's mighty satisfying."

Grandma was shy no longer. She looked up beyond the tallest pine tree, right into the deep sky. She waited for the words to form in her mind. Then she sang them out:

" 'The angel of the Lord stood among the myrtle trees.' "

Maureen's and Paul's eyes met and smiled knowingly.

"'And the morning stars sang together, and all the sons of God shouted for joy.'"

Grandpa's hand went up to the bristles in his ears. "Ida," he chortled, "that's a hull sermon of itself! I like 'em short like that. If I could be in your class, don't know but what I'd be first there ever' Sunday. I'd even brave all them womenfolks."

Grandma's face beamed as she ladled chicken gravy over every plate. Then she sat down.

No one had to be urged to eat. Plates, wiped clean with biscuits, came up for second and third helpings.

"A good thing biscuits don't have pits inside 'em," Paul grinned, reaching for another. "Nobody can count how many I've had."

They ate until they could eat no more. And then instead of going off to chores, they stayed a moment as if caught in some spell no one wanted to break.

"This week is embroidered in my heart," Grandma said. "Just think of little Misty sending Clarence Lee to college!"

Grandpa chuckled. "Y'know," he said, "I kin see the diploma hangin' onto the parlor wall already, and writ on it as plain as plain is the name, 'Clarence Lee Beebe, Jr.' And I'm goin' to print out Misty's name alongside it. And that's all I'll ever read on it," he laughed. "College people wastes words."

Paul swung one leg over the picnic bench and faced out to sea. A silence washed over them, a cozy silence, not sad at all. And running through it were the tiniest sounds that made it even cozier. The wind riffling the pine needles and rustling along the grasses. A duckling trying its wings. Guinea hens scratching. And deep in the woods a wren spilling a waterfall of notes.

Grandpa dropped his voice to fit the quiet. "Me and yer Grandma have had a good many head of children," he mused to himself, "but when each one went off to work or to war, we always got a little dread inside us. Lasted for days. But then . . ."

"Then what?" asked Maureen.

"Always somebody was left behind to stay a spell with us. Even when all our childern was growed up and didn't need us, then you two come along and the empty feelin' was gone."

Paul let out a cry, cut off in the middle. He leaped to his feet. "Look!" he yelled. "Look what's coming!"

Maureen whirled around, almost falling off the bench in her haste. Coming into view at the bend of the lane was a tall, lank man leading a splashy brown-and-white mare. The mare limped a little on her near hind foot, and her head kept turning around as she hobbled along. But it was not her foot that worried her. It was a little brown colt nuzzling along beside her.

"Ahoy, Paul! Ahoy, Maureen!" yelled Wilbur Wimbrow. "Come get your colt and mare. I got to go down the bay oysterin' tomorrow. I can't be wastin' my time on these two. They're yours!"

Paul and Maureen flew to meet them.

"You — know — what?" Paul asked, a little breathless as he ran.

"What?" puffed Maureen.

"Sea Star's come to adopt *us!*"

He called to Mr. Wimbrow. "We're coming! We're coming to open the gate!"

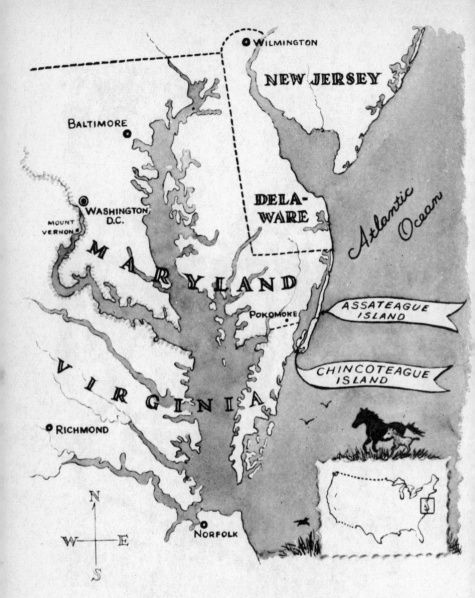

Four miles off the eastern shore of Virginia lies the tiny, wind-rippled isle of Chincoteague. It is only seven miles long and averages but twenty-one inches above the sea.

Assateague Island, however, is thirty-three miles long. Just as Paul Beebe says, Assateague is an outrider, protecting little Chincoteague from the rough seas of the Atlantic. The outer island is a wildlife refuge for wild geese and ducks and the wild ponies.

STORMY

MISTY'S FOAL

STORMY
MISTY'S FOAL

By MARGUERITE HENRY

Illustrated by Wesley Dennis

DEDICATION

Dedicated to the boys and girls everywhere
whose pennies, dimes, and dollars helped restore
the wild herds on Assateague Island,
and who by their spontaneous outpouring of love
gave courage to the stricken people
of Chincoteague.

CONTENTS

Prologue

LAND ACROSS THE WATER

IN THE GIGANTIC ATLANTIC OCEAN just off the coast of Virginia a sliver of land lies exposed to the smile of the sun and the fury of wind and tide. It almost missed being an island, for it is only inches above the sea. The early Indians who poled over from the mainland to hunt deer and otter and beaver named this wind-rumpled island *Chin-co-teague*, "the land across the water."

Today a causeway, five miles long, connects it with the eastern shore of Virginia. Sometimes, when the sea breaks loose, it swallows the causeway. Then the people on the island are wholly isolated.

But most of the time Chincoteague enjoys the protection of a neighbor island, a great long rib of white sandy hills. The

Indians called it *Assa-teague*, or "outrider." They named it well, for it acts as a big brother to Chincoteague, protecting it from crashing winds and the high waves of the Atlantic.

For many years now Assateague has been preserved as a wildlife refuge for ponies and deer and migrating waterfowl. On clear days herds of the wild ponies can be seen thundering along its shores, manes and tails flying in the wind.

Assateague, then, belongs to the wild things. But Chincoteague belongs to the people—sturdy island folk who live by raising chickens and by gathering the famous Chincoteague oysters and clams and diamond-backed terrapin. The one big joyous celebration of their year comes toward the end of July on Pony Penning Day. Then the volunteer firemen round up the wild ponies on Assateague, force them to swim the channel to Chincoteague, and pen them up for tourists and pony buyers who come from far and near. Of course, only the young colts are gentle enough to be sold. The money from the auction is used to buy fire-fighting equipment to protect the fisherfolk and chicken farmers who live on Chincoteague.

There is one family whom the firemen look upon as friendly competitors in their yearly pony sale. They are the Beebes— Grandpa and Grandma and their grandchildren, Paul and Maureen. Except for Grandma, whose father was a sea captain, they call themselves "hossmen." They are in the pony business the year around. Their place at the southern end of the island is known simply as Pony Ranch.

STORMY
MISTY'S FOAL

Chapter 1

BEFORE THE STORM

THE CLOCK on the shelf pointed to five as young Paul Beebe, his hair tousled and his eyes still full of sleep, came into the kitchen. Paul did not even glance at the clock, though it was a handsome piece, showing the bridge of a ship with a captain at the wheel. For Paul, his banty rooster was clock enough.

Grandpa Beebe was bent over the sink, noisily washing his face. He came up for air, his head cocked like a robin listening for worms.

"Just hark at that head rooster!" he grinned, his face dripping. He reached for the towel Grandma was handing him. "That banty," he went on as he mopped his face, "is

better than any li'l ole tinkly alarm clock. Why, he's even more to depend on than that fancy ticker yer sea-farin' father brung us from France." He gave Grandma a playful wink. "What's more, ye never have to wind him up, and I never knowed him to sleep overtime."

"Me neither," Paul said, "even when it's cloudy."

The old man and the boy went thudding in their sock feet to the back hall, to their jackets hanging over the wash tubs and their boots standing side by side.

Grandma's voice tailed them. "Wrap up good now. Wind's bitter." She came to the doorway and looked sharply at Paul. "I got to brew some sassafras roots to perten ye up.

I declare, ye look older and tireder than yer grandpa."

"Who wouldn't look tuckered out?" Grandpa asked in pride. "Paul took the midnight watch on Misty."

"This household," Grandma sputtered, "does more worritin' over Misty having a colt than if she was a queen birthin' a crown prince."

"Well, she is!" Paul exclaimed. "She's a movie queen."

"Yup," Grandpa joined in. "Name me another Chincoteague pony who's a star of a movin' picture like Misty is. And her being famous—well, it's made a heap o' difference to Pony Ranch."

Paul nodded vehemently. "Yes, Grandma. You know we sell more ponies because of her, and we can buy better fodder, and this summer I'm going to build her a fine stable and . . ."

"And I'll never hear the end of it!" Grandma grumbled. "Our place is a reg'lar mecca for folks comin' to see her, and when she has her colt—land o' mercy!—they'll be thicker'n oysters in a pie."

Paul and Grandpa were out the door. Grandma's sputtering bothered them no more than a mosquito before the fuzz comes off its stinger.

A faint light had begun to melt the darkness and there was a brim of dawn on the sea. The wind, blowing from the southwest in strong and frequent gusts, rippled the old dead marsh grasses until they and the waves were one.

As Grandpa and Paul hurried to the barn, a golden-furred collie leaped down from his bed in the pickup truck and came galloping to meet them.

"Hi, Skipper!" Paul gave him a rough-and-tumble greeting, but his heart wasn't in it. He caught at his grandfather's sleeve. "Grandpa!" he said, talking fast. "Buck Jackson's got some she-goats up to his place."

"So?"

"Well, if Misty should be bad off . . ."

"What in tarnation you gettin' at?"

"Maybe we'd ought to buy a goat, just in case . . ."

"In case *what*?"

"Misty couldn't give enough milk for her colt."

The old man pulled himself loose from Paul. "Get outen my way, boy. What's the sense to begin worryin' now? We got chores to do. Listen at them ponies raisin' a ruckus to be fed, and all the ducks and geese a-quackin' and a-clackin' and carryin' on. Everybody's hungry, includin' me."

"But, Grandpa!" Paul was insistent. "You yourself said April or May colts have a better chance of living than March ones."

The old man stopped in mid-stride. "It just ain't fittin' fer colts to drink goat's milk," he said gruffly. "'Specially Misty's colt." He clumped off toward the corncrib, muttering and shaking his head.

Paul skinned between the fence rails and ran toward the made-over chicken coop that was Misty's barn. He heard her whinnying in a low, rumbly tone. His heart pumping in expectancy, he unbolted her door. She came to him at once, touching nostrils as if he were another pony, then nibbling his straw-colored hair so that he couldn't see what he was looking for. Gently he pushed her away and stepped back. He looked underneath and around her. But there was no little colt lying in the straw. He looked at her sides. They were heavily rounded, just as they had been at midnight, and the night before, and the night before that.

"Surely it'll come today," Paul said to her, trying to hide his disappointment. "For a while it can live right in here with you. But soon as school's out, I got to build us more stalls. Maureen can help."

"Help what?" came a girl's voice.

Paul turned to see his sister standing on tiptoe looking over his shoulder. "Help me pump," he added hastily.

"Paul! Maureen!" Grandpa shouted from the corncrib. "Quit lallygaggin'! Water them ponies afore they die o' thirst."

Most of Grandpa's herd were still away on winter pasture at Deep Hole on the north end of the island. There the pine trees grew in groves and the whole area was thickly underbrushed so the ponies could keep warm, out of the wind. And they could fend for themselves, living on wild kinksbush and cord grass.

But here at Pony Ranch Grandpa kept only his personal riding horses—Billy Blaze, and dependable old Watch Eyes—as well as a few half-wild ponies from Assateague. All winter long this little bunch of ragged creatures ran free out on the marshland, fenced in only by the sea. But every morning they came thundering in, manes and tails blowing like licks of flame. At the gate they neighed shrilly, demanding fresh water and an ear or two of corn. It was Paul's and Maureen's duty to pump gallons and gallons of water into an old tin wash tub and dole out the ears of corn.

"It's your turn to pump," Maureen said. "I'll let the bunch in, and I'll parcel out the corn."

"Don't you start bossing me!" Paul retorted. "One grandma to a house is enough." Then he grinned in superiority. "You pump too slow, anyway. Besides, it develops my muscles for roundup time."

As Maureen let the ponies into the corral, two at a time, they dashed to the watering tub and drank greedily. Paul could hardly pump fast enough. He drew in a breath. Cold or no, this was the best time of day. And no matter how hard and fast his arms worked, nor how many times he had to fill the tub, he liked doing it. It made him feel big and strong, almost godlike, as if he had been placed over this hungry herd and was their good provider. He liked the sounds of their snorting and fighting to be first, and he liked to watch them plunge their muzzles deep in the water and suck it in between their teeth. He even liked it when they came up slobbering and the wind sent spatters against his face.

Usually Misty was first at the watering tub, for she ran free with the others out on the marsh. But now that her colt was due she was kept in her stall, where she could be watched constantly. So Paul watered her last. He wanted her to take her time and to drink her fill without a bunch of ponies squealing and pawing at the gate, getting her excited. But today, even with the tub all to herself, she acted skittery as dandelion fluff—not drinking, but playing with the water, blowing at it until it made ripples.

Paul grew alarmed. Why wasn't she drinking? Did that mean it would be soon? Or was she sick inside? He stopped pumping and gave himself up to bittersweet worry. It could be this very morning, and then he'd have to stay home from school to help dry off the colt and to see that Misty was a good nurser.

"Paul! Maureen!" Grandpa's voice boomed like a foghorn. "Put Misty in and come help me feed." He stood there in the barnyard with his head thrown back, shrilling to the heavens: *"Wee-dee-dee-dee! Wee-dee-dee-dee!"*

The call was a magnet, pulling in the fowl—wild ones from the sky, tame ones from the pasture. Geese and ducks and gulls, cocks and chickens and guinea hens came squawking. Above the racket Grandpa barked out his orders. "You children shuck off this corn for the critters." He handed them a coal scuttle heaped high with ears. "I got to police the migrators. Dad-blasted if I'll let them Canadian honkers hog all the feed whilst my own go hungry."

Faster than crows the children shelled out the corn until the scuttle held nothing but cobs, and at last the barnyard settled down to a picking and a pecking peace.

Grandpa scanned the sky for stragglers, but he saw none. Only gray wool clouds, and an angry wind pulling them apart. "Looks like a storm brewing, don't it?"

Paul laughed. "You should've been a weatherman, Grandpa, 'stead of a hossman. You're always predicting."

"Allus right, ain't I? Here, Maureen, you run and hang up the scuttle. I can whiff Grandma's bacon clean out here, and I'm hungry enough to eat the haunches off'n a grasshopper."

24

It was a bumper breakfast. The table was heaped with stacks of hotcakes and thick slices of bacon. Grandpa took one admiring look at his plate before he tackled it. "Nobody," he said, "not nobody but yer Grandma understands slab bacon. Over to the diner in Temperanceville they frazzle all the sweetness outen it so's there ain't no fat left. Tastes like my old gumboots."

Grandma beamed. If someone had given her a string of diamonds or a bunch of florist flowers, she couldn't have looked more pleased. "Clarence," she asked in her best company voice, "will you have honey or molasses on your hotcakes?"

"How kin I have *mo'* 'lasses when I ain't had *no* 'lasses at all?"

Paul and Maureen giggled at Grandpa's old joke—not just to please him but because it tickled them, and when they went visiting they sprang it on their cousins every chance they got.

Quiet settled down over the table except for the clatter of forks and Grandpa slurping his coffee. With second helpings talk began.

"Grandma," Paul asked, "how'd you like a few goats? A billy maybe, but a she-goat for sure? Y'see, she could be a nurser just in case."

Grandma put down her fork. "Paul Beebe! I swan, it must be mental telegraphy. Why, only last night I dreamt we had a hull flock of goats, and Misty friended with a nice old nanny and she let her kid run with Misty's baby and they'd butt each other and play real cute."

Grandpa clamped his hands over both ears. "I'm deef!"

25

he bellowed. "I heerd nary a word!" He got up from the table. "Six o'clock!" he announced. "You children light out and clean Misty's stall. Schooltime'll be here afore ye know it. The sea's in a fret today and there's a look to the sky I don't like. No time for gabbin'."

"Pshaw," Grandma said. "My daddy, who was captain of the . . ."

"Yes, Idy," he mimicked, "yer daddy, who was captain of the *Alberta,* the last sailing vessel here to Chincoteague, he'd say—wa-ll, *what'd* he say?"

"He'd say," Grandma repeated, proud of her knowledge of the sea, " 'There's barely a riffle of waves in the bay. Glass is down low, and we're due for a change in the weather.' But, Clarence, aren't we always in for a change?"

Chapter 2

A DUCK IN THE HORSE TROUGH

WHEN MISTY's stall was mucked out and her manger filled with sweet hay, Paul and Maureen burst into the kitchen, laughing and out of breath.

"*You* say it, Maureen."

"No, you."

Paul shuffled his feet. He glanced sidelong at Grandma. "Me and Maureen . . . I and Maureen . . . Maureen and I . . . Well," he blurted, "we'd like to say some Bible verses, with a little change to one of them."

Grandma almost dropped the cup she was wiping. She spun around, smiling in surprise. "There's no call to blush about quoting from the Good Book," she said. "It's a fine thing."

27

Paul swallowed hard. His eyes flew to Maureen's. "You say it," he urged.

Maureen looked straight at Grandma. "Last Sunday in church," she spoke quickly and earnestly, "Preacher read: 'There's a time to sow and a time to reap.' "

"Yes, that's what he said," Paul nodded. "And he said, 'There's a time to cry and a time to laugh.' "

" 'And a time to love and a time to hate,' " Maureen added.

Paul began shouting like the preacher. " 'There's a time to make war and a time to make peace.' "

"How 'bout that!" Grandma's eyes were shinier than her spectacles. "You heard every bit of the message, and here I thought you two was doing crossword puzzles all the time! Now then, what's the made-up part?" she asked encouragingly.

The answer came loud and in unison: "There's a time to go to school and a time to stay home."

"And just when is that?" Grandma demanded.

"When a mare is ready to foal," Paul said with a look of triumph.

The kitchen grew very still. Grandma shook out the damp towel and hung it above the stove. To gain thinking time she put the knives and forks in the drawer and each teaspoon in the spoon rack. Then she glanced from one eager face to the other. "You two ever see a wild mare birthing her young'un?"

They both shook their heads.

"Nor have I. Nor yer Grandpa neither." She looked far out on the marsh, at the ponies grazing peacefully. "Well, the way the mares do it," she said at last, "is to go off a day, mebbe more, and hide in some lonely spot. And the next time you see her come to the watering trough, there's a frisky youngster dancing alongside. Why, one mare swum clean across the channel to Hummocky Isle to have her baby, and three days later they both come back and joined the herd— even that little baby swum."

"But *they're* wild, Grandma," Paul said. "Misty's different. She's lived with people since she was a tiny foal."

Grandma took an old cork and a can of powder and began scouring the stains on her carving knives. She nodded slowly."And Misty's smart. If she needs help, she'll come up here to the fence and let us know right smart quick, same's she does when she's thirsty. Now you both wash up and change yer clothes. You touched off the wrong fuse when you quoted Bible verses to get excused from school."

"But, Grandma," Paul persisted, "how can Misty tell anyone she needs help when Grandpa's in town shucking oysters, and we're trapped in school and . . ."

Grandma didn't answer; yet somehow she interrupted. She handed Maureen a pitcher of milk and a saucedish. As if by magic Wait-a-Minute, a big tiger-striped cat, appeared from under the stove and began lapping the milk even before Maureen finished pouring it.

"Tell you what," Grandma said after a moment's thought. "I promise to go out every hour and look in on Misty."

"You will?"

"That I will."

"And will you telephone school in case she needs us?"

"I'll even promise you that. Cross my heart!"

Somewhat appeased, Paul and Maureen washed and hurried into their school clothes. When they dashed out of the house, Grandpa was climbing into his truck. "Hop in," he said. "I'll give ye a lift." He put the key in the ignition, but he didn't start the car. A blast of surprise escaped him. "Great balls o' fire! Look!"

"What is it, Grandpa?"

He pointed a finger at a big white goose up-ended in the watering tub. "Jes' look at him waller! Now," he said in awe, "I got a sure omen."

"Of what?" both children asked.

Grandpa recited in a whisper:

> "A goose washin' in the horse trough
> Means tomorrow we'll be bad off."

"Who says so?" Paul wanted to know.

"My Uncle Zadkiel was a weather predictor, and he said geese in the trough is a fore-doomer of storm."

Grandpa started the car, a troubled look on his face.

The day at school seemed never-ending. Maureen answered questions like a robot. She heard her own voice say, "Christopher Columbus was one of the first men who believed the world was round. So he went east by sailing west."

"Very good, Maureen. You may sit down."

But Maureen remained standing, staring fixedly at the map over the blackboard. Her mind suddenly went racing across the world, and backward in time, to a tall-masted ship. Not the one that Columbus sailed, but the one that brought the ponies to Assateague. And she saw a great wind come up, and she watched it slap the ship onto a reef and crack it open like the shell of an egg, and she saw the ponies spewed into the sea, and she heard them thrashing and screaming in all that wreckage, and one looked just like Misty.

"*I said*," the teacher's voice cut through the dream, "*you may sit down, Maureen.*"

The class tittered as she quickly plopped into her seat.

In Paul's room an oral examination was about to take place. "We'll begin alphabetically," Miss Ogle announced. "Question number one," she said in her crisp voice. "With all books closed, explain to the class which is older, the earth or the sea, and where the first forms of life appeared. We'll begin with Teddy Appleyard."

Teddy stood up, pointing to a blood-splotched handkerchief he held to his nose. He was promptly excused.

"Now then, Paul Beebe, you are next."

Dead silence.

"We'll begin," the teacher raised her voice, "with Paul Be-ee–be-ee," and she stretched out his name like a rubber band. But even then it didn't reach him.

He was not there in the little white schoolhouse at all. In his mind he was back at Pony Ranch and Misty had broken out of her stall and gone tearing down the marsh. And in his fantasy he saw the colt being born, and while it was all wet and new, it was sucked slowly, slowly down into the miry bog. There was no sound, no whimper at all. Just the wind squeaking through the grasses.

Tap! Tap! Miss Ogle rapped her pencil sharply on the desk. "Boys and girls," she said, "you have all heard of people suffering from nightmares. But I declare, Paul Beebe is having a *daymare*."

The class burst into noisy laughter, and only then did the mad dream break apart.

Back home in Misty's shed all was warm contentment. There was plenty of hay in the manger, good hay with here and there some sweet bush clover, and a block of salt hollowed out from many lickings so that her tongue just fitted. She worked at it now in slow delight, her tongue-strokes stopping occasionally as she turned to watch a little brown hen rounding out a nest in a corner of the stall. Fearlessly the hen let Misty walk around her as if she liked company, and every now and again she made soft clucking sounds.

Out on the marsh Billy Blaze and Watch Eyes, pretending to be stallions, fought and neighed over the little band of mares. Misty looked out at them for a long time, then went to her manger and slowly began munching her hay. The hen, now satisfied with her nest, fluffed out her feathers and settled herself to lay one tiny brown egg.

Contentment closed them in like a soft coccoon.

Chapter 3

A BODY WITH A PURPOSE

RIGHT AFTER school Paul and Maureen rushed into Misty's stall, almost in panic. Things should be happening, and they weren't. Grandpa Beebe joined them. "You two hold her head," he ordered. He put his stubbly cheek and his ear against Misty's belly.

"Feel anything? Hear anything?" Paul whispered.

"Not jes' now. Likely the little feller's asleep." He bent down and felt of Misty's teats. Gently he tried to milk them. "Some mares is ticklish," he explained, "and they kick at their colt when it tries to nurse. I aim to get her used to the idee."

"You getting any milk?" Maureen asked.

Grandpa shook his head. "Reckon Misty ain't quite ready to have her young'un. But no use to worry. Now then, I'd like for ye two to do me a favor."

"What is it, Grandpa?"

"I want ye to climb aboard Watch Eyes and Billy Blaze, 'cause today noon it 'peared to me Billy was going gimpy. You children try him out and see which leg's causin' the trouble."

Paul and Maureen were glad of something to do. The way Grandpa talked made them feel like expert horsemen. Quickly they bridled the ponies, swung up bareback, and took off. Paul stayed a few lengths behind on Watch Eyes, calling commands to Maureen on Billy Blaze.

"Walk him!"

Ears swinging, head nodding, Billy stepped out big and bold. Almost bouncy.

"Trot him!"

Again he went sound, square on all four corners.

"Whoa! Turn! Come this way."

Maureen pulled up, laughing. "Except for his being so shaggy," she said, "he could be a horse in a show, his gaits are so smooth. Grandpa knew it all the time."

"Of course. He just wanted us to stop fussing over Misty. I'll race you, Maureen."

It was fun racing bareback across the marsh. The rising wind excited the horses, made them go faster, as if they wanted to be part of it. And it was fun to round up the mares and drive them down the spit of land, stopping just short of the sea. It was even fun arguing.

"Maureen, you got to do the pumping tonight."

"I don't either. I got to gather the eggs."

"All right, Miss Smarty, then you can just mend that chicken fence, too."

It ended by both of them repairing the fence and both

taking turns pumping water. Afterward, they charged into the house, glowing and hungry.

Grandma promised an early supper of oyster pie. "And then," she said, "if you can trust me to keep watch on Misty, you can drive with yer Grandpa over to Deep Hole to the Reeds' house. Mrs. Reed's got a pattern I want to copy for our apron sale."

"*I'll* take ye up on yer offer, Idy," Grandpa agreed quickly. "It'll give me a chance to see how my herd's doin' up there on winter pasture."

But about that time odd things began to happen. A lone marsh hen came bustling across the open field toward the house. Paul saw her first. He was at the table in the sitting room, painting a duck decoy.

"Look! Come quick!" he shouted to the household. "A marsh hen's coming to pay us a call!"

Maureen hurried into the room to see. Grandpa and

Grandma almost collided, trying to get through the door at the same time.

"Jumpin' mullets!" Grandpa whistled. "In all my born days I never see a marsh hen walkin' on dry ground."

"Can't say I have either," Grandma agreed. "They're timid folk, ain't they?"

"Yup, only feel safe in a marsh, like a rabbit in a briar patch."

"I saw one, one day," Paul said, "walk right across the causeway."

"Pshaw!" Grandpa whittled him down to size. "*Everyone's* seen 'em do that. They're just makin' a quick trip acrost, from one marsh to another. But *this* little hen has made a journey. For her it's like travelin' to the moon."

Grandma nodded. "To my notion, she's a body with a purpose. She's tryin' to find a hidey-hole. Wonder what's frighted her?"

They all watched as the hen made her way to the high ground near the smokehouse and settled down on the doorstep as though she'd found a safe harbor.

Everybody went back to work except Grandpa. He crossed the room to the window that faced the channel. "Great guns!" he exclaimed. "Look at how our lone pine tree is bent! Why, the wind's switched clean around from sou'west to nor'east! And look at the sky—it's black as the inside of a cow." Suddenly he sucked in his breath. "The tide," he gasped, "it's almost up to our field!"

"Only nacherel," Grandma called from the kitchen. "We're in the time of the new moon, and a new moon allus means a fuller tide."

But Grandpa wasn't listening. He began pacing from one room to the other. "Any storm warnings on the radio today, Idy?" he asked.

"No," Grandma said thoughtfully, "except the Coast Guard gave out small-craft warnings this morning. But three outen five days in March, they hoist that red flag."

"Even so," Grandpa said, "me and Paul better light out and put the ponies in the hay house for safety."

Paul dropped his paintbrush and started for the door.

"Bring in more wood for the stove," Grandma called after them.

Darkness was coming on quickly and the wind had sharpened, bringing with it a fine whipping rain. The old

man and the boy whistled the ponies in from the marsh. They came at a gallop, eager to get out of the weather. It wasn't often they were given all the hay they could eat, and warm shelter too.

Paul grabbed a bundle of hay and ran to Misty's stall. He found her stomping uneasily and biting at herself, but he blamed the little colt inside her, not the weather. The wind fluttered the cobwebs over the window at the back of her stall. He nailed a gunny sack to the frame to keep the cold out. Then, feeling satisfied, he gave Misty a gentle pat on the rump. As he went out, he bolted both the top and the bottom of her door.

He joined Grandpa, who was gathering up four fluffy black mallards, too young to fly, and putting them in a high cage in the hay house. The peacocks and banties were already roosting in the pine trees. Wherever Paul and Grandpa went,

Skipper ran ahead, enjoying the wind and the feeling of danger and excitement. At the kitchen door he left them, jumping into his bed in the truck. Habit was stronger than the wind.

Inside the house, all was warmth and comfort—the fire crackling in the stove, the oyster pie sending forth rich fragrances, and from the radio in the sitting room a cowboy's voice was throbbing:

> "Oh, give me a home
> Where the buffalo roam,
> And the deer and the antelope . . ."

The word "play" never came. The music stopped as if someone had turned it off. At the same instant the kitchen went black as a foxhole.

A strange, cold terror entered the house. For a long moment everyone stood frozen. Then Grandma spoke in her gayest voice, which somehow didn't sound gay at all. "We'll just eat our supper by candlelight. It'll be like a party."

She found the flashlight on the shelf over the sink, and pointed its beam inside a catch-all drawer. "I got some candles in here somewheres," she said, poking in among old party favors and odds and ends of Christmas wrappings.

Grandpa struck a match and held it ready. "Yer Grandma looks like Skipper diggin' up an old bone. Dag-bite-it!" he exclaimed. "I'm burnin' my fingers." The match sputtered and died of itself.

"I'm 'shamed to say," Grandma finally admitted, "but I recommember now, I gave my old candles to the family that moved in on Gravel Basket Road. They hadn't any electric in the house. What's more, I loaned 'em our lantern."

Grandpa's voice was quick and stern. "Paul! You drive my pickup over to Barrett's Store and get us a gallon of coal oil. Maureen, you crunch up some newspaper to —"

"Clarence!" Grandma was shocked. "Paul's not old enough to drive, and hark to that wind."

"Idy, this here's an emergency. I'm the onliest one knows jes' where in the attic to put my hand on the old ship's lantern off'n the *Alberta*. Besides, Barrett's is jes' up Rattlesnake Ridge, as fer as a hen can spit."

Paul was out the door in a flash and Grandpa was pulling down the ladder in the hall to the crawl-space in the attic. As he climbed up he muttered loud enough for Grandma to hear, "Wimmenfolk and worry, cups and saucers, wimmenfolk and worry!"

When he came back with the lantern, he handed it to Maureen. "Like I said, honey, you crunch up some newspaper and give this chimney a good cleaning, and then pick the black stuff off'n the wick. Here, ye can use my flashbeam to work by."

Seconds passed, and the minutes wore slowly on. It was past time for Paul to be back. Grandpa peered out the window, trying to pull car lights out of the dark. He wished Grandma would not just sit there, hands folded in prayer. He wished she'd sputter and scold. He wished she'd say something. Anything.

He even wished Maureen would say something. But she was intent on her work. "That's good enough, honey. Better shut the flashbeam off now. We may be needing it for trips to the barn," he added seriously.

When at last Paul burst into the house, he set the can of coal oil on the table without a word. Grandma quickly opened it and poured some in the base of the lantern.

"Wa-al?" Grandpa asked as he struck a match and lighted the wick. He turned it slowly up and watched the flame steady. "Where ye been? Yer Grandma's nigh crazy with worry over ye. What took ye so long?"

"I drove around to see how bad the storm is."

"And how bad is it?"

"Bad. *Real* bad."

"What you lookin' so ashy about?"

"I got bogged down in the sand on Main Street. The bay water's coming right over the road and lots of cars are stuck. Fire Chief had to push me out."

"Oh . . ." Grandpa looked concerned. "Ye'd better run my truck up to that high place by the fence, Paul. If this wind keeps up, no tellin' how far she'll shove the tide."

Chapter 4

LET THE WIND SCREECH

THE STORM was sharpening as Paul moved the truck. If he hurried, he could look in on Misty once more. Skipper read his thoughts and leaped out with him, but he didn't dash ahead. He hugged close to Paul, his action saying, "Two creatures against the storm are better than one."

The wind swept down upon them and struck with an iron-cold blast. It took Paul's breath. He had to fight his way, reaching up, grasping for the clothesline. He might not be able to get out again. Suppose Misty'd already had her colt and was too frightened to take care of it? Suppose it suffocated in its birthing bag because no one was there to tear it open?

He stumbled over a tree root, and only the clothesline kept him from sprawling. But now he had to let go. He had reached the post where the line turned back to the house. He was almost to the corral. Now he was there. He squeezed through the bars. He reached the shed, crying out Misty's name.

She came to him, her breath warm on his face. He put both arms around her body. The colt was still safe inside her. A wave of love and relief washed over him as he leaned against her, enjoying the warmth of her body. He stood there, wondering what she would say to him if she could, wondering whether she was thinking at all, or just feeling content, rubbing up against a fellow-creature for comfort.

Skipper nosed in between them, nudging first one and then the other, wanting to be part of the kinship.

"You can stay in here tonight, feller," Paul said. "You'll keep each other warm." Reluctantly he left them and headed toward the house. The wind and rain were at his back now, pushing him along as if he were in the way.

The kitchen felt cozy and warm by contrast, and the acrid smell of the coal oil seemed pleasant. The light, though feeble, didn't hide the worry on Grandma's and Grandpa's faces. But Maureen was humming and happy, her head bent over small squares of paper. Wait-a-Minute was perched on her shoulder, purring noisily.

Paul picked up the cat, warming his fingers in her fur. "What you doing, Maureen?" he asked.

She folded one of the squares and held it up in triumph. "Isn't it exciting, Paul?"

"What's it supposed to be?"

"Why, a birth announcement, of course."

"Gee willikers! Horsemen don't send out announcements!"

"I know that. But Misty's different. Everybody's heard

44

how she came from the wild ones on Assateague and chose to
live with us 'stead of her own kin."

Paul held the folder close to the light. He studied it
curiously and in surprise. On the top sheet were three sketches
of horses' heads. The one on the left was unmistakably Misty,
and the one on the right could have been any horse-creature
except that it was carefully labeled *"Wings."* Between the
two, in a small oval, there was a whiskery colt's face and underneath it a dash where the name could be printed in later.

"Right purty, eh, Paul?" Grandpa asked.
"Look at the inside," Grandma urged.

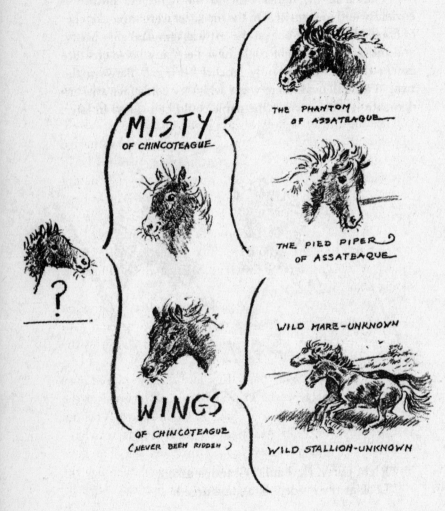

?

MISTY
OF CHINCOTEAGUE

THE PHANTOM
OF ASSATEAGUE

THE PIED PIPER
OF ASSATEAQUE

WILD MARE — UNKNOWN

WINGS
OF CHINCOTEAGUE
(NEVER BEEN RIDDEN)

WILD STALLION — UNKNOWN

Paul opened it and read aloud: *"Little No-Name out of Misty by Wings. Misty out of The Phantom by The Pied Piper. Wings out of a wild mare by a wild stallion."* He pulled at his forelock, thinking and studying the pedigree.

"One thing wrong," he said with authority.

Maureen's lips quivered. "Oh, Paul, I can't help it if I can't draw good as you."

"It's not that, Maureen. The pictures are nice. Better than I could do," he admitted honestly. "But in pedigrees the stallion's name and *his* family always come first."

"But, Paul, remember how Misty's mother outsmarted the roundup men every Pony Penning until she birthed Misty? The Pied Piper was penned up every year, and if it hadn't been for Misty, likely The Phantom never, ever would of been captured. Remember?"

" 'Course I remember! I brought her in, didn't I?" He stopped and thought a moment. "But I reckon you're right, Maureen. This pedigree *is* different. Misty and The Phantom should come first."

"These children got real hoss sense, Idy," Grandpa bragged. "I'm so dang proud o' them I could go around with my chest stickin' out like a penguin." He strutted across the room, trying to stamp out his worry.

Suddenly the lights flashed on and a voice blared over the radio: ". . . is in the grip of the worst blizzard of the winter. Twelve inches of snow have fallen in central Virginia and still more to come. At Atlantic City battering seas have undercut the famous board walk. Great sections of it have collap . . ." The voice was cut off between syllables as if the announcer had been strangled. Again the house went dark, except for the flame in the lantern and a rim of yellow around the stove lids.

"Supper's ready," Grandma sang out in forced cheerfulness. "Guess we can all find our mouths in the dark. These oysters," she said as she ladled the gravy over each plate, "is real plump, and the batter bread is light as a . . . as a . . ."

"As a moth?" Paul prompted.

"Well, mebbe not that light," Grandma replied.

They all sat down in silence, listening to the sound of the wind spiralling around the house. Suddenly Grandpa pushed his chair back. "I can't eat a thing, Idy," he said. "But you all eat. I just now thought 'bout something."

"'Bout what, Clarence?"

"'Bout Mr. Terry."

Grandma put down her fork. "That's the man who moved here to Chincoteague last fall, ain't it?"

As Grandpa nodded his head, Paul broke in. "He's the man who has to live in a kind of electric cradle."

"That's the one. His bed has to rock, Idy, or he dies. And now with the electric off, he may be gaspin' for air like a fish out o' water. Me and Paul could go over and pump that bed by hand."

He hurried into the sitting room, to the telephone on the little table by the window. "Lucy," he told the operator, "please to get me Miz' Terry. She could be needin' help."

Grandma put Grandpa's plate back on the stove. Everyone stopped eating to listen.

"That you, Miz' Terry?" Grandpa's voice boomed above wind and storm.

Pause.

"You don't know me, but this here's Clarence Beebe over to Pony Ranch, and I was jes' a-wonderin' how ye'd like four mighty strong arms to pump yer husband's bed by hand."

There was a long pause.

"Ye don't say! Wal now, ain't that jes' fine. But ye'll call me if ye need hand-help, eh?"

Grandpa strode back to the table, sat down and stuffed his napkin under his chin.

"What did Miz' Terry say?" asked Grandma, setting his plate in front of him.

Grandpa ate with gusto. He slurped one oyster, then another, before he would talk. "Why, ye'd never believe it, Idy, how quick people think! First, Charlie Saunders, who's in charge of the hull Public Service—he calls Miz' Terry and warns her 'bout the wind bein' high and the electric liable to go out, so she calls Henry Leonard down to the hardware store, and almost afore she hung up there was a boy knockin' at her door with a generator and some gasoline to run it."

Grandpa sighed in satisfaction. "So let the wind screech," he said, "and let the rain slap down, and let the tide rip. We're all here together under our snug little roof."

A good feeling came into the room. The lantern flame seemed suddenly to shine brighter and the homely kitchen with its red-checkered cloth became a thing of beauty.

Chapter 5

NINETY HEAD

BEFORE SECOND helpings the storm struck in full fury. It came whipping down the open sea like some angry, flailing giant. It shook the house, rattled the shutters, clawed at the shingles.

The kitchen, so snug and secure a moment ago, suddenly seemed fragile as an eggshell.

Grandpa and the children rushed to the sitting-room window. They could not see beyond the windowpane itself. Only wind-driven rain, streams of rain, slithering down the glass, bubbling at its edges. Every few moments one ghostly beam from the lighthouse over on Assateague sliced through the downpour—then all was blackness again.

Maureen tugged at Grandpa's sleeve. "Grandpa! What if Misty's baby is being born? Right now? Will it die?"

Paul, too, felt panic. "Grandpa!" he yelled. "Let's go out there."

But Grandpa stood mesmerized. He wasn't seeing this storm. He was in another storm long ago, and he was thinking: " 'Twas the wind and waves that wrecked the Spanish ship and brought the ponies here. What if the wind and waves should swaller 'em and take 'em back again!" In his darkened thoughts he could see the ponies fighting the wreckage, fighting for air, fighting to live.

And suddenly he began to pray for all the wild things out on a night like this. Then he thought to himself, "Sakes alive! I'm taking over Idy's work." He turned around and saw her at the sink washing the dishes as if storms were nothing to fret about. A flash of understanding shuttled between them. They would both hide their fears from the children.

Paul's voice was now at the breaking point. And Grandpa knew the questions without actually hearing the words. But he had no answer. He, too, was worried about Misty. He put one arm around Paul and another around Maureen, drawing them away from the window, pulling them down beside him on the lumpy couch.

"There, there, children, hold on," he soothed. "Buckle on your blinders and let's think of Fun Days. I'll think first. I'm a-thinkin' . . ."

In the dark room it was almost like being in a theater, waiting for the play to begin. And now Grandpa was drawing the curtain aside.

"I'm a-thinkin'," he began again, "back on Armed Forces

Day, and I'm a-ridin' little Misty in the big parade 'cause you two both got the chickenpox. Recomember?"

"Yes," they agreed politely. And for Grandpa's sake, Paul added, "Tell us about it."

"Why, I can hear the high-school band a-tootlin' and a-blastin' as plain as if 'twas yesterday. And all of 'em in blue uniforms with Chincoteague ponies 'broidered in gold on their sleeves. And now comes the Coast Guard, carryin' flags on long poles, marchin' to the music, and right behind 'em comes me and the firemen a-ridin'."

Now the children were caught up in the drama, reliving the familiar story.

"Misty, she weren't paradin' like the big hosses the firemen rode. She come a-skylarkin' along, and ever'where a little riffle of applause as she goes by. But all to once she seen a snake—'twas one of them hog-nose vipers—and 'twas right plumb in the middle of the street, and she r'ared up and come down on it and kilt it whilst all the cars in the rear was a-honkin' 'cause she's holdin' up the parade."

Grandpa stopped for breath. He gave the children a squeeze of mingled pride and joy. "Why, she was so riled up over that snake she like to o' dumped me off in the killin'. But I hung on, tight as a tick, and I give her a loose rein so's she could finish the job, and . . ."

Maureen interrupted. "Grandpa! You forgot all about our pup."

Grandpa winked at Grandma. His trick had worked. He had lifted the children out of their worry. "Gosh all fish-hawks," he chuckled, "I eenamost did. What was that little feller's name?"

"Why, Whiskers!" Maureen prompted.

" 'Course," Grandpa said, scratching his own whiskers as he remembered. "Well, that pup was a-ridin' bareback behind me, and when Misty r'ared, he went skallyhootin' in the air. But you know what? He picked himself up and jumped

53

right back on, after the snake-killin' was done. And Misty won a beautiful gold cup for bein' the purtiest and bravest pony in the hull parade."

"And that was even afore she became famous in the movie," Paul added.

Grandpa stopped, groping in desperation for another story. In the short moment of silence a gust of wind twanged the telephone wires and wailed eerily under the eaves.

Maureen's face went white. "Oh, Grandpa!" she whimpered. "Is Misty's baby going to die?"

"No, child. How often do I got to tell you I'm the oldest pony raiser on this here island, and if I know anything at all about ponies, Misty'll hold off 'til the storm's over and the sun's shinin' bright as a Christmas-tree ball."

Paul leaped from the couch. "Grandma!" he challenged. "Do *you* believe that?"

Grandma was putting away the last of the dishes, and did not reply. The question was so simple, so probing. She wanted to tell the truth and she wanted to calm the children. "As ye know," she said at last, "I had ten head o' children, and it seemed like *they* did the deciding when was the time to appear. But from what yer Grandpa says, ponies is smarter'n people. They kin hold off 'til things is more auspicious."

Grandpa brushed the talk aside. "I got another worriment asides Misty," he said. "She's safe enough on high ground and in a snug shed. But what about all my ponies up to Deep Hole?" He jerked up from the couch. "I got to call Tom Reed."

"Clarence," Grandma reproached, "Tom Reed's an early-to-bedder. Time we bedded down, too. It's past nine."

"I don't keer if it's past midnight," he cried in a sudden burst. "I *got* to call him!" But he didn't go to the phone. He suddenly stood still, his hands clenched into fists. "Somethin' I been meanin' to tell ye," he said with a kind of urgency.

No one helped him with a question. Everyone was too bewildered.

"All I know in this world is ponies. Ponies is my life," he went on. "And ever' Pony Penning I buy me some uncommon purty ones." Now the words poured from him. "Some fellers salt their money in insurance and such, but I been saltin' mine in ponies. And right now I got ninety head. And they're up to Deep Hole in Tom Reed's woods. I *got* to know how they are!"

"Ninety head!" Grandma gasped. "I had no idea 'twas so many."

"Well, 'tis." Grandpa's voice was tight and strained. "If the ocean swallers 'em, we're licked and done." He looked at the children. "And there'll be no schoolin' for this second brood o' ours." He rubbed the bristles in his ears, the worry in his face deepening. "One of the ponies is Wings."

"Oh . . . oh . . ." Maureen's lips trembled as if she had lost a friend. "Not Wings!"

"Not Wings!" Paul repeated.

"Who's Wings?" Grandma demanded.

"Why, Grandma," Paul said, "he's the red stallion who stole Misty away for two weeks last spring. Don't you remember? He's the father of Misty's unborned colt."

Maureen went over to Grandpa and took his gnarled old hand into hers and pressed it against her cheek. "Tonight I'm going to send up my best prayer for Wings. And for all ninety head," she added quickly. "But, Grandpa, we don't mind about school. Honest we don't."

" 'Course not," Paul said. "We'll just raise more ponies from Misty."

Chapter 6

OCEANUS

"TRY ONCET more, Lucy! Just oncet more!" Grandpa was imploring the operator.

Paul and Maureen were on the floor at Grandpa's feet, listening anxiously. Grandma brought in the lantern and set it/on the organ near him as if somehow it would help them all hear better.

After an unbearable wait Grandpa bellowed, "Tom! That you, Tom? How are my ponies?"

A pause.

"What's that? You're worried about your son's *chickens!*" Grandpa clamped his hand over the mouthpiece and snorted in disgust. He summoned all of his patience. "All right, tell me 'bout the chickens, but make it quick." He held the receiver slightly away from his ear so that everyone could listen in.

"My son," Tom Reed was shouting as loud as Grandpa, "raises chickens up to my house, you know."

"Yup, yup, I know."

"He's got four chicken houses here, and he comes up about eight o'clock tonight, and wind's a-screeching and a-blowing, and the stoves burn more coal when the wind blows hard."

"I know!" Grandpa burst forth in annoyance. "But what about . . ."

"He puts more coal on and he asks me to help, and tide wasn't too far in then. But when we'd done coaling, he goes on back to his house. And an hour or so later he calls me up all outa breath. 'Tide's risin' fast,' he says. 'Storm's worsening. I can't get back up there. Will you coal the stoves for me?' So I goes out . . ."

Grandpa stiffened. "What'd ye find, Tom? Any o' my ponies?"

"All drowned."

A cry broke from the old man: "All ninety head?"

"They was all drowned, two thousand little baby chicks. They was sitting on their stoves like they was asleep. The water just come right up under 'em. I guess two-three gasps, and they was all dead."

"Oh." Grandpa held tight to his patience. He was sorry about the chickens, but he had to know about his ponies. He cleared his throat and leaned forward. "Tom!" he shouted. *"What about my ponies?"*

There was a long pause. Then the voice at the other end stammered, "I don't know, Clarence, but no cause to worry —yet. Stallions got weather sense. They'll just drive their mares up on little humpy places."

Grandpa wasn't breathing. His face turned dull red.

"They must of sensed this storm," the voice went on. "Tonight after I watered 'em, they just wanted to stay close to the house. But I drove 'em out to the low pasture like always. I'll go out later with my flashbeam. You call me back, Clarence."

There was a choking sound. The children couldn't tell whether it was Grandpa or a noise on the line.

"You hear me, Clarence? I'll go out now. Call me back."

Blindly Grandpa put the receiver in place. He went to the window and stood there, his head bowed.

No one knew what to say. Their world seemed to hang like a rock teetering on a cliff.

The quiet felt heavy in the room, with only the wind screaming. Suddenly Grandpa turned around. His eyes seemed to throw sparks. "Idy! Play something loud. Bust that organ-box wide open. March music, mebbe. Anything to drown out that wind. And Paul and Maureen, quit gawpin'. Get up off'n the floor and sing! Loud and strong. Worryin' won't do us a lick o' good."

Grandma was relieved to have something to do. She plumped herself on the organ bench, spreading out her skirt as if she were on the concert stage. "Now then," she turned to Grandpa, "I'll play 'Fling Out the Banner.' "

"I don't know the words," Paul said.

"Me either," Maureen chimed in.

"Ye can read, can't ye?" Grandpa barked. "Here's the song book. Go ahead now. I'll be yer audience."

The organ notes rolled out strong and vibrant, and the children sang lustily:

"Fling out the banner, let it float
Skyward and seaward, high and wide . . ."

When they were well into the second verse, Grandpa silently tiptoed into the hall, put on his gumboots and slicker, and let himself out into the night.

A flying piece of wood narrowly missed his head as he went down the steps, and a piece of wet pulpy paper hit him full in the face. He wiped it off and focused his light to see the path to the corral. But there was no path; it was covered by water. He drew his head into his coat and sloshed forward, bent double against the wind. "'Tain't a hurricane, it's naught but a full tide," he kept telling himself. "Still, I don't like it, with Misty so close to her time."

Inside the shed all was dry and warm. Misty was lying asleep, with Skipper back-to-back. The light brought the collie to his feet in a twinkling. He almost knocked Grandpa down with his welcome. Misty opened wide her jaws and yawned in Grandpa's face.

He couldn't help laughing. "See!" he told himself. "Nothing to worry about. Hoss-critters is far smarter'n human-critters." He fumbled in his pocket and found a few tatters of tobacco and said to himself, "Watch her come snuzzlin' up to me." And she did. And he liked the feel of her tongue on his hand and the brightness of her eye in the beam of his flashlight.

Affectionately he wiped his sticky palm on her neck and said, "I got to go in, Misty, now I know ye're all right. See you in the morning, and by then all the water'll slump back into the ocean where it b'longs."

When he came into the kitchen, Grandma was standing with a broom across the door. "Praises be, ye're safe!" she exclaimed. "I been holdin' these young'uns at bay. They wanted to follow ye."

"Grandpa! Has the colt come?" Maureen and Paul asked in one breath.

"Nope. And if I'm any judge, 'tain't soon. Now everybody to bed. Things is all right. We got to think that."

"Paul and I, we can't go to bed yet," Maureen protested.

"And why can't ye?"

"We haven't done our homework."

"Clarence," Grandma said, "you're all tuckered out, and you can't call Tom Reed 'cause our telephone's dead as a doorknob. So you go on to bed. I'll listen to the homework so's no more members of this household tippytoe out behind my back."

Grandpa patted everyone good night and went off, loosening his suspenders as he went.

"I feel like Abraham Lincoln studying by candlelight," Maureen said, bringing her pile of books close to the lantern.

"Wish you looked more like him," Paul teased, "instead of like a wild horse with a mane that's never been brushed."

"Humph, *your* hair looks like a stubblefield."

"Children, stop it!" Grandma interrupted. "Ye can have yer druthers. Either ye go to bed or ye get to work."

Paul weighed the choices, then reluctantly opened his

science book. But at the very first page he let out a whistle. "Listen to this! 'If the ancients had known what the earth is *really* like, they would have named it Oceanus, not Earth. Huge areas of water cover seventy per cent of its surface. It is indeed a watery planet.' "

"Now that's right interesting," Grandma said, putting a few sticks of wood into the stove.

"Yes," Maureen pouted, "a lot more interesting than trying to figure how many times 97 goes into 10,241."

Paul waxed to his lesson as a preacher to his sermon. "Listen! 'People used to say the tides were the breathing of the earth. Now we know they are caused by the gra-vi—gra-vi-ta—gra-vi-ta-tion-al pull of the moon and sun.' "

"I do declare!" Grandma said. "It makes my skin run prickly jes' thinkin' about it."

"Go on!" Maureen urged. "What's next?"

Paul read half to himself, half aloud. " 'When the moon, sun, and earth are directly in line—as at new moon and full moon—the moon's and the sun's pulls are added together and we have unusually high tides called spring tides.' "

Grandma sat rocking and repeating, "I declare! I do declare!" until her head nodded. Suddenly she jerked up and looked at the clock. "Paul Beebe! Stop! It's way past ten and, lessons or no, we all got to get to bed. *This instant!*"

Chapter 7

THE SEA TAKES OVER

ALL NIGHT long Paul heard the driving rain and the wind lashing the dead vine across his window. Even in his dreams he heard it. As gray daylight came, his sleepy voice kept mumbling, "They should've named it Oceanus . . . Oceanus . . . Oceanus."

His own words brought him awake. Scarcely touching his toes to the cold floor, he leaped to the window and pulled the curtain aside. He stared awestruck.

The sea was everywhere, all around. The tide had not ebbed. It had risen, its waves dirtied and yellowed by sand and jetsam. They were licking now against the underpinning of the house. Suddenly Paul knew it was more than rain he had heard in his dreams. It was the sea on its march to the house.

All at once fear was sharp in him, like a pain. Misty had drowned! She had drowned because she was trapped in a stall. He himself had bolted and locked and trapped her. If only, long ago, he had sent her back to Assateague with the wild things where she belonged! Then she could have climbed the White Hills and been saved. If only . . . If . . . !

Angry at himself, almost blaming himself for the storm, he pulled on his blue jeans over his pajamas. And he yelled for Grandpa as he tore through the silent house to the back hall.

The old man was already there, struggling into his hip boots. "Shush! Shush!" he whispered. "You'll wake yer Grandma and Maureen. Ain't nothing they can do to help. Mebbe," his voice was tight and bitter, "ain't nothing anybody can do."

Paul hoped Grandpa wouldn't notice the tremble of his hands as he buttoned his jacket. But Grandpa was busy gathering up a pile of supplies—some old, worn bath towels, a thermos jug of hot water, a box of oatmeal, and a small brown paper sack. He stuffed the towels inside his slicker, picked up the jug, and gave the oatmeal and the sack to Paul.

"Mind you keep them dry," he cautioned. "The sack's got sugar inside . . . in case o' emergency."

He opened the door, and the old man and the boy stepped out into a terrifying seventy-five-mile-an-hour gale. The sudden pressure half-knocked Paul's breath out. The rain blew into his eyes faster than he could blink it away. He felt Grandpa thrust a strong arm through his, and linked tight together they flung themselves against the wind, floundering

ankle-deep in the choppy water. Paul's heart hammered in his chest and he cried inside, "Please, God, take the sea back where it belongs. Please take it back."

As they stumbled along, Grandma's new-hatched chicks swept by them and out to sea on the tide. And they saw two squawking hens, their feet shackled by seaweed, struggling to reach their chicks. But they were already out of sight. Paul and Grandpa, too, were helpless to save them.

Numb and weary, they reached the shed, and to their relief it was a windbreak. They caught their breath in its shelter. At least, Paul thought, the wind won't rush in when we open the door.

Grandpa set down his jug. Paul opened the door just a crack. Fearfully, uncertainly, they peered in. They stared unbelieving. Maureen, looking like a wet fish or a half-drowned mermaid, sat dozing on Misty's back. Skipper was sleeping at her feet, curled up in a furry ball.

As the door creaked on its hinges, Misty shied and Maureen fell off in a surprised heap. She bounced up like a jack-in-the-box.

"Wal, I never!" Grandpa clucked as he and Paul went inside. "Seems like we're intrudin'. Eh, Paul?"

Paul's surprise turned to resentment. "Least you could've done, Maureen, was to wake me up."

"And who usually goes off alone?"

"Who?"

"You! Remember when you sneaked Grandpa's boat and went to Assateague all alone?"

"Oh, that! That was no place for a girl."

"Stop it!" Grandpa shouted. He gave Maureen a gentle

spank, then turned to Paul. "We've got all the makings here. You and Maureen fix a hot mash for Misty. I'll wade over to the hay house and see to Watch Eyes and Billy Blaze and the mares. You two wait for me here."

Later, at breakfast, Paul started to tell Grandma about her chicks, but he couldn't bring himself to do it. She was spooning up the porridge, trying to hide her fears with nervous chatter. "As you said, children, there's a time to go to school and a time to stay home. Well, this-here is the time to stay home. I won't have you going out again and catchin' the bad pneumonia."

"Guess ye're right, Idy," Grandpa agreed.

Paul and Maureen merely nodded. For once, a holiday from school did not seem attractive. They ate in silence.

"I've a good mind to feed you sawdust after this," Grandma went on. "Not a one of ye would know the difference."

Halfway through, Grandpa pushed his bowl of porridge aside. "It's stickin' in my gullet," he said. He got up from the table and stood over the stove, flexing his fingers. "Any way ye look at it," he sighed heavily, "we're bad off. Our old scow tore loose in the night—it's gone. And likely our ninety head up to Deep Hole are gone, too." His body shivered. "But even so," he added quietly, "we're lucky."

Maureen sat up very straight. "You have me and Paul," she said solemnly.

"That's 'zactly what I mean! We got us two stout-built grandchildren, and they're not afeard to buckle down and pull alongside us."

Paul stood up. He felt strong and proud, as if he could tackle anything. "I'm going with you, Grandpa."

"How'd ye know I'm going anywheres? But I am! I got to get over to town. Human folk may need rescuin'."

Grandma's lips pressed into a thin line. "Ye can't go! There's no road! Water'd come clean up over your boots."

"There, there, Idy. The wind's let up some, and Billy Blaze and Watch Eyes is used to plowin' through water. If they can't walk, they kin swim. Boy, ye ready?"

Paul shot a look of triumph at Maureen and immediately felt ashamed.

"Clarence!" Grandma pleaded, trying to keep her menfolk at home. "I won't have you going off and over-straining yourself. You, and me too," she added quickly, "is getting agey. Besides, soon the telephone will come on, and the electric, and we can all set cozy-like and listen to the news on the radio."

"If everyone was to stay home, Idy, a lot of folk might go floatin' out to sea like yer baby chicks." He clapped his hand over his mouth. He hadn't meant to tell her. But now it was too late.

Grandma's eyes filled. She covered her face with her hands. "Pore little chickabiddies," she whispered, "with their soft yellow fuzz and their beady birdy eyes." She wiped her tears with her apron. "All right, go 'long," she said. "I just hope your herd up to Tom's pasture ain't met the same fate."

Grandpa put a gentle hand on her shoulder. "That's another reason I got to go," he said. "When I'm fightin' the elements, I can't be grievin' about my herd. If they've weathered the night, they'll last the day. And if they ain't . . ."

"I'll keep watch on Misty," Maureen offered. "And if there's any trouble, Grandma knows all about birthing."

Chapter 8

PAUL TO THE RESCUE

B Y THE TIME Paul and Grandpa set out on Watch
Eyes and Billy Blaze, the wind had dropped to fifty miles an
hour. Yet the water from the ocean was stealthily creeping up
and up as if to reclaim this mote of land and take it back to
the sea. Spilling and foaming, the tide continued to rise—
flooding chicken farms, schoolyards, stores, and houses—in
its surge to join ocean and bay.

Watch Eyes and Billy Blaze were used to surf and boggy
marsh, for they had been on many a wild pony roundup.
Feeling ahead for footholds they pushed forward, step by step,
not seeming to mind the water splashing up on their bellies.

72

Grandpa, on Blaze, cupped one hand about his mouth and yelled above the wind. "Turn off at Rattlesnake Ridge, Paul. We'll stop at Barrett's Grocery first and get the news."

Paul nodded as though he had heard. He was staring, horror-struck, at the neighbors' houses. Some had collapsed. And some had their front porches knocked off so they looked like faces with a row of teeth missing. And some were tilted at a crazy slant.

Anger boiled up in Paul—anger at the senseless brutality of the storm. He rode, shivering and talking to himself: "The big bully! Striking little frame houses that can't stand up to it, drubbing them, whopping them, knocking their props out."

A street sign veered by, narrowly missing the horses' knees. *98th Street,* it said. Grandpa turned around to make sure he had read it aright. "My soul and body!" he boomed. "It scun clean down from Ocean City! That's thirty mile away!"

Without warning, Watch Eyes suddenly slipped and went floundering. Paul's quick hand tightened on the reins, lifting his head. He felt Watch Eyes jolt, then stretch out swimming. "Go it! Go it!" he shouted, and he stood up in his stirrups, feeling a kind of wild excitement. This was like swimming the channel on Pony Penning Day. Only now the water was icier and it was spilling into his boots, soaking his blue jeans and the pajamas he still had on. Yet his body was sweating and he was panting when they reached the store.

In front of Barrett's Grocery two red gas pumps were being used as mooring posts for skiffs and smacks and trawlers. A Coast Guard DUKW, called a "duck," and looking

like a cross between a jeep and a boat, came churning up alongside Grandpa and Paul. The driver called out: "Mr. Beebe! We need you both." His voice was a command. "Tie up your horses in Barrett's barn and come aboard."

From under the tarpaulin a child's voice cried excitedly, "Paul, how's Misty?"

And another spoke up. "Has she had her baby yet?"

Paul shook his head.

Mr. Barrett's barn had a stout ramp, and Watch Eyes and Billy Blaze trotted up and inside like homing pigeons. After Paul and Grandpa had loosened the ponies' girths and slipped the bits under their chins, they waded out to the DUKW. The passengers squeezed together to make room. Then the DUKW turned and chugged toward the village.

"Sir!" Paul asked the driver. "Could you take us up to Deep Hole to see about Grandpa's ponies?"

Grim-faced, the man replied, "Got to save people first."

As they turned onto Main Street, which runs along the very shore of the bay, Paul was stunned. Yesterday the wide street with its white houses and stores and oyster-shucking sheds had been neat and prim, like a Grandma Moses picture. Today boats were on the loose, bashing into houses. A forty-footer had rammed right through one house, its bow sticking out the back door, its stern out the front.

Nothing was sacred to the sea. It swept into the cemetery, lifted up coffins, cast them into people's front yards.

Up ahead, a helicopter was letting down a basket to three people on a rooftop. Grandpa gaped at the noisy machine in admiration. "I itch to be up there," he shouted, "lifting off the old and the sick."

Paul too wanted to do big rescue work.

As if reading his mind, the driver turned to him. "Son," he said, "do you feel strong enough to save a life?"

"Yes, sir!"

"Good. You know Mr. Terry—the man who has to live in a rocking bed?"

Paul nodded. "It rocks by electric, but he's got a gasoline generator now. Mrs. Terry was telling Grandpa last night."

"Yes, but along about midnight the gas ran low. It took the firemen an hour to get through this surf to deliver more gas to keep the generator running. He's still alive . . ."

"Then what can I do?" Paul asked.

"Plenty, son. The whole island's running out of gas, and until helicopters can bring some in, that respirator's got to be worked by hand."

"Oh. 'Course I'll help."

The driver now turned to Grandpa. "These folks," he said, indicating his passengers, "are flooded out. We'll take them to the second story of the Fire House for shelter. Then we got to chug up to Bear Scratch section and rescue a family with six children. Whoa! Here we are at the Terrys'."

The DUKW skewered to a stop in front of a two-story white house.

"Good luck, Paul. When the gas arrives, grab any DUKW going by, and we'll meet you back at Barrett's Store along about noon."

76

Paul got out and plowed up to the house. The door opened as he stumbled up the flooded steps, and Mrs. Terry greeted him. Her face was pale, and there were deep circles under her eyes, but she smiled. "You've come to man the generator?"

"Yes, sir—I mean, yes, ma'am," Paul stammered. "I'm Paul Beebe."

"Oh," she smiled again. "So you're the Beebe boy. You're the one who rescued Misty when she was a baby and nearly drowned."

"Yes, ma'am."

"And to think that now she's going to have a baby of her own."

"Yes, ma'am. Any minute."

All the while she watched Paul pulling off his boots and jacket Mrs. Terry talked to him, but her head was cocked, ears alert, listening to the steady hum of the generator in the next room.

"We've so little gas left," she said. "The doctor says I'm to save it in case relief-men get worn out." She led the way down the hall to Mr. Terry's bedroom.

Paul blanched. Hospitals and sick rooms gave him a cold clutch of fear. But the moment he saw Mr. Terry smiling there in his rocking bed he was all eagerness to help. Maybe he could do a better job than an old machine. Maybe he could pump stronger and faster, so Mr. Terry'd get a lot more air in his lungs and his face wouldn't look so white.

Mrs. Terry showed Paul how to work the controls. "He's used to just twenty-eight rocks a minute," she explained. "No faster."

77

"Hi, son." The voice from the bed was weak but cheerful. "It's good of you to help."

Paul bent to his work, pushing up and down in steady rhythm, twenty-eight strokes to the minute. Maybe, he thought as the minutes went by, now I can qualify for a volunteer fireman. He was glad he was used to pumping water for the ponies. And that set him thinking of Misty, and the bittersweet worry rushed over him again so that he barely heard Mrs. Terry.

"How wonderful people are, Paul," she was saying. "With their property wrecked and their own lives endangered, they are so concerned about us. And we aren't even Chincoteaguers. We just came here to retire."

Paul heard the words far off. He was thinking: Sometimes newborn colts don't breathe right away and horse doctors have to pump air into their lungs with their hands—like this, like this, like this. Down, up, down, up, down, up. Would it be twenty-eight times a minute for a little foal? Or more? Or less? How would he know? Why hadn't he asked Dr. Finney, the veterinarian from Pocomoke?

Runnels and rivulets of sweat were trickling down his back; his face and hair were dripping as if he were still out in the rain.

"Paul!" Mrs. Terry was saying, "Look! A whole beautiful tank of gas has come. And the DUKW man is waiting to give you a ride back. High time, too. You're all tuckered out, poor lamb!"

Mr. Terry smiled and shook hands with Paul. "In my book, you are a hero," he said.

In Barrett's store the smell of fresh-ground coffee and cheese and chewing tobacco was mixed with the stench of wet boots and dead fish. Paul stepped inside and closed the door. Groups of men were standing, knee deep in water, gabbling to each other like long-legged shore birds. Paul waited by the door until Tom Reed beckoned him over.

"Yes, sir-r-r!" a man with a cranelike neck was saying, "I figure two, three pressure areas come together and made a kind of funnel."

Mr. Barrett was waiting on customers and listening at the same time. He leaned over the counter. "To my notion," he said, "this storm made a figure eight and come back again afore the tide ever ebbed."

Paul tugged at Tom's sleeve. "Mr. Reed," he whispered, "what about Grandpa's ponies up to your place?"

"Don't know, Paul. And we won't 'til we can get back into the woods. Water's too deep to walk in, and the DUKWs are too busy rescuin' people."

The storekeeper leaned across the counter, nosing in between Paul and Tom Reed. "Who's next, gentlemen?"

Paul felt in his pocket, counting his money. "I have thirty-nine cents," he said. "I can buy two cans of beans."

"If only we'd of got some notice of this storm," Mr. Barrett was saying as he spilled the coins into the drawer. "With a hurricane you know ahead, and when it's over, it's over."

"Yup," the men agreed. "A hurricane blows crazy, then it's gone. But a tidal storm sneaks up on you and stays."

Wyle Maddox, the leader of the roundup men, had been listening as he crunched on an apple. He came over now to Tom Reed. "Tom," he said, "you're blest with mother-wit. You're the one knows most about sea and sky. How do *you* figure it?"

The small, spare man blushed. "Pshaw, Wyle, I'm no authority, but as I see it, the storm looped and come back, and kept a-pressin' and a-pressin' the water into the bay instead of letting it go out at ebb time."

"But why is the water so high on the bay side nearer the mainland?"

" 'Cause usually it's a nor'west wind that helps the tide flow back out of the bay, but this time, wind blew nor'east and the water jes' swelled up into a bulge at the narrows, and it had to go somewheres."

The door suddenly opened, letting in the sound and cold of the wind, and with it came Grandpa Beebe, looking hale and ruddy alongside the lean fisherfolk.

"What's the news?" Mr. Barrett called out.

Grandpa looked from face to face. "Bad," he said. "Government's declared Chincoteague a disaster area."

A cry of scorn went up. "Disaster area? That's no news."

"But *this* is! A hull fleet of heelyacopters is comin' in from the military this afternoon and we're all supposed to e-vac-u-ate over to the main."

"*Evac*uate?" The word dropped like a time bomb. Then the explosion.

"Why?"

"What fer?"

"Mebbe okay for sick folk."

"Yeh. Or the homeless."

"Me, I got a second story."

"Me, too."

Everyone was talking at once. Everyone but Paul. He felt a hard lump in his stomach. He would refuse to go . . . unless they took Misty, too. The storekeeper rapped on the counter for silence. "Fellers, let's hear Mr. Beebe out."

Grandpa took a moment before he went on. "Tide's supposed to come up higher," he announced. "Four feet higher."

"*Four feet!* Why, that'll flood the whole island. Every house, every store. Even the Fire House and the churches!"

"But that's only half the reason. Government says there could be an epidemic of the typhoid, 'cause of all the dead chickens and fish a-rottin' and mebbe"—Grandpa avoided Paul's eyes—"mebbe dead ponies."

The talk ceased. There was a sudden exodus. Men sloshing heavy-footed out of the store, getting into their boats, going home to their families, figuring out how to break the news.

"Come, Paul," Grandpa beckoned.

Paul followed along. "I bought us two cans of beans," he offered, not knowing what to say.

"Ain't goin' to need 'em," Grandpa said gruffly; then he turned to look at Paul. "They might taste real good, though, come to think of it."

Chapter 9

WAITING FOR THE WHIRLYBIRD

GETTING HOME was rough going and agonizingly slow. The horses plodded through the water when they could, and swam when they had to. Paul and Grandpa stopped once to let them blow. Then they pressed on, man and creature eager for Home.

Almost there, Paul saw the higher ground of Pony Ranch with the buildings still standing brave and whole—the cottage, its green roof darkened by the rain, the made-over chicken coop and the hay house and the smokehouse—but they looked littler than before, and somehow frightened, with the sea creeping up on them.

83

At the gate Grandpa made his decision. "Ride down to the smokehouse, Paul," he said. "Pick us out a big ham. If we got to go, we ain't showin' up over on the main empty-handed. I'll dry off Billy Blaze and see about Misty."

Skipper swam out to meet Paul, then paddled alongside

all the way to the smokehouse. Round as a silo and perched on the highest spot of the ranch, the smokehouse was a landmark for ships in the channel. Inside, it was a friendly place, with its exciting smells, sweet and smoky. In the little while it took Paul to select the biggest ham and to cut a piece of rind for Skipper, the rain turned to icy sleet.

Grandpa was throwing an old red blanket over Misty

when Paul looked in. "Grandpa!" he cried. "Misty's standing in water!"

"So'm I!"

"But you're not going to have a colt!"

"Wisht I was. Then maybe I'd get a bit o' coddlin'."

"But, Grandpa! What are we going to do with her?"

"The only thing left to do."

"What's that?"

"Take her smack into the kitchen."

"Into *Grandma's kitchen?*"

"The very one. And that's where she's goin' to stay 'til tide ebbs."

"Whew! How're you going to ask her?"

"I ain't askin'. I'll jes' put her halter on and lead her up the steps and onto the porch and in through the door."

"No, I mean how you going to ask Grandma."

"O–h. I ain't askin' her, neither. I'll jes' tell her, quiet-like."

But Grandpa didn't tell her quietly. He led up to it like a growing storm. "Idy! Maureen!" he thundered as he and Paul stomped in. "Yer menfolk are home."

"Praised be the Lord!" Grandma exclaimed. "I been so worried I couldn't do a lick o' work. Just sat by the window praying double-quick time."

"Tell it now," Paul whispered to Grandpa.

"Now ain't the time."

"But Misty's feet are wet."

"Won't hurt her none. Salt water's good for feet, man or beast." He turned now to Grandma. "Idy, dear, don't set the table. We'll jes' stand up and eat beans and sop up the 'lasses with some of yer good bread. Then we got some packin' to do, Idy dear."

Grandma mimicked. "Don't you 'Idy-dear' me, Clarence Beebe! What you up to? Yer face is red as a gobbler's wattle."

Paul giggled nervously. Often he had thought their tom turkeys and Grandpa looked alike, but he had never dared say it. He couldn't stop giggling. And soon Maureen was laughing along with him.

Grandma began to chuckle without knowing why. "I declare to goodness! Hearing people laugh is like sunshine flooding the house."

"It's floodin' I want to talk to ye about, Idy."

The laughter stopped.

Grandpa's voice was stern. "All morning heelyacopters been carryin' off the sick. Now they're comin' for folks as is well."

"Not me, they ain't!" Grandma flared up. "They can jes' count me out! I'm too old to start riding acrost the sky in an eggbeater."

"All righty! Mebbe ye prefers stayin' here and havin' sharks and crabs slinkin' into yer house and grabbin' ye." He winked at the children. "Recomember the day when that crab pinched yer Grandma when she was bendin' over, gatherin' oysters? Why, she went off like one o' them big rockets from Wallops Beach."

Grandma turned her back and began slicing bread with a vengeance.

"But what'll happen to Misty?" Maureen asked in alarm.

"*I'll* stay with Misty," Grandma announced without turning around. "Much as I dislikes treating ponies like folks, I admit to a kinship when she's having a baby."

Grandpa cut open the can of beans with his knife. "Paul," he growled, "mebbe *ye* can explain things to yer Grandma."

"It's true, Grandma," Paul said, helping himself to the heel of bread. "Tide's coming back four foot higher, and the island's going to be contamin—going to be spoilt rotten with dead chickens and stinky fish and snakes and mushrats and maybe even dead horses." He looked at Grandpa, wishing he hadn't said that. Then he went on quickly. "Health officials want everybody to clear out. They say there could be a fierce epidemic."

No one spoke. Grandma sat down at the table and stared vacantly. She brushed imaginary crumbs into her hand.

"Wa–al, Idy," Grandpa said, "ye can have yer druthers. Do ye want to stay and take a chance on losin' Paul and Maureen to the typhoid? Or do ye want to light out now, afore the tide pushes us out?"

For the first time Grandma began to waver. "Why, I had no idea 'twas that bad, Clarence."

"Wal, 'tis! Way to look at it is: people *got* to go. Why, up to the north end of the island there was one big fat lady, weighed nigh two hundred pound, and this lady and her teen-age girl and her girl's beau was a-sittin' in their house just talkin' away, and all to once a big whoosh o' the sea come spang into their sittin' room, and they was scramblin' atop tables and chairs, and they would've clumb into the attic if they'd a had one. But they didn't. An' that young boy, he had to saw a hole in their ceilin', mind ye, and he clumb up into the teensy air space there under the roof, and with him a-pullin' and the girl a-pushin' they squeezed the mother up through the hole." Grandpa stopped for breath.

"What happened to them?" Maureen asked. "Were they there all night?"

"Yup, and 'long 'bout daybreak the boy sawed a hole in the roof and they all clumb out, and later one o' them whirly-birds come down and rescues the three o' them from the roof-top, all shivery and wet and hungry.

"Now, Idy, how'd ye like it if we had to cut a hole in our purty green roof, and I'd have to haul ye up like a sack o' potatoes?"

Paul nudged Grandpa. "Tell her now."

"So ye see, Idy, we could be next. Already flood waters is seepin' into Misty's stable. She's comin' into yer kitchen," he announced, "and that's where she's going to stay 'til the tide's out."

"Good heavings!" Grandma looked beaten.

"Now then," Grandpa went on heartily, "ye better start packing. We'll want a blanket apiece and we're takin' a beautiful ham to surprise the mainlanders. And speakin' o' eatin', these beans is Paul's treat."

At last Grandma accepted the truth. She began to scurry about, talking to herself. "We got to take some soap for sure, and we'll have to have a comb and . . ."

Grandpa and the children left her to her bustling. There was much to be done before the helicopter came. Misty had to be brought into the kitchen and, before that, the marsh ponies in the hay house had to be made comfortable.

"Let's lift down the top bales," Grandpa directed when

they reached the long shed. "We'll pile 'em two deep over the hull floor. That way even their feet'll be dry."

"And if we don't break open the bales," Paul said, "it'll take them just that much longer to eat the hay."

"They could live for a week in here," Maureen said.

" 'Zackly!" Grandpa nodded. "No need to worry 'bout them."

Then it was Misty's turn. Paul had expected to lead her out of her stall quietly and that she would foot her way along carefully, as any broodmare should. But the moment he put on her halter, she began quivering as if the wind and waves called up the wildness in her. Her head went up, her tail went up, her ears pricked sharply. And even in the bitter cold she broke out in sweat.

"Whoa there, girl, whoa," Paul soothed. He slid his hand through her halter as he opened her door. But with one leap she was in the water, lifting him off his feet. She didn't want to be led. She wanted to splash and play like any Chincoteague pony.

Grandpa grabbed her from the other side. "Maureen!" he yelled, "you hop on and ride her to the steps. Me and Paul'll guide her from behind."

Maureen climbed aboard. Through her legs she could feel Misty's heart pounding. The water was up to Misty's knees. Then a swirl of it hit her belly. She tried to jump over it.

Maureen grabbed a handful of mane. "Yahoo!" she cried in startled surprise.

Misty tried one more leap, then settled down and went steadily forward. She reached the steps well ahead of Paul and Grandpa, who came wading up, out of breath.

"Now here's the touchy part," Grandpa panted. "Steps're mighty slippy and we don't want her fallin' and hurtin' herself."

But Misty had been up these steps before. She clomped up happily, lifting each foot high. On the top step she paused, mesmerized. A little brown rabbit sat stock-still on the porch rail, not a whisker twitching. It seemed more statue than real. The two creatures stared at each other, the big soft brown eyes and the small beady ones. Misty snorted as if to say, "What you doing here? Go on back to your briar patch!" But the rabbit never budged, not even when Misty stretched out her neck and breathed right in its face.

Grandpa guffawed. Even then the cheeky little thing stood its ground, more afraid of the rising water than of people or ponies.

"He's sassing Misty," Paul laughed. " 'Don't eye me, ma'am,' he's saying, 'I been flooded out. Same as you.' "

At last Misty grew bored and ambled across the porch, through the back hall, and right into the kitchen. When they were all crowded inside, Grandpa took off his hat in a sweeping bow. "Meet Idy, my wife," he said.

Grandma winced. "We met before," she said drily. Then her heart melted. "Take off yer purty red shawl, Misty," she said, entering into the game, "and make yerself to home." She went to the refrigerator while Misty followed after, snatching a streamer of her apron.

Grandma jumped in fright, almost stumbling over her apron on the floor. "Why, that ungrateful rascal! I've a good notion to put these carrots back in the box." But she didn't. She held them out and let Misty lip them. "Feels tickly, her lips and whiskers, don't they?"

Paul and Maureen exchanged glances.

Grandma stiffened. "You're all dripping pools of water on my clean floor." She sighed. "But no matter now, I guess. How soon will the heelyacopter come for us?" she asked.

"Right soon," Grandpa replied. "Come on, son, we better hurry and haul in plenty of straw for Misty."

After they had made a deep rustly bed for her in the kitchen, there was nothing left to do. Four blankets and the ham were ready and waiting, and Misty was already at home, contentedly munching wisps of hay while Maureen combed her mane.

As the minutes dragged on, Grandma grew pale and fidgety. She busied herself pouring an extra bowl of milk for Wait-a-Minute. Then she began watering her sweet potato vine and her fern.

"That's my girl," Grandpa came over and patted her

shoulder. "That's my girl." Then he broke into a sudden howl as he caught her wetting down a plant of artificial violets.

Even Grandma laughed at herself and her color came back. "Believe now I'll just sit down and play us a hymn," she said. "I hate waiting for anything, 'specially heelyacopters."

She opened up the organ and began playing and singing. Her voice quavered at first, then grew stronger as if she wanted to reach God in his heaven, direct.

> "*Je*-sus, *Sav*-iour, *pi*-lot *me,*
> *O*-ver *life's* tem-pest-uous *sea;*
> *Un*-known *waves* be-fore me *roll,*
> *Hi*-ding *rock* and treach-erous *shoal;*
> *Chart* and *com*-pass *come* from *Thee;*
> *Je*-sus, *Sav*-iour, pi-lot *me.*"

"That's great, Idy. Misty's ears is keeping time, turning ever' which way."

Then Grandpa saw the helicopter breaking through the dun-colored sky. "Play it once more," he urged. "Just once more!" No use worrying her too soon, he thought.

Again Grandma's trembly voice filled the little house.

> "*Je*-sus, *Sav*-iour, *pi*-lot *me,*
> *O*-ver *life's* tem-pest-uous *sea.*"

Chapter 10

BACKYARD LANDING

THE HELICOPTER was chewing into the wind, coming closer and closer to Pony Ranch. Almost over the house it stopped in midair, engine roaring. It silenced even Grandma's music.

Everyone flew to the window, including Misty. They watched as the noisy machine hung over their heads.

"He's trying to decide!" Paul yelled.

"Who is? What?" Maureen wanted to know.

"The pilot, silly. He's figuring out where to land."

Grandpa was spellbound. "Ain't that beautiful? It's hangin' in the air jes' like a hummer-bird."

"Oh, mercy me!" Grandma cried as the helicopter tilted drunkenly, and began a steep vertical descent. "Oh . . . oh! It's going to set right in my daffydil bed!"

Like a bird aiming for its nest, the helicopter hovered over the mounded-up flower bed, then squatted down on the tiny patch.

Grandma watched in dismay as its rotors spit sand and water in every direction. She hid her face in her hands. "Oh, Clarence! Oh, Clarence!" she sobbed. "I can't go. I can't!"

"And why can't ye?" Grandpa demanded.

"Because, because . . ." She groped for a reason. "Misty'll ruin my linoleum and . . ." Here the sobbing became a wail, ". . . she'll chew on my nice new table with the let-down leaves."

"No, she won't!" Paul was on the defensive. "I'll stay and watch her."

"You listen to me, Paul Beebe," Grandpa exploded. "Anybody stayin' behind'll be me, head o' the household. Quick now! Everybody grab a blanket. I'll go out and explain things to that pilot." He started for the door.

Grandma reached it first and made a barricade of herself. Her crying was done. "If'n you stay behind, Clarence, we all do. Either we go as a fambly or we stay as a fambly."

Grandpa sighed, half amused, half annoyed. "Then everything's settled. Throw yer mind outa gear, Idy, and get yer duds on."

While Grandma was struggling into her overboots, Grandpa and the children were doing last-minute chores: opening a window from the top, just a crack, taking vegetables from the refrigerator and scattering them in amongst Misty's hay. Last of all, Grandpa put the stopper in the sink and turned on the cold water. "Makes a neat water trough, eh?" he chuckled, avoiding Grandma's eyes.

"You think she can manage without us?" Maureen asked.

"We got to think that, honey. And even if the tide seeps in, I made this straw bed so thick the little colt won't even get his hinder wet."

"Sure," Paul added. "And see how Wait-a-Minute is cozying up to Misty. They'll keep each other company. And see how calm she is, watching that 'copter. She's saying, 'I've seen big birds flapping their wings before.' "

"Oh, Paul, I wish I could read critters' minds the way you do."

"That's easy, Maureen. You just got to be smart as them."

Mr. Birch, the Coast Guard man, welcomed the Beebes at the foot of the stairs. Standing there in the water he looked like a preacher, ready to baptise his flock. "Wisht everybody was prompt, like you folks," he said as he herded them toward the helicopter, "and willing to cooperate without arguin'."

"We did all that afore you came," Maureen said.

Mr. Birch laughed. "Leave it to the young'uns to come out with the truth!" He helped Grandma up the steps and into the shuddering plane. "See, Mrs. Beebe, it's easier than boarding a train."

Maureen started to follow but suddenly turned to Paul, and almost in unison they let out one cry. "Skipper! Skipper!" They both called frantically. *"S–k–i–p–p–e–r!"*

Mr. Birch was shaking his head. "Sorry, children. We just have room for folks on this trip. All dogs stay behind."

"Put him in the kitchen, too," Grandma offered.

"Skipper! Here, Skipper!" The children whistled and screamed. But there was no sign of him. Only the water swirling, and the trees bending with the wind.

"All aboard!" the pilot called out. "We got another pick-up to make before dark. All aboard!"

Likely Skipper's drowned, Paul thought but didn't say aloud. He got into the helicopter and took a seat where he could look out at the house. But he refused to look.

"Fasten your seat belts!" the pilot ordered.

"Now, ain't this excitin'?" Grandpa yelled, as the blades overhead began whirring madly and the helicopter rose slowly off the earth and climbed straight up and up. "It's just like bein' in a elevator."

Grandma shook her head. She leaned toward the earth. taking a long last look at Pony Ranch, saying good-bye to it. Grandpa squeezed her hand comfortingly, and he looked down, too, down at the little house growing smaller and smaller.

"Such a racket!" Maureen cried. "Sounds faster than we're going."

Grandma held her hands over her ears. "Feels as if a thousand dentists are drilling inside my head."

"On your store teeth?" Paul grinned.

"Oh, Paul, stop teasing. I wish . . . I wish you and Maureen was littler. If only I had a baby to hold, I'd feel braver."

Grandma soon got her wish. At the next stop they picked up the Hoopers and the Twilleys and young Mrs. Whealton with her squalling baby. Just as the father of the baby was about to board, the pilot poked his head out the window. "Sorry, sir. We're full. You'll have to wait for the next one."

Quickly the young man tried to hand in a pile of diapers, but a gust of wind tore most of them away and they went flying off like kites.

Mrs. Whealton, clutching her baby, started to get out.

"Stay put, lady. Everybody! Stay put!"

"I'll be along soon," Mr. Whealton called. And before the door closed, he thrust in the remaining diapers and the baby's bottle.

As the helicopter took off, Mrs. Whealton began sobbing louder than her baby. The passengers looked at one another, helpless and embarrassed. All except Grandma. She opened wide her arms.

"You just hand that little tyke acrost to me," she smiled, "and wipe yer eyes. You kin busy yerself foldin' the few diapers you got left."

Willingly Mrs. Whealton passed the baby across the aisle and into experienced hands. The crying stopped at once.

The northeast wind shook the helicopter, but it obeyed the pilot's stick. "We take no back talk from the elements," Mr. Birch said to reassure his passengers.

The plane was heading into the wind, flying low over the channel and over the long rib of sand that was Assateague. Everyone scanned the hills and woods for wild ponies.

"I see a bunch!" Paul cried.

"I knowed it! I knowed it!" Grandpa exulted. "They're atop the White Hills."

The pilot tried to hold the plane steady, but the gale buffeted it mercilessly. Twice he circled the herd, then climbed and headed due west. The island of Assateague seemed to be sailing backward, and now they were over Chincoteague again.

"Mr. Birch!" Maureen shouted. "Look at the people on that raft. They're waving a white flag."

"I see it," Mr. Birch answered, "but it's a housetop, not a raft, and they're waving a bedsheet. They don't know we got a full load."

From the cockpit the pilot called back, "We'll get 'em on the next trip. No, we won't!" he contradicted. "I see another chopper heading this way. They'll beat us to it."

Mr. Hooper, a quiet little man, said his first words of the trip. "Sky's so full o' whirlybirds we're goin' to need a traffic cop up here."

In spite of all the tragedy, the passengers couldn't help smiling at Mr. Hooper's joke.

"Yup," Grandpa agreed. "I can eenamost see a policeman mounted on a cloud like a parson in a pulpit."

But the make-believe fun didn't last. Now they were over the big bay of water, and now they could see the wavy shore of the mainland. Slowly the helicopter came down from the sky onto a landing field at Wallops Station. A thin fog was closing in and the night lights were already on as the Beebes and Hoopers and Twilleys and Mrs. Whealton tumbled out of the plane like seeds from a pod. A gust of wind swept them into a little huddle.

Suddenly the adventure and excitement were over. Standing there in the rain, Paul felt what he was, a refugee, homeless and cold and hungry. And half his mind was far away in a hay-strewn kitchen.

Chapter 11

REFUGEES

WALLOPS STATION is on the mainland of Virginia, just across the bay from Chincoteague Island. Once it had been a Naval Air Station, teeming with activity—planes roaring off and gliding in; signal crews waving orders; officers and men, pilots and engineers, radio technicians and clerks all criss-crossing from building to building. Then the government closed the base, and for three years the buildings stood empty, like a forest of dead trees.

But when the helicopter landed that stormy March evening, lights were blazing in every window. The whole place had come to life. Fire trucks were racing to meet helicopters, rushing sick refugees to the emergency hospital and others to the barracks and even the administration building.

The storm was now twenty-four hours old. Wind still blowing strong. Rain gusty. Clouds low. No moon, no stars.

At the edge of the landing strip the little clump of passengers stood huddled, clutching their blankets, staring at the yellow headlights coming toward them.

"Which building?" a fireman called out as he drove the truck within earshot.

Grandpa Beebe shouted back, "Don't know. Be there a fire?"

The driver replied with a boom of laughter, "There's no fire, Old Timer. I simply got to ask each family if they want to go where their friends are. Climb in, folks."

"Hey, Chief," Grandpa addressed the driver, "we don't any of us know one building from t'other. But if it's all the same to you, it'd be best to see to little Mis' Whealton first. In that shawl she's got the teensiest baby you 'most ever see."

The driver nodded. "Good idea," he said, backing and turning and roaring away. He dropped Mrs. Whealton and her baby at the hospital, left the Hoopers and the Twilleys at one of the barracks, and took the Beebe family to the mess hall. "There's more children here," he explained.

Wet and weary, Grandpa and Grandma, Paul and Maureen climbed the flight of stairs to the second floor, clutching their blankets. Paul still had the ham, now slung over his shoulder. An arrow on the wall pointed to an open door down the hall. Light streamed out and voices buzzed.

The room, half filled with refugees, was large and bright, and it smelled of wet wool and rubber boots, and fear and despair.

"Make yourself to home," an earlier arrival greeted them. "Just find a little spot to call your own. Lucky thing you have blankets. These floors are mighty hard for sleeping."

For a moment the Beebes stood looking around, trying to accustom their eyes to the light. Benches were lined up against the walls and scattered throughout the room. Most of the people were strangers to them, refugees from Nag's Head probably, or other islands nearby. They sat paralyzed, like animals caught in a trap, not struggling any more, just numbed. Only their eyes moved toward the entrance as each new family trudged in.

"They all look sad and full of aches," Grandma said, searching for a place to sit down.

"I see an empty bench," Maureen called, and led the way in and out among suitcases and camp chairs and children.

An old grizzled seaman in a ragged jacket came over and confronted Grandpa. He swore loud oaths to sea and sky. "Can't believe it could happen here," he said, pounding his fist on his hand. "Why, ye read 'bout it elsewheres . . ."

"Yeah. Tidal waves slam up in faraway places, but you never dream about it happening here."

At the far end of the room women from the Ladies' Aid were bringing in platters of sandwiches and a huge coffee pot.

"Take our ham over to them, Paul," Grandma said. "Mebbe they'd like to cut it in chunks and bake it with potatoes for tomorrow. I'd feel a heap happier if I could help," she confided to Maureen.

When the table was readied, people began forming in line. And all at once they were no longer trapped animals. They were human beings again, smiling at one another, sharing stories of rescue. Drawn by the smell of food, a long-eared pup shot out of a blanket and ran toward the table, his mistress after him.

Paul and Maureen joined the chase. "How'd you do it? How could you bring your dog?" Paul asked.

"Why, he's all the family I got, and I just rolled him up in his blanket. This afghan is really his," the woman explained, "and he burrowed into it like a turtle in his shell. The pilot didn't even see him. Tonight," she added with a smile, "he's got to share his blanket with me, for a change."

Maureen admired the dog, thinking of Skipper. "We couldn't find our Skipper," she said as she stroked and petted the little pup.

The lady was all sympathy. "Tell me about your dog."

"We had a big collie right up until time to leave," Paul answered.

"And we got a pony in our kitchen back in Chincoteague," Maureen spoke up.

The woman seemed suddenly to recognize Paul. "Why.

you're the boy who caught a wild mare over to Assateague
and set her free again."

The children nodded.

"And the pony in your kitchen—is it Misty?"

"Yes, ma'am, it's Misty, all right."

The woman was excited. "Why, they been talking about
her on the radio. Children who saw her movie are swamping
the stations with calls, wanting to know if she drowned."

"She's safe," Paul said. "That is, she . . ." He stopped.
He could feel his heart throbbing in his ears. In a split-
second dream he was back on Chincoteague with the ocean
rolling and pounding in under the house, and with a horrible
hissing sound it was breaking the house apart, and in the same

instant Misty was swept out to sea until her mane became one with the spume. Paul shook off the dream as the woman called three young children to her.

"You youngsters," she said, "will be glad to know that Misty's safe in the Beebes' kitchen. And this is Paul and Maureen Beebe."

Wide-eyed, the children pelted them with questions. In the pain of uncertainty Paul answered what he could. Then he turned away, pulling Maureen along back to their bench. Grandma put an arm around each of them. "More folks are coming in," she said, trying to put their world back together. "Now mebbe we'll get some heart'ning news."

In a daze Paul and Maureen listened to the bits and pieces of talk.

"Old Dick Evans died trying to save his fish nets. Got plumb exhausted. His heart give out."

"When we flew over, I saw how the waves had chawed big chunks out of the causeway, and six autos were left, half-buried in sand. Even one of the DUKWs was stuck."

"When *we* flew over, the sea had swallowed up the causeway. Why, Chincoteague is cut off from the main like a boat without an anchor."

"I heerd that a lady over to Chincoteague had a husband and two children that couldn't swim. She swum two blocks in that icy water for help. Nearly died afore one of them DUKWs fished her up and drug her, sobbin' and drippin', to the Fire House. Then they goes back for her husband and kids." The speaker paused. "But guess what?"

"What?" someone asked.

"Why, between whiles a whirlybird airlifted 'em off'n the

106

roof and they thought *she'd* drownt and she thought *they'd* drownt. And later they all got together at the Fire House."

"See, children," Grandma whispered, "some of the news is right good."

A young reporter carrying his typewriter joined the gathering. "I heard," he said, "that a hundred and fifty wild ponies were washed right off Assateague."

"O–h!" The news was met by a shocked chorus.

"Before I write that for my paper, I'd like you folks to give me your comments." He took out a notebook and pencil.

A strained silence followed. The reporter looked around at the tight faces and put his notebook away.

Then the talk began again.

"I s'pose we oughtn't be thinking about wild ponies when people are bad off," a white-haired woman said.

"But what would it mean to Chincoteague," the reporter asked, "if Pony Penning Day had to be stopped for lack of ponies?"

Grandpa Beebe roused up. "Why, Chincoteague has took her place with the leading towns of the Eastern Shore. And mostly it's the wild pony roundup did it."

"That's what I say," a chorus of voices agreed.

"And if we had to stop it," Grandpa went on, "Chincoteague and Assateague both would be nothin' but specks on a map."

The reporter scribbled a few notes. Then he looked up. "Any of you hear about the man swept out to sea on a dining-room table while his wife accompanied him on the piano?"

His joke met with grim silence. It was too nearly true to be funny.

Grandma tugged at Grandpa's sleeve. "Clarence," she said, "we been hearing enough trouble. You tell the folks 'bout me and my violet plant."

Grandpa forced himself to smile. For the moment he put the worry aside. "Folks," he said, "my Idy here commenced waterin' her plants afore we took off. She give 'em a right smart nip. And then, split my windpipe if she didn't wet down the artyficial violet the kids give her for Christmas. She even saucered the pot to catch the come-through water, and dumped that in too!"

A young woman laughed nervously. "I can match that story," she offered. "The sea kept coming in under our door and kept pushing up my little rug, and I took my broom and tried to whisk it away, and then I got my dustpan and tried to sweep the water into it! A broom and a pan against the sea!"

A man, looking sheepish, said, "I tried the same stunt in my barn, only I used a shovel and a wheelbarrow!"

The talk petered out. Then a minister got up and prayed for a good night's sleep and for the tide to ebb and the wind to die. Gradually the people went back to their benches. One by one the lights were switched off, except for the night lights over the doors.

As the Beebes settled down in their corner, Grandpa whispered, "Close your eye-winkers, chirren, turn off your worries, and snore away the night." Then he got down on the floor, wrapped himself up like an Indian, and began breathing in deep, rhythmic snores.

"What better lullaby?" Grandma sighed.

And Paul and Maureen caught his calm, and they too slept.

Chapter 12

WAIT-A-MINUTE COULDN'T

B Y SIX O'CLOCK the next morning the men had been outside summing up the weather, and had come in to report: "Wind's slacked up a bit. Still blowin' nor'nor'east. Sky's cloudy, but no rain."

By seven o'clock a new parade of church ladies marched in with big pans of sweet rolls and pots of steaming hot coffee.

At eight o'clock a Coast Guard officer, square-jawed and handsome, strode into the room. He was a big man, and when he pounded for order, the few leftover rolls jumped on their plates. "Folks," he boomed out, "I've good news for you." He waited a moment until his scattered audience finished folding their blankets and quieted down. "You'll be pleased to know," he announced, "that the Red Cross is coming in, bringing canned goods and a steam table so you can have nice hot meals."

One of the church ladies walked out in a huff.

"And they are bringing cots and pillows, so there'll be no more sleeping on the floor."

A shocked silence followed. Who wanted to stay another night? Even on a cot? Everyone wanted to get home.

"Bear in mind, friends," the brisk voice went on, "this is not a one-day evacuation. More refugees will be coming in."

"Where'll we put 'em?" several voices demanded.

The officer ignored the interruption. "By order of the State Department of Health, no women or children can return to Chincoteague until all the dead chickens are removed and the other carcasses, too—goats, dogs, pigs, and of course dead ponies. There could be a plague—typhoid or worse."

Grandpa's arms seemed big enough to take in his whole family. "Don't listen at the man. Ponies got sense. They'll hie theirselves to little hummocky places and wait it out. And Misty, of course, is dry and comfortable."

The officer let the mumblings and grumblings die down. He rapped again for silence. "The Mayor of Chincoteague has asked for volunteers—only able-bodied men—to fly back each day to clean up the island and repair the causeway. Only able-bodied men," he repeated, scrutinizing the group. "Will all who wish to volunteer come to the front of the room."

Grandpa leaped forward as if he'd been shot from a cannon. Paul was a quick shadow behind him.

"Paul Beebe!" Grandma called out. "You come back!"

But Paul seemed not to hear. He locked step with Grandpa and they were almost the first to reach the officer.

Grandma sighed. "Who can stop a Beebe? We can be proud of our menfolk, can't we, Maureen?"

Maureen burst into tears. "Oh, Grandma, being a girl is

110

horrible. Paul always gets to have the most excitement. And he'll be first to see Misty's baby. Oh, oh . . ." And she buried her head in Grandma's bosom and sobbed.

"There, there, honey. We'll find something real interesting for you to do. You'll see."

A handful of lean, weathered fishermen were now lining up as volunteers. The officer began counting from the tail of the line. As he came to Paul, he stopped, trying to make up his mind if he were man or boy. For the moment he left Paul out and went on with his counting, ". . . eleven, twelve, thirteen, fourteen." At fourteen he paused.

"But, sir!" Paul heard his own voice sounding tight and urgent. "The 'copter holds fifteen, and Grandpa needs me. Don't you, Grandpa?"

The officer turned inquiringly to the old man.

"Fact is," Grandpa said proudly, "when it comes to handlin' livestock he's worth ten men."

"That settles it," the officer smiled. "We've completed our first load."

When the helicopter set down on Chincoteague right beside the Fire House, the Mayor was waiting for them, standing in the cold and the wet, slapping his hands together for warmth. He poked his head inside the cabin, quickly studied the occupants, then clipped out his orders: "Split into three bunches, men. Beebe, you and Paul go up to Deep Hole to check on the dead ponies and mark their location for removal by airlift. Charlie and Jack, you arrange for crews to pile up the dead chickens at convenient loading points. We'll need the rest of you to work on the causeway so's we can truck the chickens across. Thank you, men, for volunteering."

111

Three DUKWs were parked alongside the helicopter waiting to take each group to its base of operation. The driver of the first one beckoned Grandpa and Paul aboard with a welcoming smile. "You men are lucky," he said, "your house is okay; at least it was last time I was down there."

"Is . . . uh . . ." Paul stopped, embarrassed. The Coast Guardsman had just called him a man, and now he was frightened to ask a question, and more frightened not to ask.

"What you lookin' so scairt about?" Grandpa wanted to know.

"I want to ask him a question," Paul said miserably.

"Go ahead!" the driver encouraged as he steered through the debris-clogged street. "Go ahead."

Holding his breath, Paul blurted, "Is Misty all right? Has she had her colt?"

"Sorry, Paul, we been too busy to look in on her. But Mayor says I can take you there before we go up to Deep Hole."

It was strange, chugging down Main Street. Paul knew he ought to have remembered how it was from yesterday. But yesterday Chincoteaguers were sloshing along in hip boots, or

riding horses or DUKWs, and they were trying their best to joke and laugh. Today there were no home-folk faces. Grim soldiers were patrolling the watery streets, rifles held ready.

"What they here for?" Paul asked.

"To prevent looting," the Coast Guardsman replied.

But what's there to loot, Paul wondered, looking at the houses smashed like match boxes, with maybe only a refrigerator showing, or a bathtub filled with drift.

They passed other DUKWs plying up and down, delivering food to the Fire House, to the Baptist Church, to the few houses on higher ground where owners had refused to leave. And they passed heaps of rubble which once were old

landmarks—the oyster-shucking house, and the neat white restaurant whose owner boasted he bought his toothpicks by the carload. Now there was not even a toothpick in sight.

As the DUKW headed eastward to the spit of land that was Beebe's Ranch, Paul winced. The pretty sign, "Misty's Meadow," was still standing, but it didn't fit the spot. There was no meadow at all. Only a skim of murky yellow water.

Paul felt a strangling fear. He had waited all night and half the morning to see Misty. Now in sight of the house, he couldn't wait another moment. He started to jump out.

Grandpa put a restraining arm across his chest. "Ye're jerky as a fish on a hot griddle, son. Simmer down. Ponies can't abide fidgety folk."

After what seemed an eternity but was only a minute, the DUKW jolted to a stop and Paul and Grandpa were out and up the steps.

Breathless, Paul opened the door a crack, and all in a split second his worry fell away. Misty was whinkering as if she too had waited overlong for this moment, and she started toward him, but stepping very carefully, lifting her feet high, avoiding something dark and moving in the straw.

"My soul and body!" Grandpa clucked, looking over Paul's shoulder. "Ee-magine that!"

Then he and Paul were on their knees, and Paul was laughing weakly as he stroked Wait-a-Minute and admired her litter of four squirming, coal-black kittens.

"Ee-magine that!" Grandpa repeated. "Misty's postponed hers, but Wait-a-Minute couldn't!"

"A whole mess of kittens in Grandma's kitchen!" Paul said. Disappointed as he was, he couldn't help laughing.

Chapter 13

UP AT DEEP HOLE

After HE had poked and felt of Misty, Grandpa threw up his hands in despair. "Could be a week yet."

Paul groaned, wondering if maybe the foal was dead inside her and that was why it wouldn't come out, wondering if she was really going to have a colt at all.

"Yup," Grandpa said, "mebbe she's goin' to wait till her stall dries out. She's still got plenty hay, so you feed the cat, whilst I take a quick gander about the house."

As Grandpa hurried down the hall, Paul searched the refrigerator. He took out the pitcher of milk and smelled it. "Phew-eee!" he said to himself. "She'll just have to be satisfied with the left-over beans."

Grandpa soon came back, rubbing his hands. "Water seeped into only one bedroom," he announced. "But the rooms is colder'n a tomb, and they stink like old fish. Beats all how nice it is here. Somethin' companionable in the smell of a hoss."

Misty, as if in appreciation, offered to shake hands.

"Sorry, gal. No time for tricks 'n treats today. Now then, Paul, come along. We can't keep the DUKW man waiting forever, and I got to see 'bout my herd up to Deep Hole."

116

Tom Reed was getting into his boat when the DUKW reached his place on the north end of the island. "Figured ye'd come along about now," he called. "Get out of that new-fangled contraption, Beebe, and climb aboard my old scow."

"How come she didn't get blowed away, same as mine?" Grandpa asked as he and Paul waded over. "And how come you and the missus didn't evacuate?"

"I tied her up to the rafters of my barn, that's why."

Paul grinned. "Is she still hanging there?"

Tom chuckled at the idea. "No, son, 'twas the boat. Truth is, Marjie just flat refused to go."

The driver of the DUKW was turning around, ready to leave. "Hey, Mr. Beebe," he shouted, "how soon should I come back?"

Tom answered for him. "No telling, captain. Could be all day. Ye'll just have to keep checking."

As Paul climbed into the boat, he noticed a bundle of sticks and a cellophane bag stuffed with pieces of cloth. "What they for, Tom?" he asked.

"They're rags from my wife's scrap bag. They're to make flags to mark where the dead animals are. Can't expect the 'copters to find 'em if they don't know where they be."

Although the air was bitter cold, the wind had lessened and holes of blue sky showed through the clouds. But the water about them was muddy-brown and full of drift. Grandpa reached for an oar.

"Wait a minute!" Tom said. "I got strict instructions from Marjie to give you coffee afore we set out. Wait a minute."

Grandpa guffawed. "We got a cat by that name 'cause she never does."

117

Paul broke in excitedly. "And she just had four kittens —Matthew, Mark, Luke, and John."

"Well, I'll be a chipmunk's tail," Grandpa chortled in surprise. "No worse'n namin' people for saints who they don't resemble a-tall."

"Easy to remember, too," Tom said, "and no hurt feelings if you call one by t'other." He was pouring thick black coffee into the lid of his thermos. "Its extry stout," he said, offering it first to Paul, "to fortify us for what's ahead."

Paul tasted it, trying not to make a face. Then he gulped it down, feeling it burn all the way.

Grandpa sipped his, meditating. "Over to Assateague," he thought aloud, "over in those dunes there's plenty hollows to ketch nice clean rain. Whatever ponies is left, there's places for 'em to drink. But here . . ." All at once he dumped the rest of his coffee overboard. "We got to rescue the live ones *right now,* or they'll bloat on this brackish water. Let's go!" he bellowed.

With Tom directing, they each took an oar and poled off into the morass. It was heavy going. The sludgy water was choked with boards from smashed chicken houses, and with briar and bramble and weedy vines so thickly interlaced it was like trying to break through a stout wire fence. Silently the three in the boat threaded their way along, stopping time and again to push rubbish aside and to scrape the seaweed from their oars.

Suddenly there came a thud and a jolt. The three oars lifted as one. All movement ceased. The men stared down in horror.

"Oh God!" Grandpa whispered. "It's my Black Warrior!"

No one spoke. Tom Reed reached down and took one colored square out of the bag and tied it to a stick. He drove the marker into the mud next to the stallion's body. " 'Twas a piece of Marjie's petticoat," he said nervously, just to say something. "I allus liked it with all the bright pink flowers."

Grandpa's eyes looked far off. "I was proud of the Warrior," he said quietly. "He used to help on Pony Penning Days to drive the really wild 'uns to the carnival grounds, and his tail was so long it swept the street, and his coat a-glistenin' like black sunshine. Recomember, Paul?" He wiped his arm across his eyes. Then his voice changed. "Move on!" he commanded. "We got to find the livin'."

The grim search went on. A quiet hung over the bog, except for the sloshing of oars and twigs snapping as the scow moved heavily along. Then a raucous, rasping sound sliced into the quiet of the morning.

"Look!" Paul cried. "Crows!"

The men poled faster until they came to a cloud of bold black birds flapping over a huddle of dead ponies.

Grandpa's face twisted in pain. "The Warrior's mares and colts," he said in utter desolation.

It was almost as if they were alive. Some were half-standing in the water, propped up by debris. They looked as if they were old and asleep.

"Guess they just died from exposure and cold." Tom's voice quavered, but his words were matter of fact. "One flag can do for all."

Grandpa got out of the boat and he grabbed the flag from Tom's hands. He stabbed it hard and fierce into the mud. Then he took a good look, and he began to name them all, saying a little piece of praise over each: "This one's a true Palomino. She had extry big ears, but gentle as the day, even though she'd never been rode. And this great big old tall mare was blind of one eye, but she had a colt ever' spring, reg'lar as dandylions. And this mare, she's got some pretty good age to her. She's somewhere in her twenty."

The crows came circling back, cawing at Grandpa. Angrily he whipped them away with his hat. "Likely she's had twelve, fifteen head in her day, and expectin' again." He sighed heavily. "That Black Warrior was a good stallion. He died tryin' to move his family to safety, but . . ." his voice broke ". . . they just couldn't move."

The heart-breaking work went on. They came upon snakes floating, and rabbits and rats. And they found more stallions dead, with their mares and colts nearby. And they found lone stragglers caught and tethered fast by twining vines. As the morning dragged into noon, and noon into cold afternoon, the pile of flags in the boat dwindled.

Sometimes an hour went by before they came on anything, alive or dead. Then Tom would chatter cheerfully, trying to lighten the burden. "Not ever'thing drowns," he said. "Early this morning I found me a snapper turtle under a patch of ice. He'd gone to sleep. Y'know, Paul, they snooze all winter, like bear."

Tom waited for an answer, but none came. "Funny thing about that little snapper," he went on, "he was a baby, no bigger'n a fifty-cent piece, and he was froze sure-enough. 'Tom,' I said to myself, 'he's dead.' But something tells me to put him in my inside pocket. And walking along I guess the heat of my body warmed him up, and guess what!"

120

"Grandpa!" Paul screamed. "I see something *alive!* In the woods!"

They turned the boat quickly and went poling through the soggy mass of kinksbush and myrtle. And there, caught among broken branches was a forlorn bunch of ponies, heads hanging low, their sides scarcely moving.

Grandpa slid overboard, trying not to make a splash,

trying not to panic them. Softly he called each one by name. "Nancy. Lucy. Polly. Gray Belle. Princess. Susy . . ."

The low, husky voice was like a lifeline thrown to drowning creatures. They lifted their heavy heads and one tried a whinny, but it was no more than a breath blowing. They were held fast, rooted in the boggy earth.

Tom and Paul were beside Grandpa in an instant. Without any signals between them, they knew what had to be done. They must drive the ponies to higher land near Tom's house, or they would die. Grim and determined, they maneuvered their way behind the ponies. Then grabbing pine boughs for clubs, they brandished them, whacking at the water, yelling like madmen, stirring the almost-dead things to life.

A pinto mare struggled free and led off in one desperate leap. The others stumbled after, trying to keep ahead of the wild thunder behind them. Scrabbling, crashing through uprooted trees, squeezing through bramble and thicket, they slogged forward inch by inch. And suddenly a mud-crusted stallion leaped out of the woods to join them.

"It's Wings!" Paul shrieked.

Men and ponies both were nearing exhaustion. But still they drove on. They *had* to. Shoving the boat, the men nosed it into the laggards, frightening them ever forward.

And at last they were in Tom's yard. Safe! As one, the ponies headed for the water barrel. Single-handed Grandpa overturned it, spilling out the dirty water tainted by the sea. He tried the spigot above it. "Pressure's good!" he exulted. "They got to blow first, then they can drink."

He and Tom and Paul were blowing, too. But it was a healthy blow. *Something* at last had gone right.

122

Chapter 14

MISTY GOES TO POCOMOKE

IN THE HELICOPTER on the way back to Wallops Station, Grandpa and Paul talked things over. They would try to seal off today's grief. No need to speak of it tonight, with folks listening in. It would be like unbandaging a wound for everyone to see. They would talk of the kittens instead. And so, when the plane landed, their faces were set in a mask.

Maureen and Grandma, bundled in coats and scarves, were there to meet them. Maureen rushed up, bursting with curiosity. Before she could ask her question, Paul said, "You'd never, *ever* guess."

"All right, Mr. Smarty. Then I just won't try."

"There's more than one!"

"Twins?" she gasped. "Oh, Paul, isn't that wonderful! One for you and one for me!"

"Nope. It's quadruplets—it's four of them."

"Can't be!" Grandma broke in as they walked toward the mess hall. "I may be a sea-captain's daughter, but I know 'nough about ponies to know they don't have four to once. Speak up, Clarence."

Grandpa took off his hat and let the wind pick up the wisps of his hair. "Yup, Idy," he nodded, "yer kitchen's a nursery now with four little ones . . ."

Grandma wailed. "Oh, my beautiful new table all bit up, and my linoleum ruint."

"Pshaw! The little ones ain't bigger'n nothing," Grandpa said, flashing a wink at Paul.

At the door of the mess hall Maureen stopped in her tracks and began jumping up and down as if she had the answer to a riddle. "It's Wait-a-Minute!" she shouted. "She's had kittens again!"

Paul smiled. "Yep, Grandma's kitchen is a mew-seum now."

The children and even Grandma and Grandpa laughed in relief, not because they thought the joke so funny, but because it was good to be together again.

The refugee room had been transformed—cots lined up against the wall, neat as teeth in a comb, and new tables and chairs, and a television set with a half-circle of giggling children.

The Beebes went directly to their corner. Maureen and Grandma were still full of questions. But the answers were short.

"Yup, Misty's okay."

"No, no sign of Skipper anywheres."

"Rabbit's gone, too."

"Yup, our house is dry, 'cept for a tiny bit of wetting in one o' the bedrooms." Here Grandpa pinched his nose, remembering. "But it's got a odor to it that'll hold you."

In her dismay over her house, Grandma had forgotten all about Grandpa's ponies. Now as she helped him pull off his sweater, she asked, "What about your ninety head, Clarence? Are they . . ."

Paul kept very still, and Grandpa's old leathery face did not change expression. He looked dead ahead. "There was losses," was all he said. He turned to Maureen, and his voice was tight and toneless. "Me and Paul have done a lot of yelling today, and we're both wore out. We just don't feel talky, do we, Paul?"

"No, Grandpa."

"Suppose you and Grandma be like Red Cross angels and tote our suppers over here. We'd ruther not eat up to the big table with ever'body."

As Maureen and Grandma heaped the trays and carried them back, Maureen's lip quivered. "Oh, Grandma, Paul didn't even ask what I did today. He doesn't even know I was at Doctor Finney's, riding a famous trotter. Oh, Grandma, why was I born a girl?"

"It's God's plan, Maureen. Oops! Take care. Ye're spilling the soup."

Friday. The fourth day of the storm. Gray skies over Chincoteague. Rain off and on. Temperature rising. Wind and tide slowly subsiding. The causeway in use again—red ambulances carrying off the sick, yellow school buses the well, dump trucks removing the dead chickens.

Misty in the kitchen at Pony Ranch is growing restless. Her hay is gone. The water in the sink is gone. She is bored with the squeaky, squirmy kittens, and tired of looking out the window. Nothing seems to happen. No ponies frisking. No dog teasing her to come out and play. No birds flying. No friendly human creatures.

The room is getting too warm. Her winter coat itches. Even the bony part of her tail itches. She looks for something to scratch against. The handle of the refrigerator! She backs up to it. To her surprise the door kicks right back at her! She

wheels around, barely missing the mewing kittens. She pokes her head in the box, sniffing and nosing. She tries to fit her tongue into a pitcher of molasses. Crash! A dark dribble spills down on the kittens, on Wait-a-Minute too.

At last Misty has something to do. Good sweet molasses to clean up. She licks Wait-a-Minute, and Wait-a-Minute licks her kittens. The steady strokes bring on rumbly purring sounds. Misty grows drowsy. She turns to lie down, but the kittens are in her way. At last she sleeps, standing over them.

Afternoon came, and with it strange happenings. Paul and Grandpa arrived at Pony Ranch. This time their concern over Misty was desperate.

"A day or two at most," Grandpa said gravely.

"You been saying that!" Paul replied accusingly.

"I know." Grandpa looked crestfallen as if he'd failed in his duty. He made up his mind on the spot. "We're carryin' her over to Doc Finney's today, *to once!"*

They led Misty out of the house and into the old truck. They stowed a bundle of hay in its accustomed place, just as if she were going off to a school or a library story hour.

"You wait, Misty, we'll be right back," Grandpa said. "Paul and me got to give the kitchen a quick lick."

"Oh, do we *have* to?" Paul was all impatience.

"Yes, son. Some way I got a hunch yer Grandma's coming home right soon."

Back in the kitchen Paul and Grandpa mucked out the old straw, and gave the floor a hasty cleaning.

"Gives you a new regard for wimmenfolk, don't it, Paul?" Grandpa asked, dipping the broom into a pail of suds.

"Why?"

"Well, how'd *you* like to get down on yer knees and scrub suds and dirt together and try to get a slick surface?"

"I'd ruther muck out stalls."

"That's what I mean. Misty is what I'd call a tidy pony. She uses one corner and keeps ever'thing mounded up real neat. But even so—!"

When they had done the best they could, they turned to inspect their handiwork. The room looked better, they admitted, with the kittens in the laundry basket and the straw swept out and the molasses fairly well cleaned up, but somehow the pattern of the linoleum was gone.

"Oh, well," Grandpa sighed, "yer Grandma'll say, 'Clarence Beebe, this floor looks like a hurrah's nest.' And then she'll get right down with her brush and pail, and she'll begin purrin' and hummin' like Wait-a-Minute with her kittens. So let's leave it to her and get on with Misty."

Driving the truck through town to the causeway took an hour instead of minutes. The streets were filled with men

and machines. Huge bulldozers were pushing sand back into the bay and rubble into piles for burning.

Every time the truck had to stop, Misty was recognized and men shouted questions.

"Where ye taking Misty?"

"To Doctor Finney's!"

"Clear to Pocomoke City?"

"But why now, when the weather's fairin' off?"

" 'Cause she needs a doctor, that s why," Grandpa answered. "She's way past her time."

"Shucks, you never done this with your other ponies."

"But they're used to wild ways," Paul broke in. "Misty's more like folks."

"My grandchildren set a mighty store by her," Grandpa said. "We just can't chance it."

In front of his house the Mayor came out and flagged them down. "Beebe," he said, looking heavy-eyed and discouraged, "we're having a time getting those carcasses airlifted."

"How come?"

"The government has approved sending 'copters to take fresh water to the ponies still alive on Assateague, but they have no orders yet to take out the dead ones."

Grandpa exploded. "Mayor! The live ones has *got* water. There's allus water in the high-up pools in the White Hills. Them ponies know it."

"You and I know it too, Clarence. But sometimes outside people get sentimental in the wrong places. They mean well enough," he added with a tired smile. "It's the same old story about the evacuation. Even though the drinking water is piped to Chincoteague from the mainland, the Health Department still says no women or children can return yet."

Grandpa's face went red. "Mayor, I guess you don't need me to tell you the wimmenfolk is madder'n fire and sputterin' like wrens. Less'n they get home soon and tote their soggy mattresses and chairs out in the air, ever'thing'll be spoilt."

"Yes, I know. I know. I'm doing the best I can to get things cleared up. Right now I have a call in for our Senator in Washington. Perhaps he can get some action for us."

"But how about all the folk who didn't evacuate?"

"We can't force them to leave their homes, Clarence. But those that are at Wallops Station just can't come back until all the dead animals are removed. And Clarence," he called as Grandpa shifted into gear, "when the order does come through, we'll want you to help with the airlifting."

On the long trip to Pocomoke, Grandpa kept grumbling and muttering to himself.

Paul couldn't keep his eyes open. With Misty close by him, where he could reach back and touch her, he suddenly felt easy and relaxed, easier than he had since the storm began. He tried to stay awake. He tried to listen to Grandpa. He tried to watch the scenery. But his eyelids drooped. Finally he crawled in with Misty and slept on the floor beside her.

When at last they turned into Dr. Finney's place, Grandpa had to shake him awake.

Chapter 15

GRANDPA MAKES A DEAL

D R. FINNEY was a big man, outwardly calm, but his face looked as if it knew patience and pain.

"What do you think, sir?" Paul asked as they stood with Misty in the paddock.

"Well, to be frank, she's a little too heavy, Paul. That is, for one so fine-boned. And that's never good at a time like this. But we'll pull her through."

Misty shouldered her way into the center of the group, ears listening and questing, as if she were part of the conference instead of the cause.

The doctor put a gentle hand on Paul's shoulder. "Misty won't be lonesome here," he said. "In the next stall she can neighbor with Trineda, a well-bred trotter. And my boy

David can comfort her and take your place—for the time being," he added quickly.

Just then Dr. Finney's son came racing out of the house. Paul almost hated the boy on sight, for Misty trotted right up to him, sniffing curiously.

"Doctor Finney," Paul said urgently, "couldn't I stay here? Please?"

Grandpa answered before the doctor had finished clearing his throat. "If ye could be of help, me and Doc'd both say yes. But ye're needed over to Chincoteague. Lots o' moppin' up to be done, and ye volunteered as an able-bodied *man*. Recomember?"

Still Paul could not bring himself to go. He slid his hand under Misty's mane, scruffing his fingers along. "Doctor Finney," he asked, "would it be a good idea for us to get a nanny goat just in case . . . ?"

The doctor was about to say it wouldn't be necessary. Then he saw the troubled look on the boy's face. Better, he thought, to keep him busy instead of worrying. "It wouldn't hurt at all, Paul. Many breeding stables keep a goat for that very purpose. By the way," he turned now to Grandpa, "you must know Buck Jackson from Chincoteague."

Grandpa flinched. "Yup, I know him. Sells goat's milk."

"Well, he's delivering a flock of goats to Girdletree today, and I'm to give them a health certificate. If you'd like to buy a nanny, I'll ask Buck if he can spare one. But you'd have to keep her at Pony Ranch, because I'm short of space."

Grandpa shrugged helplessly. "Allus it's me against the world," he said, half joking, half in earnest. Then he stared down the highway in amazement.

A shining white truck was barreling along toward them. Now it was slowing, and in big black letters on its side Grandpa made out the words:

BUCK JACKSON DELIVERY—GOAT'S MILK.

With a screeching of tires the truck turned into the driveway and came to a stop. A big-shouldered man jumped down from the cab and opened the tailgate. "Hi, Paul and David," he called. "Hi, Doc. Hi, Mr. Beebe. Hi, Misty. Heavens-to-Betsy, I didn't expect a welcoming committee!"

Misty and Paul and David were first to peer inside. The two boys were suddenly friends, buyers, judging an odd assortment of goats.

Grandpa stuck his nose into the truck and sniffed noisily. "I jes' don't like 'em," he insisted. "They smell from here to Kingdom Come. To me, a polecat smells purtier."

But Paul was ecstatic. "They can't help it, Grandpa.

And besides, Misty needs someone to play with, now that Skipper's gone."

"She'll have her colt," Grandpa reminded.

Paul was not listening. "I like that brown nanny with the little white kid."

"So do I," David agreed. "And if I was your Grandpa, I'd let you have the whole truckload," he offered generously.

"Who says I want to sell any?" Buck Jackson asked.

That did it. Grandpa was a born trader. "Buck," he said, "there's lots o' goats over to Chincoteague. Some nicer'n yours. Cy Eustace has a hull flock, and Ben Sykes has . . ."

"Not any more they don't. They're drowned."

Grandpa ignored the interruption. "But since my grandson has took a fancy to that brown one and her kid, what'll ye take for the pair?"

Buck winked at Dr. Finney. "I'll take Misty and her unborn."

Now Grandpa's blood was up. "Quit yer jokin'!"

"Who says I'm jokin'?"

In the waiting silence Misty poked her head inside the truck and the brown goat gave her a friendly butt. Misty came right back, asking for more.

"I give up!" Grandpa sighed. He pulled out his ancient leather purse and began fumbling inside, transferring bits of string and wire to a pocket. At last he held out a much-folded five-dollar bill. "This may seem mighty little to ye, but hoss-keepin' ain't what ye'd call profitable. Here, take it."

Buck Jackson chewed on a toothpick, thinking. "If I didn't say yes," he said at last, "even Misty here'd hate me. It's a deal, Clarence, and I'll throw in a bale of hay besides."

The transaction was quickly completed. But even with the nanny and her kid in the pickup, Paul didn't find it easier to say good-bye to Misty. "Don't ride her," he cautioned David. "She's going to have a colt."

"I know she is," David replied in disgust. "*Everybody* knows that."

Dr. Finney held onto Misty's halter. "Don't you worry, Paul. I'll sleep in the stall next to her, and I'll stay within sight and sound during her foaling period."

"You promise?"

"I promise."

It was almost dark when Grandpa and Paul crossed the state line back into Virginia.

"Tradin' whets my appetite," Grandpa confided to Paul. "What d'ye say we stop by Wallops Station and have some nice hot Red Cross food with Grandma and Maureen?"

"What about our goats? Shouldn't we hurry home and put them in the hay house with Billy Blaze and Watch Eyes? They got to get used to being with horses."

Grandpa wasn't listening. A flicker of a smile crossed his face. "Don't interrupt me, son. My mind's turnin' over important thoughts."

The refugee room looked much the same, except for more cots and more people. And it still smelled of old rubber and leather and steamy woolen socks.

As the family sat down at the long table, Paul whispered to Maureen, "I like the smell of goats better'n people, and we got two—a nanny and a kid."

"Oh, Paul, how beautiful!"

"They're not beautiful; they're really kind of funny-looking with their eyes so different from horses'."

"I know. They're bluey-yellow, and they look glassy, like marbles."

136

Paul and Maureen could hardly eat for all they had to say to each other.

"Misty's at Doctor Finney's, Maureen. She can't keep on postponing forever and she can't go on living in Grandma's kitchen. Ain't healthy and airy for her. And besides . . ."

"Besides what?"

"I overheard the doctor say there could be complications."

Grandma and Grandpa were deep in conversation, too. Grandpa seemed to have forgotten he was hungry. "Idy," he said, "Pony Ranch is now the owners of a nanny goat and her kid. A billy-kid, at that! It's got whiskers as long as yer sea-captain pa."

"Clarence Beebe! Don't you talk like that. I'll not have ye comparin' my father to a billy goat!"

"Oh, come now, Idy. I'm jes' bein' jokey. Besides, yer father smelled real good—of tobaccy and things. By the way," he asked, trying to appear casual, "you and Maureen had yer arms scratched against the typhoid?"

Grandma nodded.

"Good! I'm turribly glad."

"Why? Is the typhoid raging?"

"No, but I need ye at home, Idy, to perten me up for what I got to do."

"What's that?" Grandma asked in alarm.

"I got to see that all my dead ponies is taken off'n Chincoteague, and the dead ones on Assateague, too."

"Oh . . . oh, how dreadful! But they say wimmenfolk can't go home now. Regardless."

"I know they *say* so." Grandpa's eyes crinkled with his secret. "But *I* say the Lord helps them as helps theirselves."

Grandma looked at him questioningly.

"Idy, how'd ye like to . . . ?"

"Like to what?"

Grandpa sopped up some tomato gravy with a chunk of bread and ate it slowly, enjoying Grandma's impatience. Then he leaned close to her ear. "How'd ye and Maureen like to be smuggled back home? Right now!"

Grandma beamed. "Be ye serious?"

"Serious as a cow at milkin' time."

"Why, mercy me, I'd feel young and chipper doin' a thing like that."

"Ye would?"

"Yes, I would."

"Even if ye had to hide in the back o' a truck under a bundle o' hay with goats eatin' through to ye?"

"Even if!" Grandma hurriedly left the table, motioning Maureen and Paul to follow. "Don't ask any questions," she said. "Just slip into your jackets and come along, and leave our blankets on the cots."

The people nearby looked up in surprise as the Beebe family put on their wraps.

"My husband has got some goats down in the truck he wants us to see," Grandma explained.

"But it's raining, Mrs. Beebe."

"I know. That's why we're bundling up." Grandma blushed. "Y'see, my husband's like a little boy whenever he's got a new pet to show me."

138

Chapter 16

WELCOME HOME, PROGGER

THE NIGHT was dark and broody with no moon or stars. Not a glimmer of light anywhere. A curtain of fine rain closed in the deserted parking lot.

With a great heave Grandpa hoisted Grandma up into the back of the truck. "It's easier loading Misty," he panted.

Grandma was too excited to answer. Feeling her way in the dark, she pushed the goats aside, took off her head scarf, and sat down on it. Then she opened a clean handkerchief for Maureen. But Maureen ignored it, lost in delight over the little white kid.

The motor made a roar in the night as the truck pulled out of the lot and headed for the highway. Almost there, Grandpa turned down a gravel lane, dimmed the lights, and parked. He and Paul jumped out and ran to the back of the truck. Hastily they broke open the bale of hay, and began shaking it over the stowaways.

Maureen sneezed.

"Hay's dusty," Paul said.

"Might of knowed it," Grandpa snorted. "No wonder Buck Jackson give it away. Now whichever of ye sneezed, we can't have no more o' that. If yer nose feels tickly, jes' clamp yer finger hard underneath it, and 'twon't happen."

Before Paul and Grandpa got back into the cab, they looked around cautiously. No one was in sight.

"I feel like the smugglers we read about in Berlin," Paul said, "sneakin' refugees to West Germany."

It was only a half-hour's ride to Chincoteague, but with no one singing or laughing, it seemed more like half a day. In silence they rode past Rabbit Gnaw Road and through Horntown and past Swan's Gut Road and across the salt flats that led to the causeway.

Almost at the end of the causeway their headlights showed up a temporary guardhouse. A soldier with a rifle came out and flagged them down. He shone his flashlight into the cab of the truck. "Hi there, Mr. Beebe," he grinned in recognition. "Hi, Paul. How's Misty?"

"She's still all right," Paul replied.

The guard flicked off his flashlight and leaned one arm on the lowered window. He seemed hungry for talk. "Funny thing," he said, "about the telephone calls comin' in from all over the countryside. Mostly they're from children. It's not folks they're worried about. It's the ponies. 'Specially Misty. Yeah," he laughed, "*she's* their prime concern."

"Mine, too!" Paul said.

Unmindful of the drizzle, the guard went on. "By the way, how's everybody over at Wallops?"

Grandpa coughed. "They're all hankerin' fer home."

"Wal, maybe it won't be long now. The Mayor got through to Washington, and they're sending four big 'copters tomorrow to work with you and Tom on liftin' the dead ponies." In a routine manner he went around to the back of the truck and flashed his light inside. "Any stowaways?" he asked jokingly.

Grandpa matched the joking tone. "Yup, we got two."

After an interminable silence the soldier's laughter filled the night. "Wal, I'll be a billy goat's whiskers if ye 'ain't got a nanny and her kid! How's the missus going to like that?"

"I figger she's going to feel mighty close to 'em," Grandpa chuckled.

"Why? How's that?"

Suddenly Grandpa panicked. The sweat came cold on his forehead. He cut off the dashlight so his face would be in the dark. He couldn't speak.

Paul came to the rescue. "We bought them for Misty's colt," he explained. "Sup-pli-ament-ary feeding, you know."

The guard snapped off his light and tweaked Paul's ear. "Ye got a bright boy here, Mr. Beebe. G'night, folks. Ye can move on now."

Home was clammy cold, and it had a stench of fish, and the bedroom rug with the roses was wet as a sponge. But it was Home! And Wait-a-Minute was there with a wild welcome, turning somersaults, then flying round and round like a whirling dervish.

"This floor is like walkin' on mucilage," Grandma said, "but no matter how messy, there's jes' no place like Pony Ranch."

Maureen sighed in agreement. Then she added soberly, "Even without the ponies."

"You forget," Paul corrected, "we still have Watch Eyes and Billy Blaze, and the mares in the hay house."

"And," Grandpa added with a crooked smile, "'Wings' herd up to Tom's Place . . . and with Misty expectin' . . . and two goats and five cats, we got the beginnin's again."

"Grandma!" Maureen cried. "What's happened to the back of your dress?"

Grandma swished her skirt around. Her eyes widened. The whole back from the waist down was gone. "Why, whatever in the world!" she gasped.

Paul and Maureen began to shriek in laughter. "The nanny goat!"

"Like I said," Grandpa roared, "Missus Beebe'll allus feel mighty close to that nanny."

Grandma flounced to the drawer where she kept her aprons. In pretended anger she took out two. "I'll just wear 'em both," she said. "One fore and one aft."

There was much to be done before bedtime—the ponies in the hay house to be grained and watered, the nanny and her kid to be tended to, kindling to be brought in. And late as it was, Grandma got down on her hands and knees and scrubbed the floor with vigor and strong naphtha soap.

When she had almost finished, Maureen, muddy but radiant, sloshed into the back hall. "Guess what, Grandma!"

"What *now?*" Grandma asked without looking up. Her lips were set in a thin line as she carefully pushed the basket of kittens back under the stove. "Now what you so tickled about?"

"Feel in my pocket!"

"Mice?"

"No, Grandma. Guess again."

"Probably some toady-frog or lizard."

"No! No! Feel!"

Grandma wiped her hands on her apron and poked a cautious fingertip into Maureen's pocket. She touched something smooth and curved. Smiling, she reached in and brought out two tiny brown-flecked eggs.

"And there's two in my other pocket! I found 'em high and dry in Misty's manger."

Grandpa and Paul came stomping into the back hall with armfuls of wood. "What's to eat?" Grandpa shouted. "I could swaller a whale."

Grandma shook her head. "Bread's mouldy. Milk's sour. Only thing we got is four little bitty banty eggs."

"Why, they're good," Maureen said in a hurt tone.

" 'Course they are, honey." Grandma placed them on the table. "Paul, you still got your boots on. Run out to the smoke-house for some bacon. We'll have a tiny fried egg apiece and plenty o' crispy bacon. I'll put the skillet on and have it spittin' hot."

When Paul had gone out, Grandma turned to Maureen and Grandpa. "Now you two wash up so's I can tell who's who. And for pity's sake, use that naphtha soap. If'n I had any sense at all, I'd go around this house with a clothespin twigged onto my nose."

Grandpa's face broadened into a grin. "Humpf! A sea-captain's daughter complainin' 'bout a little bilge water."

Suddenly Maureen shushed Grandpa and held up a warning finger. "Listen!"

Faint and far off, like something in a dream, came a sound like a dog's barking. Then it faded away and stopped. They all stood still—waiting, listening. For long seconds they heard nothing. Only the clock hammering and the fire crackling in the stove.

But there! It came again. Louder this time. Nearer! A gruff, rusty bark, then three short yaps, familiar, beloved.

In one stride Grandpa was at the door. He flung it wide

and a flash of golden fur bulleted into the room, skidding
across the wet floor until it reached Maureen.

"Skipper! Skipper!" she cried, hugging him passionately,
wildly.

Grandpa and Grandma seemed to forget they were
grown. They let Skipper come leaping at them, let him put
his front feet on their shoulders. Who minded muddy paws?
Who minded the icy-cold nose? Who minded the wet tongue-
swipes? And the tracked floor? Not even Grandma! Only
Wait-a-Minute hissed and spat at him.

Everyone was laughing and crying and talking all at once.

"Where you been, feller?"

"*I* thought you'd been caught in a mushrat trap."

"*I* thought you'd drowned, for sure."

"Why, ye're strong as a tiger."

"And yer coat's got a nice shine."

Paul came in then, a wide smile spread across his face. "He *should* be fat and shiny. He's been in the smokehouse eatin' his way through hams and salt pork."

Grandma wiped her laughter-tears away. "He allus was crazy on smoked meats," she said.

Maureen buried her nose in his ruff. "He's even got a smokehouse smell to him," she said. "Remember, Paul? Last thing you did was to go get a ham before we left on the helicopter."

Grandpa went to the sink and plunged his face into the wash basin, making a sound like a seal. He came up bellowing: "Skipper's a progger!"

"What's that?" Maureen and Paul wanted to know.

Grandpa scruffed his beard, thinking. "It's a old, old Chincoteague word, and it means . . . wa–al, it jes' means someone as is smart enough to grab a livin' when things is dire bad." And he cupped his hands around his mouth and boomed, "Welcome home, ye old Progger!"

Chapter 17

SAWDUST AND SADNESS

SATURDAY. News briefs from around the world were coming over the radio like flak:

"India agrees to a conference with Pakistan. . . . African leaders at the United Nations are exploring the Common Market. . . . Russia accuses the United States of warmongering. . . . Jordan and Israel again at loggerheads over the River Jordan. . . . England's Queen Elizabeth and Prince Philip return in triumph from Australia and New Zealand."

The newscaster paused and took a breath as if all this were far away and only a prelude to the real news. His tone became neighborly now and concerned.

"And here on the home front, the tiny flooded island of Chincoteague has aroused the sympathy of the whole nation. The islanders, whose livelihood depends on chickens and sea-food and ponies, have suffered a savage blow to all three industries. Their oyster beds are gone; their chickens are gone. And today's report indicates that only a remnant of the wild pony herds on Assateague Island have survived. These are the ponies that made Chincoteague famous for the annual round-up and Pony Penning celebration, and that have brought visitors by the thousands. How seriously this loss will affect the tourist industry can only be estimated.

"Yet the Chincoteaguers are showing indomitable courage. With bulldozers and scoop shovels they are pushing tons of sand off streets, off lawns, out of cellars, and back into the channel. Clean-up crews are making bonfires of rubble and debris.

"Oh . . . flash news! Two notes were just handed me. One says Misty, the movie-star pony, has been evacuated from her owner's kitchen to an animal hospital in Pocomoke, Maryland, where her colt is expected momentarily.

"The other says the Second Army at Fort Belvoir is flying in helicopters within the hour to remove the dead ponies from Chincoteague and Assateague . . ."

At Pony Ranch Grandpa snapped off the radio in mid-sentence. "I got to go now," he said in a tone of finality. "Them's my orders." He kissed his family good-bye as solemnly as if he were going away on a long journey and might never return.

"No, son." He shook his head in answer to Paul's asking look. "No, ye're needed here today to work on Misty's stall.

Somebody's got to ready it for her homecoming. Besides, Grandma and Maureen can't lift that wet rug out on the line by theirselves. They need an able-bodied man."

"But who's going to help lift the dead po—"

Grandpa cut off the word with a sharp glance. His eyes said, "Less talk, the better." And his voice said, "Each 'copter has a crew of four stout army men, and there's Tom Reed and Henry Leonard to help me."

Grandma's eyes were bright with unshed tears. Quickly she went to the cupboard and took out a small brown sack. "I was saving these peppermints for Misty's baby. But here, Clarence, you take them. For extry strength," she whispered, "when things is rough."

Paul and Maureen were soon so busy with preparations for Misty's return that they forgot Grandpa. The phone might ring any minute, long distance, with big news from Pocomoke. And if it did, the made-over chicken coop had to be dry and snug and warm, and waiting.

The day was spent in a fever of activity. At first they tackled the heavy, sodden straw with enthusiasm. They were used to cleaning Misty's stall every morning before breakfast. It took only a few minutes—fifteen at most. But now clumps of seaweed made the bedding slithery as soup and heavy as lead. With fork and shovel they pitched and tossed for an hour. Each wheelbarrowful seemed heavier than the last, until finally it took both of them, one at each handle, to push it and dump the muck in the woods.

Skipper found an old pulpy potato and asked Paul and Maureen to play ball, but they were too busy and too tired.

At morning's end the floor of the shed was emptied of wet bedding, but what remained was a churned-up, slimy mass of mud. Maureen leaned against the wall, rubbing an arm across her face. "How are we *ever* going to get it dry?" she said, bursting into tears.

Paul felt defeated too, and his head and body ached. "What we need," he groaned, "is a thousand million blotters. But where?" Suddenly his face lighted in inspiration. "Sawdust!" he cried. "That's what we need!" He ran sloshing toward the road, calling back over his shoulder, "You wait, I'm going to see Mr. Hancock."

Mr. Hancock was a long-time friend. He was a woodcarver, and had given work to Paul and Maureen when they were earning money to buy Misty's mother. Often for fifty cents apiece they had swept his shop clean of sawdust and shavings.

By the time Maureen had finished her cry and wiped away her tears, Paul and Mr. Hancock were driving into the yard in his newly painted truck. She gaped in astonishment as she watched them unload bushel basket after bushel basket of sawdust at the door of the stall.

"Ain't near enough," Mr. Hancock said as he helped dump the yellow sawdust on the floor and saw it turn dark and wet in seconds. "Tell ye what," he said, noticing Maureen's tear-streaked face, "it's eatin'-time now and we all got to eat, regardless. That'll give this stuff time to absorb all the wet it's a-goin' to. Then ye got to heave it all out, and I'll bring more sawdust, and some chips too. Lucky thing I had it stored high and dry in my barn loft."

Paul piled the empty baskets into Mr. Hancock's truck.

151

Then he and Maureen headed wearily for the house. Maureen was trying not to cry.

"See what I see?" Paul pointed to the back stoop. And there was Grandma milking the nanny goat, who was tied to the stair railing.

"Sh . . . sh!" Grandma warned as the children came up. "Don't frighten her. This ain't easy, but I got eenamost enough to make us a nice pot of cocoa."

All during lunch Grandma kept up a stream of conversation to cheer them. "Children," she said brightly, "a she-goat was 'zackly what we needed. If not for Misty, then for us. Ain't this cocoa *de*-licious?"

Paul and Maureen nodded, too tired for words.

"You can each have two cups. And all the biscuits you can eat, with gooseberry jam. I figger the starving people of the world would think this a Thanksgiving feast, don't ye?"

"Yes, Grandma."

"And since you still got work on Misty's stall, you don't need to hang my rug outside today. I got all the windows open and there's a good breeze blowing in."

"Thank you, Grandma."

"Now, you two perten up. Everything's going to be better this afternoon. Life's like a teeter-totter. Heartbreak, happiness. Happiness, heartbreak. You'll see. Everything'll be better this afternoon."

Grandma was right. By the time the wet sawdust was shoveled out, Mr. Hancock was back again with a small tow wagon hooked onto his car.

"Got a big surprise fer ye," he chuckled. "The road people was putting down some ground-up oyster shells, and I got 'em to fill my wagon plumb full. With them shells first, and the shavings atop that, ye'll have the driest stable this side o' Doc Finney's."

The rest of the afternoon flew by in a fury of work. Paul dumped the oyster shells onto the floor. Maureen raked them even. Then came layer on layer of chips and shavings. For a final touch they took a bale of straw and cut it up, a sheaf at a time, into short wisps.

153

"Why can't we just shake it airy?" Maureen asked. "My fingers ache. Why do I have to cut it?"

"Do you want his pipestem legs getting all tangled up and throwin' him down?"

" 'Course not. When you tell me why, I don't mind doing it. But, Paul, how do you know it's going to be a 'he'?"

"I don't, silly. People always say 'he' when they don't know."

"Well, *I* say 'she.' "

With the work done, Paul flopped down on the straw and lay there quite still.

"You sick?" Maureen asked in fright.

"No!"

"Then what are you doing?"

"I'm a newborn colt and I'm testing to see if there are any draughts. Doctor Finney says they can't stand them."

"I feel the wind coming in through the siding. I can feel it blowing my hair."

"That's easy to fix." Paul got up and plastered the cracks with straw and mud. Meanwhile Maureen stripped some pine branches and scattered the needles lightly for fragrance.

By twilight any horse-master would have tacked a blue ribbon on the old chicken-coop barn. Maureen called Grandma to come out and inspect. "You've got to see, Grandma. It's beautiful. Misty's going to be the happiest mother in the world."

Grandma, holding her sweater tight around her neck, stepped inside the snug shelter. She beamed her approval. "I declare to goodness, I'd like to move in myself. Just wait 'til yer Grandpa sees this. Likely he'll do a hop-dance for joy."

But that night Grandpa never even looked at Misty's stall. It was dark when he came home. Without a word he made his way toward the kitchen table and sat down heavily. His face seemed made of clay, gray and pinched and old. Without removing his jacket he sat there, hands folded, just staring at the floor.

The noisy clock was no respecter of grief. Each stroke of the hammer thudded like a heartbeat. The seconds and minutes ticked on. Paul and Maureen sat very still, saying nothing, doing nothing. Just waiting.

"Yer Grandpa's had a mill day," Grandma whispered at last. "He's all cut to pieces. Jes' leave him be."

It was as if the gentle words had broken a dike. The old man hid his face in his arms and wept.

"Don't be ashamed to cry, Clarence. Let the tears out if they want to come." Grandma put her clean, scrubbed hand on the gnarled, mud-crusted ones. "King David in the Bible was a strong man and he wept copiously." Her voice went on softly. "In my Sunday School class just two weeks ago I gave the story of King David. There was one verse and it said, 'The King covered his face and wept.' Just like you, Clarence."

Neither Paul nor Maureen made a sound. They were too stunned. They watched the heaving shoulders in silence. Grandpa, who had always seemed so strong and indestructible, now looked little and feeble and old. When his sobs quieted, he wiped his eyes and slowly looked up. "I ain't fit to talk to nobody," he said, his voice no more than a breath.

"Oh . . . oh, Grandpa!" Maureen cried. "Your voice! It's gone! You ain't bellerin'!" And she ran to him and flung her arms about him, sobbing hysterically.

"There, there, child. Don't you cry, too. I'm plumb 'shamed to break down when we're lots luckier than most folks." He smiled weakly. "We got our house and each other and . . . "

"And Misty," Paul said earnestly.

"And Misty," Grandpa nodded. "It's jes'. . . ." He swallowed hard and his hands gripped the table until the knuckles showed white through the dirt. "It's jes'," he repeated, "that all the days of my life I'll hear that slow creakin' of the crane liftin' up the dead ponies, and I'll see their legs a-swingin' this way and that like they was still alive and kickin'." Now the words poured from him in a tide; he couldn't stop the flow. "And some had stars on their faces, and some had two-toned manes and tails, and some was marked so bright and purty, and most o' the mares had a little one inside 'em." His voice broke. "I knowed all my herd by name."

"How many were there in all, Clarence? Yours and the others?"

Grandpa's breath came heavy, as if he were still at work. "We lifted off more'n we could count," he said, "includin' the wild ones over to Assateague. And when the trucks was all lined up with their dead cargo, ever' one of us took off our hats, and the army men and us Chincoteaguers all looked alike with our sunburnt faces and white foreheads. And we was all alike in our sadness.

"Then the preacher, he come by and he said somethin' about these hosses needin' no headstone to mark their grave, and he put up a prayer to the memory of the wild free things. He said, 'Neither tide nor wind nor rain nor flight of time can erase the glory o' their memory.' "

Everyone in the little kitchen let out a deep sigh as if the preacher's words were right and good.

After a moment Grandpa got up from the table and put his arm around Grandma. "Now ye see, Idy, why I had to smuggle ye home. I needed ye for comfort."

Grandma wiped her spectacles with her apron. "Must be steam in the room," she said.

Grandpa had one more thing to say. "Fer jes' this oncet in my life I wisht I was a waterman 'stead of a hossman. When oysters die, ye can plant another bushel, and when boats drift away, ye can build another. But when ponies die . . . how can ye replace 'em?"

Paul glanced around in sudden terror. It was as if a cold blade of fear had struck him. His eyes sought Maureen's. They were very dark and wide and asking.

Was Misty all right?

Chapter 18

WITHIN THE FOALING BOX

O N THE same day that Grandpa was airlifting the ponies and Paul and Maureen were drying out Misty's stall, Misty herself felt strangely unhappy.

She had a freshly made bed in a snug stable, and she couldn't have been lonely for she was never without company. If she so much as scratched an ear with a hind hoof, young David Finney tried to do it for her. If she lipped at her hay, he tore handfuls out of the manger and presented it joyously to her. If she lay down, he tried to help her get comfortable.

And there were newspaper men coming and going, taking pictures of her in her stall, out of her stall, with David, without David. One caught Misty pulling the ponytail of a lady reporter. There was plenty of laughter and a constant flow of visitors.

But in spite of all the attention she was getting, Misty felt discontented and homesick. She was accustomed to the cries of sea birds, and the tang of salt air, and the tidal rhythm of the sea. And she was accustomed to going in and out of her stall, to the old tin bathtub that was her watering trough. But here everything was brought to her.

She kept shaking her head nervously and stamping in impatience. Occasionally she let out a low cry of distress which brought David and Dr. Finney on the run. But they could not comfort her. She yawned right in their faces as much as to say, "Go away. I miss my own home-place and my own children and my own marsh grass."

In all the long day there was only one creature who seemed to sense her plight. It was Trineda, the trotter in the next stall. The two mares struck up a friendly attachment, and when they weren't interrupted by callers, they did a lot of neighborly visiting. If Misty paced back and forth, Trineda paced alongside in her own stall, making soothing, snorting sounds. The newsmen spoke of her as Misty's lady-in-waiting, and some took pictures of the two, nose to nose.

When night came on, Trineda was put out to pasture, and Misty's sudden loneness was almost beyond bearing. She shied at eerie shadows hulking across her stall. And her ear caught spooky rustling sounds. Filled with uneasiness, she began pacing again, not knowing that the shadows came from a lantern flame flickering as the wind stirred it, not knowing that the rustling sounds were made by Dr. Finney tiptoeing

into the next stall, carefully setting down his bag of instruments, and stealthily opening up his sleeping roll.

When at last there was quiet, Misty lay down, trying to get comfortable. But she was even more uncomfortable. Hastily she got up and tried to sleep standing, shifting her weight from one foot to another.

Suddenly she wanted to get out, to be free, to high-tail it for home. She neighed in desperation. She pawed and scraped the floor, then banged her hoof against the door.

Trineda came flying in at once, whinnying her concern. Trying to help, she worked on the catch to the door, but it was padlocked. She thrust her head inside, reaching over Misty's shoulder, as much as to say, "There, there. There, there. It'll all be over soon."

Dr. Finney watched, fascinated, as the four-footed nurse quickly calmed her patient. "It'll probably be a long time yet," he told himself. "Nine chances out of ten she'll foal in the dark watches of the night. I'd better get some sleep while I can." He was aware that many of his friends would pity him tonight, shaking their heads over the hard life of a veterinarian. But at this moment he would not trade jobs for any other in the world. Each birth was a different kind of miracle.

Sighing in satisfaction, he slid down into his sleeping bag and settled himself for a long wait. The seconds wore on, and the minutes and the slow hours. He grew drowsy and he dozed, and he woke to check on Misty, and he dozed again. Toward morning his sleep was fitful and he dreamed that Misty was a tree with ripening fruit—just one golden pear. And he dreamed that the stem of the fruit was growing weak, and it was the moment of ripe perfection.

A flush of light in the northeast brought him sharply awake. He peered through the siding and he saw Misty lying down, and he saw wee forehoofs breaking through the silken birth bag, the head resting upon them; then quickly came the slender body with the hindlegs tucked under.

He froze in wonder at the tiny filly lying there, complete and whole in the straw. It gave one gulping gasp for air, and then its sides began rising and falling as regularly as the ticking of a clock.

Alarmed by the gasping sound, Misty scrambled to her feet and turned to look at the new little creature, and the cord joining them broke apart, like the pear from the tree. Motionless, she watched the spidery legs thrashing about in the straw. Her foal was struggling to get up. And then it was half way up, nearly standing!

Suddenly Misty was all motherliness. She sniffed at the shivering wet thing and some warning impulse told her to protect it from chills. Timidly at first, she began to mop it dry with her tongue. Then as her confidence grew, she scrubbed in great rhythmic swipes. Lick! Lick! Lick! More vigorously all the time. The moments stretched out, and still the cleaning and currying went on.

Dr. Finney sighed in relief. Now the miracle was complete—Misty had accepted her foal. He stepped over the unneeded bag of instruments and picked up a box of salt and a towel. Then, talking softly all the while, he unlocked Misty's door and went inside. "Good girl, Misty. Move over. There, now. You had an easy time."

With a practiced hand he sprinkled salt on the filly's coat and the licking began all over again. "That's right, Misty. You work on your baby," he said, unfolding the towel, "and I'll rub *you* down. Then I'll make you a nice warm gruel. Why, you're not even sweating, but we can't take any chances."

Misty scarcely felt Dr. Finney's hands. She was nudging the foal with her nose, urging it up again so that she could scrub the other side.

The little creature *wanted* to stand. Desperately it thrust its forelegs forward. They skidded, then splayed into an

162

inverted V, like a schoolboy's compass. There! It was standing, swaying to and fro as if caught in a wind.

Smiling, Dr. Finney stopped his rubbing. He saw that all was well. Reluctantly he left the stall.

Minutes later he was on the telephone. Young David stood behind him, listening in amazement and disgust. How could grownups be so calm, as if they'd just come in from repairing a fence or pulling weeds? He wanted to do handsprings, cartwheels, stand on his head! But there was his father's voice again, sounding plain and everyday.

"Yes, Paul. She delivered at dawn."

"A mare colt, sound as a dollar."

"Yes, I'm making Misty a warm mash. Just waiting for it to cool a bit."

"No, Paul, she's just fine. Everything was normal."

"No, don't bring the nanny goat. Misty's a fine mother."

"Don't see why not. By mid-afternoon, anyway."

Dr. Finney put the receiver in place, stretching and yawning.

"Dad, what don't you 'see why not'?" David asked.

"Why they can't take Misty and her foal home today."

"Can I go out and see her now?" David pleaded.

"No, son," Dr. Finney replied. Then he saw the flushed young face and the tears brimming. "Of course you can go later. Just give them an hour or so alone."

Chapter 19

GLORY HALLELUJAH!

PAUL TURNED from the telephone and let out a war whoop loud enough to break the sound barrier. He grabbed Maureen and they pulled Grandpa between them and went dancing around the kitchen table, lifting their knees high, bugling like wild horses. It was a free-for-all frolic. Grandpa was suddenly himself again, spry-legged and bellowing.

Grandma laughed in relief. She dropped her spoon in the pancake batter and half ran to the organ. Recklessly she threw back the lid and, with all stops open, made the notes thunder and throb as she sang in her full-bodied voice:

"Glory, glory, halle-*loooo*-jah,
Glory, glory, halle-*loooo*-jah,
Glory, glory, halle-*loooo*-jah,
His truth is marching on."

Around and around the table marched the three Beebes.
Skipper burst into the house, joining the dance, howling to

the music. At last Grandpa had to sit down, and Paul and Maureen fell limp and exhausted on the floor.

Grandma turned from the organ, her eyes crinkled with joy. She clapped her hands for attention, then chanted:

> "*Come* day, *go* day;
> God send *Sun*-day.

And where do we go today?" she asked.

"To Pocomoke!" Maureen burst out.

"But before that, where? And who do we thank today?"

"Misty!" Paul shouted. But he grinned as he said it, knowing what Grandma had in mind.

Grandpa twisted uncomfortably. "Me and him," he said, scratching Skipper behind an ear, "we got to clean out the truck and do a passel o' things. We'll jes' do our churchin' while we work."

"Clarence Beebe, you'll do no sech a thing! Today is a shining special day and we won't argify. To church we go. *As a fambly!*"

Promptly at nine forty-five the truck, now clean as water and soap could make it, rattled out of the yard with Grandpa and Grandma sitting dressed up and proud in the cab, and Maureen and Paul in back, feet dangling over the tailgate. The sun was shining for the first time in a week, and the sky was a luminous blue.

"Seems almost like it's Easter," Maureen said. "Seems different from other Sundays. Wonder why?"

" 'Cause we're wearing shadow rolls over our noses, just like race horses."

Unconsciously Maureen felt of her nose.

167

"Can't you see, Maureen? We're not even looking at the houses with their porches ripped off and mattresses and things drying in the sun. We're seeing bigger."

"Like what?"

Paul looked up. "Like that flag flying over the Fire House, painting stars and stripes on the sky. And the sea smiling and cheerful as if it'd never been nasty-mean."

Maureen nodded. "And even if the houses *are* all bashed in, Paul, you hardly notice them for the clumps of daffydils."

It was true. The world seemed reborn. The blue-green water of the bay was unruffled and washing softly against the drift. Gulls were gliding on a seaward breeze with scarcely a wing-flutter. And here and there in all the mud and muck, hosts of yellow daffodils were nodding like spatters of sunshine.

Up in front Grandpa and Grandma were feeling the same joy. "The storm sure bloomed the place up," Grandpa said.

Grandma sighed in deep contentment. "Takes a wrathful storm to make us 'preciate bonny weather, don't it?"

As the Beebe family took their seats in the rapidly filling church, the men of the Coast Guard filed into the front rows.

"Paul!" Grandpa whispered loud enough for the whole congregation to hear. "There's Lieutenant Lipham. He's the one rescued you the day you snuck over to Assateague and your boat drifted away."

The lieutenant turned around, smiling broadly. Paul's cheeks reddened.

Maureen had secretly brought the birth announcements to church so that she and Paul could fill in the hour and date, everything except the name. But they never even opened the package. From almost the beginning of the sermon, they leaned forward, listening with every fiber.

"The earth is the Lord's," the deep voice of the preacher intoned. "He hath founded it upon the seas, and established it upon the floods."

And just by listening to the resounding voice, Paul and Maureen could see God commanding Noah to build the ark, big and flat-bottomed, and they could see the flood waters rising and the animals marching in, two by two.

"God is in the rescue business," the preacher's words

rolled out, "and every believer is a member of His rescue force. Today we pay special tribute to the United States Coast Guard. In the sight of God, men who do not know the harbor of His love are like men lost at sea, grasping for something or someone to save them. The Church is God's rescue force, just as the Coast Guard is the government's rescue force."

The preacher half-closed his eyes. "On Thursday night," he said, "when the last of the refugees staying here in our church had been taken to their homes or to the mainland, I walked down the streets and saw the havoc and the emptiness of our once lovely island. Yet no Chincoteaguer had lost his life, and I paused to thank God.

"Then I came back to the parsonage. All was dark and quiet. I was alone. Darkness was all around. Then a flash across the sky! The only light left shining came from the old lighthouse on Assateague Island. It was spreading wide its beam of hope and guidance. So it is when the lights of this old world are snuffed out, and the storms of life would destroy us, the steady light of God's love still shines. As our great Coast Guard keeps the light flashing from the lighthouse, so it is our task to keep our lights burning here at home.

"Let us sing."

Paul and Maureen were almost sorry when the sermon ended. They rose with the congregation, and sang as lustily as Grandma. Even Grandpa made his lips move as if he knew the words:

> "Brightly beams our Father's mercy
> From His lighthouse evermore,
> But to us He gives the keeping
> Of the lights along the shore."

170

Just as the final "Amen" faded, the preacher was handed a message. He read it to himself in apparent pleasure. Then he stilled the congregation.

"Friends," he said with a smile, "I have an important announcement." He cleared his throat and glanced at Paul and Maureen before he began. "On this day, in a stable in the city of Pocomoke, a foal was born—a tiny mare colt." He paused. Then he added, "And her mother is Misty."

There was a rustle as everyone turned to look at Paul and Maureen, then smiles and murmurs of "Misty . . . Misty" from every pew.

Quickly the congregation moved out into the bright sunshine. Preacher Britton was greeting the members, and Paul and Maureen, blushing in embarrassment, were standing beside him. Everyone was shaking hands with everyone else. Hands that all week had lifted and scrubbed and prayed now clasped each other in joy.

"It's the happiest news to reach Chincoteague in a week of terror!"

"The very happiest."

For once Grandpa didn't bolt for home as if his house were on fire. He shook hands heartily with the preacher. "Reverend," he said, "ye jes' put up one o' the greatest sermons I ever heerd!"

"Come oftener," the preacher replied with a grin.

Chapter 20

HOME AT LAST

A<small>FTER RETURNING</small> home from church, all of the
Beebes hurried into old clothes and went to work in a kind of
happy frenzy. Everything needed doing at once.

Paul crushed oats in Grandma's coffee grinder and
mixed them with bran and linseed, all ready for the hot
water when Misty came home. He filled the manger with
good-smelling hay. He washed the salt block.

"Wouldn't surprise me none if ye licked it clean with yer
own tongue," Grandpa laughed as he went by with Nanny's
kid tugging at his pants leg.

In the kitchen Maureen was sewing strips of tape on an
old blanket. Every now and then she ran to try it on Grandma to see if the ties were in the right place. "If it fits you,
Grandma, it'll fit Misty."

Grandma made a wry face. "Reckon I should be complimented," she snorted, " 'stead of laying my ears back. Beats me!" she added as she wrapped jelly sandwiches in waxed paper. "There's barely a speck o' meal in the house for biscuits or bread, and scarce a dry thing to cover folks with, but there's allus oats and bran a-plenty, and a royal blanket for Miss Misty."

"Missus Misty!" Maureen corrected.

Grandma disappeared into her bedroom for a moment and came back with a shy smile. "Here's my contribution," she said. "Likely I'll have no more use for this soft baby blanket. With a couple of safety pins to fasten it under her belly, it'll be just the right size for Misty's young'un. That long ride home will be kind o' drafty for a newborn."

By half-past noon Grandpa and Paul and Maureen were waving good-bye to Grandma and were on their way to Pocomoke City. To their amazement, the causeway to the mainland was jammed with a long procession of cars coming from Maryland, Delaware, and even Washington, D.C.

"Why in tarnation they coming to Chincoteague today?" Paul asked, opening up the lunch box.

"I'll tune ye if I catch ye sayin' 'tarnation' again," Grandpa scolded. Then he cackled in laughter. " 'Tain't fittin' except fer an old feller like me."

"But why *are* they?" Maureen wanted to know.

"Folks is funny," Grandpa mused. "Some jes' nacherly likes to waller in woe like pigs in a pen. Sure as shootin' they're comin' to gawp at the wreckage and to take pitchers o' the boats in the streets, and the soggy beddin' and things dryin' in the sun. Curiosity folks, I calls 'em."

A station wagon with a Maryland license flagged them down. Brakes screeched for a mile as cars behind honked in a mad chorus. A young man with a shock of red hair called out, "How do we get to the Beebe Ranch? We want to see Misty's colt."

Grandpa stopped the truck and guffawed. "News out already?" he asked in amazement.

"Yes, sir! Network had it on the radio, and my kids gave me no peace—"

"Wal, what do ye know! Sorry, young feller, but you passed plumb by her. She's over to Pocomoke City, to Doc Finney's house." Grandpa drove on, chuckling.

"See!" Maureen said. "Not everybody comes to look at trouble."

"Ye're right, honey. Lucky thing yer Grandma stayed to home. She would've flew into the air, hearin' me talk like that."

When they reached Dr. Finney's place, the doctor, who had been watching from the house, came to meet them. With a welcoming smile he unlocked the gate and motioned Grandpa to drive in and park alongside the corral. Then without a word he led the way. In absolute silence the three Beebes walked one after the other Indian file behind him. They moved across the paddock as if it were hallowed ground. Still in silence they eased up to the barn. And then, after almost a year of waiting, the moment had come!

Unconsciously Grandpa took off his hat and tucked it under his arm. Paul and Maureen stood on tiptoe, peering in without breathing. They were utterly still, not wanting the scene to change. There, at the far end of the stall, stood

Misty. She eyed them dispassionately as if they belonged to another world and another time. Like a bird brooding a chick she was hovering over a wise little, fuzzy little, scraggly little foal. For a moment the tiny thing took fright and leaned quivering against her mother, who made soft whuffing sounds. Then, comforted, she nosed her way to Misty's teats and began nursing.

"Wa-al, I never!" Grandpa sighed in deep contentment. "Them sucky-smacky sounds is purtier 'n a hull flock o' meadow larks!"

Maureen brushed away a tear. How could a creature be so young and breakable-looking, and yet so spunky? "Why, I feel like I'm its grandma!" she whispered shyly. "And hasn't it got the longest eye-winkers and the curliest tail you most ever saw?"

Paul whispered too. "Look at the strange marking on her forehead—it's in the shape of a new sickle moon! I know!" he exulted. "That's 'cause she was born in the time of the new moon."

Grandpa stared. "She's the onliest colt I ever see with a markin' like that."

"Yes," Dr. Finney said. "There's nothing like her on the Eastern Shore."

"Likely not in all the world," Paul said.

After the colt had drunk her fill, Misty came to the door and nickered happily, sniffing Paul and Maureen by turns.

"She's inviting us in," Paul said.

Slowly, quietly, not to startle the little one, the Beebes went into the stall, and the gentlest of hands lifted her forelock that was only beginning to be a forelock. "Here's a girl's got a head on her," Grandpa approved. "There's enough Arabian into her to make that purty head. And ain't she marked up nice? Not a reg'lar map on her shoulders like her mommy, but she's got her four white stockings."

"And her color is sorrel, like Wings," Maureen said.

Dr. Finney looked at his watch, thinking of the calls still to be made.

Grandpa followed his glance. "If'n ye'll excuse us," he said, "we got to hyper along now. Any last-minute advice, Doc?"

"For now," Dr. Finney said, "avoid bulky food for Misty. Nothing rich or hard to digest."

"How about ground oats and bran and linseed?" Paul asked hopefully.

"Couldn't be better! And no need to remind you children that daily mucking-out is a MUST."

Grandpa nodded vigorously, an "I-told-you-so" twinkle in his eye.

"Right now their stall is the cleanest in the whole wide world," Maureen said proudly.

With quiet confidence she and Paul tied Misty's blanket in place for the trip back. Grandpa took the soft baby blanket and laid it on the little one. Then he crouched down and lifted her up in his arms and carried her out, with Paul leading Misty alongside.

As she approached the truck, Misty planted her feet and balked. Plain as day she bellered: "I'm *not* getting into that thing without my baby!" But when she found out that her foal was safely stowed in the cab in front, she hurried up the ramp, poked her head through the window, and nickered in relief.

Dr. Finney started to wave good-bye, then had a last-minute request. "Mind driving by David's window?" he asked. "I had to put him to bed this morning with a case of old-fashioned measles. Poor lad hasn't seen the colt. He's heartbroken."

Paul felt a prick of shame. "I'm sorry, Dr. Finney, I didn't even miss him." He reached into a pocket and pulled out a tiny wooden gull. "I made it to sell to the tourist folk," he explained, "but I want to give it to David instead. And some day," he added, warming to his own generosity, "I might make a carving of Misty and her foal. Just for him."

Grandpa drove home very carefully, avoiding ruts and bumps. He didn't want to jar the little filly, who lay asleep across Paul's and Maureen's laps, her soft woolen blanket rising and falling with her breathing.

Going over the causeway, they slowed to a crawl. One driver spotted Misty and put on the brakes so suddenly that his two children almost flew through the windshield. "There she is!" he shouted. "Hey, Mister, wait!"

Grandpa came to a stop, grinning. He felt good toward the whole world. "Want a picture?" he asked.

"Do we!" And now other cars were stopping and out popped dozens of children and dozens of cameras. Traffic stalled while shutters clicked on all sides.

178

After a few moments Misty began stomping and whinnying. There was a curious urging in her mind, a tremendous
pull for home.

"Let's go," Paul said. "Misty's getting nervous."

Grandpa stopped the picture-taking and drove on. And
at long last they were going down Beebe Road into Pony
Ranch. Once the tailgate was lowered Misty slow-footed
down the ramp like a queen returning to her kingdom.
Skipper, the official greeter, welcomed her in ten-foot bounds,

jumping, rolling, yelping in pure joy. And out on the marsh, Wings added his voice in a great cry of triumph.

Grandma rushed out of the house, calling, "Where's Misty's baby? Where?"

For answer Paul and Grandpa lifted her out of the truck and carefully set her down beside her mother. She tried a little caper, lost her balance and fell in a heap. Bravely she scrabbled up again, then staggered to her mother and began drinking thirstily. Satisfied, she blew bubbles, sending little beads of milk running down her whiskers.

Misty whickered in contentment. "Home at last," she seemed to say. And she gave the little rump at her side a nip, ever so gentle and motherly.

Chapter 21

A GRAVE DECISION

THAT NIGHT, when Pony Ranch had simmered down into a semblance of peace, Maureen brought out the birth announcements and piled them on the kitchen table. She and Paul were alone. Grandpa had gone to an emergency meeting of the Pony Penning Committee, and Grandma was attending the evening church service.

"You put the date on," Paul said to Maureen. "You write better than me. Besides, I got some important thinking to do."

"Oh?"

Paul flicked open his pocketknife and began working on a block of wood. Out of the corner of his eye he saw Maureen dip her pen in the ink bottle and wait with it poised in the air.

"I declare, Paul Beebe, you can be downright mean! What *are* you thinking?"

"And you can be such a *girl!*" Paul said in disdain. "Always poking and prying."

"All right, I won't ask. 'Cause I already know. So there!"

"What do you know?"

"You're trying to think of the right name for Misty's baby."

"Okay then. I reckon you got what Grandpa calls 'woman's tuition.' Now you know what's occupying my mind, whyn't you keep quiet and do your work?"

Sunday, March 11, 6 a.m. Maureen wrote again and again until her fingers were tired.

At last Paul was ready to talk. "There's three ways to do it. One is by her markings . . ."

"Like *New Moon* or *White Stockings,* Paul?"

"Uh-huh. And the second way is by using her family's names—like *Misty Wings* or *Pied Phantom.*"

"And what's the third way, Paul?"

Just then Grandpa's truck roared into the yard, brakes screeching. Grandpa himself banged into the house like a Fourth of July firecracker. He threw his hat on the peg, then with both hands began rubbing the bristles in his ears.

"I say there's *got* to be a Pony Pennin' this year like allus," he stormed. "Why, it's the oldest roundup in America! We jes' can't let folks down 'cause of a little flood. Why, come July and roundup time, folks are goin' to pack their night things and set out for Chincoteague hopin' to give their kids a real hollerday. And they're goin' to drive fer miles an' miles, and when they get here—NO hollerday! No

182

Pony Penning!" He snorted in disgust. "I won't hear to it! I jes'—"

"Grandpa!" Paul interrupted. "Who says there won't be a Pony Penning?"

"Why, the Mayor's committee and the firemen, they say ain't enough wild ponies left over to Assateague to make it excitin', and no money in the treasury to buy new ones.

"What's more," he bellowed, "they're right! But I ain't told 'em so! 'Cause without ponies this-here island is dead. Do ye think folks comes here to see oysters and clams and biddies?"

"No, Grandpa."

"Ye're dead right they don't! They come to see wild ponies swimmin' across the channel, and feudin' and fratchin' in the pens. Pony Penning Day! That's what they come fer. Can't see it nowhere else in the world."

Paul and Maureen were aghast. July without Pony Penning was unthinkable. "All year I been answering letters about Misty," Maureen said. "And in every one I invited people to come to Pony Penning, people from all over the United States. Even one to Alaska."

Paul broke in. "And this year folks'll come special on purpose to see Misty's baby."

Grandpa began pacing, thinking out loud. "If only we had the ponies! If only the Town Council could buy back some of the colts that was auctioned off last year and the year afore that."

He quickened his pace. "Why, we could load 'em onto a big old barge, and chug 'em acrost the channel to Assateague, and they'd go wild again jes' like they'd never left."

Now he spoke out with great conviction. "Why, then we could put up one o' the greatest Pony Pennings in Chincoteague history."

Grandpa ran out of breath. He gulped for more. "But all that'd take a heap o' money," he sighed.

"Maybe," Maureen said excitedly, "maybe Paul and me could earn a lot of money like we did to buy Misty's mother. We could rake clams or help people clean up their houses."

Paul looked pityingly at his sister. "When you going to grow up, Maureen? Why, it took us three whole months to earn enough to buy just one mare and her colt. Besides, folks here lost most everything in the flood. They can't afford to hire us."

"Paul's right, honey."

"But, Grandpa," Paul asked, "even if we had the money, would people sell back their ponies?"

"Likely some'd be right anxious to help," Grandpa replied, "and some'd sell fer other reasons. A lucky thing me and the Fire Company got a record o' each sale, and if only half them people say yes, that'd give us the start we need."

Grandpa suddenly remembered that his feet hurt. He collapsed into the nearest chair and began unlacing his Sunday shoes. "Can't abide 'em!" he grumbled. "I jes' stormed outen that meetin' afore it was done—half 'cause my hackles was up, but half 'cause my shoes squinched me."

The phone rang insistently. "You answer, Paul. There's another thing I can't abide. Phone-talkin'. A contraption o' the devil."

"It's for you, Grandpa. It's the Mayor and he sounds real important."

Grandpa thudded to the phone. "Hall–oo–oa!" he bellowed.

"Grandpa doesn't need a phone," Paul snickered. "He could just open a window."

"Sh!" Maureen put up a finger, listening.

"*Who* called you?" Grandpa questioned.

There was a pause.

"What in tunket *he* want?"

Another pause.

"He did!"

Paul and Maureen looked inquiringly at each other.

"Wa-al, Great Jumpin' Jehoshephat! Now ain't that nice? . . . What's that ye say?"

A long pause.

Still holding the receiver, Grandpa turned and looked penetratingly at Paul and Maureen. His voice sobered. "Sure I like the ideer, Mayor, but 'tain't fer me to say. I'll have to put it to Paul and Maureen and get their yes or no. The colt, nor Misty neither—they ain't mine, y'know."

Grandpa hung up the receiver and walked back to the table, collecting his thoughts. Paul and Maureen stared at him, unable to ask the question except with their eyes.

Grandpa hummed and hawed. "Now I ain't a-goin' to influence ye," he said. "It's *yer* druthers, an' no one else's."

"But what is it?"

"Y'see, uh, it's this way. One o' the big chiefs from the movie company that made Misty's picture—he jes' telephoned the Mayor long distance. From his home, mind ye."

"What did he want?" Maureen asked. "Does he want to make a picture of Misty's baby?"

"Stop interruptin'," Paul scolded. "Let Grandpa finish."

"Wa-al," Grandpa went on, "seems he'd been readin' 'bout the storm and how so many ponies had drowned. And he wants to do somethin' to help. Why, he's willin' to let theaters borry the picture of Misty free; that is, *if* the money tooken in goes to build up the lost herds."

Paul did a flying leap over his chair. "That's great, Grandpa. You don't have to get our okay on that."

"But I ain't told ye the kernel yet," Grandpa explained. "Y'see, the Mayor and the Council wants to start a disaster fund, and call it the Misty Disaster Fund." Grandpa stroked his chin and a far look crept into his eyes. "They want to cast Misty in the biggest role o' her life; even bigger'n bein' a star in a movie."

The children listened, speechless.

"Even bigger," Grandpa added, "than birthin' a colt."

"What could be bigger?" Maureen asked.

"They want Misty and her young'un to make a personal tour wherever her picture is playing, and go right spang up onto the stage. And part o' the ticket money'll be used to tidy up the island, but most of it to buy back the ponies. Mind ye, it'll all have to start right away. Mebbe in two weeks—that is, if there's to be a roundup this year."

Paul turned to his sister. "What do you say, Maureen?"

Maureen's face clouded and she thought carefully before replying. "If Misty's baby wasn't so new and tiny, I'd say yes."

Paul picked up the block of wood and his knife, and made a few fierce jabs. "Exactly the way I feel." He looked

at Maureen. " 'Course, it'd be fun to be excused from school and all."

"Mostly it'd be on Saturdays," Grandpa said drily.

"But suppose," Paul was serious now, "suppose they caught the shippin' fever, or bad coughs from travelin' and going in and out of hot theaters. Or even broke a leg."

All three of them lapsed into silence. No one knew what to say. Maureen screwed the cap onto the ink bottle as if she would never have need of it again. Paul threw his piece of wood into the stove and closed his knife. The silence was a growing power. Grandpa sat down and crossed his arms, using his paunch as a ledge. He looked up at the ceiling and across at the clock. He picked up one of the birth announcements and studied it. The corners of his mouth twisted into a smile of sympathy and understanding. "It'd be chancy," he admitted. "Mighty chancy."

"But suppose," Paul spoke slowly, earnestly, "suppose we let Misty and the colt go to just one theater, and if they come home feeling frisky, they could go again. But if they got sick or were off their feed for just one day, they'd *never* have to go again."

Grandpa's eyes shone like twin meteors. "Sometimes I think you two is the livin' image o' me! I'm so proud of ye I could strut like one o' our peacocks in full sail. I'll take it up with the Council first thing in the—"

Bong! Bong! . . . The clock struck the hour of ten, and with the last *bong* the telephone rang shrilly. Grandpa clapped a hand to his forehead, then grabbed for his shoes. "Great balls o' fire! I plumb forgot to pick up yer Grandma from the meetin' house. You answer, Maureen. I'm gone!"

Chapter 22

THE NAMING BEE

OVER THE WEEKEND the schoolhouse had been dried out, and on Monday it re-opened with only the high-tide mark showing. Paul and Maureen were present and on time. But it was a hard thing to remember the provinces of Canada, or to stand up and recite: "Washington, Adams, Jefferson, Madison, Monroe . . ." when Misty's filly had to be named. The Town Council was insistent. They had to have a name at once. And the more Paul and Maureen were pressed to make a decision, the harder it was to decide.

For the next few days, in school and out, they thought up names and just as quickly discarded them. None seemed right. Either they were too long, or when you called them out across the marsh they sounded puny. It wasn't like naming just any colt.

For three days they struggled. Then on Wednesday almost at dusk Mr. Conant, the postmaster himself, arrived at Pony Ranch with a whole bag of mail for the Beebes. When Grandma spied him striding across the yard, she quickly set an extra place at the table and sent Maureen to the door.

"Evenin', Mr. Conant," Maureen said politely, but her eyes were on the mailbag.

"How do you do, Maureen and Mrs. Beebe?"

"How-do, Mr. Conant. I declare," Grandma chuckled, "you look jes' like Santa Claus with that leather pouch ye're carryin'. Let me hang it on a peg whilst you set down. Mr. Beebe and Paul will be in right soon. Now then," she beamed, "do stay to supper. We got us a fine turtle stew with black-eyed peas, and light bread, and some of my beach-plum preserves."

"I'd be very honored to stay!" Mr. Conant replied. "My wife has taken her mother to Salisbury for over night, and while she has no doubt prepared some tasty treat for me, what is food without good talk to digest it?"

Grandma looked pleased. "That's what I allus tell Clarence, only I don't say it so elegant."

Maureen was still eyeing the mailbag, her curiosity at the bursting point.

"Oh, I almost forgot," Mr. Conant smiled broadly. He reached into his inside pocket and drew out an envelope bearing a bright red Special Delivery sticker. "It's for you and Paul," he said, handing it to Maureen. "Since it's marked *Special,* I decided to bring all of your mail along, instead of letting it wait until tomorrow." Pointing to the mailbag, he added, "It's the biggest batch of mail ever to come to Chincoteague for one family in one day."

There was a clatter and a stamping in the back hall as Grandpa and Paul came in. "Why, if 'tain't Mr. Conant,"

Grandpa said, putting out his hand. "I'm as pleased to see ye as a dog with two tails!"

"Look, Paul!" Maureen cried. "A letter, Special Delivery! For us!"

Paul took the news with outward calm, but his eyes strained to see the postmark and his fingers itched to snatch the letter and run off, like Skipper with a bone.

"You children put that letter with the others and wash up now," Grandma scolded gently as she stirred the stew. "Turtles is hard to come by, and I ain't minded to let our vittles get ruint. Besides," she said, "if it's good news, it'll keep, and if it's bad, time enough to read it after we've et. Everyone, please to sit. You here, Mr. Postmaster."

In spite of company, supper that night was, as Grandpa put it, "a lick and a gallop." Everyone was in a fever of excitement to start opening the letters. But first the table had to be cleared, and the crumbs swept clean. Then Grandma spread out a fresh checkered cloth to protect the top. "We allus use the kitchen table for everything," she explained to Mr. Conant, "fer readin' and writin', fer splintin' broken bird legs—whatever 'tis needs doin'." She nodded now in the direction of the mail pouch.

The postmaster took down the bag and dumped the letters onto the table. With the hand of an expert he stacked them in neat piles, placing the Special Delivery on top.

"It's like Christmas!" Maureen gasped.

"It's *bigger* than Christmas," Paul said.

"Who they for?" Grandpa wanted to know.

"Some are for you, Mr. Beebe, and some for Paul and Maureen."

192

Wait-a-Minute jumped on the table and began upsetting the piles. Paul swept her off with his arm. "You tend to your kittens," he said not unkindly. "We got important business!" He took out his pocketknife. "I'll do the slitting," he announced.

"I'll do the pullin' out and unfoldin'," Grandpa offered.

"You read them to us, Grandma," Maureen said. "You make everything sound like a storybook."

Grandma blushed. "Mr. Conant's got the edification. I'd be right shy readin' in front of him."

"Not at all, not at all, Mrs. Beebe. I agree with Maureen. Many a Sunday I've gone by your class and heard you reading from the Bible. I feel complimented you let me stay and be part of the family."

For a moment the slitting of the envelopes and the crackle of paper were the only sounds in the room. Then Grandma picked up the Special Delivery letter, took a deep breath, and in her best Sunday voice began:

> *"Dear Paul and Maureen,*
>   *I am sorry the storm came. But I am glad Misty had a baby. Was I surprised!*
>   *I hope some day I can visit your island or maybe even live there. I hope to go to Pony Penning Day and maybe buy a pony.*
>   *I hope you don't mind if I send you a name for Misty's baby. I think 'Windy' would be nice."*

"By ginger!" Grandpa exclaimed. "That's uncommon purty. Let's have another, Idy."

Mr. Conant took pencil and paper out of his pocket and wrote down *Windy* with a checkmark after it.

"This one is to Misty herself," Grandma went on. "Why, it's a regular baby card, and it says, *Congratulations to you and the new little bundle of joy."*

"Turn it over, Grandma, there's a note on the back," Maureen said.

"So there is! Listen:

> *"Dear little Misty,*
>   *I've heard so much about you I feel like I know you. I love horses and I was worried about you*

*during the storm. You have a wonderful master
and mistress to bring you into the kitchen.*

*You should name your filly 'Misty's Little Storm
Cloud.'*

Isn't that beautiful, folks?"

Grandpa looked inquiringly at the children. "To my
notion," he hesitated, "it'd be too long a handle fer such a
little mite—even if we was to boil it down some."

Maureen was impatient. "More, Grandma. More!"

"Here's one from a fifth-grader up to Glassboro, New
Jersey:

*"I am a boy ten and a half years old. This is not a
very long letter, but I like the name 'Windy' for
Misty's colt."*

Mr. Conant made a second checkmark after *Windy.*
"Two for *Windy*," he announced.

"Doggone, if this ain't jes' like an election," Grandpa
said. "Vote countin' and all."

Grandma broke out in smiles. "This one's mostly
questions:

"Dear Paul and Maureen,
*How are you? I am fine. I read in the paper that
Misty is safe.*
How do you pronounce your island's name?
*If I should come to your island, would you show
me how to eat oysters?*
*How are your Grandpa and Grandma? I think
you are one of the greatest families in the U.S.A.*
*P.S. Do you think you'll have a Pony Penning this
year?"*

"See?" Maureen said. "Folks are asking already, but I just won't answer this one until later. Go on, Grandma."

"Here's one from a lady teacher:

> "*We read in the paper that Misty had a filly and also that 145 ponies died. My heart just sinks.*
>   *One of my pupils said that colts have such twinkly legs he thought 'Sand Piper' would be a good name for Misty's baby.*"

"Hmmm," Paul said approvingly. "See what I mean, Maureen? *Sand Piper* would honor her granddaddy, the Pied Piper."

Mr. Conant wrote down the name with one checkmark and a star beside it.

"If she was a horse-colt instead of a mare-colt," Maureen said, "I'd like it fine. But we got to think about when she's grown up."

Mr. Conant erased the star.

Grandma pursed her lips as she read the next letter to herself.

"Land sakes, Idy, I'll be a bushy-whiskered old man by the time ye make that one out."

"Oh, it's easy to make out," she replied. "The writing's beautiful. It's to you, Clarence." She held it up for all to see. Then she cleared her throat:

> "*Dear Sir:*
>   *I cut a picture from the state paper yesterday of Misty's filly, born Sunday, March 11th. The caption said she was foaled at an animal hospital, but I am hoping that someone in your town can give me more information about her. Is she healthy? And is she for sale?*"

196

There was a stunned silence. Grandpa's face went red and the cords of his neck bulged.

Mr. Conant looked at him in alarm. "Mr. Beebe," he said, "I know the answer to that one. If you'll allow me, I'd like to do the replying."

Grandpa didn't trust himself to speak. He managed a nod of thanks.

"Grandma, try another!" Maureen urged.

"Here's a real short one," Grandma said cheerily, "and it says:

"If I owned Misty, I would name her colt 'Stormy.'"

Paul's eyes met Maureen's and held. Then he leaped up from his chair, stood on his head, and cried, "Ya-hoo!" In an instant he was right side up again. He shouted the name, "STORMY!" Then he whispered it very softly, *"Stormy."*

Maureen clapped her hands. "Why, it sounds good both ways!"

Promptly Mr. Conant wrote it down. "I'll give this one two stars," he said.

And still there were more letters and more names— *Gale Winds* and *Rip Tide* and *Sea Wings* and *Ocean Mist* and *Misty's Shadow* and *Mini Mist* and *Foggy* and *Cloudy* —until at last they were down to one letter.

Grandpa loosened his suspenders, yawning and stretching. "Out with that last one, Idy. Sandman's workin' on me, both barrels."

Grandma's face lighted with pleasure. "Why, it's signed by a whole bunch of school children over to Reisterstown, Maryland." She adjusted her spectacles and began:

"Our class read the book about Misty. Now we are reading about the awful storm that flooded your island. We are glad Misty was not drowned. As soon as we heard the news about her colt, we decided to write you. We think you should name her 'Stormy' because she was born in a storm. Would you like that? We would. We had a secret ballot, and 'Stormy' won first place with twenty votes."

Paul drew in his breath. "That does it!" he said. "Remember, Maureen? Sometimes they name 'em for markings, sometimes for ancestors, and the third way is for natural phenom . . . happenings of Nature."

"Like the storm?"

"Exactly." Paul got up from the table and spoke now in great seriousness. "Mr. Conant, how many votes do we have for *Stormy?*"

"Twenty-two, Paul."

"All those in favor of *Stormy* please say Aye."

The Ayes were loud and clear.

Maureen heaved a great sigh. "Oh, Paul, now we can fill in the announcements."

Chapter 23

DRESS REHEARSAL

IT WAS unanimous! The Town Council, the Firemen, the Ladies' Auxiliary, Preacher Britton, and of course the Postmaster—everyone approved the name *Stormy*. Stormy, they said, was the one good thing to come out of the storm.

News of the Misty Disaster Fund swept the Eastern Shore. Theater owners all up and down the coast wanted to present the famous ponies on their mission of mercy.

Now that Paul and Maureen had agreed to a tryout, they entered into the project with enthusiasm. "It's got to be good!" Paul kept repeating. "If children are going to spend their allowance money, they're entitled to a real show."

"Why, Paul, the movie of Misty is a beautiful show," Maureen said in a hurt tone.

"Sure it is. But lots of folks have seen it. What they want now is to see Misty herself and little Stormy. Even the Mayor says so."

The performance in the big city of Richmond was scheduled for a week from Saturday. That left only ten days to do a million things, big and little.

They scrubbed Misty's stepstool and gave it a fresh coat of paint, bright blue. And the moment it was dry, and a dozen times each day, they made her step up on it and shake hands vigorously, just for practice. Often while she shook hands, Stormy nursed her.

"Makes Misty seem ambi-dextrous," Paul said.

Grandpa chortled. "Reckon you could call it that. I swan, the way that gal shakes hands on the slightest excuse it looks like she's campaignin'."

"She is!" Maureen said. "She's campaigning for the Misty Disaster Fund."

"Maureen, you go get my nippers," Grandpa ordered. "I better trim them hoofs. She's shakin' hands so high she's liable to plant her hoofograph on some little younker's head."

As for Stormy, working on her was pure joy. Every night after school Paul and Maureen curried and combed her, not to make her less fuzzy, but to get her used to something besides Misty's tongue. And gradually they halter-broke her. Of course, there wasn't a halter anywhere on the island—or even in Horntown or Pocomoke—tiny enough to fit. Paul had to make one out of wickie rope, just as he had done for Misty when she was a baby. And after a little urging Grandma gave up her favorite piece of chest flannel to wrap around the noseband of the halter.

"Just feel of it now, Grandma," Paul exclaimed. "It's as soft as the lamb's wool they use for racehorse colts."

"Don't need to feel it. I know," Grandma said drily.

Stormy accepted the halter with only a little head tossing. Occasionally as she was being led about, she turned to gaze at Skipper and the kid as much as to say: "Hey, you! Why can you two run free?"

For answer they blatted and barked and dared her to join in the fun. But Misty wouldn't let her. When they came too close, she leaped at them, lashing out with her forefeet, head low, teeth bared. They quickly got the message, scattered in panic, and stayed away for hours.

As Saturday approached, everything was ready except the old truck. How ugly and drab it seemed for a movie star and her filly! It needed paint and polish and a new floor and a new top. But there was no money and no time to do anything about it.

Then late on Friday, just before darkness closed in, Mr. Hancock arrived looking pleased as a boy. He took a long bundle from his car and with a proud flourish unrolled two enormous pieces of canvas. On each he had painted a life-size picture of Misty and Stormy. "To cover the sides of your truck," he said proudly. "I want the folks in Richmond to know that us Chincoteaguers do things up right."

Now even the truck was resplendent and gay!

By six o'clock the next morning, chores were done and Grandpa and the children were loading up the truck. Grandma and Skipper, Nanny and the kid were clustered about, watching, as Misty walked up the ramp in eager anticipation. She could smell the sweet hay aboard and the juicy slices of a Delicious apple tucked here and there. Little Stormy skittered along after her, with Paul and Maureen on either side, arms spread-eagled to keep her from falling off.

"I feel so left-behind," Grandma said, folding and unfolding her hands in her apron. "Like a . . . well, like a colt that's bein' weaned."

Grandpa was about to break into laughter, but when he saw Grandma's woebegone face, he came over to her, his voice full of tenderness. "Tide o' life's flowin' normal again, eh, Idy? The goin' out and the comin' in."

"Sure, Grandma," Maureen said, "and we'll be home afore dark."

"And hungry as bears," added Paul.

Grandma blinked hard. "I reckon the storm's brought us so close I hate to lose sight o' ye, even for a day." Big tears began running down her face.

"Idy!" Grandpa bellowed. "You come with us. Call up them Auxiliary ladies and tell 'em you can't sew on the children's band uniforms today. What if the old ones did float out to sea? Tell the kids to play in their birthday suits! Tell 'em anything. Tell 'em we can't load and unload the ponies without your help."

Suddenly the tension was gone. Grandma wiped her tears with a corner of her apron and began laughing at the thought of her lifting the ponies. "Now be off with you. I can't stand out here all day. I got a pile of work to do."

But as the truck swung out of the drive, she didn't go into the house. Her eyes followed it to the road, as she continued wrapping and unwrapping her arms in her apron. Then suddenly she took off the apron and waved good-bye.

Paul turned and waved back. He could see Grandma growing smaller and farther away, standing in front of the sign that said "Misty's Meadow." And even while he was feeling sorry for her, having to do up the dishes and go to the Ladies' Auxiliary and all, his mind raced ahead to Richmond. In sudden panic he wondered, Would there be anyone at the theater at all? Maybe the day was too nice, and children would be shooting marbles and flying kites and playing baseball, and they had seen the movie anyway.

Chapter 24

STORMY'S DEBUT

I N RICHMOND, a hundred and twenty miles away, children of all ages were waking up, springing out of bed, aware that this morning held a delicious sense of adventure and wonder. They dressed more quickly than usual and fretted at grown-ups who dilly-dallied over breakfast. They wanted to be sure of getting to the theater on time.

A few of the children could boast of having seen real actors making personal appearances, and some had even seen animal actors like Trigger and Lassie. But no one ever had seen the live heroes of a story that had really and truly happened. It was almost too exciting to think about.

The employees of the Byrd Theater, too, felt an enthusiasm they could not define. By nine o'clock the manager arrived, just out of the barber chair. He was followed closely by the projectionist, who disappeared into his cubicle under the ceiling. Then came the cashier, the popcorn-maker, and the ticket-taker, followed by the musicians with their cellos and piccolos and kettledrums.

And last of all, the ushers and the doorman in bright blue uniforms with gold braid and buttons.

By ten minutes after nine all was in readiness: the lights blazing, the film threaded properly, the orchestra tuning up, popcorn popping and filling the lobby with its tantalizing smell; and, most important, a special ramp was snubbed up tight against the stage. To test it, the manager stomped up the ramp and stomped back down again as if he were a whole cavalcade of horses. "Solid as the Brooklyn Bridge!" he said in satisfaction.

By nine-fifteen the ushers took their posts, the doorman opened the plate-glass doors, and down in the pit the orchestra began playing "Pony Boy, Pony Boy, won't you be my Pony Boy?" At the same time the pretty cashier climbed to her perch in her glass cage.

By nine-sixteen she was looking out the porthole saying, "How many, please?" "Thank you." "How many, please?" "Thank you." Her fingers flew to make change and tear off the right number of tickets.

No one, not even the manager, was prepared for the swarms of people coming all at once—Boy Scouts and Cub Scouts, Girl Scouts and Brownies, Campfire Girls and Bluebirds, classes from schools, from churches, from orphanages, families of eight and ten, with neighbor children in tow. It was a human river, so noisy with shuffling and shouting that even the drums in the orchestra could scarcely be heard.

By nine-forty every seat on the first floor was taken. By nine-fifty the balcony was filling up, and by one minute to ten there was not a seat left anywhere, not even in the second balcony. From floor to ceiling the theater was packed.

At the stroke of ten the asbestos curtain went up, the ponderous red velvet curtains parted, and the house lights dimmed, except for the tiny red bulbs at the exits. With a crash of cymbals the music stopped. A hush spread over the theater and rose like heat waves from a midsummer hayfield.

Then in all that breathless quiet the picture flashed on the screen, and suddenly Time ceased to exist. A thousand people were no longer in a darkened theater. They were transported to a wind-rumpled island with sea birds crying and wild ponies spinning along the beach. By pure magic

they were playing every role. They were roundup men spooking out the wild ponies from bush and briar, and suddenly coming upon the Phantom with her newborn foal, Misty. And then they *were* that foal, struggling to swim across the channel, struggling to keep from being sucked down into a whirlpool. And in a flash they were a daring tow-headed boy, jumping into the sea, grabbing Misty's forelock, pulling her to safety.

Even the ushers in the aisle were caught up in the spell —cheering when the Phantom raced Black Comet and won; laughing when Misty came flying out of Grandma's kitchen; gulping their tears when Paul bade farewell to the beautiful wild mare who was Misty's mother.

An unmistakable sniffling filled the theater as THE END

207

flashed upon the screen. Grownups and children smiled at each other through their tears as if they had come through a heartwarming experience together.

Then a handful of boys in the balcony began shouting: *"We want Misty. We want Stormy!"* And the whole audience took up the chant.

From the wings the manager walked briskly onto the stage. His face was one wide happy smile. He raised his hand for silence. "Boys and girls!" he spoke into the microphone. "Thank you for coming to this gala performance. All of the proceeds today—every penny you paid—will be used to restore the island of Chincoteague and to rebuild the herds of wild ponies on Assateague."

The applause broke before he had finished. He opened his lips to say more, but the same handful of boys shouted, *"We want Misty. We want Stormy."* And again the whole audience joined in. *"We want Misty. We want Stormy!"*

When the chant showed no signs of diminishing, the manager shrugged helplessly, then signaled to the stagehand. As if he had waved a wand, the lights went out, one by one, until the theater was in total blackness. An utter quiet fell as a slender beam of light played up and down the left aisle. It steadied at a point underneath the balcony.

And there, from out of the darkness into the shaft of light stepped two ponies. They were led by a spry-legged old man and flanked by a boy and a girl, but no one saw them for they were lost in shadow. Every eye was riveted on the two creatures tittupping down the aisle—one so sure-footed and motherly, one so little and wobbly.

From a thousand throats came the whispered cry,

"There they are!" And the murmuring grew in power like water from a dike giving way. The children in the balconies almost fell over the railing in their urgency to see. And down below, those on the aisle reached out with their arms, and those not on the aisle crowded on top like a football pile-up, and the fingers of all those hands stretched out to feel the furry bodies.

The theater manager cried out in alarm: "Don't touch the ponies—you might be kicked!" But it was like crying to the sun to stop shining or the wind to stop blowing.

With his body Paul tried to protect Stormy and Misty. But they didn't want protection. They were enjoying every minute of their march down the aisle.

And now the little procession has reached the ramp to the stage. Misty walks up calmly, in almost human dignity, and with only a little pushing from behind, Stormy joins her. The stage is ablaze with light so that the audience is nothing but a black blur, far away and quiet now. Misty looks around her at the big bright emptiness. It is bigger than her stall at home, bigger even than Dr. Finney's stable. Her eyes give only a passing glance to the artificial palm trees. Then they pounce on the one thing she recognizes. Her stepstool! In seeming delight she goes over and steps up with her forefeet, nickering to Stormy: "Come to me, little one."

Stormy shows a moment of panic. Her nostrils flutter in a petulant whinny. Then, light as thistledown, she skitters across the stage. And with all those faces watching, she nuzzles up to her mother and begins nursing, her little broomtail flapping in greedy excitement.

209

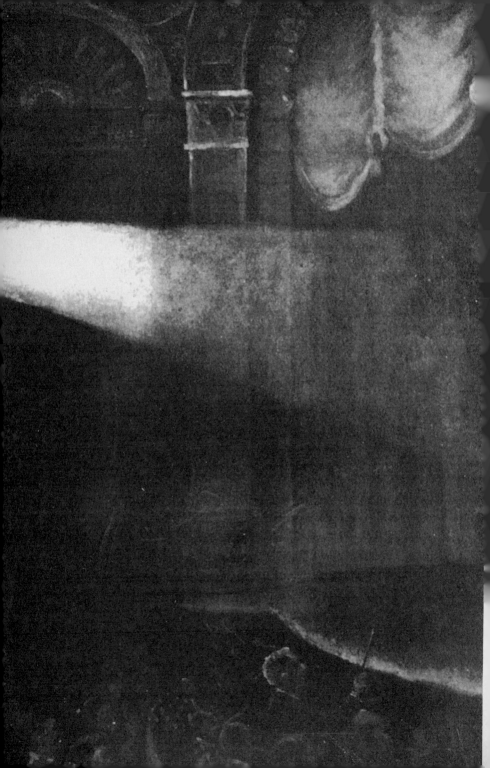

So deep a silence hangs over the theater that the sounds of her suckling go out over the loud speakers and carry up to the second balcony. In quiet ecstasy each child is hugging Stormy to himself in wonder and love.

Done with her nursing the filly turns her head, wiping her baby whiskers on Paul's pants leg. The audience bursts into joyous laughter.

The spell is broken. Misty jostles her foal and nips along her neck just in fun; then she licks her vehemently as if to make up for that long separation during the ride from Chincoteague.

All this while none of the human creatures on the stage had spoken a word. But suddenly Grandpa was over his stage fright. "If Misty ain't careful," he bellowed to the last row in the balcony, "she'll erase them purty patches off'n Stormy."

The children shrieked. When at last they had quieted down, Grandpa thanked them in behalf of all the people of Chincoteague, and the ponies that were left, and the new ones which their money was going to buy.

"And Stormy thanks you, too." Grandpa set her up on the stepstool alongside her mother, and they posed with their heads close together even when a flash bulb popped right in their faces.

Then Grandpa selected one boy from the audience and one girl and invited them up on the stage so that Misty could shake their hands and so thank everyone. Eagerly the two children ran up the ramp, but once on the stage they suddenly froze, their arms rigid at their sides. It was Misty who without any prompting offered her forefoot first. Then timid hands reached out, one at a time, to return the gesture. But again it was Misty who did the pumping and enjoyed the whole procedure.

Grandpa threw back his head and howled. Still chuckling he explained, "In my boy-days I was an organ-pumper on Sundays. If only I'd of had a smart pony like Misty, she could've done it fer me!"

Then a man went up the aisles with a microphone, and children asked their questions right into it.

"Was Misty really in your kitchen during the storm?"

"Was it funny to see a pony looking out your kitchen window, instead of Grandma?"

"Why are colts mostly legs?"

"How many days old is Stormy?"

"How many ponies will the firemen buy with our money?"

"Will they go wild again on Assateague?"

"Did Grandma get mad at Misty messing in the house?"

"Did Wings live through the storm?"

Grandpa patiently answered each question, with a nod and smile of agreement from Paul and Maureen. With dozens of eager hands still waving for attention, time ran out. The musicians started playing "America, the Beautiful," while Misty and Stormy went down the ramp and up the other aisle this time so that more hands could reach out and touch.

The sun seemed brighter than ever when the little procession reached the door of the theater. Paul and Maureen drew a deep breath. It had been a rousing, heart-lifting performance, and they knew they had never been so happy.

213

Chapter 25

THE LAST SCENE

IT WAS afternoon before Misty and Stormy were loaded into the truck for the long drive home. All the way Grandpa and the children sat in quiet contentment, too full for words. They rode in silence, each one tasting his own memories of the performance, each one filled to the brim with a deep, almost spiritual happiness.

The pine trees were throwing long shadows and the sun was slipping into Chincoteague Bay when they arrived back at Pony Ranch. Grandma came hurrying out to meet them, her eyes asking a dozen questions. She waited expectantly for the news, but all she got was a "Hi, Grandma. It was great!"

Grandma buttoned her sweater against the evening breeze and sat down to watch the unloading. "No use pressin' now; else I'll only get half the story," she told herself. "Allus the ponies come first. I'll bide my time." Nanny shouldered up to her, butting very gently. Unconsciously Grandma tucked her skirt out of Nanny's reach. Then she settled herself to watch and wait.

Grandpa and the children were like actors working in pantomime. Each one knew exactly what to do. Paul lowered the tailgate of the truck and led Misty down to the fence. Grandpa picked up Stormy, carried her out and set her beside Misty. Maureen took off Stormy's halter. Then she and Paul quickly went around to the gate to let the bars down. But before even the top one was lowered, Misty did something she had done only as a yearling. From a standing start she leaped nimbly over the bars and landed inside. Then she turned around as if wondering what to do about her youngster. Stormy let out a frightened squeal, then with head and tail low, she scrambled under the bars and found her mother.

The twilit quiet ended in a crash of noise. A gaggle of geese rose in a honking cloud, the peacock let out a hair-chilling scream, Skipper yelped, the goats blatted. Even Grandpa swelled the racket. "By thunder!" he boomed. " 'Twas quieter in that there movie house with a thousand kids screeching."

In the midst of all the confusion Misty let Stormy nurse, but only for a matter of seconds. After the long hours of being a sedate mother, she suddenly had to be a wild pony again. She took off down the pasture in a quick streaking run, Stormy hopping along behind.

"Look at that little tyke go!" Paul exclaimed.

Maureen cried out in sudden alarm as Misty began crow-hopping, twisting, swerving, kicking at the sky. "Stormy'll get hurt!" she screamed.

But Stormy was trying out little kicks of her own, kiting away, falling to her knees, picking herself up, yet always keeping out of reach.

"She knows just how far to stay away," Paul laughed proudly.

"Why, they're brimful of spirit after all the doin's!" Grandma exclaimed. "Wisht I felt like that."

216

"*I* feel spry as a hopper-grass," Grandpa boasted.

"So do I," Maureen said.

"I don't," Paul declared. "I feel better . . . and bigger . . . and wilder."

"How do you mean, Paul?" Grandma asked.

He pointed a finger to the darkening sky. "See that gull 'way up yonder heading into a cloud?"

"Uh-hmm."

"Well, I can fly up there right alongside him."

Grandma took off her spectacles to study the white soaring wings tipped with the last gold of the sun. "You can?" She smiled at him in pleased wonder. "Even without wings?"

Paul nodded, embarrassed, not knowing how to explain.

There was a strained silence. At last he spoke in a hushed voice, "Grandma, today in the theater I felt and knew things I never knew before."

Grandpa put an arm around Paul and another around Maureen. "I know jes' what he means, Idy. And I don't think no one—not their teacher, nor the postmaster, and mebbe not even Preacher Britton—could really put it to words. Idy, to those city kids in Richmond, today was like a fairy story come to life. It meant something real to 'em. And you'd of thought Misty and Stormy was borned actors, the way they played their parts." He sighed in deep satisfaction. "Fer oncet everything come out jes' 'zackly perfect. And fer oncet in my lifetime I'm too happy to eat."

Misty and Stormy seemed to feel the same way. Their kicking and cavorting done, they turned tail on their friends and walked down the meadowland toward their pine grove by the sea.

It was like the end of a play, their walking off, slow-footed and contented, side by side. Without benefit of words they were playing the last scene. It was good to be out under the big sky. And good to breathe in the fresh, clean air. And how cool the marshy turf felt to their feet. Home was a good place to be.

Epilogue

TO MAKE THE STORY COMPLETE

MISTY AND LITTLE STORMY showed no ill effects, even the next day, because of their trip to the theater. They were, as Grandpa Beebe said, "borned actors." They seemed to burst into bloom like the daffodils after the storm. And so they traveled to more and more theaters. Each time they seemed eager to go, eager to meet their enraptured audiences, and deliriously happy to come back home.

At the end of the tour there was money enough to start the Volunteer Firemen buying back the ponies sold in other years.

But this is only half the story. While Misty and Stormy were doing their part, boys and girls all over the United States were helping, too. They deluged Chincoteague with a fresh tide—of letters! From big cities and tiny hamlets they came, and tucked inside were pennies, dimes, and dollars.

The letters are stories in themselves:

Here is a check for four dollars and four cents for the Misty Disaster Fund. It is an odd number because we earned it weeding dandelions and they grow odd. We hope the money will come in handy. Please excuse our poor writing. We are doing this in my tree house.

We had a lemonade stand and Mother didn't charge us for the lemons. We made three dollars to help restore your herds. We think the new ponies will be glad to go wild again.

I was sad to hear of your disasterous flood because I feel like Misty and Phantom and the Pied Piper are my friends. I know that a quarter is just a drop in the bucket, but I hope that enough people send in "drops" to fill it up.

The radio said your ponies and chickens drowned. I will send you a surprise with this letter. It is one dollar. I know that isn't much, but that's how much I can give.

We all voted to give our class treasury of five dollars to the Misty Disaster Fund so you can buy a whole pony in the name of us fifth graders. We want Pony Penning Day to go on forever.

I been picking blueberries all day and here's my fifty cents. Give my regards to Misty.

During our Story Hour we set out a jar marked "For Pony Pennies," and we marched around the library until 386 pennies were dropped in.

We are a group of 4-H girls, 10 to 16 years old. Every year we have a horse show and we do all the planning, fixing rings, making jumps, and getting prizes and ribbons. From our proceeds this year we want to give a hundred dollars to help replenish the herds that were drowned.

Day by day the Misty Disaster Fund grew and grew. By June the firemen had bought back enough ponies to restore the herds on Assateague. And on the last Wednesday of July the annual roundup and Pony Penning took place just as it has for over a hundred years. Thousands of visitors came, and they marveled at how quickly the new ponies had gone back to their wild ways. The celebration was a rousing success.

Of course Stormy and Misty were on hand where everyone could see and pet them. *They* were not wild at all. Yet they were the heroes of the day.

For their help the author is grateful to

RALPH AND JEANETTE BEEBE, uncle and aunt
of Paul and Maureen

SAM BENDHEIM, SR., AND SAM BENDHEIM, JR.,
President and Vice President of the
Byrd Theaters, Richmond, Va.

THE REVEREND RAYMOND BRITTON, Chincoteague

WARREN CONANT, Postmaster of Chincoteague,
and his wife, PAULINE

DR. GARLAND E. FINNEY, JR., veterinarian
of Pocomoke, Md., and his wife, MARAH

MILES HANCOCK, terrapin trapper and woodcarver, Chincoteague

LT. WILLIAM LIPHAM, U.S. Coast Guard

WILLIAM E. NICHOLS, JR., Councilman of
Chincoteague

ROBERT N. REED, Mayor of Chincoteague

TOM REED, naturalist, Chincoteague

JOYCE TARR, map maker, Chincoteague